Noah wanted to take Mercy in his arms so badly, but he knew he needed to separate himself from her. Shove her away. He had no right to have an ounce of happiness. He didn't deserve a woman like Mercy. He didn't deserve a second chance. "Don't you see I can't give you what you need? What you deserve?"

"I never asked you to help me," Mercy said quietly but firmly. "Not once."

"That's not what I mean and you know it."

She rested her hands on her hips and she lifted her gaze to meet his in challenge. "Then what did you mean?"

He shook his head. *"No Mercy."*

Her brow creased. "What?"

"No mercy. You never give me any mercy." He took a hesitant step toward her. "You never just let me give up, give in."

He felt as if he were falling. Mercy was pushing him off the ledge from where he watched the world but didn't have to participate in it. He was digging in his heels, but she was shoving hard.

And he loved her for it.

Noah caught a wisp of her honey hair with his finger and thumb. It was so soft. He wanted to take her in his arms. He needed her. He was so damned tired of being alone.

"I don't know what you want me to do," Mercy said. To his surprise, her voice was shaky. He didn't think anything scared her. "What . . . what do you want from me?"

Noah took another step closer, entranced by her blue eyes that begged him to kiss her. Begged him to make love to her.

"I think you do," he whispered.

Books by Colleen Faulkner

FORBIDDEN CARESS
RAGING DESIRE
SNOW FIRE
TRAITOR'S CARESS
PASSION'S SAVAGE MOON
TEMPTATION'S TENDER KISS
LOVE'S SWEET BOUNTY
PATRIOT'S PASSION
SAVAGE SURRENDER
SWEET DECEPTION
FLAMES OF LOVE
FOREVER HIS
CAPTIVE
O'BRIAN'S BRIDE
DESTINED TO BE MINE
TO LOVE A DARK STRANGER
FIRE DANCER
ANGEL IN MY ARMS
ONCE MORE
IF YOU WERE MINE

Published by Zebra Books

IF YOU WERE MINE

Colleen Faulkner

Zebra Books
Kensington Publishing Corp.
http://www.zebrabooks.com

ZEBRA BOOKS are published by

Kensington Publishing Corp.
850 Third Avenue
New York, NY 10022

Copyright © 1999 by Colleen Faulkner

All rights reserved. No part of this book may be reproduced
in any form or by any means without the prior written consent
of the Publisher, excepting brief quotes used in reviews.

If you purchased this book without a cover you should be
aware that this book is stolen property. It was reported as "un-
sold and destroyed" to the Publisher and neither the Author
nor the Publisher has received any payment for this "stripped
book."

Zebra and the Z logo Reg. U.S. Pat. & TM Off.

First Printing: April, 1999
10 9 8 7 6 5 4 3 2 1

Printed in the United States of America

Prologue

Nevada Territory, 1864

"God, you there?" Mercy sank her shovel into the dark soil, leaned against the handle, and peered upward. The twinkling stars above looked like sugar crystals sprinkled across a puddle of molasses. "It's me, Lord, Mercy Atkins out Nevada way."

She paused and sighed deeply, her heart weighted with a heaviness she'd never known. "I . . . I realize there's no need me confessing, Lord. You know what I've done. You saw it all from Your perch up there in those clouds." Her voice caught in her throat. "I just hope You understand."

She twisted the shovel in the garden soil. Though it was already mid-April, the night air that blew out of the foothills was so cold that it numbed her fingers. "I hope you can forgive me, and not be too hard on me the day I come knocking on Your pearly gates." She gazed into the sky again. "I just want You to know I'm not trying to hide anything from You, or pass off the blame. I did what I did, and even though I knew it was wrong, it would have turned out worse if I hadn't. You know what I mean."

Surprised by the single tear that slid down her cheek, Mercy wiped it away with the back of her hand that smelled of sun-baked soil and rye flour. She took a deep, cleansing breath. "That over, God, I've got a request to make.

"I know." She released the spade and offered open palms heavenward. "It's probably not right, me asking for something now, considering what I just did. But I've got to ask. I've got to ask for my Jacob."

She paused, drawing her crocheted wrap tighter around her shoulders. "God, will you look after us? Keep us in food, with a roof over our heads?"

Mercy glanced at the two-story ramshackle hotel that loomed in the darkness beyond her small garden. "Or what roof there is."

She smiled in spite of the ache in her heart and the constriction in her throat. "Please protect my secret. Not for me, but for Jacob and for Pap. Give my son a chance to grow up happy. To be someone. To give something more to this world than his father did."

She waited. "Well, guess that's all I've got to say."

Mercy's gaze drifted from the star canopy overhead to the Nevada soil turned by her own hand. The compost pile she kept nearby had made the parched Nevada soil so rich and dark. Her papa said this had to be the best soil in all the territory.

Her gaze lingered over the freshly turned patch for another moment and then she grabbed the shovel with firm determination, determination she knew it would take her to survive alone in this cold, hard world she'd found herself in.

When she spoke again her voice was lighter. She felt better. Stronger. "I think I'll plant my peas right there. What you think of that, Haman?" She didn't smile as she made her way back across the dark yard toward the hotel and her responsibilities. "Never did like peas, did you?"

One

Nowhere, Nevada
Four Years Later
April 1868

"Why do you have to carry out the potato peelings?" Mercy asked, halting in the middle of the kitchen, broom in midstroke. She was hot and tired and it was only mid-morning. She'd been up since four, making ready for the first paying customer the Tin Roof Hotel had had in years. "Because I told you to, that's why, Jacob," she said sharply. "Because I'll fan your bottom if you don't, Mr. Sassy."

The moment she lifted her finger to shake it at her six-year-old son, she regretted her actions. Her own mother had been nothing but harsh words and shaking fingers and Mercy had vowed she'd never become like her.

Jacob's eyes teared up as he tucked his tin whistle into the back of his patched pocket and reached for the bucket of potato peels.

"Why?" Mercy repeated, softening her voice. "Because I love you too much not to make you haul potato peels to the chickens. Because I love you too much not to make a decent man out of you."

To her relief, Jacob broke into a shy smile. "Be right back and then I'll finish the sweepin' for you if you like."

"Sweeping," she corrected, returning to her chore. "We

speak the queen's English in this house. You know that, Son. *Sweeping.*"

"Swee*ping,*" Jacob repeated. Halfway to the back door, he stopped and turned back to her. "Mama, I know we speak the queen's English, but just who is the queen? Would that be President Johnson's mama?"

Mercy's father, who sat at the table playing cards, burst into laughter. Mercy lifted her eyebrows indignantly and tapped him with the broom to get him to lift his feet so she could sweep under them. Both of her "men" loved to see her get indignant.

Now Jacob was laughing, too.

"It's just a phrase," she explained. "It means we speak proper English, like the queen of England, that's all. You know we were English before we were Americans. That's why we speak English."

"And not Chinese," Jacob added.

"And not Chinese."

The boy nodded, satisfied, and pushed through the squeaky back door. "Be right back."

Mercy continued to sweep. Tinny kept his feet high off the uneven plank floor.

"Your turn, Joe," her father, Tinny, said. "Been your turn for half an hour."

Joe made no reply, of course, because there was no Joe. Joe was her father's invisible friend. Joe played cards with Tinny, though not well. He sat on the front porch in late afternoon, and walked him to the outhouse in the dark at night. Joe even snitched a peek at the red petticoats of the local saloon girls for Tinny on occasion.

Mercy had long ago given up trying to convince her father that Joe didn't exist. What harm did Joe do? He kept her father company and made him happy. Sometimes Mercy wished she had a Joe of her own.

"You can put your feet down, Pap."

When Tinny made no response, she laid a gentle hand on his knee. "Pap, put your feet down."

Tinny lowered them to the floor, not looking up. "I'll not wait all day, Joe. Take your turn, or lose it."

Mercy swept toward the back door. "When you and Joe are done with that hand, would you mind going out and catching a chicken from the coop? I thought I'd fry one up for supper. Something special for our first paying customer."

Tinny gave a hurrumph. "Don't know why we have to let someone in our house. I don't want him to come."

"It's not a house, Pap, it's a hotel. You live in a hotel," she said patiently. "And boarders stay in hotels."

Tinny thrust out his tobacco-stained lower lip. "Don't know why he has to stay in *our* hotel."

Mercy swept the dust onto a piece of newspaper and dumped it out the back door. "I told you. It's how I'm going to make enough money to feed us. The egg and the hen money and what little laundry and sewing I've been able to do isn't enough. We've got to have more money to live on."

Tinny discarded two dog-eared cards and retrieved two fresh ones from the deck. It was the sixth or seventh time he'd discarded. Tinny always played until he won. "If you'd let me go to California, I could bring back some of that gold. They got gold in California, you know."

Mercy brushed back a wisp of honey-blond hair that had fallen from her chignon. "You can't go to California, because I need you here." She hung the broom on its nail beside the door and returned to the cast-iron cookstove to check the heat of the oven. Two loaves of bread waited to be popped in to bake. "You know I couldn't care for Jacob without you."

"If that worthless, cheating, lying, whoring man of yours would come and get a decent job, you wouldn't have to let strangers into your house." Tinny laid down his cards. "Straight. Looks like you lose again, Joe."

Mercy ignored Tinny's comment about Haman. She just wasn't up to it this morning. "Pap, the fact of the matter is that Haman isn't here, and I have to take care of us. I have to see Jacob fed, and put a pair of decent shoes on his feet for once. Mr. McGregor is talking about starting a school in the fall in the back of his store. I want to send my son to school in shoes."

Tinny began to collect his cards. "You want Joe and me to do what, again?"

"Kill a hen."

Slowly he pushed out of his seat and rose, dropping his bollinger hat on his head. The dress hat looked out of place on a man wearing patched denims, suspenders, and long underwear, but Tinny liked the hat so Mercy let him wear it. He'd found it in an alley behind a saloon somewhere years ago.

"Be better if we had a hog." He walked to the door, surprisingly spry for a man his age. "I like pork chops."

"It *would* be better if we had a hog." She crossed her arms over her chest. "It would be better if I had two loaves of silver ore from the Comstock lode on top of this stove, too, instead of just bread. But I don't."

As Tinny passed her, he touched her chin lightly. "And you call the boy sassy. Wonder where he got it?"

Mercy smiled bittersweetly. A human mind was a strange thing. How could her father be so crazy, and yet so sane and perceptive at the same time? "I'll boil the water for you to pluck the hen, but I want *you* to pluck it, Pap," she called after him. "Not Joe. Joe never does it after you tell him to!"

The door slapped shut in response and Mercy reached for the bread to pop it in the oven. Mr. Cook, from the bank, would be here any minute with the outrider and his first week's room and board. If she were going to wash her face and repin her hair, she'd have to hurry.

Noah Ericson stared at his muddy boots. He hadn't seen a boot scrape on the front porch, but he guessed he should have at least stomped his feet before he walked into the front hall of the hotel. Not that it was a fancy place or anything. Far from it. The porch sagged, the roof looked like it leaked, and more than one shutter hung crooked. But Mr. Cook said it was the only hotel in Nowhere, Nevada. Besides, the bank was paying his room and board. What did he care so long as the Tin Roof had a bed and no lice?

Mr. Cook, the man who had hired him to escort the stagecoach from the bank, south to Carson City, rapped his small white fist on the door. He waited, his hands tucked behind his back.

Noah waited behind him.

A moment later, the door pushed open and a young blonde woman appeared. It wasn't like him to be curious about anyone, but Noah swung his forelock off his forehead and glanced at her from beneath the brim of his hat. She was pretty in a wholesome, earthy way, with blue eyes that sparkled and a mouth . . . a mouth that . . .

Noah lowered his gaze to his muddy boots again, surprised by the stirring he felt inside. It had been a long time since anyone stirred him.

Mercy smiled and nodded as the banker introduced her to Mr. Ericson, though she couldn't help noticing the outrider's dusty boots. He'd tracked dirt all the way across her freshly swept porch and into the front hall. It was true enough that a woman faced a losing battle against the dry, sun-baked soil of the region, but it wasn't a battle any decent woman surrendered to easily.

Mercy should have known that a man who hired himself out as a gunman would be careless, with no respect for carpets or decent manners.

But she didn't protest. She didn't say anything because she desperately needed the bank's money. And frankly she didn't care if Satan himself was one of her boarders, just as long as he paid his bill in advance and in cash.

Mr. Cook repeated the original agreement between them, his waxed mustache twitching as he spoke. He handed her Mr. Ericson's first week's payment. With a jaunty nod, he returned his hat to his head and went around Mr. Ericson.

"Good day," Mr. Cook called as he stepped out the door.

Mercy slipped the envelope with the precious greenbacks into her apron pocket. "Good day. See you next week," she called cheerily.

Then suddenly she was alone, face-to-face with a man with an old army-issue Colt .45 strapped to his hip. Unable to stop herself, her gaze slid from his mop of chestnut hair and hard, angled face to his dusty boots. He shifted his weight in the boots but still didn't move. She wondered if he was stuck to the floor.

"Um . . . sorry about the mess." He glanced at the ridges of red dirt that had fallen on her floor.

There was something about Noah Ericson that made Mercy feel strange inside. Uneasy. Had she made a mistake in allowing a hired gunman into the hotel? Sure, it was a hotel, but it was her home, too. Would Jacob be in danger around such a man?

She tried to look him in the eye, but he averted his gaze beneath the fringe of ragged hair and the brim of his leather hat. "Just try to knock the dirt off before you come in next time, all right?"

He gave a nod. "Yes, ma'am."

At least he wouldn't talk her to death.

She eyed the leather-brimmed hat that had seen better

days. She didn't let Jacob or Tinny wear a hat inside. She was tempted to tell Mr. Ericson so, but decided against it. What did she care if he had manners or not? "I'll show you your room so you can unpack your bags— Bag," she corrected herself, realizing he carried only one small canvas duffel tossed over a broad shoulder. Obviously he wasn't planning on staying long or changing clothes often. "Travel light, don't you, Mr. Ericson?"

She waited on the bottom tread.

He seemed to hesitate, but then finally freed himself from the spot in her front hall. He followed her up the steps toward the second floor. "All I need."

At the top of the stairs she pointed right. "Family quarters. Rooms to rent are this way." She adjusted a rag rug that covered a floorboard she'd recently replaced. She wasn't much of a carpenter, so the new piece didn't fit well, but at least it kept the rats out of the hall.

"Meals are at six, one, and six. If you miss a meal, there's always something in the kitchen, but it might just be a cold cheese sandwich."

The outrider grunted a response she took to mean that was all right. Not that she intended to change her mealtimes even if he didn't. Mercy didn't have time to fiddle with men and their peculiarities. She was too busy just trying to take care of Tinny and Jacob. Just trying to survive.

Mercy pushed open his door. She still had the strangest feeling about this man. He was trouble. She could feel it in her bones. Somehow, he was going to change her life. She wondered if she ought to turn him away. She already had enough problems. But she needed the money.

"This is your room." She rested her hand on the white glass doorknob. "Clean towels on the sideboard. My boy will bring up a pitcher of hot water morning and night for your shaving, bathing, and such. Sheets'll be changed once a week. The dining room is down the stairs, through the parlor. Outhouse is directly out the back kitchen door, or out the front and around the house. I've got a barn if you've a horse that needs stabling." She paused. "That'll be a dollar and a half more a week, though," she dared.

"Bank's stabling my mount at the livery." He tossed his canvas bag on the bed covered with a green-and-blue patchwork quilt she'd stitched herself. All five rooms, three upstairs, two down, that she'd prepared for boarders had similar quilts spread neatly on their beds, but this one was her favorite. She wished now she'd put it on a different bed.

"Well." Mercy lifted her hand from the doorknob. "I'd best get back to the kitchen. Like I said, dinner's at one. You're always welcome to bring someone else. Only thirty-five cents a head for a hearty meal."

She didn't know why she said that, except out of nervousness. Something told her Mr. Ericson was the kind of man who dined alone.

Again, he just nodded his bristly chin.

She started to pull the door shut behind her, then turned back with a swish of her petticoat and sprigged calico skirt. "The rules, Mr. Ericson. No women. No drunkenness. No indecency."

"I don't drink," he said quietly. "I don't have a woman, and I'll keep my pants on."

She nodded, not in the least bit embarrassed. "Good. Well . . . I'll see you shortly."

Noah listened to the woman's light footsteps as she went along the hall and down the steps. He sat down on the edge of the rope bed and ran his hand over the quilt's star design, feeling the texture of the tiny, even stitches. Blue and green. Alice had loved blue and green together.

His gaze shifted to the four walls of the small room as he pushed thoughts of Alice and cozy quilts from his mind. He was good at redirecting his thoughts like that. He'd been doing it a long time.

The room was plain, and small, only eight by eight. The walls were freshly whitewashed; he could smell the paint. They were unadorned except for a small oval mirror over the sideboard that looked as if it might have come from a woman's dresser. There was a slightly chipped washbowl, a pitcher, and two neatly folded, but thin, towels on the sideboard that served as a washstand.

Noah lifted his hat from his head, set it on the bedpost and lay back, taking care to keep his boots off the quilt. He stared at the ceiling. It looked much the same as all the other ceilings he'd lain beneath in the last three years, a little more cracked than some, less cracked than others. He wouldn't need to escort the first stagecoach to the train station for two days. That would mean he'd have plenty of time to stare at the plastered ceiling. Plenty of time to torment himself.

Noah ground his teeth. The Nowhere Bank of Nevada had been robbed twice in the last three months—both times, during transportation of their funds from the bank to Carson City south of here. Noah had been hired to escort the coach with the money. The pay was good because the work was considered dangerous. A man had been shot and injured in the last robbery. But Noah didn't care about the money. Sometimes he didn't even collect his fee before moving from one job to another. He only cared about the danger. He liked the danger. He liked the fear. He deserved it.

Noah bolted upright as he heard a sound in the hall outside his door. There was a shadow beneath the crack in the door. Someone was there. He waited for Mrs. Atkins—Mercy—to speak. When she said nothing, but just stood outside his door, Noah's brow creased. Odd behavior for a woman. If she wanted something, why didn't she say so?

"Yeah?" Noah called.

No answer. But the shadow didn't move.

"You need something, Mrs. Atkins?" Still nothing.

Noah rose from the bed. The ropes that held up the mattress squeaked.

He turned the doorknob. "Can I help you Mrs.—" Noah halted in midsentence. This was a boy. A young boy with dark hair and blue eyes the same shade as those of the missus.

The boy just stood there and stared.

Noah stared back. He didn't like children. Especially children that stared at him. "Yes?"

The boy slipped his hands into his pockets and rocked in his holey shoes. "My name's Jacob." He peered up at Noah. Most children were afraid of him and avoided him, which was probably smart on their part. Only this one didn't seem to be afraid. "What's yours?" he asked.

"Noah Ericson." Noah spoke sharply, hoping the boy would get the hint to move on.

Jacob nodded as if Noah had revealed something profound. "Then you must be our outrider boarder."

"Guess so, seeing as how I'm the only boarder." Noah didn't smile.

Jacob leaned to look through the doorway. "Can I come in?"

"No."

Still, the boy didn't back down. He stared at the duffel on the bed. "I could help you unpack."

"Don't need any help."

His gaze fell to Noah's boots. "I could clean up your boots for you. Shine them up—"

Noah cut him off. "My boots are fine."

Again, Jacob nodded. "Well . . . you need anything, I—"

"I don't need anything." Noah closed the door.

For a minute Noah stood there, his hand on the knob. He didn't hear a sound. The child continued to stand on the other side of the door, even though Noah had practically slammed it in his face.

Finally the voice on the other side said, "Well, I'll see you at suppertime. We can talk more then. Bye."

Noah waited until the skipping footsteps fell away before he lay back on the bed again.

Where was I? he thought. *The ceiling.* As he stared up, he mentally made a grid on the eight-by-eight surface and began to analyze each square-foot section. Cracked. Not cracked. Possible water stain.

Only half an hour passed before Noah sensed someone was at the door again. And again, he'd heard no footsteps. It wasn't like Noah to let people sneak up on him. It wasn't like him to let people near him at all.

"I said I don't need anything!" he called sharply. Mr. Cook hadn't said a pesky boy came with the free room. He'd guaranteed Noah wouldn't be bothered.

"What's that?"

Noah was startled by an old man's gravelly voice. He sat up as the door swung open.

"Good day to you." A stooped, thin man in suspenders tipped an expensive bollinger hat to Noah. The hat seemed comically out of place on a man wearing long underwear and pants that were too short for him by three inches.

Noah stared at the intruder. He hadn't recalled inviting the man in, but that didn't seem to matter.

"Name's Tinny, Tinny Parker. I'm the man of the house. Mercy's my girl. Her good-for-nothin' husband hasn't found his way home from the war yet, so I look after her and her boy." He hitched up his pants proudly and bare legs appeared even farther above his shoes.

"I don't need anything, Mr. Parker. You can go and pull the door behind you."

The man frowned, his papery, suntanned skin creasing across his brow like a lady's fan. "What do I care what you need? Hell, boy, I'm not the maid. I come to ask if you want to play a hand of poker. Joe's not up to it. Wore himself out pluckin' that chicken, I suspect."

"I'm not much of a card player." Noah lay back on the bed. "Thanks anyway." He closed his eyes.

"Phew-ee! You got some seriously dusty boots there."

Noah opened his eyes. What was this family's preoccupation with dirty shoes? Hadn't they ever seen a little mud on a working man's boots before?

"Mr. Parker—"

"Tinny. Call me Tinny. All my friends do."

It was on the tip of Noah's tongue to tell the old man he wasn't his friend. That would get rid of him. But for some reason it wouldn't roll off his tongue. Noah sensed that there was something about Tinny that wasn't quite right, and he couldn't bring himself to hurt his feelings. "I'm a little worn out, Tinny. I thought I'd just rest a while."

Tinny gave a hurrumph. "Don't know why a young man like you would need to rest in the middle of the day." He squinted, looking Noah over head to foot. " 'Course it's a wonder a man as buzzard-leg skinny as you can walk. You need a little meat on your bones. Wait until you taste my Mercy's cooking. I give you a few weeks at her table and we'll have to wheel you away Mr. . . . ." Tinny paused, waiting for Noah to fill in his last name.

When Noah didn't bite, Tinny repeated himself. "Sorry, I didn't catch your name Mr. . . ."

Noah sighed and stared at the ceiling. "Ericson."

"Got a first name there, Ericson, seeing as how we'll be sleeping under the same roof?"

"It's Noah," he said softly. When he spoke his first name, somewhere deep inside he heard Alice's voice. It had been four years since he'd heard her call his name, but it still hurt.

"Noah." He nodded the same way the boy had, as if Noah had said something profound. He squinted. "You look like a Noah."

Noah knew the best thing to do was nothing. If he didn't say anything, Tinny would go away. But he couldn't resist. The man, like the boy and his mother, sparked his interest. Noah couldn't remember the last time anything or anyone had interested him. "And how does a Noah look?" he asked dryly. "Do I seem like a man who could build an ark?"

Tinny stared for a moment, as if he didn't know who the biblical Noah was, then suddenly burst into laughter, slapping his hand on the thigh of his faded denims. "Build an ark! That's a good one. Build an ark." He cackled. "I'll have to tell Joe that one."

Noah couldn't resist a wry smile. The old man was easily amused. For some reason Noah was envious.

The men's gazes met, and for a moment Tinny seemed to see through Noah's shaggy hair, through his eyes, right to his heart.

Noah tucked his arm beneath his head and stared at the ceiling again.

Tinny shuffled his feet. "Well, guess I'll leave you to yourself. But if you find yourself looking for a card game, most likely I'll be on the front porch. That's where my daughter puts me to keep me out of her way."

"I don't see myself looking for a card game, Tinny."

"Just the same, invitation is always there. See you dinnertime, Noah. One sharp."

The door closed and Noah tried to recall which grid on the ceiling he'd left off with. As he found his place and once again began to catalog the bare white squares, he wondered if he was making a mistake going downstairs for meals. Something told him he'd be better off in the kitchen with the cheese sandwich later in the day. Something told him that if he went downstairs to try Mercy's chicken, his miserable life would forever be changed.

The thing was, he was perfectly content to be miserable. It was what he did best.

Two

Mercy set out the fifth plate and turned it so that the blue willow pattern was straight. Jacob followed behind her, adding a fork and a knife to the place setting. As he walked around the table, she straightened the knife at Mr. Ericson's seat.

What am I doing? she wondered as she drew back her hand. What was she so nervous about? The hen was fresh and young and she'd fried it up crispy brown. Her peas were sweet. The bread was still warm from the oven. The meal would be fine.

Mercy wiped her hands on her apron and headed for the kitchen. Who was she kidding? It wasn't her cooking she was nervous about. It was that man upstairs. Mr. Ericson. *Noah.*

His name rang strange in her head. It set her stomach uneasy, but not like she'd eaten something bad. This was different. She wondered if she was having some sort of premonition. The thing was, she was uneasy, but she wasn't afraid. She wasn't afraid of Mr. Ericson, just wary of him.

In the past, she'd always been able to depend on her intuition to keep her and Jacob safe. It had always warned her when her husband, Haman, was liquored up and feeling mean.

Mercy took a loaf of bread wrapped in muslin from the

back of the stove, set it on the clean wooden table, and began to slice it.

If she was uneasy about Ericson in the house, she should just tell him to leave. Yes, she needed money desperately, but Jacob and Tinny had been her first responsibility since Jacob had been born and her father had arrived shortly thereafter. Before Haman had gone to war she'd had to protect her father and son from him. She'd had to keep Tinny out from under foot and Jacob quiet. There had been nights when she'd walked a colicky Jacob on the front porch, even though it was bitter cold out and she'd had to wrap him up in half the quilts in the house, just so Haman wouldn't hear him. She'd kept her infant in the dark and cold so he wouldn't disturb his father's poker game, or his alcohol-induced sleep. It was the only way she knew to keep him safe.

Mercy knew the war had been bad for most families, but for hers, it had been a miracle. If the Army hadn't taken Haman, she knew she and Jacob wouldn't have survived his heavy hand.

Bastard, Mercy thought, sawing hard on the bread, harder than she needed to. Haman's name left a bad taste in her mouth, worse than the blood she'd tasted when he hit her. The Bible said a man paid for his sins. To her way of thinking, Haman's debt had to be awfully steep.

She shifted her thoughts back to the man in her upstairs bedroom. Should she be afraid of him? Her gut instinct told her no. He wouldn't harm her or her family. Maybe she was just wary of him because she was wary of all men.

"Mama?" Jacob stuck his head in the doorway. "Want me to fill the water glasses?"

She glanced up and smiled. "Please."

"Then you want me to call Mr. Ericson?"

She arranged the bread in a round basket she'd woven.

"He's not a hog. He needn't be called to trough." Covering the breadbasket with a clean piece of muslin, she passed her son in the doorway. "We can't spend our time calling guests to the table. As we have more guests, we'll only get busier. Mr. Ericson knows what time I serve the midday meal. He can come or not come." She set down the bread and checked to be sure there was a plate of fresh butter on the table.

Mercy traded butter for eggs with Annie on a weekly basis, because Annie had an affinity to cows but hated chickens worse than a barn cat hates a rat. It was a convenient arrangement for them both, and it kept Mercy from having to come up with precious coin to set her table.

Mercy heard her father shuffle into the room.

"Want me to call the gunman?" He hung his hat on a rack and slid into his chair. He'd washed his hands and face and slicked back his gray hair, still damp from the water at the pump out back.

"He ain't—" Jacob eyed his mother. *"He's not* a hog to be called to trough, Pap." He slid into his own designated seat. "He can come to the table or not. We don't care."

"Please don't call Mr. Ericson a gunman, Papa." Mercy fussed with the butter dish. "It makes him sound like he's some sort of outlaw. He's been hired by the bank to protect the coach. He carries a gun to safeguard the bank's profits."

Tinny made no response.

Mercy glanced at the clock on the corner shelf just as it clanged one o'clock. "I'll get the chicken and peas. Jacob, you'll honor us by saying the grace."

"Yes, Mama."

By the time Mercy returned to the dining room with the plate of fried chicken and bowl of peas, Jacob had carefully placed his napkin on his lap and bowed his head to wait for her. His eyes were squeezed shut so tight that he grimaced, his hands clenched in prayer.

Mercy untied her apron and hung it beside Tinny's hat. She slipped into her place at the head of the table. "Go ahead, Jacob." She bowed her head.

As Jacob prayed, Mercy listened for the sound of footsteps on the staircase overhead. Mr. Ericson's footsteps.

Won't that be something, she thought. She'd gone to all this trouble for him and he wasn't even going to show his face for the meal. Cheese sandwich, hell, it would be a pea sandwich for Mr. Can't-Be-Bothered-To-Come-Down-For-Dinner.

As Jacob went on with his litany, thanking the good Lord for the hens in the hen house and the corn to feed them, the hollow sound of footsteps echoed above.

"Amen," Jacob finished quickly. He glanced up at the parlor doorway.

"Amen," Mercy and Tinny murmured.

Mercy reached for the platter of chicken, surprised to find her hand shaky. She wondered if this was a mistake, sitting down to eat with her boarders, including them with her family meal.

Her idea had been that men far from home or without kin might enjoy eating with a family. If the recent silver strike two miles from Nowhere panned out, the town would fill with men who came to work the mines. They would need hot meals and a bed to sleep in. And it was Mercy's intention to feed and put those men up. But she hadn't anticipated she'd be so nervous. She wasn't comfortable with the male of the species and that was that. Nothing but heartache had come out of most of the men she'd known.

Mercy heard Mr. Ericson reach the bottom of the steps as she took a chicken thigh and passed the plate to Tinny. Mr. Ericson seemed to hesitate. She wondered what ailed him. Surely he could find the dining room.

Then she heard footsteps again, only instead of coming through the parlor to the dining room, he went straight out the front door.

"Where's Mr. Ericson going?" Jacob took a drumstick from the plate his grandfather held for him. "Ain't—*isn't* he going to eat with us?"

Mercy scooped a spoon of peas from the bowl. Now she was really annoyed. She'd made it clear that they ate at one. When she'd said if he missed a meal, he could get something in the kitchen, she'd meant if he missed a meal because of his job. She didn't mean he could come and go in her kitchen day and night as he pleased.

"Not your concern, Jacob," she chastised. "I want to see a full spoon of peas on that plate. Boy does not live by drumsticks and bread with a mountain of butter alone."

Her son obediently took a portion of the vegetable, though he counted the number of peas on the spoon before dropping them onto the plate.

Mercy heard the front door open again. She frowned. What *was* that man doing?

When she heard his footfall in the parlor, she made an event of placing her napkin on her lap just as she had taught Jacob, as her mother had taught her.

"Didn't mean to be late. Sorry," Mr. Ericson said, appearing in the doorway. He deposited his hat on the rack. "Cleaned off my boots."

Everyone's gaze fell to his boots. Mercy noticed they were still dirty, but at least they weren't mud-encrusted anymore.

"I appreciate that, Mr. Ericson." Mercy didn't look directly at him.

Ericson studied the two place settings left open. "Where you want me to sit?" He tipped his head slightly so that his hair fell over his eyes.

"There." Tinny pointed. "Across from my grandson.

That one there's Joe's." He pointed with his knife that balanced a pat of butter to the seat beside Mercy, directly across from him.

Ericson nodded.

Mercy passed him the chicken as he took his chair.

Everyone was silent as he added bread and peas to his plate.

Realizing both Jacob and Tinny were staring at him, and not eating, Mercy cleared her throat. Who would come to her hotel to eat if they were constantly being stared at?

"Jacob," she said, stumbling to start a conversation. "Eat up and tell me what news Miss Annie had for us when you fetched the butter."

The boy took a big bite of chicken. "She said Sissy's going to drop a calf any day. Oh, and the sheriff had to arrest a man last night for putting his hands on Letty down at the saloon. She said he put his hand right up her—"

"Jacob," Mercy cut in.

Tinny snickered.

"That's not appropriate conversation. Not in front of guests. Annie knows better than to tell such tales."

Her son shrugged. "You asked for the news."

Mercy pushed several peas onto her fork with the aid of half a slice of bread. "So, Mr. Ericson . . . where'd you come from last?"

She heard his fork scraping his plate.

He took his time in answering. "Utah."

She nodded. "You worked for a bank there?"

Again, a pause. "No."

"I see," Mercy said. Obviously the man wasn't looking for engaging conversation.

"Who'd you work for?" Jacob asked excitedly.

"Railroad. Guarding cargo."

"See any wild redskins? Kill any? We got a few redskins

in town, but they're not so wild. Mr. Crow, he's a redskin, but he's not so wild. Mostly he chews tobacco, spits, and—"

"Jacob." Mercy set down her fork and stared sternly at her son.

His mouth clamped shut the moment she spoke.

"It's not necessary that we grill Mr. Ericson," she said. "He's welcome to tell us whatever he wishes. His life is not our business and it's rude to inquire of another's business."

As she spoke, Tinny continued to shovel his food from his plate to his mouth, barely taking a breath between bites. Her father rarely spoke during meals. He was a serious man when it came to food.

Jacob grimaced as he gnawed at the gristle on the end of his drumstick. Then he looked up quickly. Before Mercy could stop him, he shot another question across the table. "You married? You got children, Mr. Ericson?"

Mercy looked directly at her guest for the first time since he'd come into the room. He'd combed back his hair as Tinny had, revealing more of his angular face. She was taken aback by how beautiful his dark-brown eyes were . . . and how sad. He would have been what she considered a handsome man if not for that sadness. "I'm sorry. I apologize for my son's questions, Mr. Ericson. You know how curious little boys can be." She gave a half-laugh.

He went on chewing as if he didn't know a thing about little boys, and Mercy wished she'd just stayed in the kitchen. She was lousy at making dinner conversation with men. This was never going to work.

"No wife. No children." He wiped his mouth with the napkin he'd placed on his lap.

Jacob's eyes widened. "Awww, you're going to get in trouble with my mama, Mr. Ericson," he piped up.

Ericson halted in midwipe, glancing up at Mercy.

"The napkins are just for looking, not using," Jacob

explained. "Mama said if we use them, we'll be out on the washboard scrubbing them ourselves."

Mercy knew she blushed. She could feel the heat diffusing through her cheeks. "Jacob. I only meant—" She turned to her guest, wishing not only that she'd never left the kitchen, but that she'd never crawled from her bed this morning.

"It's all right, Mr. Ericson. I only meant the napkins were for guests, not *grubby-faced boys.*" She eyed Jacob.

For an instant, the briefest instant, Mercy would have sworn she'd seen a twinkle of humor in the man's dark eyes. Then it was gone.

He pushed back his chair, wood scraping wood as he rose. "Good meal. Thank you, ma'am." He pushed his chair in and walked around the table to retrieve his hat. He dropped the hat low over his brow so that, once again, she couldn't see his eyes. "Reckon I'll see you at suppertime." He nodded and disappeared through the parlor doorway.

Mercy held her breath and waited until she heard his footfall on the stairs overhead. With a heavy exhalation, she pushed out of her chair. "Jacob Atkins, if you can't behave yourself at the table, you'll eat on the back porch."

"I'm sorry, Mama." He rose, taking his cleaned plate with him. "I was just asking about his family. I was trying to be polite like you told me."

Sighing, Mercy halted in the doorway. It was so difficult to raise a child. She was never sure if she was doing right by him. She often wondered why God didn't send the darned little buggers with some sort of primer.

With one hand, she reached down and caressed a lock of Jacob's sun-kissed hair. "I know, sweetheart," she said softly. "But you have to learn how to read people. Mr. Ericson wasn't interested in talking with us."

She walked into the kitchen and he followed.

"Well, why not?"

"I don't know, Jacob."

"You think he's done something bad?"

"No." She turned to him. "Mr. Cook wouldn't send anyone of shady character to board with is." She took his plate. "Mr. Ericson's personal life is not our concern. Our concern is to make our guest as comfortable as possible." She scraped her plate into a small bucket on the sink. "If we're lucky, he'll tell others what a wonderful cook your mama is, and we'll have a dining room full of hungry men in a few weeks."

Jacob grinned. "That would make you happy, wouldn't it, Mama?"

She smiled back. "It would. Now, go see if your pappy is done with his meal. If he is, clear the table and then the two of you can take a walk through town. Just keep Pap out of trouble."

Jacob ran from the kitchen. "Come on, Pap," she heard him say as he disappeared into the dining room. "Finish up your plate and we can take a walk."

Mercy turned to the sink and sank the dirty dishes into a pan of water to soak.

Dinner hadn't gone as she'd planned, but what did she care if Mr. Ericson talked or not? She had a week's worth of room and board in the top drawer of her dresser. As long as the money kept coming in, it didn't matter to her if he ever spoke another word.

Noah stared at the ceiling. As the day passed, the shadows shifted from wall to wall. When the sun began to set, the room glowed orange for a brief time and then began to dim.

As he lay on his back on the blue-and-green quilt, his hands tucked behind his head, he tried not to listen to the homey sounds below—the laughter in the kitchen, the boy skipping rope in the front hall until Mercy sent him out on the porch.

Mercy. It had been a long time since a woman caught his eye like she did. He hadn't been able to keep from stealing a glance at her as he'd shoved his peas into his mouth as fast as he could. The minute he'd sat in her dining room chair, he'd wished he hadn't come down to eat with the family. It reminded him too much of mealtime with his own family. *She* reminded him too much of Alice.

Well, not so much of Alice but of the way she made him feel when they'd first met. Warm. A little nervous, but a good nervous.

Noah knew he didn't deserve to feel that way. Not ever again.

He had half a mind to walk over to the bank now and tell Cook he'd changed his mind. He wasn't going to escort the Nowhere Bank coach. He could pack his bag— hell, he'd never unpacked it—and just ride whichever way the wind blew him. Maybe he'd go to Texas. Maybe even Mexico.

All afternoon Noah contemplated heading out of Nowhere before anything got too complicated. Instead, he drifted off to sleep, listening to the fetching sound of busy female footsteps and the smell of apple pie in the oven.

Three

Mercy slid the biscuits out of the oven and dropped the pan onto the black stovetop. "Ouch!" she cursed under her breath as the iron skillet burned her hand through the rag.

She shook her injured hand and grabbed the bread-basket, gingerly transferring the breakfast biscuits. If she was going to make it to church on time, she'd have to hurry.

Overhead she heard Mr. Ericson's door squeak open. He'd be down for breakfast in a moment and it wasn't ready. She grabbed the blackberry jam from the pantry off the kitchen and then the breadbasket.

He was an odd man, this Mr. Ericson.

Last night Mercy had served him a supper of leftover cold chicken, fried potatoes, and fresh apple pie. He ate the meal in silence and then excused himself. He had eaten so fast that Mercy had thought he must have been in a hurry to get somewhere, a card game or the arms of a dance-hall girl, maybe. But to her surprise, he had not headed into town as she assumed an unmarried man would on a Saturday night. Instead, he'd simply returned to his room, hat low over his brow, boots still dirty.

She wondered if he was a teetotaler.

Mercy dropped the biscuits and jam on the table and went back for the egg pie. "Breakfast!" she shouted toward the back door. "Jacob! Pap! Breakfast!"

"Coming," she heard faintly.

Mercy slipped back into the dining room, and stopped short. "Oh. Mr. Ericson." He'd startled her.

Her first reaction was to tuck the stray strand of hair that habitually escaped her chignon back behind her ear.

"Sorry." He kept his gaze cast downward as he dropped his hat on the rack. "Am I early? I can go—" He pointed toward the parlor.

"No, no," she interrupted, flustered and not sure why. "You're right on time. It's Jacob and my papa that are late. And me." She set the egg dish on the center of the table and ran her hands over her apron for no reason other than that she didn't know what else to do with them. "I just couldn't seem to get moving fast enough this morning."

He stood awkwardly behind his chair.

"Sit, please." She gestured. "I'm sure they'll be in directly."

As he waited politely for her to sit first, Mercy felt the urge to retreat to the kitchen. She wanted to go back for something, but the meal was already on the table. She had no choice but to sit or look like a ninny. She sat.

"I just don't know what's keeping them." She glanced at the clock. "We'll be late for church if they don't hurry."

Mr. Ericson studied his plate for a moment, then touched the edge. There was a strange look on his face. Strained.

"Something wrong with your plate, Mr. Ericson? My father helped me do the dishes last night." She leaned over and stared at the plate with a critical eye, in search of a speck of potato or a greasy smear of butter. "Didn't he rinse well enough?"

For a moment the man said nothing. He just stared at the plate, his finger on a splash of the blue willow pattern. Then suddenly he withdrew his hand as if the plate was hot. "No, it's fine." He stumbled over his words. "It just reminded me of someone else who had similar plates."

Mercy wanted to ask who, but she didn't. Mr. Ericson's brown eyes were too filled with sadness, and Mercy had enough sadness of her own. She didn't think she could handle the burden of another's.

"Please eat," she said gently, not knowing why she felt the need to coddle him. "My men will be in when they're in, and if they miss breakfast, they'll just be all the hungrier come noon, won't they?"

When he made no move to serve himself, she scooped baked egg and onions and cheese from a pan in the center of the table. "Lift your plate."

He nodded, offering it. "I'm much obliged."

She served herself, glancing at him. He was dressed in blue denims again, and a soft green shirt that had faded from washing and the sun to the color of an apple. His dark-brown hair was clean, but it hung straight to brush his collar and partially obscure his face. He looked like a man who needed a little female attention. A haircut and new shirt would do his appearance wonders.

"I do laundry," she said, tasting the rich pie. "If you've anything that needs washing, just leave it outside your door and Jacob will pick it up."

"I've been doing my own wash for a while."

She shrugged, unoffended. "Suit yourself. I'm just making the offer. There'd be no charge," she added as an afterthought. "Not with you boarding here."

He halted his fork in midair as if he wanted to say something.

Mercy waited.

"Look, Mrs. Atkins—"

"You can call me Mercy. Atkins was my husband's name." She stared at her own plate. "I never really took to it." The truth was that the name left a bitter taste in her mouth. She'd just as soon not be associated with the

Atkins name, not with Haman or his sister or any of his good-for-nothing brothers.

"*Mercy . . .*" Her name seemed to come painfully to him, like the last breath of a dying man, and yet there was a sweetness to that last breath. "I appreciate your hospitality, but"—he set down his fork and stared at his plate, his hair hanging to hide his face from her—"I'm pretty much a loner. I appreciate what you're trying to do, but the food and room are enough."

She understood. He wasn't looking to be friendly. He just wanted his hot meal and clean sheets, and to be left alone.

Mercy knew she should appreciate his honesty, but instead, her feelings were hurt. She didn't know why. She had no interest in being friendly with Mr. Ericson or any other man for that matter.

"I see," she said coolly, rising and taking her half-eaten breakfast with her. Her appetite was gone. "It looks like Jacob and Pap will be walking to church with empty stomachs." She stepped through the doorway into the kitchen, not bothering to look back. "We're off to church. Just leave your plate where it is and I'll clean up later. Good day, Mr. Ericson."

Noah lifted his gaze from the blue-and-white plate that made his heart ache and caught a glimpse of Mrs. Mercy Atkins as she sashayed out of the dining room, petticoats swinging like a church bell. He'd hurt her feelings. He heard it in her voice. Not that this was anything new to him. He'd left a trail of hurt feelings across most of Utah and a good part of Nevada. This was just the first time he cared.

After the morning church service Mercy allowed Jacob and her father to walk ahead of her. She stayed long enough to inquire on Widow Laret's health. The poor girl was far gone with child and expected to deliver any day. Then Mercy strolled home in peace. She loved her son and father dearly, but she needed these few precious minutes alone each week to keep her sanity.

Today, the hot sun on her face and the clear blue sky above gave her a strange sense of hope. For months she'd been so careworn that she'd not felt like herself. Nothing seemed to be going right. The roof of the hotel that she had no customers for was leaking. She was so short on money she'd been forced to sell her wedding band just to make ends meet. Tinny's mind seemed to be getting worse and he was beginning to stray from home. And now Jacob was beginning to ask far more questions about his father than she was ready to answer.

Now, perhaps, everything would change. If the silver discovery north of Nowhere panned out, men would begin to come in search of the silver and the work it would generate. Mr. Cook had put up their new employee at her place, and for once she had cash money in her pantaloon stocking.

As Mercy walked down the plank sidewalk of the one and only street in Nowhere, she greeted the townsfolk who passed on foot and in buckboard wagons. " 'Afternoon Mrs. Reynolds, Mr. Reynolds." Mercy smiled from beneath her straw spoon bonnet.

" 'Afternoon Mrs. Atkins."

"Ma'am."

They were all friendly enough, but Mercy knew they gossiped about her. Her husband had been gone a long time. Everyone said he was dead, another casualty of the war. Not to her face, of course. To her face they were sickeningly sympathetic, falsely reassuring.

"I'm certain he'll be home soon, dear," an older woman said.

"He's sure to come riding in any day," said a man.

That's what they'd been saying for nigh on three years.

Haman's brothers and the other men of the town who survived the war had returned home long ago. Mary Cain's husband had taken the longest to show up after the war and even he'd been home by spring of '66—a full year after Lee's surrender at Appomatax. Poor Leroy had been laid up in some hospital in Tennessee with one leg rotting. He'd ended up having the leg amputated at the knee, and then hobbled home halfway across the country before managing to buy a horse.

No, everyone in the town, except Haman's family, knew he was dead. Tinny, on one of his better days, had said that the men in the Twin Pianos Saloon agreed the government would probably declare Haman Atkins dead soon. Everyone knew that a man who didn't return from war after three years was dead, his bones rotting in some lonely field. Everyone but the Atkins family.

Mercy's thoughts turned to her in-laws and her stomach soured. It was too bad the war hadn't taken all the Atkins in one fell swoop. The world would have been a better place for it.

Two of Haman's brothers, Ahab and Jehu, had gone off to war with Haman but had managed to return alive. The word was that they'd spent a good deal of their time pretending to be sick, or wounded, or running some other equally detestable scam. The Army hadn't taken their brother Potipher, Ahab's twin, better known as Pots, at all. The Union Army said he wasn't quite right in the head. He'd been called up, but when he reported for duty with a tin bucket full of honey overturned on his head and a broomstick for a gun, the recruiter had sent him home with his sister Jezzy.

The truth was that anyone who knew Pots knew he was crazy, but not any crazier than any of his other brothers. He'd just been smart enough to keep from being drafted in the first place. At the time, Mercy had been relieved that her own husband hadn't been that bright, else he'd have been sent home as well.

Walking, Mercy passed a rain barrel with a big black crow perched on it. The crow took flight as she waved her arm, and she watched it circle overhead, its beady gaze still on her. That was how the Atkins family made her feel now, as if they always had *their* beady, black-eyed gaze on her.

Mercy had never gotten along with her in-laws, not from the day she'd arrived in Nowhere as a mail-order bride. The men didn't like her because she wouldn't tolerate their hands on her buttocks, and she stood up for herself. Jezzy didn't like her because she said Mercy thought herself too smart, too good for the likes of the people in Nowhere. That wasn't true. Mercy liked everyone in Nowhere—everyone but her husband and his good-for-nothing family.

At first, Mercy had tried to get along with her new family. She invited them to dinner, offered to do mending, and even sent pies and cakes out to the ranch. But the men took advantage of her offer of friendship. They took food home from her pantry without asking, set fire to her kitchen, killed her chickens for sport, and backed her into corners when Haman was at the outhouse or passed out from drink. On more than one occasion Jehu had brought a whore with him, thinking Mercy would allow him to use one of the rooms in the ramshackle hotel. He was too cheap to pay for the whore and a room at the saloon, too.

Mercy had never really had any confrontations with Jezzy. Mostly she kept to herself on the ranch and rarely came into town.

Mercy and Haman had been married four years when the war came and took him away. Jacob was only one when his papa marched off, so he barely remembered him now, which was good. Mercy prayed he wouldn't remember the shouting and the drunkenness, the cruelty of his tone, and the harshness of his fist. The only thing Jacob remembered was what Mercy planted in his head. She knew her lines by rote. *Haman Atkins was a fine, upstanding young man who had loved his son dearly. He had joined the war effort out of patriotism and had surely died in the trenches for his country.* Mercy saw no reason for Jacob to know the truth.

Mercy spotted her hotel at the far end of the street. She was almost home. With a sigh, she removed her bonnet and smoothed the stray blond strands that fluttered in the hot, dry breeze. She wasn't looking forward to going inside. She had all those dishes from breakfast to do and then dinner to make. At least she had Mr. Ericson's company to look forward to.

Mercy smiled at her own joke as she climbed the rickety front steps to the porch. He wasn't a talkative man. What outrider was?

But something told her that this outrider wasn't like the others she'd known. It was just a hunch, but what man could get sentimental over an old plate, except a man with a tale? A sad one, she guessed.

Mercy walked into the front hall, the screen door slapping shut behind her.

"Guess I'd best get those dirty dishes," she said to herself as she headed for the dining room through the parlor. She knew Tinny and Jacob wouldn't be home for a while. Though they'd left church ahead of her, she knew they'd stop somewhere to talk, maybe share a sarsaparilla.

Mercy stepped into the dining room and stopped short, her bonnet dangling from one hand. The dirty dishes . . . they were gone. She stared in disbelief. Gone? A thief had taken her dirty dishes?

She walked into the kitchen. Lo and behold, there were her blue willow dishes, all clean and dry on the sideboard on the sink.

Someone had washed her dishes.

She broke into a grin. Not someone. Noah.

Four

Mercy stood frozen in wonder, one hand resting on her hip. She couldn't stop staring at those blue-and-white dishes on the sideboard, all shiny and clean. No one had ever washed dishes for her in her life. No one had ever been so kind.

Oh, sure, Tinny and Jacob helped her when asked, but they never volunteered on their own, or thought to do them by themselves, without her aid.

Mercy glanced up at the kitchen ceiling as if she could see right through the water-stained wood. She wondered if he was up there now. She wanted to march right up those stairs, knock on his door, and thank him.

But Mercy knew she shouldn't . . . couldn't.

She hung her bonnet on a peg by the back door and slipped her apron over her head to cover her Sunday dress. She knew the cool brown linen fabric with its high waistband and pleated front bands at the bodice was sadly out of fashion, but it was the only good dress she owned.

She still wanted to go up and thank Noah for what he did, but she couldn't because she was afraid. Mercy was afraid of what he might say. What he might not say.

Instead of following her heart, she made sandwiches for dinner from yesterday's leftover biscuits. But she kept glancing up at the ceiling and thinking about him. Once she thought she heard the creak of the old bed frame in his room.

She wondered what he was doing up there all alone hour after hour. Was he reading a paperback he carried in that bag of his? Or was he staring at the ceiling? And why had he washed her dishes? What would possess a man like Noah Ericson, an outrider, to wash a woman's dishes? Was it the dishes themselves? He said they reminded him of someone. Had he washed those dishes for the someone they reminded him of?

Or had he done it for Mercy?

Her hand trembled as she sliced another biscuit and added cheese and cold sausage. She couldn't risk getting friendly with this man—any man. Legally she was still a married woman. Until Haman was declared dead by the government, she was still his wife and she had a whole ranch of in-laws to remind her of that fact.

Mercy set the plate of sandwiches on the dining table and went back for a pitcher of cold milk and a basket of apples.

Besides, what made her think Noah was interested in being friendly with her? Hadn't he said he wasn't just this morning?

That reason brought her smack back to her question. Why *did* he wash the dishes?

Mercy was just setting down the milk pitcher when Noah appeared in the parlor doorway.

"Afternoon, ma'am."

She glanced at the clock. He was right on time. "Afternoon. Dinner's ready. Have a seat. Tinny and Jacob ought to be rolling in any minute." She chattered on nervously, trying to figure out the best way to broach the subject of the dishes. She didn't want him to think she wasn't grateful, but she didn't want him to know how deeply his gesture had touched her, either. She breathed slowly, composing herself.

"Mr. Eric—Noah." She leaned on the back of Tinny's chair. "I want to—"

"Mama! Mama!" Jacob shouted from the front door as Mercy heard him rush inside. "Mama! You have to come quick. Pap's in trouble again."

Mercy ran for the front door, meeting Jacob in the middle of the parlor's worn hook rug. "In trouble? What do you mean?" She grasped her son's shoulders, looking him straight in the eye.

Jacob took her hand and tugged, leading her toward the door. "He's had a run-in with a bad man. Some miner passing through town. He's already busted Pap's lip bloody."

Mercy ran after Jacob, out the front door and down the steps on the wooden walk. She didn't bother to take the time to remove her apron. "Where? Where is he?"

On the street, Jacob led her west toward the bulk of the town's buildings.

Behind them were only a few residential houses, a ladies' shop and a saloon that had both closed a year after the war began. The last building on the street was a livery stable that housed no horses, only plank tables for men to gather around and play checkers.

"How did he get into a fight with a miner?" Mercy demanded, keeping up with her son.

Jacob shrugged. "I tried to stop him, but you know Pap and his mouth. One minute he's grinnin' and tippin' his hat to a stranger on the street, the next minute they're having words."

"God be my strength," Mercy whispered, glancing heavenward. The sun was bright on her face and made her squint. Jacob's words were true enough. Her father did pick fights with strangers and over the damnedest things.

"I know it's not your fault," Mercy said, trying to console her son. "You're not your grandfather's keeper." They hurried past the Twin Pianos Saloon, closed on Sundays, several houses, and the bank. A crowd gathered around Black Pete's barber shop. Everyone had on his or her Sunday best. The Widow Locke had her pink parasol popped up, blocking Mercy's view.

"There he is." Jacob pointed to the center of the commotion.

"All right! All right!" Mercy shouted above the sound of the crowd. "That will be enough, Tinny Parker."

The sea of Sunday linen dresses and starched black suits parted to let her through, and Mercy spotted a brawny, bearded man in a hat just as he drew back his fist and swung.

Mercy cried out a warning as Tinny dodged left, just out of the man's way.

"Tinny! Did you hear me? I said that's enough!" Mercy hollered. "Fighting on the Lord's day, you ought to be ashamed of yourself!"

Tinny didn't seem to hear her as he danced this way and that, fists high. He'd shed his Sunday coat and hat, and his striped suspenders drooped over his thin shoulders. The blood from his split lip had dripped onto the only white shirt he owned.

Tinny looked like one of the fighters Mercy had once seen in a traveling show. Just before the war, a man in long drawers and leather gloves had come to Nowhere, fighting men for cash. That fighter had been all dance and fancy steps. He'd set up a ring with rope and onlookers were invited to place bets.

"Pap!" Mercy shouted again.

Tinny bounced this way and that, taking swings in the air as if he saw invisible opponents all around him.

Just then, the man stepped forward and threw a punch with his left hand, clipping Tinny in the chin.

"I said that will be enough!" Mercy swung around to face her father's attacker. "He's an old man, for heaven's sake!" She took a step toward the miner, her voice shaking with fury. "What kind of man are you that you get pleasure from fighting the old and feeble-minded?"

"Feeble-minded, my puckered asshole."

The townsfolk gave an audible gasp.

"He's the one that started it." As the miner spoke, he bobbed this way and that, swinging at the dodging Tinny.

"You started this?" She threw up her hand at Tinny, trying to block the next punch. "You started another fight, Pap?"

"Outta my way, woman. Give me room." Tinny bobbed and dodged comically. "It's men like this that need a good lesson. Insult me, will he? I'll take this young whippersnapper and turn him over my knee."

"Insult you? Ye're the one that insulted me first, you old coot!"

Mercy threw up her hands as the miner attempted to take another poke at her father. "I said that will be—"

The miner grabbed her left shoulder and shoved her aside. Mercy stumbled, hit one of the posts of the barber shop's overhang, and caught herself before she fell.

Tinny took the miner's next punch full in the jaw before Mercy could get to them.

Tinny flew backward and went down.

"Pap!" She fell to her knees at her father's side and helped him sit up. "Pap, are you all right?"

"That'll be enough."

Mercy heard a man's voice behind her, low but forceful. He sounded like a man who meant business. A man to fear.

It was Noah. She knew it before she turned and her gaze met his.

Tinny struggled against her to get to his feet, flailing his fists. "Let me at him. Let me teach that sorry, mother-lovin'—"

"Pap!" Mercy insisted through clenched teeth as she pinned his arms back. She could tell by the wild-eyed look in the miner's eyes that Tinny had nearly pushed him over the edge of reason. "Will you hush before he lays you an early grave?"

"What'd you call me?" the miner shouted, taking a step closer. "What'd you say about my mama, old man?"

The miner came at Tinny, not seeming to care that Mercy was between the two of them.

As the miner rushed them, Mercy threw herself over her father in an attempt to protect his feeble bones. The miner rose over her, blocking out the glare of the sun. He smelled of whiskey and sour sweat.

"I said that will be enough!" Noah boomed.

Mercy only caught a glimpse of Noah as he grabbed the miner by the scruff of his neck and pulled him backward. As she turned, both knees on the sidewalk, she saw the miner twist around and throw his fist into Noah's middle.

God above, she thought. *Pap's going to get us all killed.*

Noah took the punch full in his stomach and Mercy cringed, yet couldn't bear to turn away. The miner easily outweighed him by two stones and towered a head above him.

But miraculously, Noah didn't buckle. He never swayed. Never flinched. In fact, he acted as if he hadn't been touched, as if a fly had swatted him instead of this ogre.

"You shouldn't have done that," Noah said softly, his gaze lowered.

Eerie goosebumps rose on Mercy's bare forearms. Noah reminded her of a bull, head down, pawing the ground just before he charged.

"You shouldn't have done it," Noah repeated. Then, before Mercy could react, he lifted his gaze and flew into the man.

The miner never knew what hit him.

Noah caught him in the jaw. Once, twice, three times, four, until the miner's head snapped left and right like a feed bag hung from a barn rafter. The miner tried to hit back, tried to catch Noah with his knee. Noah knocked him to the ground, slamming him again and again with his fists, sinking his boot into the man's stomach.

"Noah!" Mercy leaped up, leaving her father seated on the sidewalk.

Noah was out of control. She had never seen such rage in a man's eyes. Never witnessed such unabandoned fury.

Noah was hunkered over the fallen man, swinging again and again, even as the miner curled into a ball and cried for mercy.

"Noah, don't. You'll kill him!" Against her better judgment, Mercy laid both hands on the gunman's shoulders. They were incredibly broad shoulders beneath the faded shirt. She could feel his muscles at her fingertips, corded and bound in power.

"Noah," she repeated softly so that only he could hear. "No more, please."

Beneath her spread palms, his shoulders relaxed. He stood absolutely still for an instant, then moved away from the injured man.

Mercy backed up out of his way, and the crowd backed with her, a little fearful of him. Who wouldn't fear a man with that kind of rage bottled up inside?

"Hee, hee, hee," Tinny cackled, stumbling to his feet. "Told that smart-lipped boy a lesson, didn't we?" He retrieved his favorite hat from the dust of the street and beat it on his knee.

Jacob followed behind his grandfather to catch the wobbly man if his legs failed him.

Noah picked up his own hat, lost in the fight.

"What's going on here? Can't a man eat in peace?"

Mercy looked up to see Sheriff Dawson coming down the sidewalk, his wife's red-and-white plaid napkin tucked into the collar of his Sunday shirt and flapping as he walked.

"It's all right," Mercy said. "No harm done, Sheriff. Go back to your supper."

"You again?" Jack Dawson halted in front of Tinny and pointed an accusing finger. "Now, I warned you, Tinny—"

"He's the one that started it!" Tinny proclaimed, pointing at the miner who still lay where he fell. "I was minding my own business, taking a Sunday stroll, when that man made a derogatory comment about my hat. Right in front of my grandson and my best friend, Joe." Tinny glided one hand over the bent rim of his hat. "A man's no man if he stands for the likes of that!"

Sheriff Dawson exhaled in frustration. "Mercy, I told you that if—"

"I'm sorry." She clasped her hands. "I'm so sorry, Sheriff. It won't happen again."

The sheriff, realizing he still wore his napkin, jerked it out of his banded collar. "You said that last week. Your father cannot pick a fight with every man who comes to town. He deserves a night in jail. That's what I promised last time."

"I know. I know." She lifted her hands to plead again. "I'll keep him inside if I have to. What's the sense in locking him up? You'll just have to sit with him all night, Sheriff. You know he's afraid of the dark."

"Afraid of the dark? Who's afraid of the dark?" Tinny passed Mercy and the sheriff and headed across the street, east toward home.

Mercy brushed the sheriff's arm. "Please, Jack. Not this time."

He grimaced and snapped the napkin in his hand. "Hell, all right. But next time, I swear to you—"

Mercy broke into a smile of relief. "Thank you. Thank you."

Sheriff Dawson glanced at the miner who rose slowly from his knees. "Tinny do that?" he asked in surprise.

"No, sir. I did." Noah appeared at her side, like a wall.

"You all right?" He touched Mercy's shoulder gently where the miner had grabbed her when he'd pushed her aside.

She nodded.

"And who are you?" the sheriff demanded.

Noah met the sheriff's authoritarian gaze, making no attempt to remove his hat or show any other sign of respect. "Noah Ericson."

"I see. The outrider the bank hired." The sheriff nodded. "So how'd you come to get in the midst of this?"

Noah continued to stare cool-eyed at the sheriff. "This gentleman overstepped his bounds. He handled Mrs. Atkins in his attempt to beat up the old man. When I tried to break it up, he struck me. I struck back in self-defense."

It was more words than Mercy had heard Noah string together since he'd arrived.

"Self-defense?" the sheriff grunted. "All right. Well, I'd best not see this again. We have a quiet town here, Mr. Ericson. We're not prone to roughness, and it won't be tolerated." He flapped his hands. "That's it, ladies and gents. Show's over. Go on home."

Sheriff Dawson walked over to the miner, crouched and leaning against the barber shop door. "Move on, mister, and I'll not take you in. But I'm warning you. I catch you in another fight in this town, and you'll be looking at it through bars. Understand?"

The miner nodded, too breathless or too dizzy to argue.

Mercy started across the street, ignoring everyone's stares. Noah fell into step beside her.

As they walked, their heels clacked in a matching rhythm. Ahead, she could see Tinny and Jacob. Her son had his arm looped through Tinny's, supporting him.

Mercy walked a full block before she spoke. "Thanks," she said quietly. She wiped the sweat that beaded above her upper lip with the corner of her apron, suddenly feeling shy.

"A man ought not raise a hand to a woman."

She gave a little laugh. His thought was heroic if not naive. "Not the first time I've been hit by a man's angry hand." She rubbed her shoulder gingerly. It was funny, but she felt the burn of Noah's touch more than the bruise of the miner's shove.

"Your father ought to be more careful. That miner could have killed him."

"It's not Pap's fault. He's not right in the head." She chuckled again. "If you hadn't already noticed."

Noah was quiet for a minute. She could feel the warmth of his body and smell a hint of his male skin on the hot Sierra breeze.

It had been a long time since Mercy had smelled a man's skin that wasn't touched by old age or youth or whiskey. It wasn't that she'd ever much enjoyed Haman when he did get close, but she suddenly realized that she missed the nearness of another human being just the same.

"There isn't a Joe, is there?" Noah asked.

This time her laugh was full and genuine. She laughed because the only alternative was to cry, and she'd already cried a creekful in her life. "No, there's no Joe. Pap made him up more than three years ago. I tried to convince him there was no Joe but finally gave up." She shrugged. "I realized that Joe's harmless enough."

Tinny and Jacob were already on the porch as they reached the hotel.

Mercy and Noah halted at the steps. She looked at him; he looked down at his boots.

Mercy had an urge to brush his hair back off his face so she could see those sad brown eyes of his. She stuffed her hands into her apron pockets. She felt overheated, and despite her undergarments, her linen dress scratched her beneath her armpits and breasts. She didn't know why she was sweating so. It was hot, all right, but she was used to the heat. She was even used to physical exertion in the heat. There was something about this man that made her always feel hotter. Maybe a drink of water would cool her down.

"Thank you again," she said. "That man might have killed Pap if you hadn't come along."

"Aw, I don't know." Slowly he raised his chin until he peered at her from beneath the brim of his hat.

Mercy was struck by how utterly handsome his smile was. For a second she lost her train of thought. The bare upturn at the corners of his mouth lit up his chiseled face, putting a sparkle in his dark eyes. His smile seemed to erase the sadness, if only for the briefest moment. Then the smile was gone and the sadness returned.

He turned his back to her. "You looked to me like you were doing pretty well on your own." He walked up the steps, hands shoved down in the pockets of his denims. "I have a suspicion that had I not shown up, you'd have had that miner on the ground of your own accord."

Mercy stood on the walk and watched him retreat. That was what he was doing, wasn't it? Running from her?

"Noah?"

He opened the screen door. "Yeah, Mercy?"

"Thank you for washing the dishes." She studied his broad shoulders wishing it wasn't so easy to recall the feel of them beneath her hands. "No one's ever done anything so nice for me."

"It was nothing," he said curtly, back to cool courtesy and monosyllables. *"Forget it."*

Mercy watched as he walked in the front hall and the door slapped shut behind him. A lump rose in her throat.

If only I could, she thought.

Five

"What'cha doing?" Young Jacob clung to one of the wooden-columned porch supports and spun around it. Noah sat on a three-legged stool pulled up beside a barrel used as a tabletop. It was where the old man played checkers at night with his invisible friend.

"Nothing." Noah stared at the chipped paint of the porch floor. Light rain pitter-pattered on the roof overhead. It was that sound that had lured him from the safety of his room to the front porch. He had always liked the rain.

"*Nothing?*" Warped floorboards creaked beneath Jacob's bare feet as he went around the pole again. "A person can't just do *nothing.*"

Noah wondered if the boy would just go away if he didn't answer. When he'd come downstairs, he hadn't anticipated company. For the last few days the family had pretty much left him alone, and that was how he wanted it. That was how he needed it to be.

Jacob raised his voice as if Noah were hard of hearing. "I said, you just can't do nothing."

"I heard you." Noah tried to hang on to the cold tightness in his heart, the constriction that could make him immune to little boys, spring rain, and the comforting smell of baking bread that wafted from the kitchen right now.

Noah knew he should never have remained at the Tin

Roof Hotel. Mercy was trouble. Jacob was trouble. Even the old man tugged at the remnant of Noah's old self. "I just don't feel much like talking."

"Mama said I should leave you alone. She said that was the way you wanted it. That you were the kind of man that wanted to be alone."

Noah couldn't resist. He lifted his head. "She said that about me? She say anything else?"

Jacob ceased spinning and came slowly around the pole. "That she was glad you were there to break up that fight the other day with Pap and the miner. That you was brave."

"That all?"

"Nope. She said you'd be handsome if you'd cut your shaggy hair and smile every once in a while."

Noah almost chuckled. "That right?"

"Uh huh. Know what else?"

"What else?"

"A decade is ten years. My mama told me. She's smart, you know." Jacob grinned, showing off a space where an upper tooth must recently have come out. Already Noah could catch the glimmer of a new, pearly tooth just breaking the surface of the boy's gum.

Noah remembered his little Becky's first wiggly tooth and the excitement it had brought to their tiny ranch house.

He ground his teeth and tried to concentrate on the cracked paint at his feet again.

"I'm glad you were there, too. I'm glad you're here." Jacob started the diversion again, spinning slowly around and around the post. "It gets lonely when Mama's busy and Pap's in a mood." His head popped up. "Hey, you want a bite of my sarsaparilla stick?"

Before Noah could turn his face away, the boy thrust the piece of candy in front of his nose. It had bits of pocket fuzz stuck to it.

Noah shook his head, averting his gaze. "No, thanks."

"Okay." Jacob returned it to his pocket and went round the pole again. "But you want some, you just have to ask. I'm good about sharing. Mama says I would have made a good big brother—if she'd ever had another baby." He paused. "She's not going to, though. She told me to just forget that idea."

Jacob's words stuck in Noah's mind. Mercy had wanted other children. He wondered why she hadn't had more, why she now discounted the possibility.

Noah couldn't keep his mouth shut. "Where's your father?"

"Aw, he went to the war when I was a baby."

Jacob said "the war" the same as he would have said "the store" or "the harness shop," and Noah knew that, like other children, he had no idea what *the war* meant. Who did, except those who had been there? Those who had smelled it, tasted it, felt its agony in their bones?

"He was a brave man who fought for his country," Jacob continued. "But he never came back." He added softly, "Mama says he's dead, killed in the war, only the paperwork just ain't . . . *hasn't* caught up with us."

Noah lifted his gaze to meet the boy's and the pain he saw in those young eyes knifed him deeply. Was this how his own Becky had spoken of her papa? Had Becky felt the same pain when people had asked her where her papa was?

Noah couldn't bear the boy's suffering and glanced away. He knew he should have stayed in his room. The cost of fresh air was too pricey in this house.

"You ought to be proud of him," Noah said. Even as he spoke, he knew he was making a mistake. With every word that passed between him and this boy, he formed a tie between them that wouldn't easily be broken. "He must have been proud of you, Jake."

He grinned. "I am. And Mama says— Uh oh." Jacob

released the pole and hopped across the porch toward the door. "Here come my uncles. I'd best tell Mama." He brought his face close to Noah's as he passed and wrinkled his freckled nose. His breath smelled of root beer. "Mama don't like them and neither do I, but we have to be nice—them being my papa's brothers and all."

Jacob disappeared into the house and Noah went on staring at the floor. There were several places where the boards had come loose and were in need of nails. He heard footsteps, but kept his gaze focused downward. There was no need for him to meet Jacob's uncles, or even speak with them. He had no intention of getting involved in Mercy's family.

"Who you?" A man came up the steps.

Noah caught a strong whiff of body odor on the breeze made damp by the rain. Immediately, he didn't like the tone of his voice. There was something ugly about it. Cold. Mean.

"Boarder," Noah replied without glancing up. He noticed the man's boots were muddy and that he made no attempt to clean them off as he walked into the hotel's front hall.

The man gave a sour laugh. "I'll be damned. Finally got herself a live one, does she?"

Two other men cackled as they passed, their boots as wet and muddy as the first man's.

Noah wondered if he ought to go inside, just to keep an eye on the three of them. But that was foolish. They were her in-laws. Family. From what the boy said, she'd been dealing with them for years. Besides, what business was it of his? He was just a boarder.

Noah waited until they went inside and then rose from the stool. He stretched his legs and groaned. All this inactivity was making him soft. Tomorrow would be his first day escorting the bank's stagecoach, and he was glad of

it. Work would get him out in the open again . . . and
out of this hotel that seemed too much like a home.

Noah ambled down the steps, then cut across the sparse
grass, headed for the backyard. The rain had slacked off
until it was barely a drizzle.

He crammed his hands into his denim pockets. He
needed something to do. Something to keep his mind
off Jake. Off the boy's mother.

If he could find a hammer and a few nails in the shed
out back, he thought he might tack down those loose
porch boards. Not for the sake of the woman, of course,
but just for something to do.

Mercy stepped over Jehu's legs that stretched across
her path between the stove and the dining room. Jehu
was dark-haired like Haman had been, and now, with his
older brother gone, he was the self-appointed leader. "Excuse me," she said for the hundredth time.

Jehu made no attempt to move his tree trunk legs as
he tossed down a card.

Mercy's three brothers-in-law had been sitting in her
kitchen for more than two hours, passing the time with
cards as they waited for her to prepare them a meal.

Mercy hadn't expected the Atkins boys for supper, so
she had to have Tinny kill another hen. The hens were
stewing on the back of the stove. Bread was out of the
oven. Now she rolled out slick dumplings to add to the
stew pot.

Mercy sprinkled flour on the sideboard at the sink and
took up her rolling pin and wiped her damp brow with
her shoulder. As she rolled out another piece of dough,
she kept her gaze fixed on the wood rolling pin.

Damned Atkins boys, she thought. It never failed. She'd
just begin to think she was getting ahead and they'd show
up wanting a free meal, and leftovers to take home, to

boot. She ground her teeth as she tried to stay calm, all the while getting hotter beneath the collar of her faded lawn dress. Now, one of the greenbacks in her drawer would have to go for more lard and flour. She picked up a knife and sliced dumplings from the rolled dough. She didn't mind cooking for her husband's brothers, but couldn't they at least, just once, bring a little something to contribute to the pot? Their ranch was successful; they sold cattle for beef, and horses for breeding. They had an interest in several gold mines in the area, one producing, she heard. They certainly had far more than she did and Jacob did, and they knew it.

Jehu hooted and Mercy heard the other two men groan as he collected their coins.

"How you like that, Mercy? I beat their sorry asses again." Jehu chuckled as he piled their coins in front of him.

Mercy made no response. She never did anything to encourage any of the Atkins boys, especially Jehu. He could get mean, just like his brother Haman. Especially when he drank.

"You hear me, Mercy? I said, I beat their sorry asses at blackjack again."

Mercy tossed more dumplings into the pot, taking care to stay out of Jehu's reach. He could get feely with his hands if she didn't watch him. "I heard you," she answered without interest.

Jehu slapped his stomach. Sweat ran in rivulets from his temples down his puffy cheeks. "Ain't you got those chicken and dumplin's cooked yet, woman? I'm damned near starved to death. You'd think a woman who wants to run a hotel ought to be able to whip up a pot of chicken and dumplin's in a reasonable 'mount of time."

"It's almost ready." She stirred the pot with a long wooden spoon Tinny had carved for her. "It will only be another half an hour."

Jehu let out a sigh. "Guess if me and the boys been waiting this long, we can wait a whilst longer." He rose and stretched his arms over his head.

As he passed Mercy, she got a strong whiff of body odor and had to turn her face away. As wealthy as the Atkins boys were, she could never understand why they couldn't buy a bar of soap on occasion.

She picked up a cutting board with four loaves of bread lined across it. As she passed Jehu on her way to the sideboard, he slapped her rear. Even through her dress, cage crinoline, and undergarments, she felt his hand on her buttocks.

Mercy spun around, cutting board in hand. "Keep your crawly hands to yourself, Jehu." She could feel her cheeks burn hot as she tried to check her anger. "I've warned you before." She balanced the board on one hand and picked up the knife with the other. "You'll have a hard time playing cards without your hands."

The twin brothers, one dark-haired and the other light, sniggered.

Mercy whipped back around, presenting her back to them. To her surprise, she found Noah standing there, a hammer in his hand. By the look on his face, he'd witnessed the whole incident, or at least a good deal of it.

Her gaze met his and, for an instant, she feared he'd say something to Jehu. The last thing she needed right now was a fistfight between her brother-in-law and her boarder.

Mercy didn't know if Noah read her mind or not, but he glanced at Jehu, then back at her, and continued on his way through the kitchen. She knew he had wanted something, but she didn't dare stop him to ask.

Mercy slapped down the cutting board and began to slice the bread. For some reason her hands were shaky. "Supper'll be served shortly, boys. If you intend to eat at my table, you'd best get yourselves to the pump out back." She tossed the bread into the breadbasket and slammed down the knife.

As she passed her brothers-in-law on her way into the dining room, she eyed them all sternly. "And you'll use soap. All three of you." She passed through the doorway and added, her sarcasm thick, "If you're unsure what to do with it, I'm sure Jacob can help you out."

Hours later, when the Atkins boys had finally cleared out, most of the supper dishes were done, and Jacob and Tinny were tucked in to bed, Mercy took the time to walk out on the front porch and get a fresh breath of night air. The rain hadn't lasted long; it never did in Nevada. But it had rained enough to give the air a thick, humid feel. And now that the sun had set, the chilly, damp air was a relief to her after a long, hot day in the kitchen.

It wasn't until she stood on the top porch step and raised her arms over her head, stretching like a cat, that she realized someone sat in the darkness behind her, watching her.

She knew who it was, of course. She could feel him observing her, even though she couldn't see his eyes in the darkness. Oddly, the thought of him watching her made her skin all warm and tingly. From her perspective, it was a strange reaction to a man.

Mercy thought about the incident with Jehu that evening in the kitchen. When Noah appeared, there had been the potential for serious trouble. She knew men well enough to know that look in his eyes. She needed this boarder's money desperately, but she didn't need trouble.

Mercy caught the porch column and turned to face him. She could feel his gaze still on her, watching, waiting.

"I don't need you to take up for me," she said quietly.

"I don't need you interfering. I've been dealing with those boys a good long time."

"I didn't interfere."

She watched him lean back in the stool until one leg rose off the porch. He pressed his back to the clapboards of the house and crossed his arms over his chest.

"No. You didn't, but you had a mind to."

She took his lack of response to mean she was right.

"They're my husband's family." She found herself defending them, though why, she didn't know. "They're crude and dumber than feather ticks, but they're relatively harmless."

He gave a snort of derision.

She leaned against the pole and crossed her arms over her chest. The cool breeze that came out of the Sierra Nevada mountains to the west felt good on her skin. "Anyway, you're just a boarder. It's not your place to come to my rescue." She couldn't resist the hint of a smile. "But I thank you for the thought, just the same. There's not many men around here to whom it would occur to come to a lady's defense."

He moved slightly and she knew that he was studying her again.

She shifted her weight from one bare foot to the other and realized the floorboards didn't squeak. She tested the board again. It had been squeaky last night. "So that was what you were doing with the hammer."

He sat quiet.

Mercy stared through the darkness at him. There was something between them. She could feel it, like the electric charge just before a thunderstorm. It frightened her. Yet, at the same moment, there was something about it that excited her. It had been a long time since she'd had any excitement in her life. "You just going to sit there and say nothing?"

"Nothing to say."

She walked toward him. She had told herself the first day he arrived that she had to be careful. She couldn't afford to become involved with this man. Not even on a friendly basis. It was dangerous. Dangerous not just to the both of them, but to Jacob, too. Dangerous to her secret.

But Mercy couldn't help herself. It had been so long since she'd felt the *need,* the *desire,* to reach out to someone. She couldn't resist. After all, she was still human.

"Want to play a game of checkers?" she asked.

"I . . . uh . . ." he stalled.

She knew he wanted to say no. "Come on." She headed for the door to retrieve a lamp. "A man who can wash dishes, bang nails without being asked, *and* fight bandits is surely a man who's not afraid to lose a game of checkers to a helpless woman."

As she stepped inside, she heard him chuckle softly. "Helpless, hell."

She smiled to herself. For some reason, known only to God Almighty, it did her heart good to hear him compliment her. And from Noah Ericson, she knew it was meant as a compliment.

Back on the porch with the lamp, and her crocheted wrap tossed over her shoulders, Mercy pulled up the other three-legged stool and set out the checkers. Noah remained rocked back in his stool, watching her from beneath the brim of his hat.

"If your husband's dead," he said, startling her with his initiation to the conversation, "you don't owe them anything. Not a meal, and certainly not the right for such actions."

"No small talk for you, eh? You just jump into the grit."

"Pointless talk's a waste of time. Yours and mine."

She sighed. "Haman's family won't admit he's dead. They still keep thinking he'll ride in at any minute, a jug of home brew in each saddlebag."

"And you?"

She tucked a stray damp lock of hair behind her ear. It was bad manners to make the first move in checkers, but she did it anyway. It gave her something to do with her hands. "I know he's dead," she said carefully. "The Army just hasn't admitted it yet."

Noah righted the stool and made his move. "He as bad as the bunch that passed through here today?"

She hopped a black game piece across the board. "Worse."

"Then you're better off without him."

"Amen to that."

"Can I ask another question?"

"Can. Don't know that I'll answer." She pretended to study the board.

"A smart, pretty woman like you with balls of iron—pardon the expression—what made you marry a man like that in the first place?"

She supposed she should have been offended by his reference to the male anatomy, but honestly she wasn't offended, so why pretend? It was a waste of time, hers and his. "I was a mail-order bride. Haman advertised for a wife in a Philly paper. I wanted to get out of my mother's house. I stepped off the train here in Nowhere and married Haman before I saw the color of his eyes. I was young and a fool."

"When you saw his true colors, why didn't you leave?"

She rubbed her damp hands on her lap, wishing he'd move a checker. "You know the tale; it's been told a million times." She sighed. "At first I told myself the problems between us were my fault. I just had to try a little harder. Be a better wife. When I realized it wasn't my fault, it was too late."

"Too late?"

"I was going to have a baby. I was stuck. My mother

had passed away by than and Pap was already here needing me. I had nowhere to go. No one to turn to."

Noah took his turn. "You've got a nice boy there. Pesky, but good-hearted."

She smiled. He seemed to understand. She had a feeling Jacob had been wiggling his way into Noah's life. Jacob was like that. Since he was a toddler he'd had a gift for making friends, even where he wasn't welcome. "I thought you didn't like children."

"Never said that. I'm just askin' why you stayed with a man who probably beat you. Certainly didn't treat you like a woman needs to be treated."

"Once you have a child, you'd be surprised how your priorities change. If you'd ever had a child you'd understand—"

"Had one."

His voice was so soft and the pounding of his checker as he moved it so loud that she wasn't sure she heard him right.

"I thought you said you weren't married."

In the dim yellow light of the oil lamp she saw his facial muscles tighten. "Widower."

Mercy watched him carefully. "I'm sorry." And she genuinely was. She made her move, capturing one of his checkers. "The child died, too?"

"Been a while."

"That doesn't matter. I lost a baby before Jacob. I love my son with all my heart, but I still miss my daughter."

As he picked up his red checker the veins in his fingers stood out in ridges. Obviously this wasn't a subject he was comfortable with. She let it go.

They finished the game in silence, but a silence that didn't seem uncomfortable. Noah took her last checker and with the same movement stood. "I best get to bed. Tomorrow I'll be escorting the bank coach to Carson City."

Mercy rose, too. "I've got to get back into the kitchen, anyway. It's amazing how many dirty pans and dishes two hens and five men can make." She followed behind him, the lantern in hand.

"No need to make me a noonday meal," Noah said, starting up the stairs. "I won't be back till late afternoon."

"I can pack something."

She watched the back of his head as he shook it, "no." His chestnut hair stuck out every which way from beneath the brim of the hat. She wondered how long it had been since he'd had a barber cut his hair.

"But I'd be much obliged if you could . . . um . . ." He paused on the stairs, his broad shoulders hunched. "Wash up a few shirts."

She almost giggled. Had to be her fatigue. He was as shy as a schoolboy, but certainly built like a man. She didn't know why his shyness amused her, but it did. Maybe because it had been a long time since her femininity had affected someone.

"Be happy to," she said. "Just leave them outside your door in the morning." She walked toward the kitchen, feeling strangely light on her feet. " 'Night, Noah."

" 'Night, Mercy."

Any two perfect strangers could have shared exactly the same simple exchange, but somehow the words that passed between them seemed different to Mercy. Personal. Almost intimate.

She smiled her way through the rest of the dirty dishes.

Six

"Papa, guess what." Six-year-old Becky tugged on Noah's sleeve impatiently. "Papa, guess what! Guess what!"

Noah set down the feed bucket and crouched in front of his daughter so that he was at eye level with her. "Guess what, Beck? Guess what?" he teased, tugging on a bright red pigtail.

The little girl giggled with delight, one finger poked in her mouth. "I've got a wiggly tooth," she said proudly. "Mama says it's going to pop out."

Noah's eyes widened in mock horror. "Your teeth are going to fall out? Oh, no! How will you chew your food? You'll be just like the old Widow Perkins who has to mash up her turnips and thin them with milk."

Becky laughed, wiggling the tooth back and forth. "Papa, that's silly." She rolled her eyes. "You're so silly."

Noah's gaze met Becky's and he smiled. She was so sweet, so smart. He was so proud. "Tell you what," he said. "When that tooth pops out, you bring it to me, and I'll give you a nickel for it."

"A nickel," she breathed. "I've never had a nickel, Papa. That's so much money."

"Now, just for a first tooth, mind you." He waggled his finger. "I can't afford a nickel for every tooth, because they're all going to come out eventually."

"And big ones are going to come in. Mama said."

"That's right." He rose and picked up the bucket. "Want to

help me feed up?" He leaned over the fence to dump the contents into the pig trough.

"Nah."

Noah watched her trot off, headed for the precious timber two-room house he and Alice had built with their own hands. Some-day he hoped to have a larger house, more children, but for now he was content. Life in Nevada was good.

"Mama says you're to come in for dinner as soon as you're done."

Just as he turned away, a scream pierced the air.

Noah's head snapped around. Somehow he knew what was going to happen, even before it did.

Becky burst into flames before his very eyes. She could only have been ten paces from him a second ago, but suddenly she was twenty, thirty paces, and the distance was increasing as the open land distorted and stretched.

Noah threw down his bucket and ran after her. But no matter how hard he ran, how fast, the distance only increased between them.

"Papa! Papa!" Becky screamed.

Tears clouded Noah's eyes. He kept running. Running. But somehow he knew he would never reach her.

"Noah!" Alice appeared out of the smoke. *"Noah!"*

"Alice!" he hollered hoarsely. *"Becky—"* He thrust out his hands. His daughter was being drawn farther and farther from him.

"Noah!" Alice screamed.

Then she, too, burst into flames.

Noah's heart hammered in his chest, pounded in his head. The smoke stung his eyes and burned his throat. He couldn't reach them. He ran, but he made no headway. His wife and daughter were dying in front of him and he couldn't get to them. He couldn't help them.

Noah tripped and fell to the ground, the heat of the fires scorch-ing his face, the stench filling his nostrils. Their screams . . . their screams . . .

Noah bolted upright in bed and opened his eyes wide. "Alice!"

He wasn't on the farm anymore. He was in a bedroom. In a hotel.

It was just a dream.

Only a bad dream.

Noah shoved away the blue quilt, clammy with his sweat, and tried to catch his breath. His heart pounded in his ears, his chest tight. He felt as if he were suffocating.

Alice . . .

Her name was still on the tip of his tongue, as sweet as yesterday's fleeting rain.

Noah swung his bare feet over the side of the bed and rested his elbows on his knees, his hands cradling his head. A sliver of moonlight fell through the window forming a patch on the floor in front of him. He focused on that light, waiting for the raw images in his mind to fade.

After three years he still had the terrifying nightmares. Three years of waking up sweating, heart pounding as if it was going to leap out of his chest.

He wiped his mouth with the back of his hand. It had been a while since he'd had the dream. He'd forgotten how intense it could be.

The whole thing was ridiculous, of course. Noah hadn't been there. His wife and daughter had never been set on fire. The bandits had broken into his home, shot his family, and then burned the house down around them. A gunshot to the head was a merciful death, Noah knew that. If a six-year-old could have a merciful death.

Noah rose from the bed and the quilt slid to the floor. He walked naked to the window and gave it a hard shove upward. It squeaked in protest and finally yielded.

Cold night air hit him in the chest in a whoosh and he exhaled in relief. Slowly his heart rate fell to a normal pace and his skin grew dry and cool.

He stared out the window. By the light of the moon, he saw the outline of the Sierra Nevada Mountains beyond the rooflines of the houses on the street. He knew that north lay Washoe Lake and on the west bank of that lake had been his homestead.

Noah closed his fists and opened them, flexing. His mind wandered, fighting to find an even keel. No matter how many times he dreamed that dream, he could never reach Alice and Becky in time.

Of course he couldn't. He'd still been a thousand miles away, headed home when the thieves had murdered his family and burned his homestead.

And it was his fault.

Alice had begged him not to return to the war when he came home to Nevada on furlough in '64. She said he'd given to his country, and now it was time to give to his family. She said she was afraid of living alone in the territory. She said she couldn't take care of herself and their daughter, but he trivialized her protests. He told her she was strong. He told her she could hang on just a little longer. He said those things because secretly he *wanted* to go back.

Noah told Alice he had to go back. It was his duty. He was a good officer. His men followed him. Listened to him. Respected him. Depended on him. What would they do if he didn't return to active duty? Who would lead them, then?

Noah told Alice the war wouldn't last much longer. They'd all but whipped the Rebels. A few months more and he'd be home for good. He promised.

He promised.

But the war stretched on longer than Noah anticipated. It took the South longer to fall than anyone had anticipated. And when he returned home, there'd been nothing left. Nothing but the charred black ruins of the little house and outbuildings that had been his and Alice's for the last eight years. Nothing left but the grave mound, already patchy with new grass, under the shade of a piñon tree.

Noah wondered what had brought on the dream. Was it because he was so near to the old homestead? It was barely ten miles north. Maybe he shouldn't have taken this job.

But then he thought of Becky's wiggly tooth. He thought of Jacob. Had Jacob brought on the nightmare?

Noah walked back to the bed and picked up the quilt off the floor. It reminded him of Mercy and her soft, low voice on the porch last night. Mercy was comfortable, like the quilt.

He was attracted to her. That was why he'd had the dream.

Noah tossed the quilt on the end of the bed with disgust and lay down again, tucking his arms behind his head.

He started work tomorrow. He'd be escorting the stagecoach that ran to Carson City, guarding the bank's money. The job would keep him busy, keep his thoughts occupied and off would-be widows.

"I don't know, Jacob."

"Please, please, Mama?"

Mercy wiped her damp forehead with her forearm. It was still early morning, but the air was already hot. She sat on a stool on the back porch, leaning over the washtub. She scrubbed one of Noah's faded shirts on her washboard. "It's early to be bothering Mr. McGregor."

"Please, Mama, pleasssssse?" He hopped on one foot and then the other. "He might have a little sweepin' for me to do. Last time he gave me two pennies for sweepin' and puttin' the cans on the shelf."

Paddy McGregor owned the general store in Nowhere.

Jacob sometimes visited with Paddy and did odd jobs. It occupied the little boy's time, kept him out of Mercy's hair, and, according to Paddy, gave him and his childless wife great pleasure. Despite Paddy's gruff exterior, he was a kind gentleman.

"Pleassse, Mama."

Mercy dipped Noah's shirt into the clear rinse water and swooshed it around. "Mind your g's Jacob. Sweep*ing*. Putt*ing*." She began to wring out the shirt. It smelled of him, of Noah, and was surprisingly distracting. "Yes, you may go to McGregor's, but I want you home by noonday for chores."

"Thank you, Mama!" He soared off the edge of the porch, arms outstretched as if he could fly, and landed feet first on the ground.

"Jacob." She tapped her cheek with one wet finger.

The little boy bounded up the steps, kissed her cheek soundly, and leaped off the porch again.

"Have a good time and mind your manners," she called as he disappeared around the corner of the house. "Please and thank you."

"I will!"

Mercy rose from her stool to hang the pile of wet wash that had accumulated at her feet. One by one, she hung the articles from the line that zigzagged across one end of the porch. She plucked a wooden pin from her teeth and secured Noah's blue shirt.

She wondered who Alice was. That was the name he had called in the night. Mercy had been awakened from a sound sleep by his cry of distress. She had wanted to put on her robe and go to him. No one deserved to lie alone in a bed, sweating, heart pounding from a nightmare. She'd had enough of her own to know that.

But she didn't go to him. She couldn't. Instead, she rose from her bed and walked to the window to stare out at the mountain ridges outlined in the darkness.

She wondered why a man would have nightmares about
his dead wife. It was a hard life here in the West for a
woman. Plenty died. Men remarried all the time, some
several times. Men just didn't normally anguish over the
women they'd loved and lost. It wasn't in them.

So why had Noah cried out her name in the darkness?
What haunted him?

The wash done, Mercy hauled the tub of dirty water to
the other end of the porch and dumped it over the side
into a bed of flower seedlings she was trying to coax to
life. The rinse water she left to be used for dirty dishes
later. In a dry land like this, she never wasted water.

"Mercy? Mercy? Mercy, where are you?"

She heard her father call her name, his voice tiny and
scared. He always slept late in the morning, but when he
woke he was often disoriented.

So much for the peace of the morning, she thought as she
hurried into the house. "Here, Pap, I'm coming."

Noah nodded as Mr. Cook rambled on, explaining his
company's commitment to keeping a bank open in Nowhere for the convenience of the townspeople. "But
should the losses become too great," he went on. "Too
great." His long sideburns seemed to rise and fall as he
spoke. "Should the robberies continue, the bank will be
forced to close and the good citizens of Nowhere will
have to travel to Carson City to do their banking."

Noah thrust out his hand to take the strongbox. "No
one's going to steal your money, Mr. Cook."

"Oh, dear, not my money, Mr. Ericson." Mr. Cook fluttered his pale hands. "Our customers' money."

"Whatever." He gestured. "Now, hand me the box. The
stagecoach will be pulling out soon."

Because it was so small and dealt with relatively small
amounts of cash, the bank transported money to Carson

City by means of the regular stagecoach. Noah's job, as an outrider, was to ride beside the coach and see the money's safe arrival at the main branch in Carson City.

Mr. Cook turned his back to Noah, crouched and spun the dial on the lock to the safe. They were inside Cook's office, which also served as the vault. It looked more like a horse stall with iron bars to Noah. If he wanted to get in, it would be easy enough. Hell, young Jake could bust in if he put his mind to it.

Noah turned away from the safe. He wondered why Jacob had popped up in his head so fast, so easily. He didn't like it, not one bit.

"Here you go, Mr. Ericson." Cook handed him a strongbox of considerable weight.

"Making this a little obvious, aren't you?" Noah asked as he took the small, padlocked wooden box and walked out of the office into the small bank lobby that also served as the post office.

"Whatever do you mean?" The heels of Cook's polished shoes clip-clapped on the sanded plank floor. "You mean?"

"Box is small enough. I'd put them in a lady's hat box or something of the like." He stepped out onto the bank's porch. "No need to make it any easier for the thieves to find it."

The stagecoach had already arrived across the street and was loading. A middle-aged woman and her twentyish daughter were handing the driver bags and bundles to tie on the roof.

"Up to you, Mr. Ericson. Up to you," Cook repeated, reminding Noah of an irritating parrot he'd once seen in a saloon. "Your job is to get the bank's money safely to Carson City. Safely. How you do it is up to you so long as you continue to use the stagecoach company we've contracted with."

"I told you. I do my job and I do it well." Noah nodded. "Good day to you, Cook. I'll drop by tonight when I get back and let you know the money arrived safely."

"That will do. That will do."

Noah walked to the stagecoach and nodded to the driver. "You ready for this?"

"Name's Clarence. Front boot under the driver's box'll do, I reckon."

Noah could barely understand him for the wad of chew in his mouth.

"But I'm warning ye. Men come at me with bandannas on their faces and loaded guns in their hand, and I'll give up the Virgin Mary to save myself." He spat a long stream of tobacco onto the ground.

Noah walked around the front of the coach to load the strongbox. Another man might have been offended by the driver's declaration, but it suited Noah just fine. He'd just as soon not have any would-be heroes to worry over. This way, the responsibility for the money was totally his.

Noah secured the strongbox under the driver's seat and walked back to the hitching post to get his horse. Sam was saddled and ready to ride, seeming as anxious as he was to get back to work.

By the time he returned to the loaded black stagecoach, scrolled in gold, the two female passengers were inside and the driver in his seat, reins in hand.

The driver was such a bulky, lumpy man that Noah didn't notice the boy on the seat on the far side of the drive until he mounted.

"Jake?" Noah urged his mount forward. "What are you doing up there?"

The driver glanced over. "He said he's with you."

"With me?" Noah stared hard at the boy. "You're not with me." He eyed the driver. "He's not with me."

"Please, Mr. Ericson, please let me ride along," Jacob begged. "I've never been on a stagecoach. Never been anywhere. Never been to Carson City."

"No."

"Pleeeease? I won't be no trouble. I swear I won't."

"Get down off that seat, Jake."

"I gotta roll," Clarence said, checking his timepiece that hung on a long chain. "Got a schedule to keep. I got another stop between here and Carson City."

"Can I hold the reins?" Jacob asked the driver.

Noah felt a strange sense of panic deep in the pit of his stomach. Fear. Fear for the boy. Fear for the boy as if he meant something to him. The idea of it scared the hell out of Noah. "Jacob, get off that seat," he said in a voice that sounded too much like a father's voice.

"Please? I—"

"Get off the seat, Jake."

The boy must have understood Noah's tone because he climbed down without another word.

"Let's move out," Noah told the driver.

The stagecoach rocked forward and rolled away, leaving Jacob standing alone and forlorn on the far side of the street. Noah thought he saw tears in the boy's eyes.

Noah's first thought was to just ride off. The boy had no business thinking he could go with him. He had no business telling the coach driver they were together. But Noah couldn't do it. He couldn't hurt his feelings any more than he already had.

"I'll take you to Carson City another time. When it's safer."

Jacob looked up, wiping his eyes with the back of his hand. "You will?"

"I will."

"Uncle Jehu is always saying he'll take me places. He don't."

"I'm a man of my word. Now go on home to your mama."

Noah sank his heels into Sam's haunches and the horse eased forward at a steady trot.

"You won't tell her, will you?" Jacob called.

"I won't tell," Noah answered. Then he leaned forward in the saddle and urged Sam into a gallop to catch up with the stagecoach, a strange feeling lodged in his throat. A feeling that closely resembled happiness.

Seven

"No, Mama," Jacob insisted stubbornly. "He said he would take me to Carson City, and he will. He told me so. He wouldn't lie."

Mercy sat on the edge of Jacob's rope bed and buttoned the top button of his favorite red nightshirt. This was the part of being a parent she found so trying. She wanted so desperately to protect her son from the harsh reality of the world, and yet she knew that if she did, it would only make the reality harsher later.

"Let's just wait and see, shall we? Mr. Ericson is going to be very busy working for the bank. He might be too busy to haul a boy all the way to Carson City and back for no reason. Or he might be too tired. That's hard work, guarding someone else's money."

"But I can go when—*if*—he asks me." He peered up at her, his eyes wide with excitement. "Right? I *can* go?"

"We'll see, Jacob." She kissed his forehead, inhaling his little-boy scent that was changing too quickly. He wasn't a baby anymore, but full of vim and vigor and male things. A boy who needed a man's company more than his mama's. "Don't forget your prayers," she said softly, taming a lock of unruly hair with a gentle touch.

"I won't. 'Night, Mama. I love you."

"I love you, Jake, who came for my sake," she teased with a ditty left over from his infancy. Then she picked up the oil lamp and left his room in darkness, closing the door behind her.

Halfway to the staircase Mercy spotted Noah standing outside his door. He was just standing there, leaning on the jamb. He'd missed the evening meal and taken two egg sandwiches and a glass of milk for his supper on the porch with Tinny. Tinny had played checkers with Joe and chatted amiably with him and Noah. Mercy could hear them through the kitchen window. Noah had mostly listened, but he hadn't seemed annoyed. He'd stayed on the porch a long time before excusing himself to turn in for the evening. He'd stayed as if waiting for something, someone.

"The boy asleep?" Noah asked.

His rich masculine voice sounded strange in her upstairs hallway. Tinny slept downstairs in one of the rooms in the addition off the back, so it had been a long time since a man's voice had reverberated off the wall. "In bed. Asleep soon, I hope." She halted at the top of the stairs, shaking her head with a smile. "He wears me out some days." She chuckled. "Most days, actually," she corrected. "It's constant chatter." She waved her hand. "Nothing but endless questions."

"They're like that at that age."

Her lamp cast a shadow across his face, hiding his expression. She wondered if he looked as wistful as he sounded.

He misses his child, she thought, her heart aching for him.

A moment of silence yawned between them. It wasn't an uncomfortable silence, but one that seemed to demand action or words from Mercy. The connection she felt with this near stranger at this moment was almost tangible.

"Well," Mercy said, wishing she could linger in the hall,

but knowing she mustn't. "I guess I'd best get back to the kitchen."

Noah slipped his hands into the front pockets of his denims and stared at the floor. "No time for a game of checkers?"

She couldn't tell if it was an invitation or a statement. A little of both, she sensed.

"I've still got egg noodles to roll out and dishes to wash and put away."

He nodded.

"But," she went on before she could stop herself, "you're welcome to come down and keep me company. Mr. McGregor's wife sent a jar of her wild strawberry jam. An old Indian recipe, she says. I've had a taste for it and a cup of tea all day."

Still he stared at his boots.

She shrugged and started down the steps, knowing she shouldn't feel disappointed when he didn't jump at her invitation. He had made it clear his first day here that he wasn't looking for a friend. "Suit yourself," she called up the stairwell.

Mercy was halfway down the stairs before she heard Noah following her in those stuck-in-the-mud boots of his. She smiled to herself. She knew she was treading in dangerous water, but she couldn't help herself.

In the kitchen, she set the lamp on the center of the table and lit another with a broom straw lit from the banked coals in the stove. The soft light made the kitchen cozy, comfortable. The shadows hid the peeling paint on the walls, and the uncertainty she knew was etched on her face.

Mercy added hot water from the stove to her dishpan and grabbed the washrag to scrub the plates she'd left soaking. Noah appeared beside her, a dry rag in his hand.

"I'll dry," he said, dropping back into his habit of monosyllables.

Used to his few words, she didn't mind chatting for him. "How was the ride to Carson City?" she questioned. "Quiet, I assume?"

When he took the plate she'd rinsed off, she was careful not to let their fingertips touch.

"Easy enough."

"No bandits leaping from the sagebrush? No wild Indians?" She glanced at him sideways and laughed.

He didn't.

"I'm sorry." She smiled, feeling utterly silly. Happy for no reason at all. "I know thievery is not something to be taken lightly. It just seems funny—"

"A man like myself escorting stagecoaches with ladies in bonnets," he finished for her.

"And someone else's money," she reminded.

"It's more precautionary at this point. Mr. Cook seems to be under the impression the bank will be doing more business shortly. After the recent robberies, he doesn't want his bank to get the reputation of a place a man can't leave his money and still sleep soundly nights." He stacked the dry blue willow plate on the table behind him and returned for a wet one.

Mercy continued to pass wet dishes as if it was the most natural thing in the world. Haman Atkins had never dried a dish in his life, and she'd lay butter to a cow, none of his brothers had either.

"Early reports on several mines in the area look good," she said. "Mr. Cook and some of the others in Nowhere think this town will be booming in six months. I'm hoping so."

He lifted an eyebrow beneath the fringe of his shaggy hair.

"Business," she explained. "If men come to town, they'll need a place to stay. Meals in their bellies. I'm hoping the Tin Roof will be where they stay."

"I suspect you're a good businesswoman. You could make this place successful."

She passed him the last clean dish. "I intend to."

Their gazes met, her smiling confidently, him without expression on his face. He was so serious. So sad. Mercy's hand ached to reach out and brush the hair from his eyes. Smooth the frown from his mouth with hers . . .

She turned away, shocked by her own thoughts. Lord help her! What was she thinking? Mouth to mouth, indeed. She was already headed straight to hell and wondered if there was a lower floor to eternal damnation.

Mercy picked up the stack of dishes on the table to return them to their place in the pantry. She heard Noah behind her, adding fresh water to the tea kettle from the jug on the counter.

"Why do you haul the water in from the pump out back? Why don't you just use that one?" He pointed to the red-handled pump at the sink.

"Broken. Been broken as long as I've been here. Haman always said—" She turned to find him watching her again. She wiped her damp hands on her apron. "My husband always said he was going to fix it, but he never got to it."

"The hotel was his when you came to Nowhere?"

She nodded. "His brothers and sister have the family ranch, but Haman had this idea he was a businessman. He apparently bought the hotel cheap at a bank foreclosure auction. In his ad for a bride, he said he ran a hotel." She carried leftover bread from dinner and the jar of jam to the table. "What he failed to say was that Nowhere was a ghost town, and he'd not had a customer as long as he'd owned the place. Before he married me, he used it for a place to play cards, get drunk, and worse, I suspect." She went back for a small tin. "Tea?"

He stood by the stove waiting on the hot water. "Never had tea. Alice—" He cut himself off, took a breath, then went on. "My wife only ever made coffee. But I'm willing to try a taste."

Mercy carefully measured tea leaves into a china teapot that had been a gift from Tinny when he had come to stay with her. That had been a few years back, when his mind was better and he still earned an income doing odd jobs. "That was her name?" Mercy asked. That was the name he called out in his sleep the night before. She glanced up at him. "Pretty."

He scuffed the floor with his boot. "Yeah."

Mercy placed the teapot on the table and added two teacups and a little bowl of sugar before taking a seat. "Water ready?"

"Just about."

A minute later, the kettle whistled and he brought it to the table and poured the water into the teapot. He lingered at the stove, replacing the kettle as if uncomfortable with the thought of going back to sit with her.

Mercy took a piece of bread and slathered strawberry jam on it. She pushed the jar and the knife across the table to the nearest chair. "Try the jam. Best you've ever had, I'll bet."

Noah sat and picked up the knife and a slice of bread. He took his time spreading the jam.

Mercy sampled the soft bread and sweet preserves. It was heavenly in her mouth. She didn't mind if Noah didn't want to talk anymore. It was nice just to sit here at the end of the long day and have the quiet companionship. For some reason it made her feel alive again. It gave her hope.

Noah took two bites before he spoke again. "Is good."

"Told you." She laughed as if she were no older than Jacob. "I'm having another piece." She grabbed the knife from in front of him. "Want one?"

"Might."

She spread jam on another slice of bread and then

served tea for them both, pouring it through a little strainer so that she could reuse the tea leaves. Tea was her one self-indulgence. "Sugar?" she asked.

He licked his fingers. "You use sugar?"

"A little." She sprinkled a pinch of brown sugar into her cup.

"I'll take a little then."

She took a pinch of the sugar and dropped it into his tea. "Now stir it." She stirred hers and passed him the only spoon she'd brought to the table.

Mercy sipped from her cup and Noah sipped from his. It struck her as quite the domestic scene, or what she had once imagined as a domestic scene. A woman with her husband at the end of a long day, sharing thoughts and a bit of bread and tea. She and Haman had never shared anything but a bed.

"So what do you think?" Mercy asked after a minute.

Noah nodded thoughtfully. "Not bad, but I think I like coffee better."

She grinned.

"Why do you do that?"

"What?"

"Smile all the time." He took another sip of the tea and reached for the last slice of bread. "You smile a lot."

"I do?" She crinkled her forehead in thought. Then shrugged. "I don't know. Laugh instead of cry, I guess. It was always my grandmother's philosophy."

He thought for a moment. "I bet you have a lot of reasons to cry."

Mercy couldn't meet his gaze. She fiddled with the spoon. Suddenly the large, airy kitchen seemed small. Close. She couldn't get away from Noah. She couldn't get away from the feelings that were washing over her like water on a riverbank. "No more than most."

"More than most, I suspect."

Mercy felt the warmth of his hand over hers and she

looked up, shocked. Her gaze met his and for the first time she saw something beyond sadness in his eyes. Hope, maybe?

"Late," he said abruptly, and pulled away his hand. He got up out of the chair so suddenly that it nearly tipped backward onto the floor. He caught it with one broad hand and righted it. "Thanks for the bread and tea." He was already halfway to the door. " 'Night."

Mercy was confused; confused by his touch and then his brusque retreat, confused by her own jumble of feelings. "Good night," she called.

Alone again in the kitchen, she finished her tea at her leisure, cleaned up, and climbed the long staircase to her bedroom. In bed, she blew out the lamp and lay back on her pillow.

Then, for the first time in years, it was not Haman's face she saw when she closed her eyes, but another man's. Noah's.

Noah sat on a barstool at the Twin Pianos Saloon and nursed a beer. It was midafternoon and there were just a few patrons, all involved in a game of poker near the door. There was only one piano that he could see and it was silent. The bartender sat on a stool behind the bar, eyes closed, mouth open, snoring softly.

Noah didn't particularly care for saloons. He had no need for them. He stayed away from whores; there had been no one since Alice. And he was wary of saloon patrons and their often-volatile natures. He didn't really want to be here right now; he just had nowhere to go.

The stagecoach only ran every other day or so, so there was nothing for Noah to do on his "off" days but sit around. In his other jobs, since the end of the war, he'd always spent his free time locked up in his private room in boardinghouses or hotels. He didn't allow himself the luxury of a dime novel or even a newspaper. He lay on his bed and stared at the ceiling. He tortured himself with memories of the past, laced heavily with regret. He'd made as much a career out of that as of being an outrider.

Noah lifted his mug and sloshed the beer first in one direction, then in the other, making a frothy whirlpool. He couldn't stop thinking about Mercy. He knew he should be thinking about Alice. About his dead daughter. But instead, he thought of the living. He thought of the woman who surely was a widow, and of her son, Jake. He even thought about the old man and his loneliness. Noah understood loneliness.

"Seat taken?"

Startled by a husky, feminine voice, Noah glanced up. Most of the saloon girls were still abed this time of day. To his surprise it was not a saloon girl but a willowy redhead dressed in a leather skirt and denim shirt. She wore a pearl-handled Colt .45 on a belt on her hips.

"Don't know, deaf, or just stupid?" she asked after a moment.

Noah blinked. "No one there." He shifted his gaze from the redhead to the cracked mirror on the wall behind the bar.

"Mind if I sit, then?" She slid onto the stool. "Or you saving it for a cheap pair of tits?" She slapped her hand on the bar, startling the bartender from his nap. "Woody, where's my rye?"

He lurched off the stool and reached for a shot glass.

"You keep falling asleep on the job like that and we're going to take you for dead and call the undertaker." She laughed, glancing at Noah. "Just passing through?"

"No."

She took her shot and downed half of it. "Here with the mining?"

"No."

"Look, if you don't want to talk, just say so."

Noah took a pull on his beer. This was why he didn't like saloons. "I don't want to talk."

She laughed heartily, sank the last of her shot, and slapped the glass on the bar. "Another, Woody." Her mouth turned up at the corners in a sassy smile. "I like an honest man," she told Noah. "No bullshit. I haven't got time for bullshit, either."

Noah continued to stare at the mirror. In its reflection, he saw the woman pull a cigar from her shirt pocket and light it up. She was pretty—some would say striking—with a mane of thick auburn hair pulled back from her face, sun-browned cheeks, and a sensuous mouth. But Noah's tastes seemed to run more to wholesome blondes these days. Blondes with sashaying hips beneath faded sprigged calico. He didn't care for women in leather who smoked cigars.

The woman blew smoke over the bar. "My name's Jezzy. You?"

Noah exhaled, thinking maybe he'd head back to the Tin Roof Hotel. Maybe he could take that pump in the kitchen apart and see what was keeping it from working. If Mercy wasn't in the kitchen, that was . . .

Jezzy waited.

"Ericson," he answered finally. "Noah Ericson."

"Ericson." She downed half her second rye and puffed on her cigar. "Ericson . . . Hell! I know who you are. You're the man the bank hired to guard the money." She chuckled. "My brothers said they ran into you over at the Tin Roof. I understand you're boarding there."

This was the first thing she'd said that even half interested him. She was Mercy's sister-in-law? She had to have known Mercy for years. He envied her and hated himself for feeling that way. "That's right," he said a little more cordially. "Bank's putting me up there. Mrs. Atkins is taking fine care of me."

She chuckled. "The woman's got spunk, I'll give her

that. I don't guess my brother Haman would have ever thought she'd have the bull nuts to run that hotel on her own." She chuckled. "He sure as hell didn't."

"He fought in the war?"

"Mmm hmm."

"So did I." He remembered what Mercy had said about her husband's family still thinking Haman would return. "War's been over for a while."

"I know. Those slower than frozen owl piss brothers of mine think he's still alive, but I know better." She lifted an arched eyebrow. "I suppose the sweet Philly wildflower is still pining for him, too."

Jezzy's derogatory remark about Mercy made Noah grind his teeth. He tipped his beer, finished it off, and slid off the stool.

She spun on her stool. "Hey, you have some free time, ride out to my place. Can't miss it, off the road to Carson City. Anyone can tell you where it is. I've got some decent horses if you're in the market. You might want to take a look."

"Got a horse." He touched the brim of his hat, scuffing his boots as he walked out. "Be seein' you, ma'am."

"I'll be countin' on it, partner," she answered huskily.

Noah wasn't such a fool as to not recognize an invitation when he heard one. It had been a long time since he'd eased himself sexually and he realized the invitation ought to have sounded good to him. Obviously Jezzy wasn't looking for anything more than a good roll in the hay.

But he was beginning to think maybe he was.

Eight

Mercy glanced up from the pea patch to see her father cutting across the small section of parched land that separated the hotel from the outbuildings and her meager garden plot. She'd tried to grow grass here, but mostly she just grew thistles.

"Just wanted to stop by and say so long. Me and Joe, we're headed over the Sierras to Californ-i-a."

He was dressed for travel in his long johns and a white Sunday-best shirt that had once been Haman's. To that, he'd added a pair of denim overalls he'd cut off at the knees last summer, and red wool socks in need of darning. To finish off the ensemble, he'd topped his balding head with his favorite bollinger, a chicken feather tucked jauntily in the band. He'd forgotten one shoe again.

Mercy leaned on her hoe and mopped her damp brow with the back of her hand. The May sun beat down heavily on her back, a forewarning of the hot summer to come. "You're not going to California, Pap," she said calmly.

"Yep. Yep, I am. Can't stand to watch my only daughter, my only flesh and blood, work as hard as you work, and me not contributing a lick." He tipped his hat. "So me and Joe, we're off to Californ-i-a. Don't keep supper for us. It might be a day or two before we find ourselves some gold and make it back."

Tinny had been so clear-headed the last couple of

weeks that Mercy was a little surprised by his declaration. She didn't know if it was the sunny days, or Noah's company on the front porch evenings that had been the reason for his improvement, but her father had seemed better. He hadn't gotten lost in town or tried to catch the stagecoach for Carson City. They hadn't seen much of the invisible Joe, and Tinny had even helped her with chores around the house.

Mercy couldn't help being disappointed that her father had reverted to his more confused state. She missed the old Tinny when he got like this. She missed the man who had been absent most of her childhood years, but with whom she'd formed a warm relationship as an adult, before his senility had set in.

"Now, don't try to talk me out of it." Tinny held up his hands. "Me and Joe talked it over and we're going; it's final."

She struck the ground with her hoe. "How are you planning to get there?" she asked casually. "Going to take the stagecoach, I suppose?"

He crossed his arms over his chest proudly. "Reckon I am."

She grimaced. "Well, darn, Pap. I'm sorry to hear that, because you've missed the stagecoach."

His silvery brows knitted. "We did?"

"I'm afraid so. Noah, you know Noah—"

"Of course I know Noah. That's my son-in-law. My girl Mercy's husband. Fine man. Strong. Hung like a stallion."

Mercy blanched. She would have laughed about the stallion part if not for the first statement. This was the first time she'd heard Tinny say he thought Noah was her husband. That was all the Atkins family needed to catch wind of.

"No, Pap. Noah— Mr. Ericson is not my husband. Haman is my husband."

Tinny fluttered his feeble hand in front of his face as

if swatting at a pesky mosquito. "Hell, he's long gone, piece of crap that he was. Mercy's married to Noah now. They got a fine boy, Jacob."

Mercy yanked the hoe from the soil. "Pap!" She took a deep breath knowing she couldn't get angry with Tinny. He only grew worse, more confused, when she became impatient with him. "Pap," she chided gently. "Mr. Ericson is not my husband and he's not Jacob's father. Mr. Ericson works for the bank. He lives here in my hotel. We live in a hotel, Pap. Men come and go in hotels all the time."

Tinny stared hard at Mercy and squinted. "You say Noah's not Mercy's husband?"

"No. *I'm* Mercy. He's not my husband." She patted her chest.

He gazed distrustfully at her. "He's not your husband?"

"I know who my husband is, Pap. It's not Mr. Ericson. I married Haman Atkins ten years ago. Remember? I left Philly, came west here to Nevada, and married him sight unseen. You left your job on the ranch in Colorado and joined me when you started feeling poorly."

He grimaced, concentrating with great effort. "And Joe and I've missed the stagecoach to Californ-i-a again?"

She rested both hands on the hoe, praying silently for strength. "You missed the stagecoach, Pap."

"Hell." He turned and shuffled off through the new grass. "Now we'll have to wait till tomorrow." He snapped his fingers. "Well, come on, Joe. Don't just stand there slack-jawed. You heard her. We've done missed the coach. Won't be another today. We might as well play another hand of cards."

Mercy watched her father cross the yard, his gait affected by the fact that he wore only one shoe. "Jacob!" she called. "Jake!"

The boy appeared a moment later from inside the shed where she knew he'd been puttering with old, rusty tools.

Noah's handiwork around the house had apparently piqued the boy's interest. "Mama?"

"Could you keep an eye on your grandfather while I finish hoeing the peas? He and Joe are headed for California again."

Jacob nodded matter-of-factly. "He missed the stagecoach."

"Thank goodness." She leaned over, swinging the hoe again. "Play cards with him, will you? He's pretty disappointed."

"Do I have to?" Jacob whined. "He cheats."

She smiled, striking the turned soil over and over again, taking care not to disturb the sprouting peas. "For me, Jake-for-my-sake?"

The boy groaned.

"I've got dried apple pie baking in the oven. There's an extra piece for any boy who does what his mother asks without being a pain in her petticoat," she said sweetly.

"An extra piece and *a half*?" he bargained.

She laughed. "You may make a lawyer, Son. Now get inside before your grandpap strikes out on his own for California."

"Yes, Mama."

He took off for the back porch and was halfway there before Mercy called after him. "And Jacob, could you find Pap's other shoe?"

The boy hip-hopped up the rickety stairs, across the porch, and disappeared into the house.

Mercy hoed for the next half hour in peace. She enjoyed working in her garden, even in the heat of the afternoon. It got her out of the kitchen and gave her time to think. It served as a form of penance, in a way, her being here in the garden where her secret lay.

As she hoed, she silently recited all the Bible verses she knew about sin and repentance and made her confessions to the good Lord.

She was just working her way through the Psalms when she heard the back door swing open and slap closed.

"Trouble coming up the front walk!" Jacob called. The laughter that she'd heard earlier in his voice was gone.

Mercy shielded her eyes from the sun with her hand. "What's the matter?"

He frowned, appearing older than his almost seven years. "Uncle Jehu."

"Pots, and Ahab, too?"

"Yup. I think they've come from the Twin Pianos. They're walking funny and laughing a lot."

Mercy swore beneath her breath. It was moving on toward suppertime. Never failed. And drunk to boot.

"All right. I'm coming." She kept her voice even, not wanting Jacob to know she hated to see them coming as much as he did. After all, they were his father's people. She vowed a long time ago not to bad mouth Haman or his family in front of Jacob if she could help it. "Why don't you take those loaves of applesauce bread and run them over to the store for me. Mr. McGregor will have flour for you."

"Yes, ma'am."

He jumped at the suggestion, as Mercy knew he would. He was always happy to get out of the house when his uncles were around.

With a heavy heart, Mercy crossed the lawn wondering how she was going to stir up enough supper to feed the swine in her kitchen.

"Mercy! We need another plate of them biscuits of yers," Jehu called into the kitchen. "And some more sweet butter."

"Some more of your sweet self'll do," Ahab, the darker haired of the twins piped in.

The Atkins boys all laughed uproariously, still obviously feeling their liquor.

"Sweet self," Pots echoed, tee-heeing.

Mercy yanked another pan of biscuits out of the oven. "Ouch!" She jerked her hand as she felt the heat of the pan through the thin towel. As she flinched, the pan tipped and all the biscuits slid onto the floor.

Mercy cursed under her breath as she dropped the pan onto the top of the stove, towel and all, and shook her smarting hand.

"Did you hear me, woman? We called for more biscuits!" She listened to Jehu rock in one of her dining-room chairs. If she'd asked him once she'd asked him a hundred times not to rock in the chairs that she had stripped and painted herself.

"You hear me," Jehu continued. "While ye're at it, you mightst well bring in the pies off'n the windowsill. We'll be ready soon enough for 'em."

Mercy crossed her arms over her chest and watched a biscuit roll past her bare feet and come to rest under the table. Now what was she going to do?

"Mercy! You deaf?"

She contemplated the biscuits lying all over the floor that hadn't yet been swept today.

"Mercy!"

"Coming," she called. "Biscuits are coming."

She dropped to her knees, gathered all the biscuits into her apron, and piled them onto a plate. She flipped them over and quickly arranged them, brushing a piece of dust from one. "Here you go, boys," she said cheerily. "Another plate of biscuits."

Mercy purposefully circumnavigated Jehu and walked to the end of the table where Pots sat. Of the three Atkins brothers, he was the safest of the bunch. "Want butter, Pots?"

"Want you," he said gruffly, staring at the biscuits.

Jehu and Ahab burst into another fit of raucous laughter as they passed a whiskey bottle between them.

"Watch your mouth," Mercy shot at Pots. "I'm a married woman. Married to your brother. You ought to know better."

The man's face turned bright red. "Yes, ma'am." He grabbed three biscuits with one hand and set them onto his plate, still keeping his gaze fixed on the food.

Jehu and Ahab laughed harder.

"I swear, Mercy. Pots has got it bad for you," Jehu said, wiping the sweat from his chin with the corner of her checked tablecloth. "If you *weren't* Haman's woman, he'd take you for his own, fer sure."

"I didn't mean you no harm, Mercy. I swear I didn't." Pots shook his head, looking as if he were going to burst into tears. Pots always got like this when he drank too much. Jehu and Ahab got wild. Haman had been the one who got plain mean.

"Eat your biscuits, Pots." She slapped his shoulder and headed for the kitchen. That seemed to be the safest ground right now.

"Still waiting for that pie, Mercy darlin'," Jehu called after her, rocking back in the chair again.

"And people in hell are still waiting for their ice water," she muttered under her breath as she went around the corner.

"What was that?"

"Pie coming right, up, Jehu!" she answered sweetly.

Mercy carried one of the pies to the dining-room table and retreated to the kitchen again. She had no intention of eating. She'd lost her appetite.

Since Jacob still wasn't home, she guessed he'd stayed with the McGregors. She hoped so. Maybe the Atkins boys would eat and just go back to their ranch, and Jacob wouldn't have to see them again tonight.

It worried Mercy that if her son saw his uncles like this

too often, the boy would begin to question what his own father was like. She didn't want to start lying to him, but she didn't want to hurt him with the truth, either. Not while he was still so young.

As Mercy began to stack up the dirty pans from supper she heard the front door open and close. It had to be Jacob. But as she listened to the footsteps cross the front hallway and head for the kitchen, she recognized the sound as a man's footsteps. Noah's. She knew the lazy stride. She couldn't help but smile with some emotion she didn't quite recognize.

"Evening," she said softly as he appeared in the kitchen doorway. She leaned against the sink, taking a moment to look at him, into his sad eyes that didn't seem to be quite as sad these days. "You're home early."

The Atkins brothers were laughing and slapping the dining table over some infantile joke. Though they were just around the corner of the kitchen and making a hellacious commotion, it seemed to Mercy as if they were far away, just the background to a painting.

Noah leaned against the doorjamb and pulled off his dusty leather hat. His face had tanned darker since he'd arrived, adding to his hard, angular good looks. His hair still needed trimming badly. He was watching her the same way she was watching him.

A lazy grin crossed his face. "You say that as if you're glad to see me."

She lowered her gaze and picked up a dirty frying pan and sank it into the wash water. Truthfully, she was glad to see him.

In the last few weeks they'd fallen into a domestic routine that was entirely too comfortable for strangers. When he came home late in the evening from Carson City he would sit at the kitchen table while he ate the meal Mercy had saved for him. If there were still dishes to do, he helped her after he'd eaten.

Mercy looked forward to the evenings he returned home from escorting the bank's money. On those nights she had him all to herself, alone in her cozy kitchen. She knew she was headed down some path she didn't belong on, but she couldn't help herself. She was so damned tired of this life. So damned tired of pretending to be the wife of a dead man. So damned lonely.

Noah glanced in the direction of the dining room. Someone had rocked back so far in one of Mercy's chairs that he'd tumbled over backward with a bang. The men were all laughing so loud that she couldn't tell who had done it.

"They been here long?" Noah asked quietly, approaching the sink.

"Long enough."

Despite the noise in the dining room beyond the doorway, the kitchen seemed small. Even standing across the room, Noah seemed close. The static energy she had felt before between her and Noah was here tonight. Present and strong. Mercy thought about that wrong path she knew she was taking, and wondered where she was headed.

Noah dropped his hat on the table, and reached for a cup of water to prime the pump he'd fixed weeks ago. "Where's the boy?"

"I sent him to McGregor's on an errand. They must have asked him to stay for supper."

He pumped the handle and water gushed into her rinsing pan. "Maybe they'll be gone by the time he gets home."

"Maybe."

She scrubbed the inside of the frying pan vigorously and realized she hadn't offered Noah anything to eat. He'd ridden all the way to Carson City and back on breakfast at dawn and a cold lunch of bread and cheese. She knew he had to be hungry.

"I'm sorry," she said, letting the pan sink into the soapy dishwater. "I need to get you something to eat." Flustered, she dried her hands on the apron. Most days she could handle anything, but between Tinny wanting to go to California and her in-laws' visit, she felt as if she were going to break into tears at any moment.

"Mercy, it's all right."

"They've eaten everything," she said quickly. "I can fry up some eggs and potatoes. I made pie—"

"Mercy." He took both her hands between his.

She couldn't bear to look at him. His hands were so warm and firm wrapped around hers. Now she knew she was going to cry.

"Mercy, I'm not all that hungry. An egg will be fine, later. Hell, I can fry up my own egg."

She shook her head, not knowing what was wrong with her. She knew she should pull away from him. If Jehu saw him touching her, there was no telling what he would do in his drunken state. But Mercy couldn't make herself take her hand from Noah's. Last night she had dreamed about these hands.

She kept her head turned, her gaze cast downward. "No. The bank is paying good money for me to—"

"Mercy." He tightened his grip on her hands. His deep, gentle voice begged her to look at him.

Slowly she dragged her gaze to meet his. "Noah," she whispered.

He swallowed, and his Adam's apple bobbed slowly down and then up. He seemed to be struggling with something, some decision.

Mercy's gaze slipped from his warm brown eyes to his mouth, and she couldn't help wondering what it would be like to kiss that mouth, just once. Right this minute she thought she might be willing to trade her soul with the devil for one kiss from this man.

Was he going to do it? Her lower lip trembled. Did he

know how badly she wanted to be kissed? She thought he did.

"Mercy!" Jehu broke the magic of the moment as if he'd shattered a plate of glass between her and Noah. "Mercy, you got another pie in there? I could of sworn I saw two."

Mercy snapped her hands from Noah's as she heard Jehu rock back in his chair to peer into the kitchen. She and Noah were around the corner of the L-shaped kitchen, but she didn't dare take the chance of letting her brother-in-law see them together.

"You're not holding back on us, are you, darlin'?"

"Darlin'," Pots echoed, completing his statement with a soft belch.

Mercy whipped around. "It's the last one, boys," she said, making no attempt to hide her disdain for them. "I promised Jacob pie, but you go ahead and eat it. Eat the child's piece of pie." She snatched the pie off the windowsill, walked past Noah and into the dining room. She dropped the apple pie so hard in front of Jehu that flakes of crust leaped and fell on to the red-checked tablecloth.

"Jesus, no need to get hostile with us." Jehu was sober enough now to realize she'd had enough of them for one night.

Mercy didn't know what had gotten into her. Normally she didn't let Haman's brothers bait her, but she'd had it tonight. Maybe it was her father's illness, or Jacob's dislike of them. Maybe it was the feeling for Noah that she was trying so hard to suppress, but hell flew into her.

"Have some pie, Jehu." She grabbed the knife from the table littered with piles of dirty dishes, food, utensils, and a shattered plate. She hacked off a huge slice of the pie, scooped it out and slapped it on the table without bothering with a plate.

"Pie, Ahab?" She grabbed up the pie and, using her

bare hand, scooped up a big piece and dropped it on top of the cold dumplings still on his plate.

"Pots, you need more pie? Haven't eaten yourself sick yet?" She dumped the pie pan upside down on the tablecloth and lifted it. Sugary syrup ran down the baked apple bits and oozed onto the red check fabric.

"N-no thank you, Mercy. I don't care for no more—"

"Eat the pie, Pots. Eat the damned pie!"

Pots grabbed up his fork and started shoveling. "Good pie," he mumbled, his mouth crammed full. "Best pie I ever—"

"Just eat, Pots. Don't talk. Eat."

"Now, what the hell has gotten into you, missy?" Jehu lumbered out of his chair. "I swear, you get more dried up and waspy every time I lay eyes on you."

Mercy stood in the doorway of the kitchen. She refused to back up, even though the look in Jehu's eyes was close to the same look Haman used to get before he started swinging his fists at her.

"I don't think my brother would appreciate you treatin' us like this, and I don't appreciate it, either." He walked toward her. "I expect a little respect. You and me and the boy, we're family, and—"

"He's dead, Jehu. Dead and gone and you don't deserve as much respect as that piece of pie."

"Now you best shut yer mouth before I shut it for you. My brother ain't dead and I don't appreciate you sayin' he is." Jehu pressed closer, his fists balled at his burly sides.

"And let me tell you something else, Jehu Atkins." She shook a finger at him. "You and Jacob and I are not family, you stupid son of a—"

Jehu raised his hand to strike her and Noah appeared out of nowhere. He stepped between her and Jehu's open palm.

"Put your hand down," Noah said.

The hair raised on the back of Mercy's neck. She'd heard that tone in his voice before, on the day Tinny had gotten into it with the miner. "Noah, please." She pressed both of her hands to his chest, but it was already too late.

"You tellin' me what to do, outrider?" Jehu said. "I'd say you best take yourself off to your room and leave family business between family afore you get hurt." He only touched Noah's shoulder, but that was all it took.

Noah drew back his fist and struck Jehu square in the nose.

Nine

Jehu flew backward under the impact of Noah's fist and hit a chair. The sound of splintering wood cracked the air and he tumbled to the floor.

Both Ahab and Pots leaped to their feet, tipping their chairs over in the process.

"Noah!" Mercy shouted. "Stop it!" She grabbed his arm, but he pulled away.

Jehu came up off the floor, nose streaming blood as he cursed a blue streak.

"Jehu, I won't having fight in my—"

Her voice was drowned out by the Atkins brothers shouting heated curses. Noah said nothing. He just stood there, his jaw tight with anger, his fists raised.

Jehu took a swing at Noah, who dodged him easily. Jehu was bigger than Noah, heavier for sure, but he was no match for him when Jehu was still half intoxicated.

Jehu caught another punch, this time in the jaw. He swung wildly with one fist then the other, bawling like a wounded bull. Noah avoided the first two swipes, but took the third at his right temple.

The twin brothers still shouted and cursed, but so far, they hadn't joined in the fight. There seemed to be some code to men fighting, though what the blazes that code was, Mercy didn't know.

Noah shoved Jehu over the tipped chair and Jehu's head slammed and bounced against the white plaster wall.

Jehu came off the wall swinging.

"Get out of my house!" Mercy shouted at Jehu, throwing up her hands in front of him. She had had enough. The two of them were going to destroy her dining room.

Jehu attempted to dart forward to get at Noah, but Mercy intercepted him. "Get out of my house!" she repeated in rage. She pressed both hands to Jehu's fleshy chest and shoved him hard. She was so angry she thought she might punch him herself.

"Get back, Mercy. Stay out of this," Noah barked.

Mercy ignored Noah. "Get out of my house. Get out, get out!" Her voice rose with every word, and she grabbed the broken chair and threw it into the kitchen doorway. "And take your trashy brothers with you."

Jehu took one step back and then another, obviously shocked by her behavior. "This ain't no way to treat your family." He panted, sweat streaming down his face as if he'd run up a mountain.

"You're not my family. No family would behave like this. You come again, you pay for a meal, same as others."

Jehu wiped his bloody nose with the back of his hand. Pieces of sticky apple pie stuck to his nose. "You sidin' with a stranger against your own family?"

"I won't have you behaving like this in my home, in front of my son. You come in here drunk and demanding food that I have to work damned hard to buy." She was still backing him up. He was almost into the parlor now.

"You can't keep me from seeing my nephew," Jehu said, trying to intimidate her. "Haman expects me to look after the boy."

"You don't come here to see Jacob," she scoffed. "You come for free home-cooked food. You come to take advantage of me. Now, get out!" She spun around to face the other two Atkins brothers. "Pots! Ahab!? What are you waiting for? Get out." She pointed toward the door.

"Get out, and don't come back for supper again unless you've got the thirty-five cents to pay me, you hear?"

Ahab and Pots slipped into the parlor, backing up, their gazes fixed on Mercy. They looked at her as if she'd gone stark raving mad.

Maybe she had.

"Get out," she repeated softly through clenched teeth. "Now."

"We're gettin'." Jehu wiped his bloody nose again. "But we're not be put off like this. We'll be back."

She followed them through the parlor, onto the front porch. "Not for supper you won't be!" she hollered as they tripped down the steps, one in line behind the other.

Mercy hung on to the rail and watched the men disappear down the street, headed for the Twin Pianos, no doubt.

After they were gone, she stayed there another minute, letting cool evening air ruffle her hair. Calmed down, she went back into the house and through the parlor, into the dining room.

Noah was righting a chair.

"Leave it," she snapped.

"Mercy, I—"

She yanked the chair out of his hand and set it firmly on the floor. "The same goes for you," she flared. "You fight, you can well get out, too. What's wrong with you, slugging him?"

"He hit me first. He was going to hit you."

She grabbed another chair and hit the floor so hard with it that she nearly tipped it over again. "Didn't I tell you not to get between me and them? Didn't I tell you they were bad news? Didn't I tell you I could take care of myself?"

Noah stood there, staring at those damned boots of his.

Mercy picked up a dirty plate and then dropped it onto

the table. It would take her hours to clean up this mess. Tears stung her eyes. She wiped at them with the back of her hand. She had never been a bawler and she didn't intend to become one now.

"I'm sorry," he said softly. "Sometimes I . . . I lose my temper."

She raised an eyebrow. She felt better now. More in control of her emotions. "You lose your temper?" she repeated. "You're telling me." She gestured grandly. "A few weeks ago you try to kill a man on the street. Tonight you start a brawl in my dining room."

"He started it."

Her eyes widened with amazement. "You sound like a child. *He started it,*" she mimicked, and threw up her arms. "He was drunk, for Pete's sake! Of course he started it."

"That's no excuse for poor manners," Noah insisted quietly but firmly. "No excuse for threatening to hit a lady."

Mercy glanced at him askance. She'd lived so long in a world where men hit women that she had to think twice to realize that Noah was right.

Her gaze met his and she softened. Here was the man she had hoped Haman would be. Here was the man she had dreamed of, ten years too late. "You're bleeding."

He touched his temple where Jehu had struck him. His fingers came away bloody. Too damned late. "I'm not hurt."

"No, but you're going to bleed all over my floor and then I'll have to clean that up, too." She walked past him, brushing her fingertips against his, beckoning him. It was probably the boldest thing she'd ever done in her life. "Come in here where there's better light and I'll take a look at it."

He followed her.

"Have a seat." She indicated one of the kitchen chairs.

Again, he did as she told him.

Mercy's hand trembled as she poured hot water from the kettle into a pan. She added a little cool water and grabbed a clean rag from under the sink. Setting the pan on the table, she dipped the corner of the rag into the warm water. "Close your eyes."

He closed his eyes.

Mercy's outer thigh brushed his as she moved close enough to get a good look at the wound. His skin had split clean across the temple. The cut was long, but didn't appear to need stitches. She pressed the wet rag to his head none too gently.

He didn't flinch.

"You can't keep coming to my rescue," she said softly.

"Why?"

"Because you'll get hurt."

"I don't care."

She dabbed at the wound. The bleeding had slowed to an ooze. "But I do," she whispered.

Noah opened his eyes.

This time Mercy didn't have time to think about a kiss. He pulled her onto his lap so fast that there wasn't time to think.

Noah pressed his mouth to hers before she could stop him.

His kiss was hard like he was . . . demanding like she was.

Mercy heard herself make a sound in her throat. She fully intended to push him away. To tell him, no. Instead, she found herself kissing him back.

Mercy had very little experience with kissing, beyond a few stolen pecks before she married. Haman had never been one for foreplay. The night of their wedding, he'd pushed up her crinoline, sank home, thrust three or four times, and then collapsed on top of her with a satisfied grunt. Her honeymoon kiss had been a slap on her bare backside as he sent her to find him a flask of whiskey to celebrate the union.

So Mercy didn't know what she was doing, but seemed to be holding her own. Noah seemed to be enjoying it well enough.

Noah's arms were firm and tight around her waist. His mouth crushed against hers. As he pressed his tongue to her lips, they parted of their own accord. Mercy had never thought she'd want a man's tongue in her mouth until she tasted Noah.

They both came up for air panting. Nose to nose they stared into each other's eyes. For a nickel, she wagered he'd have carried her right up those steps to his rope bed. If she'd had a nickel, she might have given it to him.

"There," she said, her voice breathy. She made no attempt to rise from his lap. What was the point? The milk was spilt. "Maybe that'll be out of our systems now."

He was still looking at her, gazing into her eyes. His gaze told her what she felt inside. It wasn't enough.

"Maybe."

She brushed her fingertips over her lips, wanting to savor the feel of his mouth on hers. "We can't do this," she said.

"I know."

"I'm a married woman." Still she made no attempt to rise from his lap; her legs were too shaky. She could feel his hard, muscular thighs beneath her buttocks. She could feel his warmth seeping through his denims, through her petticoat and skirt, right to her heart.

He lowered his gaze, his hands still around her. "I'm sorry."

"Don't be." She smiled sadly. Of course she couldn't climb the stairs and bed him. What of Jacob? Tinny? The pea patch?

"Don't be sorry." Mercy pressed her hands to his shoulders and made herself rise off his lap.

He let her go, but with obvious reluctance.

"It was as much my fault as yours." She leaned over to pick up the damp rag, stained with his blood. She didn't know when she'd dropped it. "Besides, that's not a wise thing to do," she teased. "Kiss a woman and then tell her you're sorry you bothered."

He glanced up. "Didn't mean that way." He brushed her hips with his hand and her cage crinoline swayed. "You know it."

She gave a little laugh, not understanding why she felt so good inside. Sure, Noah had kissed her, but that kiss could lead to nothing but trouble, and she'd never been a woman looking for trouble. "I know you didn't," she said, letting her hands fall at her sides. She could still feel the heat of his mouth on hers. She could taste him. "It's just silly. We're adults who have had our share of hard times. No use pretending I didn't want it. Like it."

Noah didn't say anything. He looked so damned guilty. Then she realized that of course he should feel guilty. For all he knew, her husband might still be alive. After all, he'd not yet been declared dead by the Army.

"Noah—"

He held up one hand to cut her off. "I have no business laying my hand on another man's wife, even if he is most likely dead. We don't know for sure."

That premise was so easy to fall into that Mercy couldn't resist. Besides, it was just a little lie, wasn't it? Haman was certainly dead. "I don't expect him to come back, Noah, but there's his family I have to worry about. And Jacob."

He rose. "Won't happen again."

His words tugged at her heart. Instead of relief, she felt disappointment. "Fine," she said. "Good." She picked up the wash basin. "I better get to work."

Mercy heard the front door open and close, followed by Jacob's footsteps. "Wow!" he hollered when he reached the dining room. He poked his head into the kitchen. "What happened here?"

"A fight," Mercy said. "Mr. Ericson and Uncle Jehu got into it." She'd make no excuses for Noah even though he was Jacob's hero these days.

The boy's eyes widened. "Wow. And I missed it?" He swung his fist through the air. "Man! I miss all the good stuff. I missed the last time Uncle Pots threw up all over the front porch and Mama washed him and the porch down with cold water, too."

Noah cracked a grin. "Sorry I missed that one. Would have liked to have seen it." He winked at Mercy as he lowered a hand to Jacob's shoulder. "Now let's see what we can do about cleaning up this mess, Jake." He rested his hands on her son's shoulders and steered him into the dining room. "It's that, or your mama will put me out on my ear for sure."

Mercy turned away to keep Noah from seeing her smile. God help her, she was in trouble. Deep trouble. Somehow she'd fallen in love with Noah.

The baby wailed, waking Jezzy from a sound sleep. She sat up and leaned over the trundle bed to pat Daisy. On the other side of the bedroom door, Jezzy's brothers hooted and hollered and turned over chairs as they stumbled into the great room.

"There, there," Jezzy said sleepily. "It's nothing but those fat-assed uncles of yours come in shit-faced again. It's all right, honey."

The little girl quieted at the feel of her mother's hand and the sound of her voice in the darkness.

"That-a-girl, that-a-girl," Jezzy soothed.

The moment her daughter lay down and drifted off to

sleep again, Jezzy climbed out of her bed and slipped out
of the bedroom, barefoot, in a flannel sleeping gown.

"Jesus Christ Almighty!" she said the minute she closed
the door behind her. "How many times do I have to tell
you not to come home making this kind of clamor!" The
smooth floorboards were cold beneath her bare feet as
she padded to the far side of the great room and poured
herself a healthy portion of rye whiskey. A massive buffalo
head loomed over her own head, mounted on the wall.

"We ain't makin' no noise," Jehu said, dropping heavily onto the horsehair settee she'd had shipped over the
mountains from San Francisco.

"The hell you didn't!" She shoved his foot off the arm
of the settee. "A stampede of buffalo would make less
noise than you all." She sat on the arm of a chair and
sipped her rye.

Ahab sat on the floor, his head cradled in his hands,
his back to a chair. He snored softly.

"Where you been?" Jezzy asked Jehu. She knew she'd
not get anything out of Ahab before morning.

"Town."

She could smell a cheap whore's violet water on Jehu
from where she sat. "I know that," she snapped.
"Where?"

"Twin Pianos," he answered, eyes closed.

"That the only place?" She eyed him suspiciously. "Or
did you get into a fight elsewhere?" The dry blood under
his nose and the puffy eye that was already turning a
green-black was evidence enough of his antics.

"Stopped by to see the boy. Meant to have a nice supper with him, but Mercy got snappy on me." He opened
and closed one hand, making a fist. "Might have to set
that bitch straight one of these days. Show her what a
real man's like."

Jezzy sighed. She had never liked her brother's wife.
Too good to suit her. Too squeaky clean, so mostly she

just avoided her. Jezzy had no female friends and had no intentions of making any. But Jehu—he'd had a thing for that uppity Mercy since the day she arrived in Nowhere. With Haman gone, Jezzy figured it was only a matter of time before Jehu took her for his own wife. Her brothers might think Haman was still coming home, but they were idiots. Jezzy knew better. Haman was rotting in some god-forsaken ditch somewhere, a Rebel bullet through his thick skull.

She swirled her rye in her glass. "She the one who cuffed you?" She laughed when he made no reply. "What of the outrider? See him?"

Jehu opened his good eye and gazed groggily at her. "Why you askin'?"

She shrugged. "No reason. Just curious."

Jehu closed his eyes again, no doubt to keep the room from spinning. "He was the one I had to set straight."

She gave a snort of derision. "You're lucky he didn't shoot you between the eyes. What the hell are you doing fighting lawmen? You ought to stick to drunks and whores."

"Leave me alone and let me sleep."

"Where's Pots?"

Jehu tried to roll over on the narrow settee. "Pots?"

"Yes, your brother—Potipher. You know, he and Ahab are a matching set. Big, ugly, dumb like you."

"He was here a minute ago. Ahab, where's Pots?"

Ahab made no reply, sound asleep where he sat.

"Christ Almighty," Jezzy muttered, finishing her rye and rising. "Where's Pots, Jehu? You didn't leave him in town again, did you? Because if you did, Sheriff Dawson is bound to pick him up. You know the sheriff said we're going to have to start paying board on you boys every time you spend the night in jail."

"I'm tellin' you, he was here." Jehu shifted his body, trying to get more comfortable.

IF YOU WERE MINE   107

Jezzy smacked the back of his head as she went by.
"Ouch," he whined.

"Get up and get your lard ass upstairs. And I'm warning you," she called over her shoulder. "You get up at
dawn, and you pull a full load, hung over or not. We got
branding to do tomorrow." She kicked Ahab with her
foot as she walked by him. "Ahab. Go to bed."

Jezzy didn't have to go any farther than the front porch
to find Pots. He was sprawled at the door, sound asleep.

"Goddamnit, Pots. Get up. It's cold out here." She
hugged herself for warmth. In the distance she heard the
whinny of horses in the barn and the shuffling of cattle
in their pens. Somewhere, far off in the foothills, a coyote
howled.

"Pots!" She rolled him over with a bare foot.

Pots groaned and rolled onto his back, crossing his
arms over his chest.

Jezzy laughed. "Christy Almighty, Pots. You look like
the undertaker's laid you out. Gets your ass up or I'm
locking the door and leavin' you to freeze your nuts off."

"Huh? Huh?" Pots sat up, blinking. "Where am I?"
He scratched his groin through his dirty pants in a daze.
"What happened?"

"Your brothers left you for dead again." She swung
open the door. "Get inside."

Pots flipped over onto his belly and crawled on his
hands and knees into the house. "I love you, Jezzy," he
blubbered. "My brothers, they don't give a pinch for me,
but I love you." Just inside the door, he fell flat out again,
passed out.

Jezzy threw the bolt home on the door, stepped over
Pots. "Fine, sleep there."

She crossed the great room, the antlers that lined the
walls casting eerie branchlike shadows across the floor.
Jehu and Ahab had apparent]y made it up the stairs.

Weary, she blew out the lamp and headed, in the darkness, for her room for a few hours' sleep before dawn.

It was difficult being the head of the family, always making all the decisions, always feeling the weight of responsibility. But her three brothers didn't have half the sense Daisy, at three, did. They couldn't run the ranch. Left to them, it would be on the foreclosure market in two years' time. Jezzy had once dreamed of marrying a man with shoulders broad enough to share the load. Images of the tall, drawn outrider, Noah, flashed through her mind. But she'd given up on that idea years ago. She was too old to settle down with a husband. Too old and set in her ways to yield to a man on any matter. Besides, she had Daisy, what did she need a man for now?

Jezzy slipped under her quilt and closed her eyes, rolling onto her side. She wasn't looking forward to morning. There was nothing worse than trying to get chores done with her three brothers hung over and puking over the corral rails.

She wagered tight-denimed Noah Ericson never drank until he puked.

Ten

"Silver! Silver! Yee ha!"

"What on earth?" Mercy slipped out of the parlor where she'd been dusting and walked out onto the front porch. As she dried her hands on her apron, she watched a scraggly-bearded man ride down the middle of the street waving a red handkerchief.

"Yee ha!" he shouted. "Silver!"

"Someone struck silver? In Nowhere?" Mercy leaned on the shaky rail and called to him as he rode by.

He wheeled his black-and-white spotted pony around and passed the hotel porch again. "Sure did, ma'am." He lowered the handkerchief and pulled off his hat. His face and beard were caked with days, perhaps weeks, of grime, but his blue eyes had a sparkle to them. "Patterson's claim. Struck a line. Pure and glittery, she is."

Mercy became caught up in the young man's exuberance. This was it. This was what she had hoped for. "That's wonderful!"

"I've got me a share." He urged his mount to the steps. "Say . . ." He glanced at the Tin Roof Hotel sign Noah had repaired and rehung only the day before. "If you don't mind me askin', you got a bathtub here? For rentin', I mean? For a man lookin' for a bath."

"The Twin Piano's got a bathhouse in the back."

He whistled between his teeth. "No, ma'am, that won't do at all. I got a wife and a baby son in Carson City. My wife catches wind I've been in a bathhouse behind a saloon, I'll be turned out on my ear. Not all the silver in Nevada will save my hide."

Mercy thought fast. She had a big tin bathtub upstairs in one of the bedrooms. The previous owners had apparently left it. She didn't use it because it took so much water to fill it, but for cash . . .

She met the young man's gaze. Filthy as he was, he seemed like a pleasant fellow. A family man. "As a matter of fact, I was considering offering bathing as one of the hotel's services. I have fine sleeping rooms, singles or bunk-house style, depending on your preference."

He put up a hand. "I got a tent set up near the claim and I keep an eye on the place come nightfall. I'm the foreman for Mr. Patterson, and he's promising me a share in the whole caboodle."

"I've got hot meals," she enticed. "No beans and hardtack here. Even if you're boarding elsewhere, you can buy a hot meal."

He lifted a dirt-encrusted eyebrow. "And get a bath?"

She chuckled. "Definitely a bath, if you intend to sit at my dining table." She glanced at his filthy red long john's shirt and drooping suspenders. "I do laundry, too."

He glanced at his dirty clothes, then back at her. "You got yourself a deal, ma'am. I'll be back late this afternoon." He sank his heels into the spotted pony's flanks. "I'm off to the telegraph office for Mr. Patterson, but I'll be back 'round sunset."

She gave a wave. "That'll be fine. We'll see you tonight. And you're welcome to bring a friend if you like," she called after him.

He waved as he rode away.

"Holy cow," Mercy muttered to herself, walking back into the house. "How on earth am I going to haul all that water up those steps? My back will be broken in a week's time."

She walked through the kitchen and out onto the back porch to check on Tinny and Jacob. Tinny was asleep in an old rocker Jacob and Noah had found in the shed. The two had been spending many an hour cleaning out the outbuilding and finding all sorts of treasures that fascinated her son.

Mercy crossed the lawn. The grass beneath her feet was warm in the sun and felt deliciously sensual. Lately she had seemed to be more aware of her physical self; how things felt against her skin, how some smells tantalized her, how the sight of a flowering weed made her smile.

"Jacob?"

"In here," her son called cheerfully from inside the shed.

Mercy passed her garden, which was growing well. The peas were growing thick and healthy and would soon produce pods.

"Me and Noah are sorting through the tools."

Without thinking, Mercy smoothed her hair. As usual, she must look a disheveled mess. "Noah and I," she corrected. "And really, Jacob, you shouldn't address Noah by his first name. It's not respectful."

Inside the shed, Noah stood at a bench, his back to her.

"You do," Jacob said.

"That's different. We're adults. You're a child."

Noah turned, a rusty claw hammer in his hand. "I don't mind, really. But whatever you prefer."

Mercy studied her surroundings. Half the junk was gone from the shed, the other half piled neatly. Even the puncheon floor had been swept. "Goodness. You men have been busy. What happened to all the rubbish in here?" She turned slowly around in amazement, her hands resting on her hips.

"Burned the nasty stuff like that old mattress and clothes." Jacob climbed up onto the bench and sat down, his bare feet hanging over the edge.

Noah turned back to the bench.

"Took the good stuff inside." Jacob swung his feet. "We found two bedsteads that Noah said you could use in the addition, should you ever need 'em. Good as new with fresh ropes."

"Well, I just *might* be needing them." She smiled, pleased with herself. "Because someone has finally struck silver."

"Silver?" Jacob leaped off the bench. "When? Where?"

"I just met someone working the claim. He says there's a man by the name of Patterson mining nearby. They struck silver this morning. He was headed to the telegraph office."

Noah gave a long whistle, turning back to face her. He wiped his hands on his denims. "Cook, at the bank, said it was only a matter of time before someone hit pay dirt. Guess he was right."

"And I've got a customer," she said proudly.

"That right?" He sounded genuinely pleased for her.

She nodded. "The man who told me about the silver, a nice young man with a wife and a baby in Carson City. He says he sleeps at the claim, but he's looking for a place to get a hot meal and a bath."

Noah's mouth turned up into the lazy grin that made her weak in the knees. "Congratulations."

She rolled her eyes. "Congratulations? I've got a man coming in a couple hours for a bath and I'm not set up for a bathhouse. I have a tub upstairs, but Jacob and I can't lug water up and down the steps indefinitely. Besides, I'm not sure I want naked men running through my house."

Jacob giggled.

Noah glanced around, then back at her. "What would you think about making this into a bathhouse?"

She studied the shed with a more critical eye, possibilities immediately coming to light. "The shed? You think I could?"

"Sure. Jake and I could haul the tub down here. You'd need to buy a couple of lamps, a mirror, some towels, and a clothes hook or two, is all. Men could bathe out here and dress before they stepped foot in your dining room."

"There's no way to heat the place, but it's getting warmer every day." She thought aloud as she walked back and forth, guessing at the length and width of the room. If she cleaned out the shed completely, she might be able to fit two tubs, with a curtain between them. "By fall I might have enough money saved to buy a little potbelly stove."

"You've got a water pump right outside. I might even be able to rig something up to run water in here. You could put a kettle to boil on an open fire outside for the heated water."

Bored with talk of bathing, Jacob wandered out into the bright sunlight, dragging a piece of horse harness behind him.

Mercy couldn't stop smiling at Noah. "You're brilliant."

His gaze rested on hers, then too quickly he looked away. His smile faded. "No, I'm not."

Ever since the kiss they had shared last week, they'd been walking a narrow plank. One minute Noah was looking at her with eyes a woman could drown in, the next minute he was staring at the floor, barely speaking more than a word to her.

Mercy just couldn't figure him out. He seemed to agree that she was just waiting for a technicality to be declared a widow. She didn't really belong to another man and he was a widower, free to seek another woman. He was ob-

viously attracted to her. Why didn't he kiss her again?
Why didn't he try to get her into his bed?

Of course Mercy knew she couldn't have a relationship
with this man or any man right now. Her position with
the law and the Atkins boys was too precarious. If Jehu
found out Noah was courting her, he might kill him. Of
course she couldn't share Noah's bed, but an invitation
sure would have made her feel good.

Mercy looked directly at Noah. "I'd appreciate your
help. You've already done so much—"

"I don't mind." He slipped his hands into his pockets.
"Glad I can be of some use to someone."

Mercy crossed her arms over her chest. She never could
stand to see anything or anyone hurting. It was in her
nature to want to help, to comfort. "I bet you were a
good husband," she said gently. She didn't know what
possessed her to say such a forward thing. It made her
sound so . . . *envious* of his dead wife. She didn't mean
it that way, though maybe she *was* a little envious. "A
good father," she finished.

He scuffed the puncheon plank floor with his square-
toed boot. "Afraid you'd lose that bet."

His words were so heavy, so filled to overflowing with
guilt, that Mercy had to ask the question that had been
burning in her mind since she found out he was a widower. "You never said what happened to her—them."

He kept his head bent. "No, I didn't."

Any woman with good sense would have known he
meant *mind your business*. But she'd come this far. She
genuinely wanted to know what illness or accident had
taken his family, because it seemed to her that his dead
family was what was holding him back. Not just from her,
but from the world.

"How'd they die?"

"Murdered."

The dreadful word hung in the air.

Mercy held her hand to her heart. She had assumed they had died of cholera, or consumption, or one of the many other illnesses faced here in the West. But *murdered?* She couldn't imagine the pain he had to feel.

"I'm sorry, Noah." She wanted to touch him. To brush his hair from his eyes. To kiss the sadness from his lips. "Indians?" she asked. They occasionally raided farms and isolated way stations, but not often. The Washoes were relatively peaceful compared to those in the surrounding states and territories.

He swallowed hard, his Adam's apple bobbing. "Indians wouldn't do a thing like this," he said, his voice flat, emotionless. "Thieves. Robbed the house. Raped Alice, most likely. Shot and killed her and Becky."

"Ah, Noah. I'm sorry. Sorry I asked." Mercy went to him and wrapped her arms around him. It wasn't a romantic kind of hug. It was a hug a person gave in hopes of taking away some of the other person's pain.

Noah just stood there. He didn't hug her back, but he didn't pull away, either.

"Did the law catch up with them?" she whispered, smoothing his thick hair.

He shook his head.

Mercy kissed him on the cheek and stepped back. His eyes were dry, but her cheeks were damp with tears. She felt as if she was crying for him because it hurt too much for *him* to cry. "I really am sorry." She didn't know what else to say.

He turned his back to her and picked up the hammer. "Jake and I will make a place for the tub and haul it down."

Mercy had more questions for Noah. She wanted to know how he felt about his family's deaths. Obviously he felt guilty. Why? Exactly what had happened? Had he been there and been unable to protect them? But she recognized his need to change the subject. She had to

respect that need. She felt the same way about Haman.
Mostly she was just embarrassed that she'd been fool
enough to marry him and then a bigger fool to stay with
him. "I can help with the tub."

"Nah. When Tinny gets done catnapping, we'll get him
to help. He likes to have a job. Makes him feel good."

Mercy wanted to thank Noah, not just for helping her
with the bathtub, but for what he'd done for Jacob, for
her father. She realized, though, that Noah had had
enough sharing for one day. She'd have to save her
thanks for another time.

"I'm going to see what I can come up with for towels
and soap and such." She turned away, making an effort
to speak cheerfully again. "Be in the house if you need
me."

Mercy walked out into the sunshine. She felt good inside and didn't know why. Maybe because Noah had
trusted her enough to tell her about his loved ones, even
if he felt guilty about their deaths. Then she passed the
garden and she realized she didn't deserve happiness. If
she weren't so prideful, she'd be feeling her own share
of guilt.

Noah rode at an easy pace into Nowhere, the sun setting over his left shoulder. Another safe, successful trip
to Carson City and back. The ride was so easy, the job so
simple, that he was beginning to wonder if he ought to
be taking the Nowhere bank's money like this. They
didn't need an armed guard. Those robberies had to have
been flukes—thieves just passing through who thought to
get a purse or two, maybe a lady's bauble, and found a
bank's cash box by sheer accident.

Noah slowed his mount to a walk. All day he'd looked
forward to returning to town, to the hotel, to—

Hell, Noah didn't know what was wrong with him. All

he could think about was Mercy; her voice when she laughed, the way the sunlight glinted off her hair in the early morning when she crawled on her hands and knees through her garden. And her hands, he loved to stare at her hands. The way they moved, peeled potatoes, tucked stray locks of hair behind her ear, locks he longed to press his lips to.

Noah pulled his horse up sharply in front of the Twin Pianos and dismounted. He knew he had no right to feel this way. No right to be looking forward to a quiet evening with Mercy when Alice would have no quiet evening. What gave him the right to wink at Jacob as he went off to bed, holding his mother's hand, when there would be no more good nights for Becky?

Noah caught the reins and squeezed his eyes shut for a moment. He pressed his face to the horse's neck and breathed in the warm, heady scent as he tried to get a hold of himself. He took a couple of good deep breaths and tied up his horse, before anyone caught him acting like a fool.

Maybe after a beer or two he'd have his head on straight and then he could go on to the hotel. Feeling like he was right now, wanting Mercy the way he did, there was no telling what he might say or do. He might carry her upstairs to his rope bed, or something even worse . . . like . . . like, hell, ask her to marry him.

Noah shoved open the swinging door, angry with himself for betraying his wife this way. Angry at the world for creating human animals who raped women and killed little girls.

Noah didn't spot the Atkins boys until after he took a stool at the bar; otherwise he'd have turned right around and left. But it was too late and he was already at the bar. "Beer," he grunted to the bartender.

Mercy's in-laws were seated at a large round table near the staircase. They were playing poker with three other men, laughing and passing around a bottle of whiskey without the couth to use a glass. Maybe they would be too drunk or too involved in the game to notice him.

Several short-skirted, mouth-painted saloon girls hung on the men's shoulders, hoping to pick up a coin or two. Supposedly, the Twin Pianos didn't deal in the whore trade, but Noah guessed that if one of the men was willing to hand over enough greenbacks, any one of those girls was willing to go up the stairs with him. And for a cut, the proprietor would be willing to look the other way.

Noah wasn't halfway through his beer when Jehu Atkins hollered out to him. The man with jowls like a hog leaned back in his chair and tipped his hat. "Ericson." He was drunk, of course.

Noah didn't smile. "Evening."

Jehu's chair scraped. "How was that ride to Carson City and back?" He had a taunting, "dare-me" tone to his voice. He might be talking civil, but Noah could tell he was looking for a fight. Maybe because he was the kind of man who was always looking for a fight.

Noah turned back to his beer. "Fair."

"Seem kind of boring to me. Escorting ladies with their dress boxes and the like. You ought to try a man's day's work sometime. Me and the boys, we spent our day castratin' bulls. Ever done it?" He took a swig from a half-empty bottle. "Wooo-weee! Those bulls can holler. Guess I would, too, if someone was holdin' me down, cuttin' my stones."

The one called Pots cackled.

Noah didn't say anything, hoping Jehu would just shut up and turn around. He had no desire to converse with a man like Jehu. Any man that treated a woman like Jehu treated Mercy wasn't worth the time of day.

The saloon doors swung open behind Noah. "Hell, there you are," came a low, feminine voice. "How'd I guess this was where I would find you?"

Noah glanced over his shoulder. It was the Atkins woman.

"Jezzy. Hey, old girl." Jehu waved his bottle. "Pull up a chair, we'll deal you in."

"Where you been?"

To Noah's surprise, Jezzy had a little girl with her. The child hung to Jezzy's pant leg and stared with big blue eyes. She had wispy blond hair that reminded Noah of Becky's hair when she was a toddler.

Noah frowned and turned back to his beer. A child had no place in a saloon.

"I said, where have you been, Jehu?" Jezzy repeated angrily.

"What do you mean, where we been? We rode out to the west corral to do that castratin', and then we come here for a little refreshment. A man deserves a little refreshment and *peace* after a hard day's work."

"Do I look like an idiot to you, Jehu?" she said sharply. "You weren't in the west corral, because I was at the west corral looking for your lazy asses. We've got a break in the north corral, west corner, and we got two dozen horses missing. I've come for you three so you can help me find the friggin' horses. But you're nowhere to be found. Then I have to haul my ass and Daisy's all the way into town to find you. You think I'm pissed? You think I am?" she shouted.

"It . . . it's a big pasture, Jezzy. We must have just missed each other."

Noah heard a chair get kicked over and glanced in time to see Jezzy grab Jehu by his shirt. "You've been in this goddamned saloon all day, haven't you?"

"No, Jezzy. We ain't been here." He pushed her hand aside. "Ask Pots and Ahab. Ask anybody in here."

She pressed the thumb and index finger of one hand to her temples and massaged them in a circular motion. The little girl still clung to her pant leg.

"Get home, Jehu," Jezzy said quietly.

The other two brothers rose and made for the door, taking care to circumnavigate their sister.

Jehu took his time, picking up his hat and settling it on his head. "I'll go on home, but because I'm ready to, not because you say so. You got that?"

Jezzy chuckled. "Sure, I got it, Jehu. I got that you're full of goose shit. I want that break in the fence fixed and those horses found," she told him as he passed her. "I don't care if it takes all night, you understand?"

Jehu pushed through the swinging doors and they slapped shut behind him.

Jezzy sighed and walked up to the bar, child still in tow. "Sammy, a double rye." She glanced at Noah. "The only thing worse than hired lazy assholes is family lazy assholes, don't you think?"

Noah glanced at the little girl who cringed each time Jezzy raised her voice. He was appalled that anyone would speak so crudely in front of such a young child.

Jezzy must have guessed what he was thinking because she hooked her thumb in the girl's direction. "Pay her no mind. She's mine. She already knows her uncles are assholes, don't you, Daisy?"

Daisy said nothing, only gazed up at her mother with big blue eyes.

Jezzy reached for her rye. "So, thought any more about my invitation?" She glanced sideways at Noah. "I'm not looking for any long-term commitment here." She smiled slyly. "Just a little fun. You do like fun, don't you, Mr. Ericson?" She winked. "It'd be a hell of ride, I promise you that."

Noah was so disgusted by the woman that he slid off his barstool. "Sorry. Not looking for that kind of fun."

She eyed him suspiciously. "Please tell me you're not a man for the pole."

Noah picked up his hat off the bar and dropped it

onto his head. "This is no place for little girls. Why don't you take her home?"

"I can't believe you're turning me down." Jezzy shook her head. "You don't know what you're missing. An offer like this doesn't come often."

Noah cocked his head toward the door. "That gunfire I hear? That one of your drunken brothers making that racket?"

"Shit." Jezzy slammed down her empty glass, pitched a few coins on the bar, and spun on her boot heels. "Jesus H. Christ. Can't they follow simple directions? I told them to get their asses home."

Noah stepped out of the way to let Jezzy pass. He watched the little girl, dressed in pants like her mother, run to keep up with Jezzy as she went through the saloon doors.

Outside he watched as Jezzy mounted a horse and pulled the little girl up in front of her. She reined her mount around and took off, following the sound of the direction of the random gunshots.

Noah didn't mount his horse, but instead walked to the livery stable, then took his time walking to the Tin Roof Hotel. By the time he reached the front steps, he had just about convinced himself to take his supper up to his room tonight and not take any chances of being alone with Mercy. It was the best way to insulate himself.

Mercy waited for him on the porch, her face tight with worry. "There you are. The sheriff waited for you for an hour and then he had to go. Mr. Cook's here with another man."

Noah pulled off his hat, scraping his boots before he followed her inside. "What's wrong?" He touched her elbow. "You all right? Jake?"

"We're fine. Fine." She brushed his arm as if it were the most natural thing. As if they were lovers . . . No, as if they were a couple who loved and respected each other. "Everyone here is fine," she said.

"Then what—"

"A stagecoach robbery, Noah. Someone else has been killed."

Eleven

"Cook?" Noah strode into the parlor off the dining room. It was a small room, sparsely furnished with an oval hook rug, a worn settee, and several mahogany Sheraton tables that had to have been thirty or forty years old. Though perhaps out of fashion, it was breezy and comfortable, like Mercy.

"Ericson." The stiffly dressed bank executive rose. A gentleman in similar attire also rose from his chair.

Noah rested his hand on his gun holster as a matter of habit. "Sit." He waved a hand. "Tell me what Mercy's talking about. What coach was robbed? I saw the Nowhere bank's money deposited safely in Carson City myself."

Mr. Cook motioned to his companion. "This is Mr. Applebee from Smithtown."

Noah nodded. "Nice to meet you, sir." He pulled off his hat. "Now, enough pleasantries. Who's been robbed?"

Cook sat again, resting his bowler hat on his lap. "We have a small branch of the Carson City bank in our town, same as you," Mr. Applebee said. "Once a week the deposits are sent by stagecoach—one that takes a different route than the Nowhere coach. It was robbed yesterday. A woman traveling with her son was killed. Hit by a stray bullet."

Noah glanced away. Somewhere in the depths of his mind he could almost understand why someone might

steal, but he could never, ever understand killing innocent women and children. "Why are you telling me this?"

"Applebee's got a request to make," Cook said. "I just
offered to do the introductions."

Noah looked at Applebee.

Applebee nervously cleared his throat. Guns tended to
make men in suits uncomfortable, though he could never
understand why. It was men like Noah with guns that
made the world safe for men like Cook and Applebee.

"I . . . I was wondering if you'd be willing to work for
us."

Noah glanced at Cook, then back at Applebee. "I already ride with the Nowhere Bank's money three times
a week."

"We could combine the runs," Applebee said. "Mr.
Cook is in agreement. Your fee would be doubled, of
course."

"Of course," Cook echoed.

Noah didn't know that he really wanted an additional
job. He didn't care for any more responsibility, and the
money meant nothing to him.

"Please, Mr. Ericson?" Applebee said. "Our town's
struggling. We end up with no bank, and stores will begin
to shut down. Our town will die."

Noah sighed. It wouldn't really mean any more work,
he supposed. He could just ride to Smithtown before the
stagecoach arrived here, and bring the money back in a
wagon. He'd just have to get up a little earlier. What difference would that make? He could barely sleep these
days anyway. "You certain this is all right with you, Cook?"

Cook bobbed his head. "All right with me. Main
branch in Carson City has given its approval. We see no
reason why you can't protect Nowhere and Smithtown's
money. You have an excellent reputation, Mr. Ericson."

Noah brushed his hat against his thigh. "I'd need a
wagon and a driver to get the money here, Mr. Applebee.

I escort. I don't ride around with cash boxes strapped to my saddle."

"Done." Applebee rose. "Anything else?"

Noah shrugged. "Guess not. Cook can give you the schedule. We run with the stagecoach. Safer that way."

Applebee bobbed his head as the two men made their way to the door. "Thank you . . . thank you."

Noah followed them to the front hall. "Day after tomorrow, I'll be there."

"Thank you, Mr. Ericson. You don't know how much this will mean to our town."

Noah pushed open the door for them. "Just a job, Mr. Applebee."

Cook nodded to Noah and replaced his hat. "See you day after tomorrow."

Noah closed the door behind them.

Mercy appeared from the kitchen, wiping her beautiful hands on a damp apron tied around her waist. "I couldn't help overhearing. You took the job."

He lifted one shoulder and lowered it, feeling awkward, though he didn't know why. It wasn't as if he needed Mercy's approval to take the extra job. It was not as if it affected her in any way. "Not really that much more work," he said, studying the rag rug on the hall floor. It had lavender flowers on a cream background. He'd walked over the rug hundreds of times probably, but this was the first time he noticed the flowers. He felt as if he were slowly waking from a long sleep, a sleep that had lasted three years. And it was Mercy who was waking him. "I'll have to leave here earlier in the morning, is all," he said, trying not to think about the purple flowers or what Mercy was doing to him.

She continued to dry her hands, though they surely had to be dry by now. "Certainly. Why not take the job?" She paused. "Even if it is dangerous."

There was sarcasm in her tone; she was concerned for

his safety. It had been a long time since anyone cared what happened to him. "Not really that dangerous. Someone's got to do it."

"Someone," she agreed. Then she was quiet.

Noah glanced up to see Mercy staring straight at him. Her gaze unnerved him. "What?" he asked, turning his palms heavenward. "Why are you looking at me like that?"

"Like what?"

"You know. Like you expect something out of me." Noah wished he hadn't said that because the hurt was immediately plain on her face. He didn't want to hurt her. Just push her away.

"I don't expect anything out of you," she said sharply.

"Good, because you shouldn't. Because I can't." Noah didn't know what lit into him. He wanted to take her in his arms so badly, yet he knew he needed to separate himself from her. Shove her away. He had no right to have an ounce of happiness. He didn't deserve a woman like Mercy. He didn't deserve a second chance. "Don't you see I can't give you what you need? What you deserve?"

Mercy released her apron, and the thin fabric fluttered, seeming to take an eternity before it settled over her faded calico skirt. Now she was staring at the rug. He hoped she wouldn't cry. He wouldn't be able to stand it if she cried. He'd have to take her in his arms then.

"I never asked you to help me," she said quietly but firmly. "Never once."

"Hell," he swore, feeling like an ass. "That's not what I mean, and you know it."

She rested her hands on her hips, hips that enticed him, even in his dreams. She lifted her gaze to meet his in challenge. "Then what did you mean?"

He shook his head. *"No Mercy."*

Her brow creased. "What?"

"No mercy. You never give me any mercy." He took a hesitant step toward her. "You never just let me give up, give in."

He felt as if he were falling. After Alice and Becky's deaths he had carefully constructed a ledge of isolation for himself. Perched on that ledge, he could watch the world, but he didn't have to participate in it. Mercy was pushing him off that ledge. He was digging in his heels, but she was shoving hard.

And he loved her for it.

Noah caught a wisp of her honey hair with his finger and thumb. It was so soft. He wanted to take her in his arms. He needed her. He was so damned tired of being alone.

"I don't know what you want me to do," Mercy said. To his surprise her voice was shaky. He didn't think anything scared her. "What . . . what do you want from me."

Noah took another step closer, entranced by her blue eyes that begged him to kiss her. Begged him to make love to her. "I think you do," he whispered. She was so close now that he could feel the heat of her body. He could smell her clean, fragrant skin and the flour on her sleeve.

Her hands came to rest on his bare forearms. "That obvious, is it?" She smiled shyly, sounding embarrassed. "That obvious I'm a wanton woman?" She gave a little laugh but he knew she was half serious.

He rested his hands on her hips. "Nothing wrong with wanting someone, Mercy. Human nature."

She lowered her gaze. "Then . . . why don't you . . . Why do we . . ." She struggled to find the right words. "You know. Is it because I'm married? Because of Haman? Because if it is—"

"It's not Haman. He's dead, I know that. You know it. Men don't come home from war three years late."

It had been so long since he'd talked intimately with

a woman that it was hard for him. Yet at the same time
it felt so good to make that emotional connection. Touching Mercy like this, whispering, made him realize just how
lonely he was and how much he hated it. "It's not you,
either. I've been attracted to you since the day my dusty
boots crossed your threshold. It's me. I don't deserve
you."

She lifted her hand from his arm and stroked his
cheek. "I don't understand."

"I know you don't." His voice was strained and he had
to remind himself that men don't cry. His eyes watered.

"Explain it to me."

He shook his head. "Can't."

"Can't or won't?"

Noah thought his reaction to her should be one of
anger. It certainly was the easiest. Most convenient. Least
painful. But she was right.

Arms still resting on her hips, he stared hard at the
hollow at the base of her throat. He watched it throb
with the pulse of her heartbeat. "Won't because I can't,"
he said.

"Noah, Noah," she whispered.

She wrapped her arms around his waist and rested her
cheek on his chest. He held her tight. He knew what she
was saying. She wanted to make love to him. She would.
All he had to do was ask.

The front porch door opened behind Noah, and Mercy
jerked away. One second he was dangerously close to lifting her in his arms and taking her up to his bed, the
next his chance was lost.

Saved in the nick of time.

"Pap," Mercy fumbled, taking another step back.

The old man couldn't have missed the embrace, but
he didn't seem to be fazed by it. Maybe his mind was too
far gone to realize what it meant.

Jacob came in the door right on Tinny's heels.

"You're home." The boy looked at Noah, then away. Had he seen them?

Noah picked his hat up off the floor; he didn't know when he'd dropped it. He wiped at his eyes and slapped his hat on his knee. "Um . . . just got in."

Tinny shuffled past Mercy toward the kitchen. "Come on, Joe. Let's rustle up some coffee."

"Me and Mama and Pap are riding out to Washoe Lake to have a picnic. Want to go?" He pulled off his hat. "It's my birthday."

Noah glanced at Mercy, uncertain. "Nice of you to ask, Jake," he stalled, "but maybe your mama wants you to herself. A family—"

"You're welcome to come," Mercy interrupted as she followed Tinny into the kitchen. "I'm borrowing Paddy's wagon to ride out."

Noah wanted to catch her hand before she got away, but he moved a second too late and she was gone.

"I don't know . . ." he hemmed.

"Please?" Jacob begged. "We're going fishing and we're going to eat fried chicken and sugar cookies, and if it's really warm, Mama says I can put my feet in the water."

A family gathering. Noah knew he shouldn't. He felt Jacob's small, warm hand tug on his own.

"Please, Noah? There's no stagecoach tomorrow. No work. You're just going to lay around upstairs or mess in the shed. Bathhouse," he corrected himself, rolling his eyes.

Noah felt stuck. A part of him wanted to go to share in the birthday celebration, to eat chicken as if he were a part of a real family again. A part of him wanted to run. "All right," he said. "Reckon I can make it."

"Whoopee!" Jacob gave a hoot and bounded off into the kitchen. "Mama! Mama! He says he can go. Noah says he'll come to the lake for my birthday!"

Noah started for the staircase, his stomach lurching as he realized what he'd just committed himself to. He couldn't go to Washoe Lake. He hadn't been there since he'd returned from the war. He wasn't ready. His old homestead was practically on the lake.

Noah gripped the stair rail, his knuckles turning white. Not more than a mile from Washoe rested Alice and Becky's graves.

"Coming?" Jacob shouted up the staircase. "Noah, you coming?"

Mercy walked through the hall, the basket lunch on her arm, her straw spoon bonnet dangling from her fingers by the ribbons. "Jacob," she told him patiently, knowing how excited he was, "he said he would be right down. He'll be down."

As Mercy stepped out onto the porch she heard Jacob shout up the stairs again. "We're leaving, Noah. Mama says we're leaving you if you don't hurry."

Mercy chuckled as she went down the steps. Tinny was already in the buckboard wagon, reins in hand. He'd dressed especially for the occasion in a pair of Haman's pinstriped pants that were too big for him, a shirt with the sleeves cut off, and a red handkerchief tied around his neck, and his old cowpoke boots. On his head, he'd perched his favorite hat. Tinny had retrieved the wagon just after breakfast and had been waiting out front of the hotel for close to four hours.

" 'Bout time," Tinny grumbled as Mercy loaded the basket in the back of the wagon next to the jars of sweetened lemonade. "Make me wait all day."

"I told you after noon, Pap." She pointed at the sun straight overhead. "It's just noon now."

He wrapped the reins around the brake lever and climbed over the seat to the rear. "I best let your husband drive. Young men don't take kindly to the old ones doing the driving."

"He's not my husband, Pap," she corrected, covering the basket and lemonade with a quilt to keep the sun off them. "Noah Ericson is not my husband."

"I'll just sit back here with the boy and Joe here." He indicated the empty plank seat. "That way you young folks can talk."

Mercy considered correcting him again, but decided against it. It was Jacob's birthday and she was going to enjoy herself. What harm could it do to let Tinny think she was wed to the lawman, if only for a few peaceful hours?

Jacob appeared on the front porch, pulling Noah behind him. Noah had a sour look on his face, the same sour look he'd worn at breakfast.

Mercy blamed herself for Noah's foul mood. Last night she'd dragged him into a conversation he obviously didn't want to participate in. Even though he'd admitted he was attracted to her, he turned down her blatant offer of sex without commitment. If she'd had any decency, she would have hung her head at the breakfast table, but she hadn't. She was too old for that nonsense.

Jacob leaped into the wagon bed and took his seat beside Tinny, leaving room for Joe.

Mercy touched Noah's sleeve. "You don't have to go if you don't want to," she said softly. She pulled her bonnet onto her head, fiddling with the ribbons. "You can make up something about the bank needing you. He'll understand."

He made eye contact with her for the first time since last night in the hall. "I want to go."

"You do?" She frowned. "That why you look as if you're headed for your hanging?"

His eyes visibly darkened. "Let it go, Mercy." He

grasped her waist and lifted her onto the wagon, forcing a squeak out of her.

"You needn't handle me," she admonished. "I can climb into a buckboard on my own." She took a seat on the front bench, and tossed him the reins.

In no time they were beyond the streets of Nowhere, headed north and slightly east toward Washoe Lake. The ride was pleasant, with a decent road to follow. The dry basin was rocky and dotted with clumps of silver-gray sagebrush and feathery golden desert grass. Occasionally they passed a knot of piñon or juniper trees. To the west of the lake loomed the Carson range of mountains and to the east, the Virginia range.

Mercy and Jacob talked about fun things they'd done in the past and Tinny entertained them with a tale of how he and a friend were once caught naked in the river by a band of curious Indians who stole their clothes. Mercy didn't know how much of the story was true, but it tickled Jacob.

At the lake, Mercy directed Noah to a shady spot beneath a clump of cottonwood and willow trees. Without being asked, he unloaded the picnic basket and set it on a quilt under the shade of a willow tree with branches hanging like the open arms of a grandfather's embrace. While Mercy set out the noonday meal, the men fished on the bank.

Thanks to the extra income she received from the foreman of the Patterson mine now coming in to town to eat and bathe several times a week, Mercy was able to put out a plentiful spread for the birthday meal. There was fried chicken, hardboiled eggs, cheese, apples, and big white sugar cookies she'd cut out with a preserves jar lid.

After the meal, Mercy produced two birthday presents for Jacob from a cloth bag under the wagon seat—a pair of new boots similar to Noah's and a shiny red iron train. Paddy had put the toy aside for her months ago, and she'd been paying on it, penny by penny. Mercy knew the store-bought toy was an extravagance beyond her means, but the hotel was finally producing income and she wanted Jacob to have the toy. She knew a train couldn't make up for the fact that he had no father, but she also knew what delight it would give him.

"A train! Wow. Wow." Jacob turned the palm-size engine over and over in his hand. "I can't believe you bought me a train," he marveled. "And boots, too. Thank you, Mama. Thank you."

Mercy smiled. "You're welcome, dear."

Tinny gave him a wooden whistle that hung on a leather cord. He'd carved it himself. Then, to her surprise, Noah produced a gift as well. From the toolbox beneath the front seat of the wagon, he brought out a bright new hammer. That must have been where he'd gone that morning, to get the present.

"For me?" Jacob asked, wide-eyed with surprise. "A hammer of my own?"

"A man who has fixing to do needs a hammer of his own," Noah said, handing the adult-size tool to the boy. "Happy birthday, Jake."

"Wow. Look, Mama. My own hammer. I'm sure I can work on those front steps for you now."

Mercy rose from the quilt to stretch and the willow's branches tickled her arms. It did her heart good to see Jacob so happy. "I bet you can."

With his train cars stuffed in his pocket, his whistle around his neck, and his hammer in hand, Jacob wandered off to pound rocks on the bank of the lake. Tinny lay back under the tree and drifted off to sleep, his hat over his face to block the bright sunlight.

Mercy walked down to the water's edge to wash her hands in the alkaline water. Noah followed her.

"Ridiculous gift, a hammer," he said, stuffing his hands into his pockets.

Mercy shook the water from her hands. She'd left her apron at home and didn't want to dry them on the new speckled lawn skirt she'd sewn last week. It was the first new piece of clothing she'd made for herself in years, the first time she'd had the money to buy the fabric, and the inclination to make something pretty for herself. "No, it's a wonderful present," she said sincerely. "Perfect for Jacob, and that's what a present is. Something just right for the person you give it to."

Noah stared at his boots.

Mercy sighed. She hated the discomfort between them. She wanted to go back to the way it had been before last night, before she practically threw herself at him.

"Noah, about last night—"

He shook his head. "You don't have to say anything."

"I understand if you're upset with me. I—"

"Not upset with you." His hat shaded his face, casting a shadow across it and hiding his expression.

"Then what is it?" she asked quietly. "You've barely spoken a word since last night. How could I not think it was because of me?"

"It's not."

She groaned in frustration. The best thing to do when he clamed up, she knew, was to just let him go. She should just let him go, period. Why was she pursuing a relationship she couldn't have anyway? A relationship that would mean nothing but trouble, and more heartache?

Because it was too late. Because she cared for Noah. The word *love* hovered in her head again.

"I posted a letter last week to the War Office in Washington asking for Haman to be declared dead," she said. "I don't want his pension or anything; I just want a death certificate. I want to be done with Haman Atkins and that part of my life."

Noah nodded.

"I need that finality. I need to be able to put it behind me and go on."

Noah glanced at her and then away. She could have sworn she saw moisture in the corners of his eyes. "Wish I could do the same," he said cryptically.

Before she could answer, he walked away.

Mercy spent the remainder of the afternoon with Jacob. They fished, saving several white bass and catfish to fry up for breakfast and the following night's dinner. They combed the banks looking for broken white pelican eggs and watched the cranes walk on their stilted legs. They laughed together and sang silly songs. Mercy even removed her shoes and stockings, lifted her skirts, and waded into the frigid water with her son.

Tinny joined in the fun, but Noah kept to himself, sleeping much of the afternoon away under the shade of the wagon. At least he pretended to be asleep. Mercy suspected he wasn't.

At dusk Mercy packed up the picnic basket and the foursome headed home. Within half an hour, Tinny, Jacob, and Joe, she supposed, were all asleep in the back of the wagon. Noah made no attempt to talk, so Mercy just rode in silence beside him.

Mercy knew something was still bothering Noah. All day she'd felt it. And finally she considered he might have been telling the truth. He had always talked straight with her in the past, even in admitting his attraction to her. Maybe this wasn't about her or last night.

At home Noah carried Jacob to bed, Tinny turned in, and Mercy and Noah said their good-nights at the top of the stairs. In her own room, Mercy brushed out her hair, washed, and put on a thin, clean linen nightgown. A part of her wedding trousseau, the gown was old and faded, made sheer by so many washings, but it was still pretty and she loved the way it felt against her bare skin.

She said her prayers, blew out the lamp, and got into bed, but she couldn't sleep. She couldn't stop thinking about Noah.

Sometime well after midnight, Mercy finally sat up and swung her legs over the bed. Before she realized what she was doing, she was at Noah's door. She didn't know if she sensed he needed her, or if her need for him had just become overwhelming. All she knew was that she had to see him.

Afraid to knock but afraid not to, Mercy tapped lightly on the door. "Noah?" She wondered if he could hear the tremble in her voice.

The bed squeaked immediately and she knew he hadn't been asleep, either.

He turned the knob and the door swung open. Only the moonlight coming through his window illuminated the small room.

"Mercy." His voice was a plea.

She knew she'd done the right thing in coming—wherever it might lead.

He looked like hell. His face was pale, framed by his shaggy hair. His eyes appeared red, as if he'd been crying. Mercy had never known a man who could cry.

At the same time, Noah looked magnificent to her. His chest was bare, showing the curves of his lean, muscular frame. He wore nothing but a pair of denims, slung low on his hips. A faint sprinkling of hair flecked his chest and formed a narrow line that disappeared at the waistband of his denims. The top button was unbuttoned, and for a moment she couldn't take her eyes off that button.

Mercy didn't say anything, because what was there to say? She put out her arms and closed them tightly around his neck, pressing her body against his. Her form molded perfectly to his, and for a moment he held her. Then he took her hand, drew her into his room, and closed the door behind them.

Twelve

"I'm not here for the reason you think I am," she said as he led her into his room.

To her surprise, he smiled, albeit a sad smile. "Too bad. I'm disappointed." He threaded his fingers through hers as if he had no intention of letting her go. All day he had tried to push her away, isolate himself from her feelings and his own. Now there seemed to be no fight left in him.

"I—I came because . . ." She paused. "Can you tell me what's wrong? Please? I know you say it's not me, but . . ." She gazed into his eyes. "You have to understand, my ground's mighty shaky these days. I had my head set on the idea of making this hotel profitable and making sure Jacob was healthy and happy. It was all I wanted, and suddenly you appear in my life . . ."

Without his hat brim, Noah couldn't hide the emotions that flashed across his face—fear, guilt, pain, desire, all tangled together. She wondered if his stomach was as knotted as hers.

"Tell me," she whispered. "I keep thinking there could be something good between us, and then I wonder if it's all in my imagination. Tell me why you were so upset today and then I'll go."

He led her to his bed with its crumpled blue quilt made by Mercy's own hands. He sat, pulling her down with him. The ropes of the bed frame groaned.

"And if I don't want you to go?" he asked.

His low, masculine voice hung in the air, tickling her senses. It was impossible for her to deny her desire for him, here so close, where she could smell his clean hair, feel the heat of his skin. His fingertips were slightly rough against her hands and she couldn't help wondering what they would feel like elsewhere on her body. Her breasts tingled with the thought of his touch.

Noah squeezed her hand tightly in his, focusing on their shadows on the clean-swept floor. "Lake Washoe," he said simply.

"Lake Washoe?"

"My old homestead."

She waited.

"It . . . it's near the lake." He let go of her hand and pressed both heels of his hands to his temples as if his head ached. "Their . . . their graves."

"Your family's?" She laid one hand on his tense thigh. He swallowed, nodding.

"Why didn't you say something? We could have gone to their graves together or you could have taken the wagon and gone alone. Jacob wouldn't have—"

He shook his head adamantly. "No. I didn't want to go— Haven't. Not since I went home and found the . . . the graves."

She tried to keep her voice calm as she imagined the horror he must have met arriving for his homecoming to be met by wooden crosses. "You didn't know they were dead?"

"Last . . . last letter I received, after I said I was headed home, she . . . Alice was fine." He sounded on the verge of tears. "She even said she had a surprise for me. Becky . . . Becky had cut her own hair. Cut half a pigtail off. Alice was furious." He gave a little laugh that threatened to turn into a sob. "Then they were just dead. Dead."

"Oh, Noah." Mercy slipped her arms around his shoulders and hugged him, her tears slipping down her cheeks to dampen his bare shoulder. "I'm sorry, so sorry."

He held himself stiff, lifting one hand in a helpless gesture. "It was all my fault."

Mercy lifted her head off his shoulder, perplexed. "Your fault? How? You weren't there."

He struck his fist into his palm as he choked on his words. "Should have been."

"Should have been?" Mercy couldn't fight her own practicality. It was the law she lived by, survived by. "You couldn't be in two places at once, Noah. You were fighting the war, fighting for our country, for men and women's freedom, for Nevada."

"She didn't want me to go," he said, remembering in a far-off voice. "She said she was afraid. She said she couldn't go it alone anymore. She . . . she feared the Indians. It was my fault. If I'd been there—"

Mercy folded her hands in her lap. "If you'd been there," she interrupted, "you'd most likely have been killed, too."

"Doesn't matter."

Mercy studied her hands in her lap. So this was the root of it all. This was why he spent so much of his time alone in his room, why he seemed to almost take pleasure in his own unhappiness. This was why he didn't think he deserved her. He didn't think he deserved any happiness, because his wife and child were dead. It didn't make sense to Mercy, but she understood how it could make sense to him . . . to a man.

Noah leaned over, resting both hands on his thighs. His broad shoulders trembled as he breathed deeply, attempting, no doubt, to calm himself.

Mercy ran her hand over his shoulder and kissed his bare skin where the hot desert sun had freckled it. The scent of his warm flesh was heavenly. "You didn't do anything wrong, Noah. These things just happen. It's not fair. It's not right. But that doesn't stop them from happening." She softened her voice. "You know, you're not the first person to lose a family. It happens more often then we'd like to think. That's why we have to enjoy every precious moment we have with them. With each other."

"I—I just wished I could have stayed home that last time."

"The Army gave you a choice?"

"No," he admitted. "But Alice, she wanted me to stay. She said she needed me."

"So if you'd stayed, you'd have been absent without leave and the Army would have hauled your rear back to the front lines anyway."

Mercy's thoughts strayed toward memories of Haman. He'd been absent without leave. That's how he'd wound up here in Nowhere in '64, instead of in Virginia where he was supposed to be. If he'd stayed in Virginia where the Army wanted him, maybe he'd still be alive today.

"Alice and Becky needed me and I wasn't there for them."

"All right," Mercy said, trying to think her way through this.

"All right?" he asked quizzically.

"Let's say you were partially at fault. I think not, but for the sake of argument."

He nodded.

"So how long do you pay for that mistake?"

He stared at the floor, trying to comprehend. "What?"

"How long do you pay for that mistake? You made a mistake, what—three years ago? How long do you pay for it before you're forgiven? Before you forgive yourself?"

"I don't know."

She rubbed his leg again. He sounded so lost. She wished she could help him find his way home again.

Noah slipped his arm around her waist. She could feel

his warm hand through her thin sleeping gown. She could feel each pad of each of his fingers pressing against her skin, sending little shivers through her body. A cool breeze from the window swept in, ruffling her hair. It smelled of the mountains in the distance.

"Mercy, I don't know that I deserve to be forgiven," he said slowly. "They were my responsibility."

"But you weren't there," she said firmly. "You couldn't help them, because you weren't there. You wished to God you were, but you weren't. It's time you accept that and move on."

"I never considered . . ." He halted and started again. "I . . . didn't think I wanted to move on, but now I've met you and . . ." His voice trailed off.

So she was the one who had set him thinking. It was Mercy who was making him want to live again, or at least consider it. And obviously that was generating another round of guilt.

But did this mean she had a chance? *They* had a chance? If this matter with Haman could be cleared, officially if nothing else, did that mean perhaps the two of them could—

Mercy didn't even want to think about it. She had come to accept her lot in life and be thankful for what she had: Jacob, the chance to know her father. She had never considered finding a man to love. She didn't want to consider it now. It would just make her crazy.

Mercy sat on the edge of Noah's bed in silence for a long time. He'd talked enough. She sensed that he just wanted her to be there. To be with him.

After a while he kissed her cheek. "Thank you," he whispered. "I don't know how much of what you say I believe, but thank you anyway."

Mercy turned her face to meet his gaze. "You're welcome."

He kissed her again, but this was no chaste thank-you

kiss of friendship. This was a real kiss, a kiss filled with all the passion and yearning a man and a woman could possibly feel for each other.

Mercy didn't resist. She wanted Noah's mouth on hers. She wanted to taste him, to feel his tongue on her mouth. That was why she'd come to his room, wasn't it? Or at least partially why.

Cradled in his arms, he pushed her back onto the bed, and still she didn't protest.

"Mercy, Mercy," he whispered when the kiss was spent. His warm breath in her ear made her feel warm and cold at the same time. "If you were mine," he murmured.

She wanted to say she could be his. Her mind screamed to say it, but then she remembered the pea patch. She felt no remorse for what she'd done, only remorse that things had ever reached that point of no return. Her concern was for Noah, for Jacob, for Tinny. The Atkins family wouldn't take kindly to the idea of Mercy starting a new life with a new man. They still thought Haman was coming home. It was hard to say how Jehu would react to the idea of Jacob having a new father.

Noah kissed her again, his mouth hard and hot on hers. She parted her lips to allow his tongue entrance. He cupped one of her breasts with his hand and she moaned as warm rivers of pleasure flowed from her hardening nipple through the rest of her body. Her veins pulsed with all the pent-up desires never realized, and she felt as if she were floating in his arms, in his touch.

Mercy had never imagined it could be like this with a man.

Her hands found the smooth planes of his muscular back. She boldly stroked his corded neck, his sinewed forearms. She drew an imaginary line from the nape of his neck, down the slight hollow of his spine, to the waistband of his denim pants. Shamelessly she ran her hands over his firm buttocks.

Noah kissed the pulse of her throat. "Stay with me," he whispered. "Will you stay with me, Mercy? Let me hold you?"

The moon had slid in the sky so that it now cast light across the blue quilt. When Mercy opened her eyes she could see his brown-eyed gaze fixed on hers.

Though Mercy throbbed with desire for him, she knew this wasn't the time to make love. This wasn't how she wanted to make love with him, not in these circumstances. She wanted him to come to her. She wanted him to make love to her because he wanted her, not because he missed his wife. "Just hold me?" she answered. "Nothing else."

He kissed the tip of her nose so gently that tears came to her eyes. "Nothing more, not tonight. I promise."

"I'll stay then," she whispered without hesitation. "But just till dawn."

He pushed his brown hair, clean and silky, over the crown of his head and it fell over his shoulders in a halo. "I believe I could love you, Mercy Atkins," he whispered. "Think you could wait for me? Be patient with me?"

That was all she needed to hear. For that chance, she thought she could wait until kingdom come. But Mercy was no fool. She knew nothing was easy. Nothing was simple. And promises were so hard to take back. "Let's just see how things go," she said quietly, pushing down her nightgown that had somehow bunched up to reveal her bare thighs. "If you're going to love me, I need you to love me for being me, not just for being around."

"I—"

Still cradled in his arms, gazing up at him, she pressed a finger to his lips. "Shh. Let's not talk anymore. Dawn comes early around here. I think we both could use some sleep."

He started to speak again and stopped himself. He kissed the top of her head and slid up onto his pillow, bringing her with him. They stretched out on the bed, side by side. Lying in his arms, Mercy nestled her cheek on his shoulder as he pulled the quilt over them and tucked it around her shoulders.

Mercy had never felt anything so comforting as his arm around her shoulders and her cheek against his bare skin. She and Haman had made a child, but Haman had never held her like this. He had never loved her like this, for a moment.

The tear that trickled down her cheek surprised Mercy. She had never been so happy before; this was an entirely new experience for her. Though her heart still pattered with the desire to make love with Noah, a part of her wished that she could lie in his arms, safe, for all eternity.

"What is it, Mercy?" Noah's voice came out of the darkness as he brushed her tears with his fingertips.

She shook her head, wiping at her foolish tears. She couldn't express to him what she felt in her heart. How could she express what she herself didn't understand? "Sleep," she said.

And they both slept.

"You gone deaf, Daisy?" Jezzy snapped at her daughter irritably.

The child stood on her stool at the sink and scrubbed the dried egg from the plate. The sun was just beginning to rise, so a lamp still burned in the windowsill, illuminating the child's wispy blond hair that escaped from her two spiky pigtails.

"I said, finish up quick. You think I don't have anything better to do than to clean up after men's filth?"

Jezzy preferred having a housekeeper to doing her own dishes, but since Consuela had taken off with one of the cowhands in January, Jezzy hadn't found time to hire a new one. With no housekeeper, Jezzy had decided to put the girl to work. She was young, but at three she was certainly trainable. Jezzy had done her own share of washing dirty dishes and emptying piss pots at that age. Her tyrant, widowed father had seen to that, bastard that he was.

Daisy dipped the plate into the rinse water and stretched to set it on the drainboard. The dish slipped from her petite fingers, crashed to the kitchen floor, and splintered into pieces as it hit the stone.

"Stupid little bitch." Jezzy reached out and smacked her on the back of the head. Not real hard, just hard enough to get her attention.

The little girl let out a squeak, but she knew better than to holler. She climbed off the stool and squatted to pick up the broken shards. Her blue eyes were red and her nose runny, but she didn't cry. She knew better than to cry, too.

"I'm going to get out of here before I lose my temper with you," Jezzy said, and headed for the back door. "You clean that mess up, sweep, finish the dishes, and get to the laundry. Pots already hauled the water and put it in the tub on the porch, seeing as how you're too weak-assed to lug the buckets yourself. Now, I want those clothes scrubbed good, you understand me?"

Daisy nodded, picking up shards and dropping them into her tiny apron she held open to collect the pieces.

Jezzy stepped onto the back porch. She knew she ought not to be so hard on her daughter, but what was the sense in coddling the child? No one had ever coddled Jezzy and she'd certainly made out fine. It was what had made her tough, made her a survivor and the mistress of all the land the eye could see.

Jezzy walked out to the porch rail and leaned over it. There was still a morning chill in the air. Someone was mucking out a horse stall and she could smell the sweet scent of horseshit on the air. She breathed in deeply.

Spotting one of her brothers, she called to him. "Yo, Ahab!"

He was hauling water from the yard's pump to the wash-tub on the end of the porch.

"Get a move on," she ordered. "We got more work today to do than we can get done before sunset. I want those fences repaired. I told you boys that."

Ahab moved along at his slower-than-a-tortoise pace, water sloshing down his leg. He made no attempt to glance up at her from beneath the brim of his new hat.

"Ahab," she called again, studying him carefully. "Where the hell you get that new hat?"

"Store in town," he grunted, dark hair falling over his face. He poured the water over the rail into the washtub and turned back for another.

"I know damned well you got it at the store! Jesus H. Christ! How'd you buy it? What with? Certainly not your good looks." She leaned over the rail, studying the shiny brass points of his toes. "And you got new boots, too?"

"I won the money. Poker game. Ask Pots."

"Poker, my ass. You've never won a hand in your life."

Just then, Pots came out of the outhouse. Hitching up his breeches and yanking on his belt, he headed for the barn. He was wearing new boots, a new hat, and a new pair of fancy chaps, as well.

Jezzy was immediately suspicious. She tended to keep a tight rein on her brothers' finances. It was the only way to keep them from gambling away the whole damned ranch. The three of them put together weren't smart enough to pour piss out of a boot. They certainly couldn't be trusted with money.

"You best not be lying to me, you worthless piece of owl shit," Jezzy warned Ahab with a shake of her finger. "I find you boys are up to no good again, there'll be hell to pay. I can't always be bailing your nuts out, you know."

Ahab watched the water pour from the bucket into the washtub with lazy unconcern.

Jezzy cursed under her breath and spun around. She might as well get saddled up. If she was going to get those fences repaired, she'd have to ride out with the boys and give them specific directions. It was the only way to get anything done right around here. "Jehu!" she shouted as she strode through the barnyard. "Let's get moving. You've already wasted half the day!"

Mercy woke to the feel of Noah's mouth on hers. He kissed her lips, then her cheek, then the tip of her chin. She hated to open her eyes and break the spell.

"Morning," she said sleepily, gazing up at him. He had already dressed and was sitting on the edge of the bed.

"Morning."

Mercy stretched her arms over her head. Even in the narrow bed, this was the best night's sleep she'd ever had. The golden sun was just coming up and the room was still shadowed in semidarkness. "Time to get up already?" she grumbled good-naturedly.

" 'Fraid so." He slipped one foot into his boot.

She could smell shaving soap. He'd already shaved, brushed his teeth, and combed his hair. The idea of a clean man fascinated her. Haman had never been a great one for cleanliness. Most often he had smelled of rye whiskey and sweaty armpits.

"I'm not ready to get up." Mercy tugged on the quilt and snuggled back on his pillow. "Don't you want to get back into bed with me?"

"Suit yourself. But I imagine Jacob and Tinny will be up and about soon." He winked. "You'll be caught red-handed and still in your nightie."

She sat up and pushed off the quilt. There was nothing

like cold reality to push a woman out of bed. "I don't think I'm ready for that."

He smiled. "Didn't think so."

She slid over to sit beside him. "Want me to fix you breakfast before you go?" She knew he had to make the ride to Smithtown early to make it back to the Nowhere stagecoach on time.

"Is food all you think about?" he teased.

She rubbed her hand down his forearm. This was what she had imagined married life would be. Funny that she would experience it now, with a man she wasn't married to, a man she'd never even had sex with. "It's my job."

"No thanks." He kissed her hair just above her ear, lingering as he breathed deeply. "I'll get some cold biscuits and cheese out of the pantry. I can make myself some coffee." He stood, boots now on his feet. "You go back to your room, sleep for an hour if you like."

She climbed off the bed, hating to leave the warmth and comfort of the blue quilt and his scent on his pillow, but knowing she had to. "No. I might as well get up. There's plenty needs doing."

"I wish you didn't work so hard, Mercy. Your father's right. You never have any time for fun." He walked to the washstand and retrieved his gunbelt.

She watched him strap it on, wishing she could be that gunbelt and ride along on his hip today. She laughed aloud at her own silly thoughts.

He smiled. "What's so funny. Me?"

"No." She padded barefoot across the room and wrapped her arms around his shoulders. "Me." She lifted up on her tiptoes and kissed him. "Have a good day. Watch yourself. I don't want you doing anything foolish like getting yourself killed over a bank's strongbox." She went to the door and rested her hand on the white glass doorknob. "Not when I haven't gotten you naked under my sheets yet."

"Just give me a chance, sweetheart," he said as she left. "You won't be able to drive me out of your bed."

Mercy was still smiling as she reached her room, her cheeks warm with the thought of his promise.

Thirteen

Mercy whistled to herself as she rolled out more slick dumplings to add to the waiting pot of boiling broth. Behind her, in the dining room, she heard the hum of men's voices and the clink of silverware as they helped themselves to seconds of her stewed chicken and dumplings.

This afternoon the young man from the Patterson Mine, Todd Dickerson, had returned again for a bath and a meal, and to Mercy's delight, he'd brought three other men from the company with him. While the men had taken turns bathing in the tub in the shed-turned-bathhouse, Tinny had killed two hens, and Mercy had popped them in a pot to boil. The four men had already eaten most of the chicken and all the dumplings and Mercy was making more. There wasn't time to cook another chicken, but the boiling broth was thick and flavorful and the dumplings would take only a few minutes to cook.

She dropped another strip of dough into the pot, tapping her foot to the tune of a jig she heard in her head. She was tickled to have business for the hotel, but the real source of her pleasure was Noah. She'd been humming, whistling, singing all day, even tapping her feet as she worked, thinking of their time together last night. She'd thought about how wonderful it had felt to lie in his arms. She thought of his lips on hers, his hand on the curve of her breast.

Mercy knew it was dangerous, but she'd made up her mind she was going to make love with him. She couldn't think about the future right now, or its possibilities, or all the ways her life could turn sour again. It was too scary. But she'd spent a lifetime doing for others and, for once, she was going to do something for herself. All she could think of was, what if no man ever came along whom she'd care for as much as she cared for Noah? What if he was her soul mate? She couldn't let him get away, not without loving him, allowing him to love her in that physical way just once.

The smell of browning biscuits wafted through the warm air of the kitchen.

"Oh, no!" Mercy grabbed a clean rag and jerked open the oven. To her relief, the biscuits had not yet burned on the bottom. She set the tray on the top of the stove, stirred her bubbling dumplings, and retrieved the bread-basket.

For the next half hour Mercy ran and fetched, poured lemonade for the men, and cleared dishes. She had just served huge slices of canned peach pie when she heard the front door open.

It had to be Noah because she could hear Tinny and Jacob on the back porch talking to each other as they finished their own pie.

Mercy barely had time to push back loose strands of hair before Noah appeared in the doorway. He cocked his head toward the sounds in the dining room. "Awful calm for the Atkins boys."

She chuckled. "Because they're not. 'Customers,' " she mouthed. She held up four fingers.

He nodded, obviously happy for her. Proud.

He walked up to her and kissed her on the lips, as if

he came home every night and kissed her. "Something I can do?"

"Would you?" she asked with relief. She'd done nothing but race about all day and suddenly she was bone-tired. And there were still dishes to clear, beds to be made, and the table to reset for breakfast in the morning. Two of the men had requested beds for the night. They'd be sharing a room next to Noah's. "Would you run and check the clothes on the line? They brought dirty shirts. A breeze kicked up before sunset. I'm praying they're dry by now."

He saluted her. "Yes, Captain."

"And will you tell Jacob to make sure the chickens have water, once he's done with his pie?"

"I'll do better than that, I'll help water the chickens. Anything else?"

She smiled, empty frying pan in her hand. "Are you for real, Noah Ericson? Are you real, or have I dreamed so long of a man like you that you've popped up, right out of my imagination?"

He caught one of the wisps of hair she'd tucked behind her ear and pulled it forward so that it curled at her jawline. "Don't build me up in your mind to be something I'm not. I wouldn't want to disappoint you."

She understood his fear because it was her own fear. Maybe she wasn't good enough for him. "Noah, you're honest, and you're clean. What else could a woman ask for?"

She listened to him chuckle as he went out the door and decided that she liked the sound of his voice in her kitchen.

Later, when the dishes were done, the tables set, Tinny and Jacob were asleep, and the men settled in their beds for the night, Mercy and Noah went out on the front porch to get some air.

Mercy sat on the top step and Noah sat behind her, casually draping one hand over her shoulder.

"You know," he said after a few minutes of comfortable silence, "I think I could get used to this." He rubbed her shoulder.

Mercy closed her eyes. She was tired from the hard work of the day and thankful tomorrow was Sunday. She would have to make a big breakfast for the men staying over, but for the most part it would be a day of rest. After church she thought she might visit Annie, who was plagued with morning sickness with her third child.

"You could get used to this?" Mercy asked, practically moaning with pleasure as he continued to massage her shoulder. "Used to what? Rubbing my back? Because I sure could."

A wagon rolled by on the street and someone Mercy didn't know tipped his hat, friendly-like. Suddenly there were a lot of people in town Mercy didn't know. With the success of the Patterson mine, not only had workers come to dig there, but more men passed through each day, in search of their own claims to stake, their own silver to strike.

"Yeah," he said. "I could get used to rubbing your back. I could also get used to helping you in the kitchen, tending chickens, fixing broken pumps. I hadn't realized how much I missed that kind of thing."

"What, and give up your exciting job as a hired gunman?" she scoffed jokingly.

He brought his nose close to her, gazing deeply into her eyes. Though the sun had already set, she could still see the sparkle in their depths and she was in awe that she could be the source of that sparkle.

"I took my first job guarding a train because it took me far from my old homestead, took me far from the life I'd led. I thought I'd changed. I thought I could be a rover. Now I think maybe not." He brushed his lips against hers. "Can I come to your room tonight, Mercy?"

His voice, the touch of his hand on her bare arm, exposed by her rolled-up sleeve, made her feel as if her entire body was pure liquid, all silky and smooth.

"I don't know," she whispered, kissing him back, taking her time to let her mouth linger over his. "I've got guests upstairs. I don't want them to think all the boarders are welcome to that privilege."

He chuckled. "Be honest with me here, Mercy darlin'. You moved Jacob downstairs today to sleep in the room beside Tinny's. Did you do that for the reason I think you did, or am I greatly mistaken and making a fool of myself?"

"I told you," she evaded him.

He traced the line of her jaw with his finger, making it hard for her to think. "You told me . . ."

"I told you, I thought I should free up the room upstairs. In case I need more room. I probably ought to move myself down into Jacob's room."

He nibbled on her earlobe. "Don't you dare."

Again she gazed into the depths of his brown eyes. He wanted her; he needed her. She wasn't certain he loved her yet, but she wasn't certain she wanted that right now. Just to have someone who respected her and wanted to hold her in his arms sounded good to her. Her own husband had never respected her; he'd never held her in his arms, either.

She whispered in his ear, nestling in the crook of his arm. "I might be persuaded to—"

"What the hell's this?"

Startled, Mercy looked up. At first glance she thought she was seeing a ghost. Haman come back from the grave? Then she realized it wasn't Haman, of course. It was Jehu. Mercy didn't know where he'd come from, how'd he'd sneaked up on them like this. This was exactly the kind of thing she had hoped to avoid.

"Jehu." She rose off the step, her bare toes curling around the plank riser.

Noah rose at the same time.

"Tell me this ain't what I think it is," Jehu said roughly. "Tell me you ain't cheatin' on my brother, woman."

"Jehu—"

"Just one minute," Noah interrupted. "There's no need to—"

"Noah." Mercy turned to face him. "Can you leave me with Jehu to speak privately?" She looked him straight in the eye, silently pleading with him to let her do this on her own terms.

Noah grabbed his hat from the porch rail and crammed it on his head. "I'll be inside if you need me."

"Thank you," she murmured. She wanted to reach out and squeeze his hand, but she didn't. She didn't want to aggravate an already volatile situation.

He crossed the porch.

"Coward," Mercy heard Jehu say under his breath as Noah walked through the door.

If Noah heard him, which he must have, he gave no indication.

Mercy turned back to Jehu. She didn't even invite him up on the porch. "What are you doing here, spying on me after dark? You taken to peeking in windows, too, Jehu?"

He thrust one boot on the lower step. The boot was new and constructed of shiny snakeskin. It looked too expensive, too refined for Jehu's tastes.

"I wasn't sneakin' up on no one. I was riding by mindin' my own business, and I see you on your porch with a man, a man with his hands all over you."

"His hands weren't all over me. But it's none of your damned business anyway."

"The hell it's not." He pointed his crooked finger at her. "You're married to my brother."

"No, I'm not, Jehu." She rested her hands on her hips. "I'm not married to him because he's dead. He's dead, been dead for years."

Jehu's eyes narrowed. He hadn't been drinking yet, she could tell by the whites of his eyes. In the faded light, he appeared dangerous. "You'd best not be speakin' such slander against my brother."

"Slander?" She laughed, but she was unamused. "That's no slander. Slander is something bad that's not true. Jehu, did you make it all the way through the second grade or did you drop out at Christmas?" Mercy knew it was a mean thing to say, but she couldn't help herself.

"He's not dead," Jehu said, huffing under his breath. "But if he was, you'd not be free for such nonsense as that."

She straightened up to her full height of five foot eight inches, towering over him where she stood three steps above him. "If I'm a widowed woman, I'm legally free to seek another man's affection."

"If you're a widow, you're an Atkins widow and our rules is different than most."

She frowned. She knew she should just turn and walk away. She didn't need to have this conversation with Jehu. It would just get her into trouble. But he made her so damned angry that she wasn't about to back down now. "Well, goodness me. I don't recall hearing that in my wedding vows. Jostle my memory, Jehu. How are the rules different with you Atkins boys?"

He came up the steps, the first, then the second. He threw back his thick shoulders, obviously trying to intimidate her. It had been Haman's way, too.

But Mercy had been pushed back enough times by men. She'd been young and naive when she'd come to

Haman in marriage, but she wasn't young or naive any longer.

She didn't move an inch.

"This place is my brother's." He was eye to eye with her now. His breath stank of rotting teeth. "If he is dead, this place is my responsibility." Jehu pointed that damned finger of his at her again. "That makes you my responsibility, too, and no woman that's mine is gonna be carryin' on the way I just saw you carryin' on with that lawman."

She pushed away his hand. "If Haman's dead, which you and I both know he is, the law says the hotel is mine. I'm a free woman—free to do as I well please. I can do what I want on my premises. Hell, I could sit on this porch and paw on every man I've got boarding with me tonight! Hell, I could bring a few in for pawing if I like, Jehu!"

He worked his jaw up and down in fury. "You keep that mouth up and I'll fix you. I'll fix you good. The law might say you got a right to this run-down place, but what about that boy?"

Mercy stiffened at his mention of Jacob. All her mothering instincts kicked in at once. Above all, her purpose on this earth was to protect that one child, that one cub.

He pointed up the stairs. "How kindly do you think the law would take to a widow woman livin' alone with all these men?"

She bristled. She couldn't have Jehu passing it around town that she was a loose woman. Where was her head when she'd been sitting here with Noah? What had made her think someone wouldn't see them so cozy? Her reputation was too important; her business was to run a decent boardinghouse.

"They're boarders, and you well know it," she snapped. "I've done nothing wrong. Nothing to be ashamed of."

He gave a low whistle, shaking his head. "I can hear

the judge now. A young widow woman, lettin' her son see strangers fondlin' her right on her front porch." Pleased with himself, he hooked both his thumbs in his front belt loops. "What do you think, Mercy? Me, I'm thinkin' the judge would send that boy to live with his uncles and his aunt where he'd be raised decent like."

Mercy's blood turned cold. Never in her wildest dreams had she imagined Jehu would use Jacob against her. She hadn't thought he was that clever. Apparently she'd been wrong.

Jehu must have realized he scared her because he smirked. "See I what I mean? A woman like you's got to be careful. Got to protect her reputation." He reached out and ran his hand along her bare arm.

She jerked her arm away from his hand with a shudder. He made her skin crawl. "I've got work to do." She turned on the steps and went up them, crossing the porch.

"What?" he cajoled. "You not even going to invite me in to visit with my nephew?"

"Jehu, it's after nine. Little boys are in bed this time of night." She stepped inside the house and slammed the door behind her.

In the kitchen, Mercy finished putting away the dry dishes. Noah came in just as she was returning plates to the pantry shelves. Suddenly her nerves were on edge.

He walked up behind her and slipped his hands around her waist. "He gone?" He nuzzled her neck.

All day Mercy had thought of nothing but Noah. All day she had longed for his gentle voice, his soft touch, his kisses. Now she just wanted to crawl into her bed and hide.

"Noah." She squeezed her eyes shut, not wanting to cry. "I'm tired," she said softly. "I think I'm just going to go to bed."

He loosened his grip on her. "Alone, you mean?" He sounded disappointed. Maybe hurt.

Mercy just couldn't deal with all this. Not tonight. She was confused. Afraid. She didn't know what to do. "Yes. All right?" She turned in his arms to face him. This was the path she thought she wanted, but she had to be certain. She had to be willing to fight for it. "All right, Noah?" she repeated.

"Something I said? Did?"

She sighed. His arms felt so good around her. So comforting. She felt safe here in the pantry with Noah, surrounded by the smells of home. He made her feel connected to something, to someone. "Jehu," she said, trying to explain but not knowing how much she wanted to tell. "He . . ."

"Put you out of the mood?" Noah's voice was light, a little teasing.

She laughed. "Thank you for understanding."

He kissed her mouth. "I want this to be right, Mercy." He ran his fingers through her hair. "Go on to bed. I'll finish here."

A short time later, Mercy climbed into bed alone, into the same bed in which she had thought she would have a companion tonight.

Fourteen

Noah rode behind and to the left of the black-and-gold Concord stagecoach, feeling every miserable bump and dimple on the rutted road to Carson City.

The air was still cool so early in the morning; rain fell, wetting his face despite the tilt of the downward brim of his leather hat. A wind that whistled west out of the mountains tore at his canvas duster, making an irritating flapping sound. No matter how he tucked the long, black coat around him, he couldn't keep it still. Mud spattered his legs and chilled him.

Noah felt as dreary as the day. He wished he hadn't had to rise so early, make the trip to Smithtown, and back to Nowhere to meet the stagecoach. He wished he didn't have to escort it all the way to Carson City in the rain. He wanted to stay at the hotel, to be near Mercy. He wanted so desperately to make love to her that he ached, an ache that seemed greater, at this moment, than the one he felt for his lost wife and child.

But Noah couldn't stay at the Tin Roof because he had a duty to his employers. He had agreed to the job, and deposited his pay in the bank. He was en route to Carson City with the two banks' deposits in his care.

Just his luck that the weather would be poor. With the rain falling as it was, the road was already flooding in places. In these parts, it didn't take much rain to turn the roads to rivers, not with the sun-baked soil as hard as mortar. The falling rain was already slowing the coach to a crawl at times. Noah doubted he'd be able to make it to Carson City and back to Nowhere tonight. He'd have to remain in the city and return to the Tin Roof in the morning.

A man alone traveling in the rain in deserted areas was just asking for trouble. A few months ago, Noah wouldn't have thought twice about making the trip, because he hadn't cared what happened to him. Looking back, he realized now that, more than once, he had put his life in jeopardy. That was what had made him such an excellent hired gun. He protected other people's money as if it were more meaningful than his own life; and at the time it was.

Now Noah felt a responsibility, to Mercy, to Jacob, even to crazy old Tinny. That feeling scared him. He didn't know if he was ready for that kind of obligation. He didn't know if he could be trusted, if he deserved to be trusted. But at the same time, it felt good. It felt right.

As the stagecoach approached a copse of cottonwoods and sagebrush, Noah caught movement out of the corner of his eye. He knocked the brim of his hat up with the back of a gloved hand to get a better look. He could have sworn he had seen a flash of movement uncharacteristic in a thicket of trees. A black-tailed jackrabbit hopped from the refuge of the low ground cover, and Noah intuitively lowered his hand to the Smith & Wesson rifle he carried in a holster strapped to his saddle. Something had startled the rabbit; why else would it leave the protection of the trees for the rain and mud?

"Clarence!" Noah called to the driver. He had intended to warn him to keep an eye out for anyone approaching from ahead. On an overcast day, it would be easy to miss a warning sign the driver might catch otherwise.

The words were no sooner out of Noah's mouth than

two men on horseback charged toward the stagecoach, long rifles cradled in their arms. A dirty bandanna masked each man so that Noah could see nothing of their faces but their eyes. One was a large man with dark hair, the other tall and thin.

Noah swore beneath his breath as he reined Sam around to the rear of the stagecoach, simultaneously sliding his rifle out of the holster. He wasn't a coward, but this was not where he wanted to be right now. Was his life really worth that money in the strongbox beneath the driver's seat? Didn't matter. He'd agreed to the job.

"Pull up, driver, or I shoot you off your roost!" one of the men hollered from beneath his bandanna.

With his face covered, Noah couldn't get a good look at the bandit, but he was a big man, heavy, with showy boots.

Clarence pulled hard on his horse's reins and the stagecoach slid sideways before coming to a halt in the muddy road.

Noah put himself between the vehicle and the two riders. The single passenger, a schoolteacher headed for San Francisco, opened the leather flap window. The moment he saw the guns drawn, he let it fall with a squeak. Noah didn't have to waste precious time telling him to stay put and out of sight.

Noah's horse danced back and forth in nervous excitement, and Noah had to squeeze his legs tightly to remain mounted. "Ride off," Noah warned. "I don't wear a badge. Ride now, and you can take your hides home with you."

The would-be robbers pulled up their mounts to face Noah. If it became a standoff, Noah figured they had equal chances. He knew Clarence had a sawed-off shotgun at his feet. If the middle-aged man could get to it, he might be able to take out one of the thieves. That would leave only one for Noah to deal with. But right this minute, Noah was looking down not one barrel, but two.

"Hand over the cash and whatever you got on you," the larger of the men said. "No one gets hurt that way."

Noah snapped his head. "Can't do that. Not mine."

The thief gave a snort. "I ain't playin' with you. Hand over the strongbox and whatever cash and such yer passengers got, and we'll just move on."

Behind him, Noah heard the leather window flap flip open. A man's change purse flew out of the window and landed in the mud. A pocket watch followed.

"Now that's more like it," the thief said. He turned his head to address his partner, the taller, thinner man. "Climb down and fetch the fob and purse."

As the second thief dismounted, the other spoke again, addressing Noah. "I'm afraid ye're gonna have to climb on down from there." He glanced up at Clarence. "You, too, old man."

Noah wasn't certain what happened next. He didn't know if Clarence tried to grab his gun and spooked the robbers, or what. The thief on the ground swung his rifle around and fired at the stagecoach driver. Clarence's gun exploded with sound and lead shot pellets. The gunshots startled the coach horses and the coach leaped forward, despite the brake that had been set.

Noah heard Clarence cry out, in pain or fear, and heard him fall over the side of the coach. The thief on foot lifted his rifle again, firing first at the empty seat of the rolling coach, then at Noah. Noah's horse shied and Noah lost his balance. He whipped his rifle around and squeezed the trigger as he tumbled from his saddle.

Noah hit the ground hard. Pain shot from his ankle, up his knee. He forced weight on the foot, ignoring the streaks of red-hot pain and cocked his weapon again.

There was no need. The thief on foot lay back in the mud, his rifle out of reach. The other thief had turned on his mount and was riding off into the rain, already nearly out of his sight, headed north.

Noah wondered for a moment if he needed to remount and follow the thief, but his first duty was to the coach driver, the passenger, and the banks' money. Limping, he grabbed the fallen thief's rifle from the mud.

The robber lay on his back, his eyes closed. His chest still rose and fell, but the dirty blue shirt he wore beneath his coat was wet with crimson blood.

Noah turned away, the bile rising in his throat. For a moment he thought he might be ill. He had learned in the war how to shoot a man, how to kill with just one shot. He had apparently learned well, because this man wouldn't live until nightfall.

"Clarence? Mr. Abbot?" Noah limped toward the stage-coach that had rolled to a halt fifty feet up the road. He saw no sign of the driver or the passenger.

"Clarence? You all right?"

The driver appeared from around the front of the stagecoach. His hat was gone, his gun gone, his lower lip bloody, but he appeared fine. "Right here!" the man shouted, waving. "No hole in me that I can see." He slapped his chest, inspecting his muddy clothes for bullet holes.

"What about Mr. Abbot?"

Clarence gave a wave of his hand. "Shot didn't hit the coach. Think it took my hat, though." He pulled open the coach door and stuck his head inside. "Mr. Abbot? You all right?"

Noah heard the man make some frightened affirmative remark.

"He's all right. No worse for the wear." Clarence closed the door again. "How's he? You shoot him or me?"

Noah hobbled back toward the dying man. He hoped he hadn't broken his ankle in his fall. Wouldn't that be a hell of a thing to tell his employer? *Yes, sir, I saved the cash, took out one bandit, and broke my ankle falling from my faithful steed.* What kind of hired gunman fell off his horse?

Noah knelt in the mud and felt for a pulse in the thief's neck. It was there, but faint. He pulled down the red bandanna, now spattered with mud. He didn't recognize the face. The thief was relatively young, in his early twenties. He had a beard-stubbled chin and a scar on his cheek that appeared to have come from a knife wound. It was Noah's guess that this wasn't the first time the young man had been in trouble. Too bad it would be his last.

Noah rose and squinted in the rain that had become a fine mist, settling over them in an eerie cloud. "Clarence, bring the coach around. We have to get this man back to Nowhere."

"Got no doctor there." The older man picked up Mr. Abbot's wallet and watch from the ground and wiped them off on his coat.

"It's the closest town. He'll never make it to Carson City. Besides, it's not advisable we go on. Could be more of them lying in wait."

Noah waited for Clarence to bring the stagecoach back. Together they loaded the dying man inside, much to the schoolteacher's dismay. Noah assured Mr. Abbot that the man was no longer a threat to anyone and that chances were he wouldn't live to reach Nowhere. Next, he tied the thief's dapple horse to the back of the vehicle.

With great effort, and pain shooting up his leg, Noah remounted Sam and they headed east in the direction they'd come.

It was a long, miserable ride back and well past noon by the time they arrived in Nowhere. They went straight to the jailhouse where Sheriff Dawson met them on the front porch. They hauled the dying man and the strong-boxes into the jailhouse. The boxes went into a cell and then the iron-bar door was locked. They laid the thief out on a cot in the only other cell.

Noah felt sick to his stomach as he sat on a stool beside the man and wiped away the blood that bubbled from his mouth with a clean, cool rag.

"Nothing can be done for him," the sheriff said, standing over them. "No need to call for a doc. It would be hours before one could get here anyway." Dawson put his hand on Noah's shoulder. "You did a good job today, Son."

"I killed a man," Noah responded without emotion.

"Nope. Saved at least two, maybe three if you count yourself. Not to mention the bank's money." He chuckled dryly. "My guess is, you'll be getting a raise in your weekly pay."

Noah scowled and dipped the rag in the cold water again. The tiny cell smelled of clean straw stuffed in the mattress tick, rain-soaked clothing, and of warm, wet blood and imminent death.

Noah dabbed the thief's face again. One minute the young man was breathing. The next he wasn't.

Dawson gave a sigh. "Shame, isn't it?"

"Damned waste of life," Noah muttered, rising. He rubbed the back of his neck and hobbled out into the front office where the sheriff did his paperwork and played poker to while away the hours.

"Don't guess you know him?" Noah asked.

"Nope. And no identification." The sheriff sat on the edge of his desk and sipped coffee from a tin cup. "But I'll ask around. He's dressed like a hired hand. That scar ought to help us track down who he was."

Noah nodded. "I'm guessing he knew the coach was carrying the strongboxes."

"That right?" Dawson scratched his chin. "Interesting."

The door opened and both men turned.

Mercy stepped in, a crocheted shawl thrown over her shoulders. "Noah? Are you all right?" She rushed in, petticoat rustling, breathing hard. "I just heard. Pap says you were shot." She clasped his arm.

Noah thought he'd never seen anyone so beautiful as this woman, with her hair that never stayed up neat, in her skirt that was a little short, and her shawl that had seen better days. She was like a breath of sunshine on a dreary day.

"I'm all right," Noah said. "I wasn't shot."

"Mr. Ericson here saved the driver, the passenger, and the money." Jack Dawson seemed as proud of Noah as if he had been one of his own deputies.

She didn't release his arm. "You're sure you're not hurt?" She gazed up at him, her forehead creased with concern. "You're sure?" she repeated.

Noah forced a smile. Surprisingly, it felt good to have someone worry over him. "Mercy, I'm all right."

She pressed her hand to her left breast. "Thank God." She clasped her hands in prayer and squeezed her eyes shut. "Thank you, thank you, God." Her eyes flew open again. "What happened? Pap said someone was dead."

"Someone is now." Noah glanced toward the cell where the thief lay. "I'll tell you later. I've business here with the sheriff, and then—"

"No, you go on," Dawson interrupted. "I've got your story. Not much to tell, is there? I can get what I need tomorrow."

Noah rubbed his temples. His ankle was swelling in his boot; he could feel the pressure, and his head was pounding. "I need to talk to Mr. Cook as soon as he gets back in town."

Dawson nodded. "The missus said he'd be back by nightfall, but it can wait till morning. I'll fill him in about what happened. He went out to the Patterson mine to work something out with Mr. Patterson. They're working

on bringing an assayer into town." He waved Noah away.
"Now, go on to your room. Let Mrs. Atkins take a look
at that ankle. I already sent your mount to the stables.
Thief's, too. Far as I see it, the horse is yours, long as he
don't turn up stolen."

Noah thought to say he didn't want the horse, but he
stopped himself. He didn't want it, but maybe Mercy
would. She'd been saying it would be nice to have a horse
and wagon of her own so that she didn't have to borrow
the storekeeper's. Jacob was getting to an age where he
ought to be riding anyway.

Noah started for the door, trying not to limp. "Be back
in the morning." He glanced over his shoulder. "Want
me to stop by the undertaker's?"

"Nah. I'll take care of it."

Mercy looped her arm through Noah's as they went
out the door. "You're hurt," she said. "Hell's bells, Noah.
Were you shot or not? Don't tell me you're being brave
while blood runs down your leg and gangrene sets in."

He winced as he came down the two steps onto the
wooden plank sidewalk that ran the length of Nowhere's
main street. They turned toward home. "I wasn't shot.
Just twisted my ankle."

"How?" She looped her arm around his waist. "Here,
lean against me."

Noah didn't like the idea of using a woman as a crutch,
but with every step, the sharp pains in his ankle grew
stronger and his balance shakier. Reluctantly, he slipped
his arm around her shoulders and shifted some of his
weight against her.

"I said, how'd you hurt your ankle?"

"Fell off my horse," he mumbled.

"What?" She frowned, her brow creasing in a most tan-
talizing way again.

God, if he didn't get her into bed . . .

"I fell off my horse," he repeated more clearly.

She snickered.

"It's not funny."

"I know." She snickered again. "It's not. I just—" She started to laugh and had to cover her mouth with her hand. "It's not funny, I'm just so glad it wasn't worse."

"Been a hell of a day, Mercy. I get shot at, I have to kill a man, I fall and damned near break my ankle, and then the woman I love laughs at me."

Her laughter stopped short.

Noah didn't know why he said it that way. It was a hell of a way to claim his love for her. Not terribly romantic and he knew women liked romance. But hell, he hadn't even realized he loved her. Not until this moment. But when the words came out of his mouth, when she looked at him with those bright blue eyes of hers, he knew it was true.

Maybe it was his brush with death today, he didn't know, but something had clicked inside him. Something made him realize that he loved her and that he wanted to fight for her, for himself, for them. Staring down a gun barrel did strange things to a man, made him realize what was important, what was worth living for. Mercy didn't say anything, maybe because nothing else needed to be said. Not right now. But in that moment, as he held her with his gaze, Noah knew they were making some kind of silent agreement. Standing in the rain, his ankle throbbing, his head pounding, he had made a commitment to this woman. Hesitantly, she seemed to accept his commitment.

Jacob and Tinny met them on the front porch of the hotel.

"How many bandits you kill?" Jacob hopped excitedly on one foot and then the other.

"Jacob, I told you. It's a terrible thing to have to kill a man," Mercy gently chastised her son. "You hush your mouth."

Tinny opened the door for them. "If I'd been with you, Noah, me and Joe would have backed you up." He gestured grandly with one spindly arm. "We could have taken them all."

"Pap, will you go into the pantry and get my white tin washpan and some clean rags from under the sink?" She reached up and brushed Noah's hair from his eyes. "You just want to go up to bed?"

It was midafternoon; no reason for a healthy man to be in bed, but the thought was too tempting. Noah was exhausted, mentally and physically. "I think so."

They started up the stairs side by side. "We'll get you off this ankle and I'll take a look at it. Think it's broken?"

She was so calm, so efficient; taking charge came so easily to her. And she was so unlike Alice. Alice had always depended on him for everything. She hadn't even been able to remove a splinter from Becky's finger; he'd had to do it.

"No." He winced as he climbed the steps. "Don't think so."

"We'll see."

In his room she helped him sit down. She took his gun holster from him, his hat, his coat, and his wet, dirty shirt. Next she squatted on the floor and pulled off his boots, first from the good foot, then the bad.

Against his will, Noah groaned in pain as she tugged off the second boot. He pressed his hands into the soft bed tick and closed his eyes. Dark shapes swirled beneath his eyelids.

"That's pretty ugly," Mercy remarked, peeling off his wool sock.

Noah opened his eyes. His ankle was bruised and swollen.

"Can you move it?" She gave him directions and came to the conclusion that he *was* still able to move it, although it was painful to do so. "I think you're right," she said, rising. "Muscles or tendons might be torn, but the bone's not broken. I'll wrap it and ice it to keep down the swelling. After that, the best thing for you is rest."

He pulled himself back on the bed and let his head fall on the pillow. "Cook may want the strongbox taken to Carson City tomorrow." He closed his eyes, lowering one forearm across his forehead.

"Good," she commented matter-of-factly. "Maybe a trip tomorrow will give you another chance to get shot. Let them finish you off."

He smiled. "No Mercy," he complained. "You never show me any mercy."

"Nope." She leaned over him and kissed him. "Hungry?"

He shook his head, so tired he was drifting off already. "No. Just tired."

"All right. Let me see what's keeping Pap with the bandages. I'll wash and wrap your foot and we'll see how it looks tomorrow."

"I can wash my own feet, Mercy," he said sleepily.

"I know you can." Her tone was sweet, gentle. She left the room and returned a few minutes later. She washed both of his feet and he let her. Then she wrapped the bad ankle with long strips of bleached cotton and tied an ice pack onto it.

Noah felt her lips on his, but he was too tired to open his eyes.

"Sleep tight," she whispered. "I'll check on you later."

Noah drifted off to sleep with thoughts of her kiss. Thoughts of his mouth on her mouth . . . and other sweet places.

Noah woke sometime in the middle of the night. His body stiff from the fall, he rose slowly and sat on the edge of the bed. Gingerly, he turned his swollen ankle

one way and then the other. Mercy must have come in
while he was asleep and removed the ice pack.

His ankle felt tight and moving it was painful but not
unbearable. As he flexed it, he closed his eyes and
breathed deeply. Mercy had left his window open a crack
so that he could smell the cool mountain breeze and feel
its chill, refreshing on his face.

Mercy . . . He had dreamed of her. He had imagined
she was here in the room, in his bed, asleep in his arms.
He glanced out the window. With no moon tonight, he
was unsure of what time it was. But it had to be late, after
midnight, he guessed. Outside it was very dark and the
house was still.

Noah's gaze drifted to the door. He wanted to see her.
To be with her. He wanted to climb into her warm bed,
wrap her in his arms, and make love to her.

He wondered what her reaction would be if he appeared in her room. Would she lift her quilt or order
him out? He wasn't certain he was up for rejection tonight. Killing that young man bothered him more than
he cared to admit. Even if the man with the scar was a
thief, he was still a human being. The war had made
Noah realize how precious life was; his family's death had
taught how precarious it was.

Noah glanced at the door again. It was only a short
walk down the hall to her bedroom. No one would see
him. He would just sneak down and listen at the door.
Maybe she was awake, too. His decision made, he rose
slowly. The first pressure on his ankle shot pains up his
calf, but by the time he reached the door it had eased
to a stiff ache.

Before he knew it, he was at Mercy's door. The entire
house was quiet, save for the occasional creak of wood
and the rhythmic snoring of one of Mercy's new boarders.

Noah listened closely, hoping to hear her. Maybe she
was awake, unable to stop thinking about him either.

Noah knew it was a foolish notion, but a man had dreams like anyone else.

After more than a minute he was forced to come to the conclusion that she was asleep.

Noah knew he should turn around and go back to his own bed. Telling Mercy he loved her put him on shaky ground. He knew he needed to reconcile his feelings for Alice and Becky; it was only fair to Mercy. But damn it, he needed her. He sensed she needed him. He almost made up his mind to go back, then turned her bedroom doorknob.

In the darkness, Noah could barely make out her form in the four-poster bed in the center of the room. He could hear her gentle breathing. He could smell the fresh, clean scent of her hair and her skin.

Noah closed the door behind him.

She slept on.

He limped to her bedside and eased down onto the tick. This close, he could see her better. There seemed to be a faint smile on her face as she slept on her back, her cheek on the pillow, her arms over her head. Her honey-blond hair fanned out on the pillowcase and he couldn't resist leaning over and breathing deeply, taking in its scent. He moved his mouth from her hair to her temple and he kissed her lightly.

She made a sound, soft, almost mewing. A sound of pleasure. He kissed her again. This time he slid one hand over her belly. It was flat beneath his hand and her thin sleeping gown. He slid his hand upward to her breast, kissing her ear.

She made the noise again, only this time it was closer to a moan.

Fifteen

Mercy sighed as the feel of his lips on her earlobe sent tiny tremors of excitement through her body. His hand, a warm, firm presence on her breast, made her shift toward him, closer, yearning for a more intimate touch.

He kissed her throat and the arc of skin above the lace edging of her nightgown. Mercy slid her hand over his, encouraging his caress. Her nipples hardened and brushed against the abrasive fabric of her wispy-thin nightgown that had been soft only a moment ago.

She felt his mouth against hers as he cupped her breast and his thumb rubbed her budding nipple. She parted her lips, slowly awakening, not wanting to. She didn't want the delicious dream to end, not yet. She didn't want to let Noah slip away again in the darkness of the lonely night.

She whispered his name.

His tongue slipped between her lips and she tasted him.

She marveled at how vivid her dreams were becoming. She was nearly awake, and yet she could still feel his touch. She could still smell his skin and the lingering scent of shaving soap that mingled with the scents of saddle leather and manliness exclusive to him. She could even taste his mouth on hers.

His kiss deepened and she wrapped her arms around him, bringing him closer. She felt the edge of the quilt lift, the sting of cool air as he slipped beneath the blanket. As he moved in beside her the seamed fabric of his denim Levi's rubbed against her exposed legs.

"Noah," she whispered again, as if beckoning him could keep him with her longer. "Noah."

"Mercy," he answered. "My sweet Mercy, my angel. Sweet Mercy mine."

She was getting good at creating these dreams. It was the first time she had heard him speak in her sleep.

She felt the mattress shift as he turned to face her. She rolled toward him, eyes still closed. It was awfully realistic . . .

Too realistic.

Mercy opened her eyes. "Oh," she whispered. She found herself nose to nose with Noah. It wasn't a dream. He was here, in her bed, under her quilt, his hand on her breast. *"Noah?"*

He pushed up on one elbow. Even in the darkness, she could see the hesitant smile on his face. "Expecting someone else?"

She blinked. "No, I just . . ." She felt silly. Shaky. "I thought . . ." She lifted her hand from his bare shoulder and brushed back her hair. She couldn't think. She couldn't talk sensibly. He entire body was awake now, pulsing. She wanted him. There was no mistaking her desire for him, not with the shameless aching heat between her thighs.

"I thought I was dreaming," she confessed softly, still surprised he was actually there.

He kissed the backs of her hands, still crossed over her chest. As she moved them, he kissed the swell of her breast. Even through the fabric of her gown, she could feel the heat of his mouth. "You've dreamed about me before?"

"Mmm hmm," she whispered, feeling shy.

"Me, too." He slid up in her bed rising directly over

her. I guess I should have knocked. But I . . . I wanted to see you sleeping. I don't know why." He lowered his head over hers, drawing her into his dark-eyed gaze. "I think I was trying to get up my nerve."

She smoothed his cheek with her hand, touched that he could admit that to her. "I'm glad you did."

There was a slight awkwardness between them now. Mercy wanted to make love with Noah, but she didn't know quite what to do with him now that she had him in her bed. It had been easier when she thought he was a dream. She hadn't felt so reserved then; she'd had no fear she might do something wrong or something that would displease him. And, of course, dream lovers didn't come with the problems of daybreak on their shoulders. It was those problems that made her reticent now.

But as minutes ticked by, Mercy began to relax. Noah seemed to be in no hurry. He smoothed her pillow-mussed hair, kissed her chin, and drew an invisible line along her jawbone with his lips. He traced the neckline of her nightgown with his finger.

"This is what you want?" he asked huskily.

She closed her eyes, trembling. "It's what I want."

He slid his hand down her side, over her thigh, and her entire body quaked in delicious anticipation. Before Mercy knew it, she was raising her head from her pillow to meet his kiss, guiding him with her hand on the back of his head.

With every kiss, she felt as if she were sinking deeper into the feather tick of the bed. With every kiss, her anxiety slipped away, perhaps into the dream Noah had emerged from.

Mercy had never made love before, because what Haman had done to her had nothing to do with love. Having no experience, except in the actual act that had only ever taken seconds, she had been afraid she wouldn't

know what to do. But it all came so naturally. And Noah
was so gentle, so patient.

Cradling her in one arm, he leisurely explored her
body with his free hand. He brushed his fingertips over
her calves, down to her ankles, then moved upward again.
As he neared the apex of her thighs, her muscles tightened. She was still nervous, but she wanted him to touch
her *there*. Needed him to touch her, *there*. When he passed
the place, only brushing his fingertips lightly over it, over
her gown, she was disappointed. That disappointment,
though, only fueled her desire. Where he didn't touch
seemed to excite as much as where he did touch.

He ran his hand over her belly, over her breasts, down
her arms. Her skin tingled with the warmth of his and
the slight roughness of his hands. He kissed her mouth
again and again, running his fingertips over the sensitive
flesh of her collarbone. Her breasts ached to be caressed,
her nipples throbbing with every beat of her heart.

He tugged at the top three buttons of her nightgown
and peeled back the thin fabric. His hand touched the
bare skin of her breast and she sucked in her breath and
held it in anticipation, only exhaling when she grew dizzy.
Her eyelids fluttered and she allowed them to fall, too
heavy with passion to keep them open any longer.

"Mercy, Mercy, you're so beautiful," he whispered. "So
perfect. Your breasts are so perfect."

No one had ever said such sweet things to her. His
voice sent chills of desire rippling over her body.

Noah slid down in the bed and she waited, watching
in the darkness with fascination as he lowered his mouth
over one of her puckered nipples. She had never known
that a man would do that. She couldn't recall that Haman
had ever touched her breasts except maybe to pinch her
nipples.

Mercy expected it to feel as it had when a baby suck-
led—warm, comforting. But it was different. Noah's

mouth was hot, wet, demanding. As he tugged gently on
a nipple with his teeth, rivers of pleasure surged through
her, radiating out from her swollen breasts.

She squirmed beneath him. The pressure in her loins
was mounting, swelling, aching.

He threw one leg over hers and she moved against him
with the instinct a woman had to be born with. Beneath
his denims she could feel his rod hard against her hip.
He wanted her as much as she wanted him.

Now he was moving too slowly for her. He was being
too patient. She clasped his hand and slid it under her
nightgown. He touched the bed of tight curls between
her thighs as she lifted her hips off the bed to meet his
caress.

"Mercy, Mercy," he groaned.

"Noah." It came out like a cry for help.

They kissed again and again, hot anxious tongues tan-
gling, lapping. He pushed her gown up to her waist. She
wiggled against him, molding her soft flesh to his hard,
muscular frame. Still it wasn't enough. Instead of easing,
the ache in her loins only grew stronger.

Mercy released Noah's broad shoulders long enough
to grasp the hem of her gown and pull it over her head.
Any sense of decorum she might have had was gone. Now
she was naked under the quilt, naked against his skin save
for his denim pants.

He ran his hands over her body, sending waves of pleasure lapping higher over her. And as she finally felt him
shift to unbutton his pants, she nearly sighed aloud with
relief.

"Now?" he whispered, his breath hot in her ear.

"Now. Yes, now."

Mercy didn't know what tomorrow would bring, or
what she would want or expect from this man at daybreak.
But tonight, right now, she wanted to be possessed by
him. Filled by him.

"Noah!" she cried, sounding as if she were in pain.

He answered with the same desperation. "Mercy."

Intuitively, he seemed to understand her need, her ache. He lifted up off the bed and rolled onto her. He wasn't heavy like Haman had been. Instead, she welcomed his weight and the pressure of his body against hers.

Mercy parted her thighs. The feel of his hardness against her bare leg was shocking. Shocking because it felt so good. She lifted her hips, rubbing against him, guiding him.

With the aid of his hand, he slipped into her. In one instant he filled her.

Mercy clung to him, arching her back, shamelessly taking him deeper.

"Oh, Mercy, sweetheart," he murmured. Not moving, he gave her time to adjust to the feeling of fullness. He brushed away the hair that stuck to her face with perspiration and kissed her hungrily.

Slowly the ache of want seeped into her again. He felt so good; he felt better than good. He felt wonderful. But she wanted more. Needed more.

But how could there be more?

Mercy lifted her hips. Noah met her halfway and they fell into a matching rhythm. The old bedstead squeaked beneath them and she heard his heavy breathing in her ear. The motion came so easily that it seemed as if they'd been making love for a lifetime, an eternity.

Mercy's breath became ragged as she struggled, feeling as if she were climbing . . . climbing. Noah moved faster, his thrusts stronger. He wrapped her in his arms, holding her as he sank into her again and again. She felt as if he was picking her up, lifting her soul. She was reaching, but still she didn't know for what.

Then suddenly, without any warning, her world burst into bright, shining shards of intense pleasure. "Oh!" she cried out, gripping his shoulders as her body convulsed. "Oh!" Her muscles tensed and relaxed, muscles she'd never known she had. The delight flowed outward, rolling over her, consuming her.

He paused, kissing her face. Then, as her breathing slowed a little, he moved inside her again. Panting, he thrust once more, twice, and then with a groan he fell still over her.

"Oh," Mercy breathed, still feeling tiny aftershocks of pleasure. "Oh, my."

He kissed her lips and rolled off her, flat onto his back. She pressed both of her hands to her chest, still amazed by what had just happened. "What . . . what was that?" she couldn't resist asking.

He chuckled and rolled onto his side to face her. He pulled the quilt over her bare breasts now dimpled with goosebumps. A cool breeze slipped in through the open window.

"What was what?" he teased.

She knew her cheeks colored with embarrassment, but his arm wrapped tightly around her gave her the confidence to go on. "You know. *That. That* that just happened. To me."

He knitted his brow. "You mean you never— Your husband never—"

She shook her head. *"Never,"* she said. "He barely gave me the time of day when he climbed on top of me. I could have done my knitting if he hadn't jiggled the bed so."

Noah broke into laughter. "I'm sorry. It's not funny; it's a crime. But you've got such a way with words."

"That was supposed to happen?"

He took her hand and kissed her palm. *"That,* my dear, is what should happen every time you make love."

"Every time?" she asked, wide-eyed.

He kissed the tip of her nose and lay back on the bed,

his head beside hers on the pillow. *"Every time,"* he repeated. "And twice on Sundays. It's a man's duty to his woman."

Mercy closed her eyes, floating in the warm aftermath of their lovemaking. "Twice on Sundays," she breathed. "Gosh, I can't wait till Sunday now."

His warm, deep, laughter filled her dark bedroom as he drew her close and they drifted off to sleep in each other's arms.

"Ouch! That hurts," Ahab whined as Jehu dabbed at the wound on his brother's arm. "Stop, that hurts like hell."

"Hold still." Jehu sat his brother on an overturned wooden crate in the horse barn so he could get a better look at his arm. They were hoping to bandage it up and not speak a word of it to Jezzy. "Stop being such a baby, Ahab," Jehu said. "You want your arm to turn green, rot and stink, and fall off?"

Pots leaned over Ahab's shoulder, the oil lantern swinging from one meaty hand. "He gonna be all right?" His voice was nervous and shaky. He and Ahab had always been tight, Jehu guessed because they had once shared the same womb. Sometimes it got on his nerves, though. Pots never asked if *he* was going to be all right.

"Ahab's gonna be all right, ain't he, Jehu?" Pots repeated. The lamp swayed and the yellow light annoyingly came and went.

"Jesus H. Christ! Hold the lamp still, Pots. I can't see a damned blessed thing with you wavin' it that way."

Pots steadied one hand with the other and the lantern ceased swaying.

"That's better," Jehu muttered. "Now, just hold it steady there whilst I get a better look at this dumb shit's arm."

"Dumb shit? Which dumb shit?"

The three brothers looked up to see Jezzy coming through the sliding barn door. She carried a lantern that cast light across her face. From the way her lips were screwed up, Jehu knew they were in trouble. *Shit. He'd never even heard her coming.*

"What's going on here? Where you been?"

Ahab let his wounded arm fall to his side and Jehu pulled back, hoping Jezzy hadn't seen anything.

"Well?" she snapped, lifting her own lantern high to illuminate their faces. "I said, what are you three dumb asses doing out here?" Her gaze immediately fell on the barn floor.

Shit. Crap. The bloody rags at Ahab's feet.

"Jesus," she swore. She looked directly at Ahab. "You bleeding?"

"No," Ahab lied, none too convincingly.

"Yes, he is! Yes, he is!" Pots cried frantically. His eyes clouded up with moisture and Jehu thought he might burst into tears.

"Ahab's hurt, Jezzy," Pots babbled. "Hurt bad. Jehu said he could fix him up, but Jehu don't know what he's doing. He keeps drinkin' the whiskey I brought him 'stead of pourin' it on Ahab's arm."

Jezzy let out a string of curses foul even for Jehu's ears.

"Shut up, Pots," Jehu snarled. "It ain't nothin' but a bullet graze, no more than a barb-wire scratch. Didn't no man ever die from a scratch."

Pots wiped his eyes with his sleeve. "But you said it would turn green, and stink, and fall off. You said, Jehu. You did."

Jezzy shoved the lantern she carried into Jehu's hand. "Hold this and shut up. All of you!"

She went down on one knee and peeled back the bandage Jehu had attempted to wrap around his brother's arm. "What happened, Ahab? A bullet wound? How the hell you get hit?"

Ahab looked over Jezzy's shoulder at Jehu.

Jehu thrust out his chin angrily. He knew what Ahab wanted. Ahab wanted Jehu to lie for him, come up with a story for him because he was too friggin' stupid to come up with his own. "Go ahead and tell her, Ahab," Jehu said, getting pleasure from taunting him. "Tell your sister what you done."

Ahab squirmed. "Uh . . . what I done?"

"What you and your fool ass twin done. You know." Jehu glanced at Pots who had taken a step back. "How about you, Pots? You wanna tell?"

Pots's eyes were wide with fright and he shook his head. He was afraid of Jezzy. "I don't want to tell. I don't want to tell nothin'."

"Bull piss! Jehu, what did you wrap his arm with?" Jezzy demanded. "Bandages we use on the horses?" She drew back as she got a whiff of the salve he'd used. "Jesus! And horse liniment?"

Jehu shrugged. "I was tryin' to save Pots and Ahab's asses. I was tryin' to fix him up so you wouldn't tear into him."

Jezzy stood and pulled Ahab to his feet. "We'll have to do this inside. It's got to be soaped and washed and clean bandages put on it. And for Christ's bony sake—" She whipped around. "No molasses liniment, Jehu!" She punctuated her words with a sharp elbow to his kidneys.

Jehu gasped and took a step back to avoid another blow. "Just trying to help."

Jezzy lowered her hands to her hips. "So, are you two going to tell me?" she asked. "Or am I going to have to beat it out of you?"

"I—I . . ." Ahab stammered.

She tapped her foot looking as mean as ever. "I'm waiting."

"I—I . . ." Pots sputtered.

"You *what?*" Jezzy gave him the evil eye.

"I—I shot him!" Pots exclaimed, startling them all. He went on faster. "I'm sorry. I done it, Jezzy. I was trying to . . . to shoot bottles on the fence and I shot him right in the arm."

"Jesus!" Jezzy started out of the barn and the three men followed. "You did what?"

Jehu could tell she was really getting pissed now. Jezzy hated it when they lied to her.

"You did what?" she repeated. She stopped for Pots to go by and smacked him across the back of his blond head as he passed.

"I shot him," he blubbered.

"You shot your own brother? Now, Pots, God knows you're stupid, but I find it hard to believe you're that stupid."

"I ain't lyin'."

Her hard gaze fell on Jehu as they walked from the barn toward the house. Darkness had settled in and light twinkled in the windows. Little Daisy stood on the porch steps waiting for them, a tiny silhouette against the backdrop of the frame and stone ranch house. Jehu liked the little girl well enough, but he figured he'd like her better once she got some teats to her.

"Is he lyin', Jehu?"

Jehu averted his gaze. Jezzy wasn't buying Pots's story. He had to think fast.

"Tell me you weren't rustlin', Ahab." Jezzy took long strides, leading the way. "You know how I feel about rustlin'. You don't take what's not yours, Ahab. Not a single calf, not a scrawny colt, not a friggin' bottle of beer."

Her last words rang in Jehu's ears. Jezzy's sense of what was right and wrong was funny. She didn't think nothing of smackin' her daughter around, but she wouldn't steal a dry bean from an Indian. Their father had been the same. Jehu had once seen the bastard beat a hired man to death for using the wrong oil on the saddles, but he never took a thing that wasn't his.

"Folks work hard for their cattle, Ahab. We don't steal what's not ours. We work for our own."

"I wasn't rustlin'. I swear I wasn't."

"Swear we weren't," Pots echoed.

Jezzy stopped at the steps to the front porch. Daisy hung back in the shadows listening to the conversation.

"Then what *were* you doing?" Jezzy's face was stone hard. "Because you know I won't tolerate thieving. I'd hang you myself for thieving."

Jehu thought quick and then said, "Tell her, Ahab. No sense in lyin'."

Ahab's face was pale. "T—tell her?" He gulped, protecting his injured arm with his hand.

"You want me to tell her?" Jehu asked.

Jezzy lifted one boot and set it firmly on the first step. "Tell me what?"

"We might as well tell, boys, because she's going to find out anyway." Jehu set the lantern on the step. "I was working on those fences, just like I was supposed." He hooked his thumb toward his brothers. "Twiddle and Twat there, they were lazin' about. Then they got the idea to go down to the river and do a little fishing."

Jezzy didn't smile. "He got shot fishing?"

"Well, they got down there and found themselves a woman alone, half Indian gal, travelin' in a wagon." Sometimes Jehu didn't know where he came up with these things. "Her man was off hunting so these two thought they'd have a little fun."

Jezzy crossed her arms over her chest.

"Well, the two have their fun, everything's goin' fine, and then the man rides up, gets all angry-like and shoots poor Ahab here." Jehu waited to see if she bought the story.

Jezzy shook her head. "Jesus, Ahab," she muttered.

Jehu waited for her to launch into another tirade, his body tensed. To his surprise, she didn't.

"You two could get yourselves hurt with that nonsense," she said in an almost motherly-fashion. "You're going to have to be more careful picking up tail. It's not worth getting your arm blown off. Certainly not a half breed bitch."

Still shaking her head, she climbed the steps. "Daisy, get my medicine bag and some clean bandages." She clapped her hands together. "Hustle, before I tan your ass bare."

The child took off at a run, blond hair flying.

"Come on, Ahab," Jezzy said, draping an arm around Ahab's good shoulder. "Let me clean your arm up and get you into bed. No harm done. Just watch yourself next time." She kissed his cheek and then let go of him, walking on ahead.

Jehu passed Ahab as they went into the house. "You owe me for this," he whispered. "You owe me for sure."

Later, after Ahab's wound had been bandaged and Jezzy had poured him two whiskeys and put him to bed, Jehu met his sister in the kitchen. She was pouring coffee into a cup. She always had liked the dregs at the end of the day.

"Want some coffee?" she asked, raising the pot.

Jehu shook his head as he sat at the table and reached for what was left of Ahab's medicinal whiskey. "Nah, you take it."

She brought her cup to the table and turned a chair around to straddle it. She leaned on the back with her elbows and reached for her coffee. "Jehu, you've got to keep an eye on those two. One of them could have been killed today."

Jehu eyed her over the rim of the whiskey bottle. "Why's it always me lookin' out for them? When they supposed to look out for me?"

"Both are half-witted and you know it." She shook a long, slender finger. "But that doesn't matter, because they're still flesh and blood. They're our brothers and we die for them if we have to."

Jehu took another sip of his whiskey, mulling over her words about flesh and blood. "Say, Jezzy."

"Yeah?"

"I been meaning to talk to you about Jacob, Haman's boy."

She rubbed her temples as if her head hurt. "What about him?"

"I was just wonderin' . . ." Jehu hesitated, unsure of how his sister might react to what he was going to say. "I was wondering if we ought to be bringing the boy out here to the ranch. Raisin' him."

Jezzy peered up. "What do you mean?"

He lifted one big shoulder and let it fall. "I'm just thinking that ain't no place for a boy to be raised. Our flesh and blood. He's got no one but that bitchy mother of his, and with her taking in men to sleep in her house, I don't know that it's the right atmosphere for a boy."

Jezzy burst into laughter.

"What?" Jehu frowned. He had no idea what his sister was laughing about and it pissed him off. "What's so funny?"

"You're worried about Miss Mercy and men boarders?" She slapped her denimed-covered knee in delight. "That's a good one, Jehu. Hell, Mercy wouldn't know a stiff cock if one was propping open her bedroom door."

Jehu stared at the bottle in his hand. Jezzy always made him feel small—damn her. "I was just thinking that if Haman don't come home—"

"I got news, Jehu. He ain't coming home."

"If Haman doesn't come home," Jehu continued stubbornly, "maybe I ought to . . . I was thinkin' maybe I ought to marry her and bring her out here where I can see the boy raised proper."

Jezzy snickered. "Marry her, you say? And you think she'd marry you? A fat-assed, lazy slob like you?"

"She married Haman, didn't she, and his ass was broader than mine."

Jezzy rocked back in the chair as if she were riding a bronco. She was obviously enjoying this conversation at his expense. "Yeah, but only because she didn't get a look at him first."

Jehu climbed out of his chair, hurt and angry at the same time. He'd had enough of his sister for one day. "She might marry me. I'd make a sight better husband than that skinny-assed, long-faced gunman she's got her thighs wrapped around now."

The minute he spoke, Jehu knew that something he'd said had caught his sister's interest. He just wasn't sure what.

"The skinny-assed gunman?" Jezzy lowered all four legs of the chair back onto the floor. "She's porking *him?*"

He answered cautiously. "Maybe. I don't know. Could be."

She scowled. "Know anything about him?"

"No. Just that he's a hired gunman for the bank. Guards the stagecoach that carries the money to Carson City."

She frowned until he thought her eyebrows might meet. "You serious about wanting Jacob here? I never thought he was much. Probably won't amount to crap, just like the rest of you Atkins men."

"I just want to do right by Haman's boy."

"Sure, right." Jezzy climbed out of her chair. "You just want to slip the virgin your meat. I know you, Jehu."

He gave her a cocky grin. "Might be she'd like it."

"And it might be that the devil serves ice cream in hell, but I'm seriously doubting it."

He shrugged again. "Just something to think about. Just wanted to know what you think, Jezzy."

She nodded the way his father had, like he was president or king or something. "All right, I'll think on it. Meantime you see what you can find out about Ericson, all right?"

"What for?" Jehu hadn't even known she knew his name.

She turned her back on him, his dismissal plain and clear. "Do what I tell you, Jehu," she said, slurping the coffee thick as mud. "If I want you to think, I'll tell you that, too."

Sixteen

"A partner?" Noah eyed Cook skeptically. He was in a good mood, but he wasn't in *that* good a damned mood. He shook his head firmly. "I don't think so. I don't do partners. I made that clear when I was hired for the job."

"Well, not partners per se. Not partners," the bank man repeated. "A deputy of sorts. You could look at it as an extra gun." The handlebars of his waxed mustache quivered.

Noah frowned. He should have seen this coming. With the bandits in action again, it was only natural that the bank would want to hire more people to protect their property.

The thing was, Noah didn't do partners. He absolutely refused to have anyone depend on him. "If I want an extra gun," he told the bank man evenly, "I'll carry my own."

"Let me explain my situation, Mr. Ericson." He paced, his steps short and controlled in the small space available to him. "It seems Mr. Patterson's mine is doing well. He'd like us to ship samples of his silver along with our cash to Carson City. Until we get an assayer in Nowhere, it's the closest town where one can be found. The bank can't afford to turn Mr. Patterson down."

Noah hooked his thumbs into his gun holster and stared at the sanded plank floor of the office Mr. Cook shared with the bank's black safe. He had half a mind to quit this job here and now. He'd been told it was a loner's job. If he'd been told any differently, he'd never have taken the position to begin with.

Quit. That's what he'd do.

But then thoughts of Mercy crept into his mind. Against his will, he softened. Last night had been something straight out of a man's dream. Their lovemaking had been incredible, but more importantly she had made him feel connected to the world in a way he'd not felt connected since before the war.

Noah didn't know where he was headed with Mercy, but he knew he wanted to stick around Nowhere long enough to find out. If he had no job in Nowhere, he'd have no reason, no excuse, to stay, would he?

Noah spoke gruffly, knowing he was making a mistake, but unable to alter his course. Mercy's scent was still too heady in his nostrils to heed his own good sense. "I suppose you've already got someone in mind."

"Matter of fact, I do." Cook held up one finger. "Just a second. Edgar!" He hurried to the doorway of his office, which opened into the main lobby of the bank.

Men and women who stood in line to make deposits or withdrawals, or send or receive mail on the post office side, glanced in Noah and Cook's direction with interest.

"Edgar, come and meet Mr. Ericson. Mr. Ericson."

A tall, lanky young man with a bad complexion appeared in the doorway. Noah guessed he was probably twenty, but he looked twelve.

This was his extra hired gun?

"Mr. Ericson," Mr. Cook said excitedly. "Meet Edgar Cook."

"Cook?" Noah lifted one eyebrow, groaning to himself. "Not your son?"

"Oh, my, no. No, no." He gestured proudly. "My nephew, just come west. I knew the bank would give him a job. Give him a chance to see this fine state."

" 'Morning to you, sir." The young man removed his hat, nodding. "I appreciate you being willing to have me work for you. My uncle says you're the best around these parts." His speech was educated, with a hint of a southern accent Noah didn't readily recognize.

A suckling, Noah thought. *They've hired a suckling. They want me to baby-sit, not escort their money.* "You know how to shoot that thing?" Noah nodded to the Colt .45 that looked out of place on the thin man's hip. It was the same piece Noah carried, originally issued by the Army during the war.

"Suppose I do. Learned at Gettysburg."

Noah had only been half paying attention to the boy's reply. He was too busy trying to think of a way to get out of this without bruising Edgar's young ego. But the mention of that battlefield immediately tapped his attention. *"Gettysburg?"*

Edgar nodded and by the look in his hazel eyes Noah knew that he *had* actually been there. A man never lost that look, not after experiencing carnage like that.

Noah immediately formed a new respect for Edgar. He might look like a boy, but anyone who survived Gettysburg was a man in his eyes. "You must have been pretty lucky." He hadn't noticed a limp or a stiff movement in Edgar's limbs as he'd walked into the office. "Not hit?"

"No. Not there. Not anywhere. Fought two and a half years and never got a scratch."

"The boy's invincible." Cook slapped his nephew on the back. "That's why he's perfect for the job."

Edgar cocked a lazy grin. "My buddies called me Lucky Bucky. They all wanted to march at my side when we advanced. They thought I was blessed or something. Men would fall all around me and I was never touched."

"Bucky?" Against his will, Noah liked the tousle-haired young man. "I thought your name was Edgar. How'd they get Bucky out of Edgar?"

Again, the lopsided grin. "The only name they could think of that rhymed with Lucky, I suppose."

Noah laughed, and the oddest feeling came over him. Within the safety of the walls of the Tin Roof Hotel he'd been laughing for weeks, thanks to Mercy. But this was the first time he'd experienced this kind of amusement beyond those walls. Without realizing it, he had taken another step away from the man he had become after his family's death. He found the sound of his own laughter strangely exhilarating.

"So, Edgar." Noah touched him lightly on the shoulder. "Got a place to stay?"

He glanced at his uncle. "Uncle Bartholomew says I'm welcome to sleep at his place, but I was thinking I might want to be on my own. Not impose. Not with Aunt Sally in the family way, pardon me for saying so." He nodded to his uncle. Then he turned back to Noah. "You have any suggestions? Pretty small town from what I've seen."

"Bank's putting me up at the Tin Roof Hotel." Noah cut his gaze Cook's way. "I imagine the Carson City Bank would do the same for you, you being my deputy."

Cook was tongue-tied for an instant. Obviously he'd been hoping to save the bank money by putting his nephew up himself. "Well, I suppose that could be arranged."

"Done." Noah walked out of the office, trying not to limp. There was no need for his employer to know he was foolish enough to fall off his own horse. "Come on, Edgar. I've got to send a telegraph to the bank in Smithtown. We're going to ride with the stagecoach tomorrow instead of the following day as planned. Sounds like a coach will be cutting through here just about every day now that summer's almost here. After I take care of that matter, I'll show you around town and get you settled at the Tin Roof." He winked as he passed the young man.

"The proprietress makes some mighty light buttermilk biscuits. You like buttermilk biscuits?"

Edgar dropped his hat on his head and followed Noah. "After the dry tack and half-rotten apples I ate on the train, biscuits sound good to me even if they're hard as nails."

Noah pushed out the bank door and stepped onto the sidewalk, smiling to himself. He wondered how late Edgar went to bed and if he could wait that long to take Mercy in his arms again.

Noah slipped out onto the back porch, lifted his arms high, stretched and groaned. Night had settled on the foothills and the air smelled of Mercy's rich chocolate cake they'd consumed for supper and the piñon pines sprouting new needles. Wagon wheels rumbled by on the street out front and Noah could occasionally make out the sound of men's voices. He couldn't hear what they were saying; they were too far away. But he could hear their presence.

More men were coming to the little town of Nowhere every day. Word got out quickly when silver was found at the Patterson mine and now would-be rich men were flocking in, staking claims and digging for all their backs were worth.

Noah knew he should be pleased for the town's rejuvenation. Even if only a little silver was found, miners would add to the town's income. It was hopeful times like these when shopkeepers and business owners like Mercy could make up for the lean years. And who knew? If the mines in the surrounding areas did pan out, Nowhere might become another bustling city like Carson City.

But selfishly, Noah didn't like the sound of the wagon wheels or the men's voices. He didn't like them because those wagons brought men not just into town, but into the Tin Roof Hotel. Today two more miners had rented rooms, and Mercy had placed them and Edgar in a room downstairs in the back addition where Tinny and Jacob slept. It wasn't that he wasn't happy for Mercy. It was obvious that the security the money could bring was important to her.

Selfishly, though, he didn't like the idea of having to share her with other men. If it was only to cook their meals and wash their linens, Noah felt as if they were intruders. He remembered the first few weeks he had come to the Tin Roof and how quiet it had been at night after supper. Then Mercy had had time to play checkers, talk, and laugh. Now she was too busy.

Light in the shed-turned-bathhouse in the backyard caught Noah's attention and he leaned over the wobbly porch rail to get a better look. The doors were flung wide and he could see movement in shadows. Someone was out there, and from the speed of the movement, he knew it had to be Mercy. These last couple of days she'd moved about the hotel with the efficiency and speed of a queen bee. She kept everything in order, everyone pleased, and most importantly, she never got flustered. If she planned for nine for dinner and twelve showed up, she was rolling out extra dumplings and biscuits before a man could get his drawers down in her bathhouse.

Noah admired Mercy; he was proud of her. What she had done here had nothing to do with him, and still he was as pleased as if he accomplished the tasks himself.

Mercy pulled back the curtain she'd hung around the bathtub and he spotted her silhouette against the backdrop of the canvas curtain. The dress she wore with its new cage crinoline and red petticoats gave her a bell-like shape that tipped out when she leaned over the tub. He smiled as she straightened and turned, hands busy lifting buckets of water.

Noah went down the porch steps, across the patch desert grass and past Mercy's garden plot. He liked getting his hand in the soil and had offered to hoe on several occasions, but her garden was the one thing she seemed possessive of. She'd asked him not to bother with it, and he'd agreed out of respect for her wishes, not because it made any sense. Maybe one day he'd have his own garden again. Maybe they'd share one.

Noah strode into the bathhouse. "What are you doing?"

"Starting a bucket brigade. Thought we'd form a fire department now that there's new buildings going up in town," she quipped. "What's it look like I'm doing? I'm emptying the tub."

"You shouldn't be doing that." He took the heavy, full bucket from her hands and set it on the floor.

"I think I owe the men clean water at least twice a week, don't you?" She caught a lock of damp hair that had escaped her loose chignon and tucked it behind her ear. As always, he made her feel self-conscious about her appearance.

She reached for the bucket again, but he beat her to it. "Let me do this," he said.

"You can't do everything for me," she protested, actually relieved to let him take a turn. The bucket was heavy. "God knows I hauled water before you came."

"I know you did." He walked out of the shed, dumped the water onto the bushy pea plants, and walked back into the dim lamplight. "But I want to do it."

She leaned over the tub and fished out a slippery bar of soap. "If you really want to help," she teased, "go lay some eggs. I'm short on eggs again. Guess I'll have to get more laying hens or take to buying eggs like a city slicker."

Chuckling, he set down the bucket and kicked one of the doors closed, blocking the view of the inside of the shed from the house.

Jacob and Tinny had already turned in for the night. Noah and Tinny had played checkers on the front porch after supper and then Noah had wrestled with the boy. He'd taught Jake a neck lock or some such nonsense and he'd gone happily to bed for once, chattering about wrestling Indians when he grew up. The boarders who were staying the night had already turned in. They would be expected at their mine sites by dawn, so they rarely stayed up late except on Saturday nights.

"What do you think you're doing?" Mercy turned around, a pair of men's wet trousers in her hand. Always trying to conserve water, she'd been soaking muddy clothes in the dirty tub water before rinsing them in clean pump water.

"What am I doing?" Noah asked, a rumble to his voice. "Doing what I've wanted to do all day." He grabbed her around the waist and pulled her tight against him.

Mercy let out a little sound of protest, but it was mild. She let the wet pants fall to the floor in a soggy heap beside her. His arms felt so good around her waist. "Noah, really! In plain view?"

He pressed his lips to the pulse of her throat, closed his eyes, and breathed deeply. "Plain view of who?" He tickled the skin at her breastbone with the tip of his tongue.

"Your father and son have gone to bed," he cajoled. "Tinny's snoring like a loose stove pipe. The others are asleep, too. It's late, after ten. All good folks ought to be abed."

She laughed, looping her arms around his neck and arching her back. "In their own beds?"

"Depends."

Mercy listened to his throaty words as she let her eyes close. His touch sent tremors of excitement rippling over her skin. She'd barely been able to get her work done today, thinking about Noah. About his hands and his mouth and what they'd done to her last night.

"Depends on what?" she whispered, letting him kiss her cheek, the lobe of her ear.

"Depends on what constitutes one's own bed. I'd say I fit pretty well in yours last night, wouldn't you?"

Mercy could feel color flush her cheeks. She wasn't really embarrassed, it just felt strange to openly talk about their lovemaking like this. "Yes," she said shyly. "I'd say you fit just fine, outrider."

He brought his mouth down against hers, crushing her in his arms. It was hot tonight, but suddenly it was hotter. Mercy felt lightheaded and weak-kneed as she welcomed his hot, wet tongue. He slid his mouth lower, over her chin, down her neck. His fingers found the hooks and eyes of her bodice and he expertly unclasped them, revealing the swell of her breasts above her corset. Even before she felt the first brush of his fingers, her breasts ached for his touch.

Noah cupped one breast with his hand and her soft flesh strained to escape her corset and layers of undergarments. "We can't do this here," she whispered.

"Why not?" He backed her up against the tool bench that now held clean towels and soap balls.

Breathless, she kissed him back. But he wasn't moving fast enough, so she fumbled with the tiny hooks and eyes of her bodice, undressing for him. "Be-because," she panted. Already she was becoming hot and achy. "Because someone might see. Might find out."

"No one will see." He kicked the other door shut with his boot heel, cloaking them in the soft light of the single oil lamp that burned on a chair on the far side of the tub.

Noah kissed her breasts, kneading them, licking them, sucking . . . Moaning, Mercy unhooked her stay cover.

Her fingers tore at the ribbons of her corset, her breasts aching to be fully free.

"Mercy, Mercy," he whispered, his breath hot in her ear.

Then he grasped her by the waist and lifted her onto the low tool bench. Mercy parted her legs so when she lifted her petticoat, cage crinoline, and chemise, his groin pressed against her woman's place.

Noah kissed her again and again, touching her, setting her flesh on fire. Her hair fell from its tortoiseshell pins and she swept it off her neck, feeling hotter by the second.

"I can't believe I'm doing this," she murmured as she reached down and tugged on the buttons of his denim pants.

He laughed huskily.

The second his pants were unbuttoned, he fell into her hands, hot and hard for her. "I can't believe I'm doing this," she said again. But even as the words slipped from her mouth, she was stroking him, reveling in the sound of his moans in her ear.

Mercy spread her legs wider and slid forward to the edge of the bench, her need for him burning all logical thought from her mind. She parted the open folds of her drawers, in too great a hurry to climb down and remove them.

"Noah," she groaned, feeling him brush against her.

"Mercy, Mercy love."

He pressed against her again, stimulating that magical place she'd not even known existed. To her surprise she cried out with pleasure and felt the same surge of release as she had last night.

"Oh," she moaned, confused, lost in the sensations of the moment. She gripped his shoulders, holding tightly to him as the tremors washed over her. "Oh," she breathed again.

He held her in his arms until the sensation nearly subsided and then slipped inside her with one hard stroke. Suddenly the waves of ecstasy splashed over her again. She grabbed his shoulders and arched her back, not understanding this wonderful thing that was happening to her again and again, but accepting it as his gift.

Again the waves subsided and then Noah began to move inside her. He gripped her buttocks and practically lifted her from the bench, holding her in his strong arms, sinking deep inside her. Mercy could do nothing but hang on as he sank home again and again, faster until she exploded again, this time at the same moment that he found release.

Noah slowly lowered her to the bench as she clung to him, her face resting on his shoulder, covered by her hair and his. Her entire body was hot and wet and sticky and trembling, and it was wonderful.

"Oh," she sighed one last time.

He caught her chin and lifted it, forcing her to look into his eyes as he held her in his arms, still inside her. "I love you, Mercy Atkins," he said. "I love you and I want to marry you, if you'd be willing to be my wife."

Mercy felt as if her heart stopped in her chest. "Marry you?"

He pulled back his hips and withdrew from her, but still held her in his arms. The air smelled thickly of pine and the musky scent that was theirs alone. "Yes, marry me. Let me be your husband, a father to Jacob."

"Noah," she exhaled, caressing his slightly beard-stubbled chin. "You mean it?"

"I mean it." He held her gaze, his dark eyes filled with sincerity. "As soon as Haman is declared dead. I want you, Mercy. I have to have you."

She smiled. Her heart had started beating again; now it pounded in her chest. "Yes," she whispered. "I'll marry you, Noah." She slipped her arms around his neck and pressed her cheek to his damp cheek. *I'll marry you,* she thought. And the hell with the Atkins family. *Dead and alive.*

Seventeen

"Pass the eggs, will you, Mama?" Jacob asked.

"More eggs?"

"A growing boy," Noah said.

"He wants to grow tall and strong like me." Edgar, Noah's new *deputy*, lifted one arm comically in a strongman's pose.

Jacob giggled and imitated the pose.

"Strong?" Noah teased. "Hell, Edgar, that boy could take you down now. I imagine old Joe here could, too, if he set his mind to it." Noah indicated the empty place setting at the breakfast table and winked at Mercy.

"Bet he could, all right." Tinny chewed enthusiastically on a thick strip of crispy bacon.

Mercy handed her son the plate of scrambled eggs as she smiled at Noah. It was a lot to ask a man to tolerate the invisible friend of an old cowpoke, but Noah didn't seem to mind. Yet another reason to keep him around.

"I can take you on." Edgar gave Noah a playful shove.

Mercy enjoyed seeing Noah so playful. It made her happy to see him happy. "Gentlemen, I won't have any brawling in my establishment, and you know it." She eyed Noah.

He chuckled and took the egg plate from Jacob and served himself another helping. Mercy had fed the other boarders earlier, before dawn. She had found that by serving two breakfasts, she could actually sit down and eat with her family, a rare occurrence these days. And Jacob enjoyed Noah's company so much, and now Edgar's, that she didn't mind the little extra work.

Her meal complete, Mercy rose from the table, taking her plate with her. "I packed a basket for you two—sandwiches in it for the coach driver, too. Don't forget it on your way out."

A minute later, Noah followed Mercy into the kitchen, as she hoped he would. He backed her up in the pantry, out of sight of the others. "How about a wifely good-bye kiss, just to get practice?"

She puckered her lips and pecked him chastely on the cheek. "How's that?"

He frowned. "Wasn't what I had in mind."

She fluttered her eyelashes. She'd never been one to play coy, but it was fun with Noah. "I thought that was how wives kissed husbands."

"Not how I want to be kissed," he answered gruffly.

Before Mercy could come up with a clever retort, he crushed his mouth to hers, rendering her breathless.

"That's better," he said when he finally released her.

Mercy's lips tingled and her mouth tasted of his. Heavens, how she loved that taste, that feel. "That kind of good-bye kiss could get a girl mighty hot and flustered," she said, her cheeks burning.

"Just the way I want you." He squeezed her hand and released it, picking up the food basket she'd packed for him. "Want me to bring you anything from Carson City?"

"Not really." She tucked her hands behind her back wishing he didn't have to go right now, wishing they could climb back into bed together instead. "Just you, that's all I want. Come home safely."

He tipped his hat. "Yes, ma'am. I promised Jacob a trip to Carson City one of these days, but I don't think it's a good idea right now. Later would be better after things have settled down. After the sheriff catches the other thief."

"I agree. Jacob will understand."

Edgar walked into the kitchen, carrying Jacob on his back. Jacob balanced their dirty plates in his hands while trying to stay astride.

"What on earth are the two of you doing?" Mercy laughed as she took the dishes from her son and set them in the sink. It was so strange to have such happiness and fun in her kitchen after all those years of misery and sometimes fear. She felt so blessed this morning.

"Playing horse and rider," Jacob said. "Get up!" He pumped his legs as if he were on horseback. Jacob's newfound friend broke into a canter of sorts and headed out of the kitchen.

"I'm going to see them off!" Jacob hollered to his mother, waving. "Back in a few minutes!"

Mercy stood beside Noah and watched the two gallop out of the kitchen. "That boy," she muttered proudly.

Noah watched him go. "A good boy," he said. "A boy I'd be proud to have call me Papa if he was willing."

Mercy smiled. "And other children?" she asked. She didn't know what made her say it. Years ago she'd given up hope of having another baby. Now suddenly here was the possibility standing right here in her kitchen.

Noah nodded thoughtfully, slipping his free hand around her waist. "I think I'd like that, Mercy. A girl maybe."

She lifted on her tiptoes and kissed him. "Or maybe another son. A young Noah?"

He grimaced. "I don't know that I'd do that to a boy. How about a young Tinny instead?"

Mercy laughed. "Think he'd be born wearing a hat with a chicken feather in it?"

They laughed together and Noah kissed her again on

his way out. "See you tonight. It might be late. I've got a few things to do in Carson City."

"Bye." She waved, so happy she thought she might burst inside. "Send Jacob home when you ride out."

"I will. Have a good day and don't work too hard." He left her kitchen whistling.

"Afternoon, Tinny." Jehu plunked his big, lumpy self down on the stool opposite Tinny out front of McGregor's store. A checkerboard on a barrel separated them. "Lookin' for someone to play a game with you?" He gestured.

Tinny squinted, eyeing his daughter's brother-in-law. Jehu was being awful pleasant; usually he couldn't be bothered to give an old man the time of day. "Might be," Tinny harrumphed suspiciously. He liked to play checkers with Joe, but playing with someone else was even better.

"I'll play you a quick game." Jehu moved his first checker. "Then I've got to get back to the ranch with that feed." He hooked a thumb toward the buckboard wagon across the street with feed bags loaded in its bed.

Tinny nodded. He didn't much like Jehu Atkins. When he saw his face he saw Haman's and he'd hated that bastard. But Tinny was lonely. Joe wasn't up to much talking today, and Tinny *really* wanted to play checkers. He hesitated, moving his chewing tobacco around inside his cheek and then cautiously sliding one of his own pieces forward.

Jehu grinned and took his turn. "So, how's the boy, and that pretty daughter of yours?" he asked pleasant-like.

Tinny moved his red checker. He always played the red; they were lucky. He wondered why Jehu was being so nice. Tinny hadn't been there, but Jacob said that Jehu and Mercy's new husband, Noah, had gotten into a brawl.

Jehu and his worthless brothers hadn't been back to eat on Mercy since. He took his time to answer. "Well enough."

"I hear she's got plenty of business these days. People are talking about her good cooking for miles around." Jehu grinned. "Your turn."

Tinny hopped his checker and took one of Jehu's.

"Hehehe," the big man cackled, his loose jowls flapping. "You're good, aren't you?"

Tinny didn't say anything.

"I guess you heard about what happened last time I stopped by for one of those good meals of Mercy's," Jehu said. "Me and the boys, we got a little out of hand."

Tinny moved another checker and took another of Jehu's blackies.

"I really am awful sorry." Slowly he slid a checker. "Mr. Ericson seems like a nice enough sort. Not particularly friendly, but—"

Tinny made a sound in his throat. He meant to just keep his mouth shut, chew his tobacco, and let Jehu blow the breeze, but he couldn't let this one by. He liked Noah. He made Tinny's little girl laugh, and any man that could make his little girl happy was a good man in his book. Tinny hadn't been around when she'd been growing up. He hadn't taken to Philly after he'd married Jean and they'd had Mercy, so he and his wife parted on friendly terms when Mercy was six, and Tinny had been wandering the West ever since.

Tinny eyed Jehu Atkins. "If you'd been through what he's been through, you'd be a mite bit sour on life, too," he grumbled.

"That right?" Jehu lifted a bushy eyebrow like he really was interested. "I heard a little about that in the Twin Pianos, but a man can never trust whiskey gossip. What happened with him, again? I heard it was something awful."

Tinny double hopped and took two of Jehu's checkers. He was going to win; he liked winning. "Came home a war hero to find his wife and daughter dead and buried. They was robbed and shot, burnt up in their house."

Tinny thought the fat man flinched, but he wasn't sure. Tinny's eyes just weren't what they used to be.

"That right?" Jehu asked, his voice sounding funny. "Dead just like that?" He snapped his fingers. It was Jehu's turn again, but he didn't move a game piece. "Ever catch the bad'uns who done it?"

"Naw." Tinny hawked and spat tobacco juice, making sure he hit the street and not the sidewalk. McGregor didn't mind Tinny sitting out front of his store as long as he didn't spit on the sidewalk the Irishman swept every morning except Sundays. "Never found who did it."

"And just where was that?"

Jehu opened a meaty hand and Tinny wondered how he ever did a decent day's work with those soft hands. In Tinny's day, a ranch hand whose hands weren't blistered and calloused wasn't worth a pinch of possum shit.

"Someone said where it happened," Jehu went on. "But I don't rightly remember. Colorado way, was it?"

"Naw." Tinny studied his choice of moves. He really wanted to win this game. "Right here in Nevada, north a piece somewhere on the Washoe."

To Tinny's surprise, Jehu popped right off his stool. "Look at the time." He glanced at the noonday sun overhead. "I gotta be going."

"Wait." Tinny watched him waddle across the street toward his waiting buckboard. "We ain't done with the game, yet!" Tinny hollered after him. "I was going to win."

But he guessed Jehu didn't hear him as he climbed up onto the wagon seat and rolled away.

* * *

Noah stepped out of the barber shop and onto the bustling sidewalk in Carson City. After delivering the strongboxes safely to the bank, he and Edgar had split up to run their separate errands and planned to meet each other in another hour to head home for Nowhere. Noah was anxious to get back, anxious to be with Mercy again.

As he walked, Noah felt his smooth cheek with his hand. Normally he shaved himself, but while he'd been in the chair getting a haircut, he thought he might as well treat himself to a shave as well.

His hair felt strange shorter like this, barely brushing his collar, but in a way it was liberating. Noah felt that as he shed his shoulder-length hair, ragged from the haircuts he'd been giving himself with his bowie knife, he was shedding the skin he'd worn the last three years. Like a rattler who had grown out of his hide, Noah had grown out of that wounded person . . . or at least was growing.

Next, Noah stopped in a general store. He bought a leather ball for Jacob and a small chalkboard and some pieces of chalk. Mercy said McGregor would be starting a school in the fall. It was time the boy started learning his letters, and if Mercy didn't have time to work with him, Noah thought he might do it himself.

Noah picked up some tea the clerk said came from China for Mercy, a new shirt and pair of denims for himself, and two wads of tobacco for Tinny. Mercy didn't approve of chew, so the old man rarely used it, but a man needed his vices on occasion, didn't he? As Noah headed up to the counter to pay for the items, a lady's sleeping gown caught his eye. It was made of a thin white cotton fabric with tiny blue flowers embroidered across the bodice. On impulse, he took the gown as well.

"What an exquisite choice. For your wife?" the salesclerk cooed as she wrapped the expensive garment in brown paper.

"I hope so," Noah answered. Taking his change and collecting his packages, he returned to the street. It was early to meet Edgar yet, but he figured he might as well go back to the bank and wait for him there. If the young man finished his errands early as well, they could be on their way.

At the bank hitching post, Noah packed his purchases carefully in the saddlebags on Sam's flanks. Then he waited, watching for Edgar.

The street was busy with wagons rolling by one after another. Some were pulled by horses, others, mules. A Conestoga wagon rolled by, loaded with a weary-looking family, bound farther west, no doubt. Men rode by on horses and a stagecoach passed, loaded top to bottom with travel trunks. Two cowpokes herded a dozen cattle down the center of the street, bound for slaughter no doubt.

Entertained by all the hubbub, Noah reached into his saddlebag and fished out a brown paper sack of sarsaparilla sticks. He'd bought them for Jacob, but he was sure the boy wouldn't mind sharing one.

Noah licked the brown stick of sticky, sweet candy and watched a wagon of tittering young women roll by. Mail order brides? he wondered.

Two black horses with black, feathered headdresses caught his eye and he froze, candy stick in his mouth. The horses pranced by, heads dancing as if they were proud of their headdresses, proud of the black glass wagon they pulled behind, proud of the black mourning shrouds draped over the glass coffin that was their baggage.

Noah slowly eased the candy from his mouth; suddenly it tasted bitter. As the funeral wagon rolled by with its glass sides, he saw the coffin, draped in black. Directly behind him walked a man in black frock coat leading two little girls, both dressed in black as well.

Noah dropped the candy stick in the sawdust at his feet.

A funeral. There had been no funeral for Alice and Becky. No coffin, most likely. Some decent neighbor had dug a single hole and laid to rest what was left of their brittle, charred bones.

For a moment Noah thought he might vomit. He hadn't been there for them; he hadn't even been there to put flowers on their graves. He should have been there to put flowers on their graves . . .

"Ready, partner?" Edgar appeared at Noah's side. He slapped Noah on the arm as he dropped several small brown parcels into his saddlebags and untied his horse.

"Noah, you coming? You want to get home to that pretty woman of yours tonight, we'd best get on the trail."

For a moment Noah stood frozen in place, numb with remorse. Mercy made him so happy. What right did he have to that happiness?

"Noah! You all right?"

Noah grabbed his mount's reins and lifted into the saddle. The sights and sounds of Carson City were a blur as he rode out of town.

Jezzy gently kneed the mare's back leg and the horse obediently lifted it. With a metal pick she carefully cleaned the hoof, taking care not to disturb the soft, spongy flesh in the center. Ordinarily she wouldn't be doing this herself, but another ranch hand, Benny Miller, had taken off. This one left without giving notice or even collecting his last week's pay, so once again, Jezzy was stuck with the extra work.

Daisy sat in the corner of the stall, her legs drawn up, singing softly to herself as she fiddled with something in her lap.

"Jezzy, can I talk with you?" Jehu came into the stall.

"Move. You're in my light. She's walking a little lame." She gestured to the mare drinking water from a tin bucket. "I don't know if she picked up a stone, or what." Jezzy went on, gently picking at the mare's hoof. "What you need?"

Jehu moved so as not to block the sunlight that poured in through the barn's open gates. "Jezzy, we might have us a problem."

"What now?" She sighed. "Ahab's not chased down another Indian woman, has he? I told him to keep his pecker in his pants unless it's invited out."

"No." Jehu kicked at the loose straw in the stall.

"Then what is it?" Jezzy turned the horse's hoof, trying to get a better look.

Jehu glanced at the little girl in the corner of the stall who continued to hum, even though she knew it annoyed her mother.

"Jesus Christ, Jehu, speak up. Daisy's a little girl. Who the hell is she going to tell? Who the hell does she know to tell?"

Jehu took a breath, started to speak, took another, and went on. "You know Ericson . . . the outrider."

"Yes."

"Well, I was talking to Tinny, seeing what he knew, like you said and . . . and it seems he met with a little bad luck a few years back."

"Yes?" Jezzy said impatiently. She couldn't find the damned pebble in the mare's hoof and the horse was beginning to get antsy standing on three legs like this. "And?" she snapped. "Get on with it."

Daisy turned in the straw in the corner, humming louder.

"Seems he lost his wife and daughter."

"Lost them? What the hell are you talking about?" She glanced up at her dim-witted brother. "Christ, people don't lose their wife and child, they lose their pocket knife or a coin."

Jehu shook his head. "Lost them like they died."

"So? Half the women and children west of the Mississippi die. Cholera, yellow fever, measles. Hell, you can die of the craps out here."

Jehu shook his head in obvious agitation. "No, you don't understand. They were killed. Shot and killed and burned up in a house."

Jezzy let the mare drop her hoof again. "You're shittin' me?"

"I'm not."

Jezzy felt the bottom drop right out of her stomach. She glanced at her daughter. "Christ Almighty, would you shut the hell up so I can think, Daisy?" she shouted, kicking at the loose straw.

The little girl immediately clamped her mouth shut and stood, something cradled in her apron. She turned her back to slip by her mother.

Jezzy ran a hand over her face. "Shit, Jehu. *Shit,*" she repeated.

Daisy walked past her mother.

"What have you got there?" Jezzy asked, her head pounding with impact of what Jehu had just said.

Daisy halted, but she didn't answer.

Of all the bad luck. Ericson? Jezzy couldn't believe it. It was too much of a coincidence. "I said, what you got there?"

The child turned her head, tiny blond pigtails brushing her shoulders. "Baby mice," she whispered, so softly that Jezzy could barely hear her.

"What?" Jezzy snapped, her patience at an end.

"Baby mice," Daisy whispered again. "They're mine, Mama. My friends."

"Jesus!" Jezzy grabbed Daisy's arm and turned her around. "Mice? Have you lost what little sense you possessed, child?" With one hand, Jezzy scooped up the little hairless pink bodies in her fist and threw them into the horse's water bucket. "No friggin' mice for pets, all right, Daisy?"

"Yes, Mama," Daisy said obediently.

"Now get back to your chores and let me talk to Uncle Jehu in private."

Daisy left the barn. She walked across the yard to the outhouse, went inside, and closed the door behind her. This was the one place no one followed her. She was safe here, at least for a few minutes.

Inside in the dark with only the moon hole for light, Daisy crouched on the floor. She hugged her knees and rocked on her bare feet. Big tears rolled down her cheeks as she swayed back and forth rhythmically.

The baby mice were her friends. She loved them because they were her only friends. Now they were drowned in Mama's horse bucket and Daisy was alone again.

Eighteen

Mercy spotted Noah coming up the sidewalk in the dark and sighed with relief. She leaned on the front porch rail. "There you are, handsome. I was beginning to worry. Edgar made it home for supper two hours ago."

Noah came up the walk slowly, his head down, his face shadowed by his hat. He carried a bulging saddlebag flung over one shoulder.

Mercy knew right away that something was wrong. This was not the man who had left her kitchen this morning, practically doing a jig. She frowned. "What's wrong?" She met him at the steps. "More trouble with the thieves?"

He shook his head. "No."

"What then?" She pressed her hand to his chest as he reached the top porch step. "I couldn't hold supper because of the others, but I saved you something. Where have you been?"

He didn't kiss her hello.

"In town," he said.

"Town?"

"Twin Pianos." He stared at his boots.

Mercy stared at his boots as well. She didn't understand. Noah rarely ever stepped foot in saloons. What was wrong with him? What had happened?

She lifted her gaze to try to look him in the eyes, but his hat was pulled down too far. She did notice that he'd gotten a haircut, though. "A haircut!" she exclaimed.

"Goodness, let me see." She tried to lift off his hat, but he moved his head out of her way.

Mercy pulled back her hand as if she'd been slapped. "Noah, what's—"

"Mercy," Tinny interrupted from where he sat on his stool along the back wall of the porch. "Could you help me out with this here boot?"

She held up one finger. "Just a minute, Pap." She was upset now. Noah had left her so happy this morning. Their future had looked so bright. What had happened? Was he just in a bad mood or was there a problem between them that she wasn't aware of?

Mercy felt a sinking feeling in her chest. Surely he hadn't somehow found out about the pea patch? No, that was ridiculous, guilt on her part talking. He couldn't know about that. No one did.

"Noah, what is it?" she asked softly. This time she kept her hands to herself.

"It's late. What say—"

"Mercy," Tinny interrupted again. "I can't get my boot off. She's stuck like hog's glue."

Again, she held up one finger to her father. "I'll be there in just a second, Pap."

"I'm sorry," she said to Noah. "What were you saying?"

Noah scuffed one boot. "I was just saying it was late. We should talk tomorrow."

"No, I think we should talk tonight." Mercy bristled. She didn't know what was wrong, but she wanted to deal with it tonight. He couldn't do this to her. Not when he'd left here this morning with talk of marrying her and making a baby with her. It just wasn't fair and she wouldn't stand for it. "If you've just had a tough day, Noah, that's fine." She crossed her arms over her chest. "But if it's me. If it's a problem between the two of us, I think we need to—"

"Mercy, Daughter," Tinny said loudly. "I still can't get the boot off my foot. Will you help me?"

Mercy spun around. "Pap! I said I'd help you in just a minute. Can't you see I'm trying to have a conversation here?"

The minute she lashed out at her father, she regretted it. Tinny sank down on his stool and lowered his gaze like a small child who'd been chastised by his mother.

Mercy sighed. "I'm sorry, Papa," she said gently. "I didn't mean to snap at you." She left Noah and crossed the porch to her father. She went down on one knee, clasped his boot, and pulled. The old boot came off easily in her hand.

"Pap." She laid her hand on his bony knee. "I really am sorry." Out of the corner of her eye, she saw Noah cross the porch and go inside. She ignored him. "That was wrong of me and I apologize. It's just that I have so much to do and Noah's upset and I don't know why, and—"

Tinny's lower lip trembled. "Pshaw, it's all right, Daughter. I'm always needin' something." He pointed at the stool across the checkerboard from him. "Me and Joe, I know we're a burden to you, two old bachelors eating plenty but not bringing a cent in."

"No. No, it's not true." She took his hand and it felt so small and fragile in hers. Tinny seemed small and fragile perched on the stool. "You and Joe are no burden. I couldn't make this place run without the two of you. I couldn't raise Jacob without you."

Tinny shook his head. "It's not right, me getting in the way of you and your husband." He picked up his boots. "I should have kept my old mouth shut. Pulled off my own damned boot or slept in it, one or the other."

Mercy made no comment about his reference to her relationship with Noah. It was a waste of breath; no matter how she tried to reason with him, in his mind, Noah was her husband. And honestly, what did it matter what he thought? Who did he hurt?

"Please don't feel that way," she said, standing. She was so upset that she had to breathe deeply to fight tears. Couldn't she do anything right? She really was turning into a dried-up wasp of a woman, just like Jehu had accused. She was always correcting Jacob, snapping at her poor old half-witted father, driving off the man she loved with her pushy, demanding ways . . .

"I never did right by you, Mercy darlin'," Tinny said. "Left you when you were still a little girl. I wasn't there in Philly to help you bury your mama. I wasn't here for your weddin' day." He fluttered a shaky hand. "And now you work like an ox to keep a roof over me and Joe's head. It ain't right." Slowly, he rose off the stool.

Mercy put her arm around him to help him to the door. "I don't work so hard. And you and Joe put plenty of hours in a day. Pap, you shelled all those peas for me today. You went to McGregor's twice, and you hung all those sheets out on the line."

He hobbled into the front hall, his battered bollinger hat tucked under his arm. "Not enough."

Mercy rubbed his back. He acted so old tonight that it frightened her. She knew she wouldn't have her father with her forever, but she didn't think she could bear to lose him right now. Not with everything in her life so unsteady. "Pap, is your rheumatism bothering you tonight? Is that what's wrong, sweetie?"

"I'm all right." He pushed her hand away. "Just let me crawl into bed. You go back to your man and make things right. You shouldn't climb under the sheets angry with each other." He waggled a bony finger. "That was half the trouble with your mama and me. I spent too many nights tryin' to sleep on that fancy settee of hers in the parlor."

Mercy watched as her father slowly made his way into

the kitchen, headed for the short hall that ran from the pantry to the addition on the back. She wanted to follow him, but she also wanted to respect his wishes. She didn't want him to feel like he was any more of a burden than he already felt.

"Good night, Pap," she called after him. "You get a good night's sleep. I've got a whole list of chores for you and Joe tomorrow."

With a sigh she went to the stove and put on water for tea. Noah's saddlebags were on the kitchen table, so she guessed he must have gone out to the pump in the yard to wash up. From the still-warm oven she pulled the plate she'd saved for him and set it down on the table. She retrieved a fork and a knife and a jar of jam for his biscuits. On impulse she went into the dining room, retrieved the small pitcher of flowers she'd picked from her garden and placed them on the kitchen table. By the time Noah came in off the back porch she'd made a pot of tea.

"Here's your supper." She stood behind his chair. "I'm having tea. I'll keep you company while you eat."

He stood with his hat in his hand, making no move toward his dinner. His hair was damp where he'd splashed water on his face out at the pump. "Not hungry," he said.

"Fine." Angrily she snatched up the plate and walked over to the compost pail and dumped his supper on top of the turnip peelings. She didn't know what had possessed her to do such a thing. What an inexcusable waste of food.

"Don't worry," she said, slamming the plate in the sink. "No one's going to make you eat my food, outrider. No one's going to make you sleep between my sheets, either, if that's what you're worried about." She grabbed her teacup, walked to the table, and set it down so hard that the cup rattled on the saucer.

"Mercy." Noah sounded as if he were in pain.

"What?" She spun around, tears in her eyes. She hurt as much as he did. "What is it, Noah? Tell me, because I'm not a pie-eyed virgin." She fought her tears of anger and hurt. "Tell me. I don't have the time or the inclination for this nonsense."

He twisted the brim of his leather hat in both his hands and stared at her swept plank floor. "I think I might have made a mistake."

"A mistake?" she asked sharply.

"What I said." He spoke as if every word was gut-wrenching agony. "About marrying you."

Mercy felt the bottom fall out of her stomach. She pressed her lips tightly to keep from making a sound. "That was a mistake, was it?" she managed between her teeth.

"Yes. No . . . I don't know."

"Damn it, Noah!" She slapped her hand hard on the table. "What's going on? This morning you said you loved me." She knew she was shouting; the boarders might hear, but she was too angry to care. Too confused. Too hurt. "So tonight you *don't* love me?"

"No," he said quietly.

She wiped her stinging eyes with the back of her hand. This couldn't be happening. Why had she let herself get her hopes up? What had ever made her think he could love her? She gritted her teeth. *"No, you don't love me, or no, I'm not right. You do love me."*

He took a deep breath and exhaled with a shudder. "Mercy, it's not that simple."

She set her hands on her hips. "It's that simple," she said flatly. "Either you love me or you don't love me."

He groaned and ran his hand over the crown of his head, pushing back his clean, silky hair. "I love you," he whispered.

"I'm sorry, what was that?" She antagonistically cupped her hand over her ear. "I didn't quite get that, outrider."

"I love you," he said louder. "I just don't know if I can marry you."

She closed her eyes, flooded with relief. He did love her. She was right; her instincts were right. If she hadn't thought he loved her, she'd never have slept with him. As long as he loved her, and she loved him, they could make this work. She knew they could.

She opened her eyes, feeling calmer now. "All right." She picked up her steeping teapot and poured the hot tea into a cup. "Let me see if I understand this." She pulled out a kitchen chair that squeaked wood against wood. "You love me, but you don't think you can marry me." She sat down. "Because you can't marry me or because you don't want to?"

"Can't."

She put two lumps of brown sugar in the tea and stirred it with a spoon. "Can't why? Alice isn't really dead?"

"Damn it, Mercy can't you ever back down a little?"

She stared him square in the face.

He twisted his hat in his hand; soon it would be beyond repair. He sighed with resignation. "No. Of course she's dead. That . . . that's why. I can't—I have no right, not when . . ."

Mercy got it now. Guilt again. She lifted the tea cup to take a sip of the dark, sweet tea. "Noah, what happened today? And don't look at those damned boots of yours and tell me nothing." She waited.

He let a full minute of silence go by. "Something I saw," he finally said.

She rose out of her chair. "What?" She softened her voice as she took his hat from his hand and set it on the table. "Tell me."

He swallowed, his Adam's apple bobbing. "A funeral

procession." His voice cracked. "A woman. Her husband and children followed the hearse."

"Oh, Noah," Mercy breathed. She wrapped her arms around him and hugged him. "I'm so sorry." She brushed back his silky hair that she loved to feel beneath her fingertips. "But it's time to let go of those guilty feelings of yours. It's time to let go," she repeated softly. His new haircut made him look younger, less thin and drawn.

"You're right. It is guilt. You've made me so happy"—there was a catch in his voice again—"and I don't deserve to be happy."

"I love you," she said. "I want to be your wife. I want to spend the rest of my life with you, but you have to get over Alice and Becky's deaths. You have to forgive yourself to make room in your heart for me and Jacob and Tinny and that baby we talked about bringing into this world." She took a breath. "Otherwise, I can't marry you. Do you understand that?"

It was probably the hardest thing she'd ever had to say, but it had to be said. And she meant it.

"I'm so sorry." He took her hand and kissed her palm. "I want to feel forgiven. I want to marry you. I want Jacob and whatever children God's willing to bless us with. I just don't know where to find that forgiveness."

She glanced away. This idea of forgiveness was almost too close for comfort. She'd sure struggled with it, hadn't she? And she had done something a damned sight more serious to forgive than he did. "You just have to ask."

His brown eyes brimmed with tears. "Ask who?"

She shrugged. She didn't want him to think she was so foolish as to believe she knew all the answers. "I don't know. God. Alice and Becky. Yourself."

He lifted her hand and brushed it against his cheek. "I love you, Mercy. I mean it."

She gave him a bittersweet smile. "I know you do. And I love you." Then she slipped her hand from his. "Now, go on to bed. Your own," she added. "What you need is a good night's sleep. Things will look clearer to you in the morning." It wasn't that she didn't want to sleep in his arms, but she had to know where this relationship was going. "We can get through this, Noah. We can do it."

He picked up his hat. "I think you're right. I just need some more time. I was so happy this morning when I left here that I think it was too much for me."

"Guilt gland," she teased. "Generally stronger in women, but not unheard of in men."

He gave her a little smile. "I brought presents." He pointed to the saddlebags.

"Save them for tomorrow. Good night."

Noah walked away brushing his hand across her shoulders as he went.

"It's going to be all right," she assured him.

After Noah went to bed Mercy sat in her cozy kitchen, drank her tea, and prayed hard that she was right.

"Mama, the sheriff's here!" Jacob skipped across the backyard chattering like a magpie. "Edgar and me— Edgar and *I*—were playing checkers on the front porch and I was winning and then the sheriff came and said he needed to speak to Noah and Edgar said to come get Noah straight away." He never took a breath. "You know where he is?"

It was the first week of June and the Nevada noonday sun was bright and hot on Mercy's face, despite the shade of her broad-brimmed straw hat. Mercy had been hoeing corn before the heat got too unbearable. She stopped and mopped her brow with the back of her hand. "Whoa, whoa. Slow down there, partner." She leaned on her hoe, gazing at her son.

Jacob had really sprouted up this spring. He'd grown

taller and his face had become thinner. What little baby fat he'd had in his cheeks was gone. He didn't have the look of a little boy anymore; her baby had grown up. "Now start again. Who's here?"

"Sheriff Dawson," he said with exasperation. "He wants Noah."

"He's in the old horse barn trying to put that door back on its hinges." She could hear his hammer banging as she spoke. "I'll get him. You see if the sheriff wants some lemonade."

"Yes, Mama." Jacob took off across the yard, headed for the back porch.

Mercy leaned her rake against the side of the bathhouse and walked around the back. "Noah!" she called. "The sheriff's here to see you."

He turned and smiled. She smiled back. He'd been quiet at breakfast but not withdrawn, and he'd kissed her in the pantry after breakfast. Mercy knew he was struggling with the guilt he felt over the deaths of his family. He was trying to make things right. And if he had the guts to try, she figured it was her part to have the patience to let him.

"The sheriff?" He climbed down off a ladder. "What's he want?"

"I don't know." She covered her brow with her hand to gaze up at the repaired barn door. "Looks good. Will it hold horses?"

"Sure will."

"Positive?" she teased.

"Well, it's holding your horse."

"My horse?" She grimaced. "I don't have a horse."

"Sure you do."

As if in response, a horse nickered from inside the small four-stalled barn. Mercy stuck her head inside. "No, I don't have a—"

In the second stall, beside Noah's mount Sam, a dappled mare, munched oats from a manger.

She looked at Noah. "Where'd that horse come from?"

"It's mine." Noah thrust his hands into his pockets, obviously pleased with himself. "Now it's yours. A present for you, and for Jake."

She went into the barn, into the stall where the dapple stood and ran a hand over the mare's haunches. "Noah, she's beautiful, but I can't take such an expensive gift. Let me pay you for her."

"No. You can't because I didn't pay for her. She belonged to the dead thief, but the sheriff said she's mine now." He stepped into the shade of the barn. "If you'd rather have a different horse, I can sell her and buy you another."

"Oh, no." Mercy stroked the mare's dappled hide. She'd been curried, and even her mane and tail had been brushed. "She's beautiful. I just don't know that I should be accepting such expensive gifts from—"

"Your fiancé?" he asked, lifting an eyebrow.

She smiled. Everything really was going to be all right, wasn't it? "Jacob will be thrilled. He'll need help. He's only ridden astride a few times and that was just on one of Mary Cain's plow horses."

"I think that can be arranged. For you, I'd do anything." Noah stood two steps from her, seeming almost bashful.

Mercy laid her hand on his bare forearm. "We're going to do it, aren't we, Noah? We're going to be a family."

He leaned over, hands still in his pockets, and kissed her cheek. "I was up half the night thinking about what you said. About forgiveness." He sighed. "And you're right. You're absolutely right. It's time for me to give up this guilt. It's almost as if it's who I've become."

Mercy listened without comment because she knew that was what he needed right now.

"I know you must think I'm crazy acting one way one minute and another the next."

"I don't think you're crazy."

He brushed the silky wisps of hair out of her eyes. "It's just hard, Mercy."

"I understand."

"I think you do." He grinned.

Smiling back, she nodded toward the house. "Go see what the sheriff wants."

He tipped his hat. "Yes, ma'am."

Mercy went back to hoeing the corn, and a short time later Noah returned. "Everything all right?" she asked, clasping the hoe.

"The sheriff tracked down the thief's identity. His name was Albert Bear. He was a ranch hand."

She shook her head. She could tell by the look on Noah's face that he was thinking, thinking hard. "Never heard of him."

"He worked for your in-laws."

"Jehu?"

"Well, for the family. The way the sheriff sees it, he worked for the sister, Jezzy. He says she's the one who wears the pants in that family."

"He's probably right there. I never went out to the ranch much. Haman mostly went alone, but the few times I did go, Jezzy spoke and everyone jumped, ranch hands and brothers alike."

"The sheriff talked to her already. She says the ranch hand took off a few days ago, without even taking his last week's pay."

"Does the sheriff think he was the one responsible for the other robberies?"

"Could be, but the descriptions witnesses gave don't match. It's always a skinny man and a heavy one, but no one can agree on what color the big one's hair is. Sometimes he has dark hair, sometimes light. The one I saw had dark hair, but one of the witnesses swears he was blond. Their mounts change, too."

She rubbed her neck absently, mulling over the information. "In the middle of a robbery I imagine it's hard to get details right. If you think you might be shot and killed, you're not looking for the color of the masked man's hair."

"You're probably right."

"I'd say your description should be the one the sheriff relies on to catch the other thief."

"The sheriff's going to send out telegraphs to neighboring towns and check into other stagecoach robberies. Maybe he'll come up with something."

Mercy studied her corn stalks, half grown and stretching upward. "He's a good man, Sheriff Dawson. I know he'll do his best."

Noah glanced at the garden, then back at her. "Mercy, I have a question. I don't want you to take offense, but I want to know what you think."

"Yes?" She swept off her hat and ran her fingers along her damp scalp. It was getting hot out and she was glad she was just about done hoeing the corn.

"Mercy, do you think Jezzy and the brothers might have something to do with the stagecoach robberies?"

"Jezzy, a thief?" She laughed. "Jezzy Atkins is a lot of things—mean, bitchy, some say loose woman—but she's not a thief. Haman once said that when he was nine or ten he stole a peppermint stick from a store and Jezzy got furious. She told their father and he beat him within an inch of his life. The Atkins boys will lie, cheat, but they don't steal. It was the way their father brought them up."

Noah stroked his shaven chin. "Funny sense of right and wrong."

"I always thought so, too." She lifted her hoe to finish off the row, but Noah reached out and took it from her.

"Let me finish for you. Why don't you go in and have some lemonade before Edgar and Jacob drink it all."

"No." She took back the hoe, setting her jaw. "It's all right," she said firmly, but not unkindly. "I've got another foot to do. You go pour some lemonade and I'll meet you on the porch in a second."

He hesitated, but then gave in. "All right. But I'm expecting you in five minutes." He started to walk away, then turned back. "Mercy?"

"Yes?" She looked up from beneath the brim of her hat.

"You said some people say Jezzy Atkins is loose. Why's that?"

"The little girl," Mercy explained. "She's out of wedlock." She shrugged. "She came from somewhere."

"I see." He thought. "Anyone know who the father is?"

"No. And no one's ever said. Jehu never mentions it, either. Jezzy just showed up in town one day with a baby a few weeks old."

"No one knew she was expecting?"

Mercy shrugged. "How would anyone? No one ever sees her and even if they did, pregnancy is pretty easy to hide under a hoop crinoline, at least until the last few weeks. A woman without a husband who's pregnant isn't likely to walk around town, shouting it."

"You're right." He turned back for the house. "Meet you on the porch."

"Be right there."

Five minutes later, Mercy sat on the front porch step beside Noah sipping from a glass of lemonade. He'd not only gotten her the lemonade, but a cool rag to wipe her sweaty face and hands. He made her feel so good, so pampered. So loved.

Mercy sipped her lemonade and watched as a wagon rolled by, piled high with new lumber. There were several new store buildings and houses going up in town and there was always something to see from her front porch now.

Jacob sat on one of the stools at the checkerboard playing marathon games with Edgar. The boy chattered and the young man seemed to enjoy the company.

"Delicious," Mercy said. It felt good to get out of the sun and sip a cool drink.

He kissed her shoulder. "I was telling Jacob that in Carson City you can get lemonade frozen. We should go sometime. Stay overnight and see the sights."

"I'd like that. How about you, Jacob?"

"Sure! Can Edgar go, too? And Pap?"

Mercy frowned. "Where is Pap, Jacob?"

The little boy shrugged. "I don't know. I haven't seen him since breakfast."

Mercy looked at Noah, her concern growing by the second. "I haven't seen him, either."

"Me, either," Edgar offered. "Last I saw him he was wearing that hat of his, overalls cut off at the knees, and red wool socks." The young man nodded. "Looked ready for a little stroll."

Mercy stood. "Oh, no."

Jacob popped up off his stool. "Oh, no, Mama."

"What?" Noah sat on the step looking at the two in confusion. "What's wrong?"

"His traveling clothes," Mercy said.

Jacob snapped his fingers, swinging his hand. "Dang it! Pap's gone to California for gold again."

Nineteen

Noah squinted quizzically at Mercy. "Looking for gold?"

"Sure. He used to take off all the time. He'd either catch a stagecoach or just hitch a ride with someone, anyone, headed west." Mercy massaged one temple, trying to think. "Jacob, run down to the store and see if Mr. McGregor has seen your pap. Ask around town."

"Yes, ma'am." Jacob ran past her, sprang off the top step, and took off running down the street.

"What time did the coach go?" Mercy asked Noah calmly. She had to remain composed because hysterics would get her nowhere. She knew she'd find her father. She always did.

"The coach to Carson City would have left midmorning, but—"

Mercy snapped her fingers. "Oh, no. The new coach run that's passing through once a week."

Noah got to his feet. "Apparently it heads north along the lake and then west."

"That's it." She threw up her hands. "I bet he took that coach." She headed for the kitchen. "I *know* he did."

Noah followed her. "I still don't understand Tinny going for gold. What do you mean he's going for gold?"

Mercy pulled a clean flour sack from a bottom shelf in the pantry and began to pack food: some apples, some dried fruit, a paper envelope of tea leaves. "He thinks that he can just walk into California and pick up gold nuggets, off the street, I suppose."

Noah scratched his head. "I'm still not getting this."

"He wants gold," she explained. "To bring here. For me. For money. He wants to pay for his room and board. To help me out." She walked into the main kitchen and scooped up some leftover biscuits from breakfast. Back in the pantry alcove, she wrapped them in brown paper.

"He does this often?"

"Yes. For a while last fall, it seemed as if he was on every buckboard or stagecoach that rolled out of town. We were just glad the railroad hadn't come through yet. Then, over the winter, the idea seemed to slip away. Once in a while he tells me he's going, but he hasn't actually left town in months."

"And you're sure that's where he's gone? He's not visiting someone or playing checkers somewhere?"

"That's why I sent Jacob to check." She squatted and dug through an old wooden crate of assorted odds and ends and came out with two battered U.S. Army canteens that had been Haman's. "But I'd lay money he took that stagecoach. He was very upset about last night."

"I see. I guess I'm partially to blame then."

"Don't be ridiculous." She took the canteens to the water pump at the sink to rinse them out. "This is my fault. I made him feel as if he's a burden, and he's not." Her voice quivered and the canteen shook in her hands.

"Whoa, whoa. What are you doing here?" Noah took one of the canteens from her.

"Packing supplies."

"For what?"

"I'm going after him, of course. Can I borrow the dapple?" One canteen full of water now, she took the other back from him.

"Of course you can." He paused. "Wait a minute . . . no."

"No, I can't?" She went back to the pantry.

"No, you should stay here and let me go after him."

"This isn't your affair, Noah. He's my father. I chased him off. I have to go after him."

He laid a hand on her shoulder. "Mercy. You can't ride out alone after that stagecoach. The other bandit hasn't been found. It's not safe. Be reasonable."

"*You* be reasonable. I chased Pap off; I have to find him. If you were in my place, you'd do the same thing."

"I'm not saying someone shouldn't go after him. I'm saying *I* should do it."

"And what if he won't come home with you? What if he can't remember who you are, who he is? What then?" She shook her head, thrusting the supplies she'd gathered into the feed bag. Her mind was already made up and he wouldn't dissuade her. "No. I have to go. I can ride astride. I've done it before." She walked out into the kitchen and dropped the flour sack on the table.

"Mercy, this is ridiculous. I can't let you ride off alone."

She shrugged. "You can go if you like, I'm not going to sit here and do nothing." She started for the stairs, headed to change her clothes. "The only thing is, chances are we won't be back tonight. You have a stagecoach run to do tomorrow."

"It can wait." He followed her up the staircase, taking two steps at a time. "Edgar can stay here with Jacob, and I'll tell Cook that the money transportation might have to run a day late this week. If it doesn't suit him, he can hire someone else. Family's more important than money."

Mercy halted at the landing and caught Noah's hand. What he said about family made her feel good. It made her feel hopeful. "We'll find him, won't we?"

"Sure we will. He couldn't have gotten far."

She released his hand and started down the hall toward her room. "I'll meet you downstairs in five minutes."

"Five minutes."

* * *

A short time later, Mercy was astride the dapple mare, headed north toward Washoe Lake. Jacob discovered that no one in town had seen Tinny in hours, but the last time he had been spotted, he'd been chatting with the driver of the northbound coach. That was enough evidence to convince Mercy that her father had taken the coach.

Edgar agreed to stay with Jacob and even promised to whip something up to feed Mercy's boarders when they rolled in for supper that night. Having Edgar there was a great relief to her, and even though she had only known him a few days, she knew she could depend on him. Although Jacob was disappointed that he couldn't go with his mother and Noah in search of Tinny, the boy was consoled by the idea that he and Edgar would be in charge of the hotel while she was gone. When Mercy and Noah left them, they were sitting on the porch rail having a contest to see who could spit apple seeds the farthest. She knew her son would be in good hands.

"He'll be fine," Noah said, as if reading Mercy's mind.

She glanced up to see him watching her intently. "I know." She shifted the reins in her hands. The dapple mare was good-natured and the saddle she had come with was comfortable. Mercy was amazed at how easily she adapted to riding again. "It's just that I hadn't realized until I left that I've never been away from Jacob, not for more than a few hours. If we don't make it home tonight—"

"Which we probably won't," he warned gently, reining in beside her.

"Which we probably won't," she agreed. "Then this will be the first time I've ever slept away from him." She lifted one shoulder. "I know he'll be fine." She gave a little laugh. "He's probably tickled to have me gone. It just feels strange."

Noah reached out and rested one hand on her forearm. "Jacob will be fine with Edgar and we'll find your father. Probably at the next stop."

She smiled. "You're right."

For a while they rode in comfortable silence. She had dressed wisely in a loose white linen shirt with long sleeves to protect her arms, and an old brown calico skirt that was worn soft by years on the washboard. She had left her cage crinoline and her petticoat at home, wearing nothing but pantaloons and cotton stockings under her skirt. On her feet she wore an old pair of riding boots her mother had bought her when she was fifteen. Tied on her head was her wide-brimmed straw gardening hat that shaded both her face and the back of her neck.

Mercy knew she didn't look fashionable, but dressed like this, with plenty of water and foodstuffs packed in her bag, she could easily keep up with a more experienced rider such as Noah, for days, if necessary.

"You know," Mercy said after a while, "you and I are talking of marrying, and I don't know anything about you."

"Sure you do." He made a clicking sound between his teeth, urging his mount closer to hers. "You know me better than I know myself."

They rode side by side, following the same rutted path that, hopefully, Tinny had taken earlier in the day. There was no breeze and the air was hot as the inside of a baking oven. Occasionally a black-tailed jackrabbit or a kangaroo rat crossed the path ahead of them, but for the most part there was nothing but them, the rocky, rolling terrain of the foothills, and the clumps of silver sage.

Mercy smiled to herself at his comment. He was right, she did know him pretty well. She knew Noah Ericson was a bright, thoughtful man who was honest to a fault.

She knew he could be tender and understanding. He was a considerate, exciting lover. She also knew he had a temper that occasionally clouded his good judgment.

"I mean that I don't know about your past. Who you were before you became an outrider for the Nowhere Bank and moved into the Tin Roof Hotel."

His ran his hand over his horse's mane. "You know I had a wife named Alice and a daughter named Becky. I was a farmer, raised a few head of beef. Nothing complicated. Then I became a soldier—an officer in the Army. Nothing else to tell."

"What about before Alice and Becky? Where did you grow up? Whose child were you? You were an officer in the Army; you must have been schooled. What brought you to Nevada?"

He chuckled. "All right, all right. It's not that I have anything to hide. It's a boring tale. I grew up in St. Louis. No brothers or sisters. My parents were older when they had me. They were both schoolteachers. After I went to St. Louis University, I taught in a boarding school for a while."

Mercy laughed, slapping her knee. "You were a schoolmaster?"

"Black frock coat, mustache, and all." He took his canteen from his saddle and offered it to her. He seemed as amused by the mental picture as she was.

Mercy accepted the canteen and took a long drink. The water had already gotten warm, but it still tasted delicious, even better because it came from Noah's canteen. "I can't imagine," she teased.

"Neither could I." She handed him back the water, and he drank his fill, then returned the container to its place hanging on his saddle. "I taught because it was what my parents wanted me to do. After they died," he grew thoughtful, "I sold the house I grew up in and went west. I hired out to ride shotgun with a small wagon train.

Alice was headed west with her family." His gaze met hers. "You know the rest. I told you, a boring tale."

She smiled at him; she knew how to read him. He had loved his parents a great deal. He'd become a school-teacher so as not to disappoint them. When they died, he'd gone west because he felt lost. Alice gave him a direction. A purpose. He had loved Alice very much. "Thank you," she said softly.

"Look ahead." He nodded to the right, just off the path.

Mercy spotted two reddish-blond coyotes followed by two young coyotes as they loped through the sagebrush and desert grass. "Aren't they beautiful?" she whispered.

"Unusual to see them this time of day." He raised himself in his saddle to gaze across the horizon.

"See anything?"

"Nah." He settled back in his saddle. "I'd just rather be cautious than sorry."

"So what do you think we ought to do?" she asked. "Ride to the next stagecoach stop and see if anyone saw him there?"

He nodded. "Makes sense to me. There's a little town called Pottsville up on the northwest side of the lake. It's not much more than a crossroad, but I suspect the coach stopped there, at least for fresh horses."

They rode in silence again. As they approached the Washoe Lake and skirted it, Mercy knew what Noah had to be thinking about. His family. After a while, because he said nothing, she did. "It would be all right if we stopped," she said carefully.

He didn't glance her way.

"You said the homestead wasn't far from the lake. The little bit of time it would take us to go wouldn't make any difference in finding Tinny."

Still he was quiet. There were no sounds except for the clopping of the horses's feet and the squeak of saddle leather. "Noah," she started again She didn't want to push him, but if they were going to have a chance—if they were ever going to become a family, he had to leave his old family behind. It wasn't that Mercy wanted him to forget Alice and Becky, only that she wanted him to feel that he deserved her and Jacob.

"You need to go to their graves," she said quietly. "You need to say good-bye."

Noah worked his jaw, making no response and Mercy chose not to say anything more. A short time later, though, she was not surprised when they veered off the road that ran along the lake and headed directly west, taking a narrow, single wagon wheel-rutted path.

No more than two miles from the lake, Mercy realized they were approaching a homestead. There was a house with smoke coming from the chimney, a small barn, some corralling, and a shed, an outhouse, and a garden. The house appeared to be new.

"Someone must have bought the place," Noah said so softly that Mercy had to listen hard to hear him.

She rode beside him in silence.

A dog barked and a woman came out of the single room, one-story house, wiping her hands on her apron.

"Good afternoon," she said with a slight Scandinavian accent and a bright smile. She was young, perhaps only seventeen or eighteen, and large with child.

"Hello," Mercy said.

Noah reined in his horse and just sat, glancing around.

Because he didn't look as if he were going to say anything, Mercy took the initiative. "My elderly father apparently went for a ride and wandered away from home and we're looking for him. You haven't seen a man in cut-off overalls and a black wool hat with a chicken feather, have you?"

She shaded her eyes with her hand. Her dog sat obediently on one of her bare feet and panted. "No, sorry

to say I haven't. But please, climb down and have some
refreshment. I don't have much to offer but cold water
and some molasses biscuits, but you're welcome to them."
She indicated the house. "You're welcome to come in
out of the sun and rest."

"That's very kind of you, but I think just a drink for
ourselves and the horses, and we'd best be on our way.
My father's mind isn't quite what it used to be, and he
gets scared sometimes. We really need to find him."

Noah dismounted, catching the reins in his hand.
"Been here long?" he asked. He spoke slowly, as if in a
dream state.

"A year. My husband Lars and I married in Colorado
Springs and came west last spring," the young blonde
said proudly. "My name's Ingrid. Ingrid Criman."

The three walked toward the pump house near the
main house. "Pleased to meet you, Ingrid. I'm Mercy and
this is Noah."

"My husband rode to the neighbor's to fix a harness,"
Ingrid said, pumping the long pump handle. "He'll be
sorry he missed you. We don't see a lot of people pass
through here. Well, miners, but no one else."

Mercy splashed cold water on her face, and drank from
her cupped hands as the woman pumped water into a
small trough for the horses.

Noah stood beside Mercy, studying the house, the yard,
the outbuildings from beneath the rim of the beat-up
leather hat she'd come to love.

"You build the house?" Noah asked.

To the young woman, Mercy was sure it sounded like
an innocent enough question, a question a passerby
would make in friendly conversation. But to Mercy who
knew what had happened here, his words were chilling.

"We did. The outbuildings and all were here, but we
built the house ourselves. The old house had burned."

Ingrid's sun-bleached blond brows furrowed. "How'd you know?"

"Oh," the woman said after a moment. "The grave."

Mercy followed her gaze to the clump of piñons on a rise behind the house. "The family here before us was burnt out." She spoke with a genuine sadness, but sadness born of a tale told by someone else about someone else. The woman thought she understood, but she didn't. She couldn't possibly.

"I don't exactly know the story. I asked, but my Lars said it wasn't our business. Didn't concern us. Wasn't Indians, though." She caressed her round belly. "I wouldn't have stayed if it was Indians. Could have been a house fire for all we know."

Noah released Sam's reins and started up the hill toward the gravesite. Mercy left her horse at the pump and followed him. The young woman chattered as they walked.

"The Washoe Indians are peaceful enough. They come to trade. Lars says that if we respect them, they'll respect us. He says that's the whole problem in some of the other states and territories. He says people aren't respecting other people. It doesn't matter what color their skin is, white, black, red." She giggled. "Green. Lars says people deserve respect from other human beings as God's creatures. Made in His image."

They came to stand before the grave. There was a single mound as if the bodies had been buried in one hole, but there were three crosses. There was one large one, flanked by two smaller ones. All three were simply marked *Ericson* with the year *1865.*

Noah plucked off his leather gloves and went down on one knee in front of the larger of the crosses. His hand trembled as he ran his fingers through tiny white flowers that grew on the slightly mounded earth. "Three. Why are there three?" he asked. "There should be only two."

"A woman and two children, God bless their souls."

"There was only one child," Noah said without emotion. "One child."

"Did you know them?" Ingrid went on, thankfully not waiting for an answer. "All I know is that shortly after we started building, our neighbor came by and asked if he could put up the crosses. He said the husband was too grieved and that he'd promised to do it. He just hadn't gotten to it with all the work to do on his ranch. My Lars offered to do it for him. Ed helped put up the rafters on the house. It was the least Lars could do for him."

Mercy laid her hand on Noah's shoulder and he closed his eyes, seeming thankful for her touch. "Ingrid," Mercy said. "You mentioned molasses biscuits. I think maybe I am hungry. We'd love to buy some from you."

"Buy! Don't be silly." Ingrid started down the hill, her little brown dog at her heels. "You come right in and help yourself. Take some with you if you want."

Mercy walked back down the hill with Ingrid. If the young woman noticed that Noah remained at the gravesite, she gave no indication. She seemed so tickled to have female companionship that she either didn't notice or didn't care what Noah did. Mercy was thankful either way. This way Noah could have a little time alone with his family.

Inside the house, Mercy shared a biscuit with Ingrid, took two more with her because she wouldn't have it any other way, then met Noah back at the pump.

His face was pale, his lips pulled back tightly.

"You okay?" Mercy asked softly. She walked by him, brushing her hand across his chest.

"I'm okay." He took a breath. "Let's ride."

"We want to thank you for your hospitality," Mercy said as she mounted with Noah's help.

"I wish you could stay for supper, or at least long

enough to say hello to my Lars. He'll be sorry he missed you."

"We'd like that, but we really do have to ride on. I have to find my pap."

Noah climbed into his saddle, took his reins, and touched the brim of his hat. "Thank you, ma'am, for the water and the biscuits. You've been kind." His voice was gentle. Peaceful.

"You're welcome." Ingrid waved as they turned their horses around to head back toward Washoe Lake. "And if you ever pass by again, you stop."

"We will." Mercy smiled and waved. "You take care of yourself and that babe who's on its way."

Ingrid grinned, rubbing her belly again. "Don't worry, I will. Bye!"

"Good-bye."

Side by side Mercy and Noah rode off the land that had once been his, and east toward the lake again. Mercy wanted to say something, anything, but she kept quiet, trying to give Noah time. Finally, as they turned north again and the sun was beginning to set, he spoke.

"You were right," he said. "I should have come back long ago. I feel better."

"Good."

"When I was here before, there was just the grave mound. No markers. Ed, said he would take care of them. I couldn't. I just couldn't do it."

Mercy rode up beside Noah and took his gloved hand in hers. "I don't know that I could have done it, either."

He cocked his head in thought. "But what I don't understand is why there were three markers. There was just Alice and Becky."

"The woman's husband just made a mistake, I'm sure."

"I guess you're right."

"But we can go back, if you want. We could wait for

him and ask him ourselves. That, or ride to Ed's and you could ask him. Another hour won't make a difference."

Noah squeezed her hand. "It's not necessary. I said what needed to be said." He turned so that she could see his face in the fading light. "We need to find your father."

"You're sure?"

He nodded. "The markers don't really matter; they'll be gone in a few years anyway. What matters is that Alice and Becky will always be here." He tapped his chest over his heart. "Nope," he said with resignation. "I'm ready to move on, Mercy. I'm ready to be forgiven and move on."

She couldn't resist a smile. "You really mean that, don't you?"

"Sure do. Let's get married."

She chuckled. "Wait a minute. One thing at a time." She thought about her secret and wondered if she could marry Noah without telling him. She wasn't sure. She'd have to think about it. "We have to find Pap first, else who'll give me away?"

Noah brought her gloved hand to his mouth and kissed it. "You lead," he said gallantly. "And I'll follow. I'll follow you to the ends of the earth."

She pulled her hand from his, giving him a saucy look. "Just to Pottsville will be far enough for now."

"I said I'll take care of it, Jehu!"

Daisy, down on all fours, froze at the sound of her mother's sharp voice on the porch overhead. Daisy had been playing under the front porch, hiding there so no one could find her and hollar at her.

She was getting good at hiding. Some days she would stay under the porches all day and pretend they were rooms in a new house. She would pretend she had a new mama and a real papa and they were always nice to her.

Sometimes the big people like her uncle or her mama or one of the ranch hands found her and hollered at her more, but sometimes they just forgot about her. It was almost dark outside and Mama still hadn't hollered for Daisy *to get her ass in the kitchen or pay for it with a strip of hide.*

If Daisy was really lucky she could snitch a dry biscuit from the pantry and sneak into bed before anyone saw her. It was always a good day when she could hide all day and not be found.

At the sound of her mother's voice, Daisy dropped on her bottom on the dusty ground and sat up, pulling her knees in close to her body. It was hot under the porch and there were spiders, but it was still better under here than under her mother's feet. Even the rattlesnake Daisy had once discovered under the steps wasn't as scary as her mother could be.

"I said we can take care of it for you," Uncle Jehu said. "I owe him."

"No!"

"Aw, you never trust me to do nothin'."

Daisy listened. She could tell by her uncle's voice that he was mad, too. Her mother was always angry, but not Uncle Jehu. Daisy liked him. Well, she didn't really like him, but she liked him better than she liked her mother. Sometimes Uncle Jehu bounced her on his knee and told her about shooting the tail off rattlesnakes and coyotes and such. Funny stuff. And he never drowned her baby mice friends.

"Of course I don't trust you." Daisy's mother's boots hit hard on the planks overhead and little flakes of dirt fell through the cracks on Daisy's head. Daisy knew better than to move, though. If her mother found out she was spying on her, she'd beat her with the razor strap for sure.

"How can I trust you or the twin numb nuts? You never do anything right. And this isn't something I want mucked up."

Daisy had heard her mother mad a lot of times, but she didn't think she'd ever heard her this mad.

"What are you going to do?" Uncle Jehu asked. "You want me to help you out? Want me to go talk to that uppity Miss Mercy?"

"What, and warn them? No, I don't want you to help me!" Jezzy spat. "I just want you to do your work and stay the hell out of the way. You stay out of this, and everything will be just fine. No one will be any the wiser if Ericson meets his fate on the road to Carson City. Men die in robberies, you know."

"You going to kill him yourself?"

Daisy held her breath. She didn't know who Ericson was, but she felt sorry for him. So sorry that tears slipped down her cheeks. Mama killed Daisy's baby mice. Mama could kill a man, too.

"You get rid of the outrider, and Miss Mercy might come to my way of thinkin'," her uncle said like he was making big plans.

She heard him strike a match and knew he had to be lightin' one of those cigars of his. She wrinkled her nose as she smelled the stinky smoke and hoped she wouldn't cough.

"One thing at a time, Jehu. First the matter of Daisy, then we'll think about Jacob. We'll make a decision later. *I'll* make a decision later."

At the mention of her name, Daisy's stomach got upset. Why was her mama talking about her? What had to be settled?

Her mother and uncle walked down the steps and out into the yard and Daisy couldn't hear anything else. But something was up. Daisy knew it. If she sneaked around some more and listened hard, maybe she could find out what was happening and what it had to do with her.

When she was sure they were gone, Daisy dropped to her hands and knees and crawled fast. If she was quick and quiet, she might still be able to get into bed before anyone saw her.

Twenty

Mercy and Noah rode into the little town of Pottsville, that really was no more than a crossroad with a few buildings, just as the sun was setting over the Sierra Nevada mountains.

As they approached the crossing, Noah tapped Mercy's arm and pointed.

Mercy smiled.

There was her father, seated on a rain barrel outside a general store that served as Pottsville's post office as well as the stagecoach stop. Tinny Parker was dressed in his traveling clothes: the cut-off overalls and red long john shirt, with red wool socks and his hat with the chicken feather. Over his shoulder he carried a lumpy canvas bag. He was just sitting on the rain barrel swinging his feet when Mercy rode up.

"Evening, Pap."

He didn't look surprised to see her. " 'Evening, Mercy." He tipped his old hat. "Noah." He greeted them as if he was perched on the front porch of the hotel and they'd just returned from church or the store.

"What are you doing here, Pap?" Mercy swung out of the saddle. "I was worried about you."

"Pshaw." He waved his hand. "No need to worry about me. Me and Joe, we was headed west to Californ-i-a to get ourselves some gold. We was coming right back."

Mercy gazed up one side of the dirt street and down

the other. "So where's the stagecoach you rode out of Nowhere on?"

Tinny thrust out his lower lip. "Put us out on account we didn't have any money to pay our way. I promised to bring the driver a few nuggets of gold on my way home, but he wouldn't have it. Contrary old codger."

Mercy had to fight a smile. How old must the stage-coach driver have been for Tinny to call him old? Tinny would be seventy-six come his next birthday.

Tinny elbowed the air. "Joe here was right upset about the whole thing. Got to cryin' about wantin' to go home and play checkers. I said not to worry. I said my Mercy would be along directly. Her and that handsome husband of hers. The one who built the ark."

Mercy brushed her father's dry, paper-thin cheek with her hand and kissed it. He smelled of cigar smoke and home. "I'm glad you're safe, Pap."

"Of course I'm safe. Just forgot money," her father groused.

Mercy glanced at Noah as he dismounted. "So what do you think? Do we start back and camp out tonight? Pap can ride behind me; he doesn't weigh much more than Jacob. Or do you think we ought to sleep here for the night in the livery stable and start home in the morning?"

"Let me talk to the shopkeeper inside." Noah tied Sam to the hitching post. "I'd feel better not being out tonight with that bandit still on the loose."

Mercy wanted to get home to Jacob, but she knew Noah was probably right. "See what you can find out," she said, taking her hat off to wipe her brow. "I'll sit tight with Pap."

Tinny watched Noah walk inside. "I'm awful sorry to cause you worry, Mercy," he said, jumping down off the rain barrel.

"It's all right, Pap," she said. And she meant it.

"I know you think I'm a crazy old man." He dug into his sack and pulled out an apple.

"I don't think that."

"Sometimes it's just easier to let people think what they want." He cracked the apple in half and fed one half to each horse. His eyes narrowed and his wrinkled brow furrowed. "I don't really think your husband built an ark, you know."

A lump rose in Mercy's throat as she wondered just what he could remember and what he couldn't. She thought back to the night of the pea patch. Of course she'd never asked him about that night and he'd never spoken of it. Of course she'd keep his secret . . . until he rested peacefully in his own grave.

A few minutes later, Noah came out the door. "All settled. We'll sleep in the stable behind the store. It's clean and warm. In the morning we'll set out for home." He took his reins and the dapple's from Mercy.

"Come on, Pap." Mercy took her father's hand. "We're going to have an adventure tonight and sleep in the straw on the bedrolls I brought." Her father walked slowly beside her, his back hunched over.

"Won't that be fun?"

Tinny eyed her and Noah. "Be fine," he grumbled, "So long as the two of you don't keep me up all night with that bumpa-bumpa you young folks are so taken with." He shook his head. "Me and Joe, we hate it when that bed of yours bangs on the wall. Keeps us up half the night!"

Mercy took one look at Noah and burst into embarrassed laughter. Noah joined in.

"No bumpa-bumpa for you tonight, I guess," she whispered and waggled her finger at Noah.

Noah leaned over and bit down lightly on her fingertip. "Guess that means twice the bumpa-bumpa tomorrow night, eh?"

"Not until you pull the bed away from the wall!"
Noah was still laughing as they went into the barn.

A few days later, with life at the hotel back to normal,
Mercy sat on the back step and snapped string beans. It
was after nine and a lantern on the rail provided light
for her to work by. It had been an unusually hot day,
even for June in Nevada, and her entire body was damp
with perspiration. Her clothes stuck to her skin and made
her itchy everywhere.

"Evening, darling." Noah walked out onto the porch
and leaned over her.

Mercy lifted her chin and accepted the kiss he offered.
"Evening. I saved your supper."

It was good to have Noah home and see him smiling.
Since their return from Pottsville she had seen no more
of his gloomy side. Mercy didn't know what Noah had
said or thought at his family's grave, she didn't know if
she would ever know, but whatever it had been, it had
seemed to put him at peace. He honestly seemed to have
forgiven himself. Noah pulled off his hat and dropped it
on a stool. He sat down beside her on the top step. "Give
me some beans to snap," he said. "Where is everyone?"

"Already gone to bed." She passed him a handful of
beans from where she cradled them on her lap in her
apron. "What about Edgar?"

"Inside eating. He said he was turning in as soon as
he was done."

Mercy started to get up to see if Edgar needed anything, but Noah caught her arm. "He'll be fine. Sit and
rest. I imagine you've done the work of two women today."

She smiled and pressed her cheek to his shoulder for
a moment. How was it that he could always read her so

well? She had accomplished a lot today and she was bone tired. "How was your day? No bad men, I take it?"

"Nope." He snapped the ends off the beans and dropped them into the basket between her bare feet. "All was quiet. So quiet I'm beginning to wonder if our bandit moved on. Maybe having his partner get shot in the gullet was enough to scare him off."

Mercy wiped her forehead with the back of her hand, pushing back wisps of blond hair. "We can hope, can't we? I know you're careful, but I still worry. It's such a relief to hear you come in the door at night."

"Hey, don't worry about me," he boasted, taking another handful of string beans. "I've got Lucky Bucky riding with me, remember? We're invincible."

"Edgar is invincible, not you." She poked his side. "And I don't want anything happening to you, you understand? I want to marry you, have your babies, and grow old with you."

"Looks like that might be happening sooner rather than later." He pulled something from his pocket. "Look what I picked up at the post office for you." He waved a letter.

Her heart seemed to skip a beat. "What is it?" She knew what it was, of course. It was what she'd been waiting for. What they'd been waiting for.

"I don't know. Wasn't addressed to me, but it looks like something official." He held up the envelope to the lamplight as if he could see inside. "Something from the Army maybe."

Mercy snatched the envelope from him, spilling beans from her apron onto the step. "I can't believe you held on to that. Why didn't you give it to me?"

"I just got home!" He ducked as she swatted at him with the envelope.

Mercy sat on the step again and held the letter in her lap.

"Well," he asked. "Are you going to open it or not?"

She smoothed the envelope addressed in sprawling letters to Mrs. Haman Atkins. This was it. Haman's death certificate. With it in her possession, she'd have the legal right to the hotel. With the death certificate, she would have the legal right to remarry. So why couldn't she bring herself to open it? What was holding her back?

Mercy glanced in the direction of her garden. She couldn't see it in the darkness because there was no moon tonight. But she knew it was there. She could feel it.

"Mercy," Noah said gently. "Open it, sweetheart."

Mercy took a deep breath and ripped open the envelope. Sure enough, there was a letter expressing the government's sorrow for her husband's death, the praise for a soldier who fell in battle whose body was never recovered . . . and the death certificate.

It was finally over. Mercy was a widow. Haman Atkins was officially dead.

"So, you want to get hitched?" Noah asked.

Mercy laughed, afraid she might cry. "You sure you want to do this? We haven't known each other that long." She lowered her gaze to the letter and death certificate on her lap because she couldn't bear to look Noah in the eyes. "And there are things . . . something you don't know about me, Noah. Something that if you knew, you might not want to marry me."

"Don't be ridiculous." He took the mail from her, tucked it in her apron pocket, and clasped both of her hands, raising her to her feet. "I want to marry you because I love you. Tell me your secret if you like." He kissed her mouth. "Or don't tell me. Just swear to me that you'll marry me, Mercy Atkins, and make me the happiest man this side of the Ohio Valley."

She laughed, tears slipping down her cheeks. She didn't know what to say. After all the unhappiness of the years, it was so hard to believe everything could be so perfect. Somewhere in the back of her mind she couldn't help thinking that something would go wrong. Somehow she'd have to pay for her sin, wouldn't she?

"Now," he said, ushering her into the house, taking the lantern with them. "Are you ready for bed, because I am."

"Noah, I've still got the beans to snap and—"

He kissed her hard on the mouth, silencing her. "I brought you something else, too, but you have to go upstairs to have it."

"What?" She rested her hands on his shoulders, intrigued. "Tell me."

"Nope. Go up to bed, put on that pretty wispy thing I bought you and wait for me. I'll close up the house."

Mercy was already hot, but his words only made her hotter. She let go of his shoulders and stepped away. "All right, I'll go after I check on Jacob. Will you bring up a glass of water?"

"I'll do better than that," he said mysteriously with a wink.

Mercy went down the back hall to the room Jacob and Tinny shared and tiptoed inside. No matter how late it was at night or how tired she was, she always checked on her son before she went to bed. It had always made Haman angry. *"Jesus, God,"* he used to say. *"Ain't nobody going to snatch the little brat out of his bed."* Mercy knew he was right, but just the same, she couldn't sleep without being sure Jacob was there, tucked safely in bed.

Mercy leaned over her sleeping son and kissed his forehead. "Good night, Jake-for-my-sake," she whispered.

There was no sound in the room except Tinny's rattling snore.

Mercy slipped out of the room and closed the door soundlessly behind her.

Upstairs, she dressed for bed with nervous excitement.

Noah had something for her? What was it and why did she have to be dressed for bed to get it?

Mercy undressed, pulled her new sleeping gown over her head, and climbed into bed. Because it was so hot, she kicked back the bedcovers and waited on top of the sheet for Noah.

Minutes later, he slipped into her bedroom, barefoot, wearing nothing but tight blue denim jeans. "I'll be glad when we're married," he said. "I hate sneaking up and down the hall."

"If Pap knows what's going on here, I'm afraid to guess who else knows."

"Don't worry, we'll be wed soon and then it will make no difference to anyone." He held something behind his back.

She scooted over to make room for him in her bed. "What have you got?" she asked, leaning one way and then the other, trying to sneak a peek.

"Close your eyes."

She squeezed her eyes shut.

Noah set something on the table beside the bed, un-buttoned his denims, and dropped them on the floor.

A shiver of nervous excitement crept up Mercy's spine as she heard his pants hit the floor.

Noah blew out the only source of light in the room, an oil lamp. He eased onto the bed. "All right, lay back," he said.

"Noah." She laughed, but she did as he said because she trusted him completely.

"Mercy, you're so beautiful," he whispered, running his hand lightly over her. "You look so beautiful in this gown. More beautiful than I ever imagined."

She opened her eyes and they adjusted to the darkness. "I love it." She ran her hand over the gown at her breasts. "Even though I am a shameless hussy to accept such a gift from a man who's not my husband."

"A mere technicality." He pressed his mouth to hers. "Now close your eyes," he said against her lips.

She closed her eyes with a sigh. He tasted so good. His hand on her waist felt so good.

"You said earlier that you were hot," he whispered, his voice low and sensuous.

"Mmm hmm," she murmured, enjoying the little tremors he set off with his fingertips as they grazed her body.

"So I thought I'd cool you off." He moved and something clinked on the bedstand, a glass and something else. The sound was familiar, but she couldn't quite identify it.

She turned her head toward the sound. "How are you going to do that?" she whispered, enjoying the mystery.

"You'll see." He brought his mouth to hers and his lips were deliciously cold. He'd had a drink of cold water. But then he pressed his tongue to her lips and it was cold, too. She opened her mouth to his and it was as cold as an underground cave.

Mercy moaned at the sensation of her hot tongue touching his cold one, searching the cool cavern of his mouth.

"Like that?" he whispered.

"Mmm hmm," she sighed.

"How about this?" He moved in the bed. "Keep your eyes closed."

She heard the clink again and then he leaned over her. Next she felt the cold wet of his mouth on her nipple, right through the fabric.

Mercy moaned with a mixture of surprise and pleasure and arched her back, instinctively wanting more. More of his touch, more of his taste.

"Cold." She wiggled.

"Cold?" He lathed his tongue over her budding nipple and her flesh felt hot and goosebumpy at the same time. It was a delicious sensation.

"Cold and hot," she said. "What have you got—ice? Is McGregor's ice house done?"

"Done, and you have a new icebox on the way. Now, shhhh," he soothed. His voice was an oasis in the darkness and heat. "Relax."

Mercy settled back on the pillows and let herself float in sensation as Noah ran his hands over her belly, down her thighs, her calves, to her ankles. He massaged her feet with slow, circular motions and she moaned with pleasure. Who would have thought having one's feet rubbed could feel so good?

"They're probably dusty," she said.

"Shh."

Again, she relaxed. She'd certainly be willing to work as hard as she did today every day if it meant nights like this . . .

Noah slowly made his way back up her body, massaging, brushing, and licking. He rolled up her nightgown, slowly uncovering her flesh that was already quivering in anticipation. Again and again he sipped the cold water and then pressed his mouth to her prickly, hot skin.

As Noah came to the apex of her thighs, she unconsciously lifted her hips in anticipation. She met with his cold mouth and a colder lump between his lips. Ice.

Mercy moaned. Cold trickles of water ran down the soft folds of her hot, moist flesh, sending tremors of pleasure downward, toward her limbs.

It felt so deliciously good. Even a little naughty, maybe because it *did* feel so good.

"You like that?" Noah asked, drinking from the glass again. "Mercy love, Mercy darlin'?"

"Yes," she sighed. "Yes, but if you don't come here"— she put her arms out to him—"you're going to make me go mad."

He chuckled and lowered his hard, muscular body over her softer, more pliant one. "That's the idea, dear." He molded his hips to hers, rocking gently, persistently. "To make you mad with desire for me and only me."

"Only you." She lifted her head and kissed his mouth, her entire body quivering. *"Only you, Noah,"* she said passionately.

Again they kissed. They touched. Mercy explored Noah's body with her hands, with her own ice chips in her mouth. Then finally they joined as one and he lifted her again and again to peaks of pleasure she was just realizing could exist.

"Noah!" she called. "Noah."

"Mercy."

And finally they peaked as one, and drifted slowly back to the reality of their cool, damp sheets, and the hot Nevada night.

"I love you, Noah," Mercy whispered as she drifted off to sleep, cradled in his arms.

"I love you, Mercy," he answered, his voice fierce in the darkness.

"Married? You?" Edgar cackled and blushed.

Noah shifted in his saddle and sat a little taller. They had left Nowhere for Carson City half an hour ago and the stagecoach was rolling right on schedule. The sky was bright and clear, there was no sign of danger, and Noah was so happy that he had to watch himself to be sure he didn't start whistling or singing or something equally inappropriate for an outrider on duty. "Sure. Why can't I be a married man?"

"I don't know. You just seem set in your ways." Edgar rode beside Noah, his tone teasing. "An old outrider, bachelor like yourself."

"I'm not *that* old. And I wasn't always a bachelor."

"I know." Edgar cut his eyes at Noah. "But I'll tell you one thing—if you don't marry Mercy, I will! A woman as smart as she is and can bake biscuits, too. I know I wouldn't let her get away." He winked. "She's right pretty if I might say so."

Noah rode directly behind the stagecoach at an easy trot. "You'd best stay away from my woman, Edgar Cook, else no one will be calling you Lucky Bucky when I get through with you."

Edgar cackled louder as he fell in behind Noah. "You know I'm just giving you a hard time. I'm happy for you. Happy for you both, and I'd love to stand up with you when you marry."

Noah tipped his hat to shield his eyes from the sun, and grinned beneath its brim. Edgar hadn't been around long, but Noah felt as if he'd found a good friend in the young man. Sometimes Noah felt so much older than Edgar; those times it almost seemed as if Edgar was a son to him. At other times, when they talked about the war, or raising Jacob, they were equals. It felt good to have a friend; it made Noah feel lucky, rich beyond any monetary standards.

Mercy was right. Everything really *was* going to be all right. After his trip to his old homestead, Noah felt as if ghosts had been exhumed from inside him. He'd told Alice and Becky he was sorry and he'd asked for their forgiveness. He'd humbled himself and asked God for forgiveness. He'd ridden away from the homestead, his shoulders surprisingly lighter for the lifting of his burdens.

Noah knew he'd never forget Alice and Becky. He would never stop loving them in a tiny corner of his heart. But he knew now that he had room to love Mercy and Jacob and even Tinny. More importantly, he honestly believed he deserved their love.

"So when's the big day?" Edgar asked.

"We don't know yet. We were thinking—"

A loud pop, something akin to a snap, rent the air. A bullet ricocheted off the coach springs.

Gunfire.

"Edgar, look out!" Noah shouted as he reined left and reached for his rifle.

As his hand found the cold metal of the trigger, he caught movement over his shoulder. Noah turned his head, the motion seeming to take an eternity.

As he turned, he saw Lucky Bucky fall from his saddle, his chest flowered in blood.

Twenty-one

No, Noah screamed inside in his head. *No, not Edgar.*

He pulled hard on his reins and his horse danced around Edgar's still body. The young man stared sightlessly at the clear blue sky.

Dead. Edgar was dead.

Another shot ricocheted off the stagecoach, and Noah was shocked into response. Edgar was dead, but there was still old Clarence, the coach driver, and the woman and her two children inside the coach.

Noah sank his heels into Sam's flanks and dodged around the far side of the coach, now careening wildly down the road.

"Clarence? You all right?" he shouted up to the driver's box.

The old coach driver had come to his feet and was holding tightly to the reins, trying to get the spooked horses under control. "Mother Mary of God!" he cried. "Where's it coming from?"

Before Noah had the chance to respond, one of the four stagecoach horses was hit by the sniper's next bullet. The horse screamed in pain and went down. The three horses in the harness immediately became a tangled mass of hooves and leather traces. One horse broke free and ran while the other two went down. The stagecoach slid sideways, stopped when it reached the end of the traces, and flipped on its side under force of its own motion.

Clarence went flying through the air, his hat going one way and his body another.

Little girls screamed. Horses bayed.

The sniper kept firing.

It was Noah's worst nightmare.

"Clarence!" Noah shouted. He'd remained astride, but kept Sam moving. It was his only chance to avoid the sniper's shot.

"I'm all right! Here!" Clarence waved his old shotgun from behind the overturned stagecoach.

"The women?"

Little girls were still screaming, which was a good sign. Only the living could cry.

Another bullet whizzed by Noah, too close for comfort, and he made the decision to dismount. From behind the cover of the stagecoach, he might be able to pick off the sniper. He was almost certain from the shot pattern that there was only one.

Noah grabbed his ammo belt from his bag, leaped off Sam, and hit the ground running. Another bullet whizzed by and the horse galloped off. Noah dove for the ground behind the overturned stagecoach.

"Don't look much like a robbery, eh?" Clarence said, leaning against the top of the coach that was now the side.

"Nope. I'd say not." Noah reloaded his Winchester.

The little girls inside the coach had quieted. "Everyone all right in there?" Noah hollered.

"We're all right," came a woman's quivering voice.

"Good. Good. Now, you just stay put until we take care of this—"

Ping. Another shot silenced Noah. He kicked a hatbox and a carpetbag that had fallen off the roof and leaned on the shiny black wood of the coach's side. Two wheels still turned uselessly in the bright sunlight.

"Ah ha," Noah whispered. Just east of the road he spotted a single figure behind a clump of trees. At first Noah just saw the outline of his form, a tall, thin man in a hat, but the figure moved and he realized that the sniper wasn't a man at all, but a woman.

"What the hell?" Noah whispered.

The figure fired on them again and Noah ducked. The bullet lodged in the bottom of the stagecoach and there was movement inside the coach as the little girls no doubt huddled closer to their mother.

Noah started to raise his head again when a volley of shots sounded.

"Jesus!" Clarence called out, flattening himself on the ground. He had crawled forward to the two horses still tangled in the harnessing and was trying to set them free.

More shots sounded in rapid succession and the horses bolted, snapping the last of the thin strips of leather, and setting themselves free. The coach jumped forward a few inches as the horses took off, then it was still again.

Noah tried to get another look. What the hell was going on? Those last shots had come from a different angle. And there wasn't just one sniper now, there were two or three. He was beginning to wonder if this wasn't something personal rather than a random hold-up.

"What the hell do you boys think you're doing?" shouted the woman sniper.

The minute Noah heard the voice, he knew who it was. Jezzy Atkins.

"What are *we* doin'? What are *you* doin?" a male voice countered.

Noah peered over the side of the coach to see three figures on horseback partially obscured by an outcrop of rocks. All three were big men with shiny boots.

Of course! It came to Noah in an epiphany.

Of course it was the Atkins boys! They had been the bandits all along. Suddenly it made sense. The thief Noah had spotted had not been the same brother as the one the last coach driver had seen. That was why the descriptions were similar, but not the same. That was why they were having such a difficult time identifying the bandits. It had been *different* brothers holding up different stage-coaches with a ranch hand tossed in to confuse them further.

Noah couldn't believe he hadn't been able to figure it out before this. If Jezzy was the leader of the family, did that mean she had ordered the robberies? No one had ever seen a woman in the robberies.

He tried to think while surveying the situation. It didn't make sense that Jezzy would order the robberies, not with what Mercy had said about her being against stealing of any kind. And what was she arguing with her brothers about now?

Noah kept his head down and peered through the spokes of one of the wheels.

"Get the hell out of here!" Jezzy shouted furiously. "I told you I would take care of this!"

"I told *you* I could make it right," one of the men shouted. It had to be Jehu. "Why don't you ever let me do anything?"

"What the blue blazes is goin' on here?" Clarence asked, his back pressed to the roof of the overturned vehicle. "Are the thieves getting into a fight or is that just my confounded imagination?"

Noah watched the brothers and the sister carefully, trying to figure out what was going on. The brothers had been the robbers all along, but why was Jezzy here? Somehow he couldn't believe she'd been an accomplice all this time. And her attack had not been like the typical hold-up. She seemed to be out for blood.

"Hey, as long as they're fighting," Noah said, hoping to calm the older man, "they're not shooting at us."

Clarence nodded. "You got that right."

"Ride out!" Jezzy shouted to her brothers. "Before one of you gets hurt."

"What you gonna do?"

"What do you think I'm going to do?" She swung her rifle around and fired on the stagecoach. "I'm going to kill them."

"You let me do the shootin', me and the boys and you hightail it out of here before you get hurt," Jehu said.

As if to emphasize his intent, he fired off three shots at the stagecoach and the twins echoed with several more shots.

Clarence flinched and sank down. "I've had just about enough of this," he muttered.

"Shhh," Noah soothed. "With any luck, maybe they'll kill each other and we can walk out of here in one piece."

"Jesus God," Clarence muttered. "I knew I was gettin' too old for this nonsense. I knew I should have taken that job in the Carson City post office."

"It's all right," Noah assured him. "It's going to be all right."

"The hell it is!" Clarence plucked a shell from his coat pocket and loaded it into the single barrel of his old shotgun. "There's four of them, and only you and me and them scared little girls and their mama in there."

"Go home!" Jezzy shouted. "Go home and see to the fences, Jehu! Go home to Daisy."

"You ain't my boss!" her brother shouted back. "You think you're my boss, but you ain't."

Jehu's horse leaped forward and he sprang from the cover of the shale rock, riding straight for the stagecoach. Directly behind him, the other two brothers followed.

Noah had no time to do anything but react instinctively. He beaded in on the closest man and squeezed the trigger. The biggest of the brothers, Jehu fell from his horse.

Jezzy screamed and fired on them.

Clarence raised his old shotgun and fired, spraying the horsemen with pellets. Another man went down.

"Oh, Jesus! Oh, Jesus, Jezzy!" the last brother cried, circling the two fallen men. "Jezzy! Jezzy, help me! Help Ahab!"

Jehu moved on the ground and lifted his hand to his brother. "Pots, gimme a hand!"

Pots gave his brother his hand. The big man tried to climb into the saddle behind him, but he couldn't make it up.

Pots's horse danced as he shot his rifle in the direction of the stagecoach.

Noah fired his last shot and caught the man on the horse in the arm. Pots fell off the far side of the horse, and to Noah's disbelief, the injured Jehu took his brother's seat in the saddle.

"Jehu, what you doin'?" Pots blubbered. "Wait! You gotta help me and Ahab." He stood and turned in a circle, swinging his rifle.

Clarence fired again, and struck Pots in the leg this time. The man screamed in pain and fell.

Jehu sank his heels into the horse's flanks and the frightened horse bolted. "Ride, Jezzy!" Jehu shouted. "They're dead! Ride!"

Jezzy seemed to hesitate for only a second before she swung onto her horse in the cover of the trees.

Reloaded, Noah fired again, but it was too late. The two took off.

Clarence stood and fired again, his shotgun exploding with an ear-splitting boom. "You best run!" he shouted. "And you best not stop running until you hit Mexico!"

The moment they were out of firing range, Noah raced around the side of the stagecoach. He guessed Ahab was dead, but Pots's injuries didn't look as serious.

Pots lay stunned on the ground. He'd been hit in the arm and the leg.

Noah grabbed Pots's rifle off the ground and tossed it to Clarence. Next he pulled a piece of rope from his belt and tied the unconscious man's hands together.

"You check the other one," Noah told Clarence. "He looks dead to me, but check to be sure."

Noah ran for Edgar, still lying in the middle of the road forty feet behind the overturned stagecoach.

Reaching Edgar, he put his rifle down in the dirt, knelt, and lifted Edgar's head. The boy was dead. Gone. Jezzy's shot had hit him right in the heart.

"Oh, Bucky," Noah whispered, his eyes tearing up. "I'm sorry. So sorry."

He closed Edgar's eyes, laid him gently on the road again, picked up his weapon, and walked back to the stagecoach.

"Fat one's as dead as a run-over rat," Clarence said, approaching Noah.

Noah nodded. "All right. I don't think they'll be back, but you keep watch while I get the women out of the stagecoach." Noah leaped up onto the side of the coach and began to pry open the door.

"Then what?" Clarence asked.

"We round up the horses, we put these ladies astride, and we take our prisoner back to Nowhere," Noah answered grimly. "I know who the thieves are now and I know where the hell to find them."

"Are you shittin' me, Jehu?" Jezzy asked, stuffing her saddlebags with anything within reach in the pantry. She threw in biscuits, tin cans of fruits, beef jerky, and dried apple slices. "Don't you get it? We've got to hightail it out of here. They'll be here any minute looking for us." She shook her head. "Jesus H. Christ. I can't believe my own brothers would be robbing stagecoaches. I ought to hang you myself!"

Jehu wiped his sweaty forehead with the back of his hand, ignoring her comment about their thieving. "I'm serious about this, Jezzy. For once I'm serious."

"We haven't got time."

"You got what you wanted. I want what I want. I owe it to Haman," he finished fiercely.

"Jesus, Jehu." Jezzy nodded. She was trying not to think right now, just act. Their lives depended on it. Of course she couldn't hang Jehu. He was the only brother she had now. "You're bleeding all over the place. You better let me have a look at that."

He held his arm against his side. "I'll be fine." He glanced up at her. "Jezzy, I won't waver on this. If we're leaving Nevada, I ain't leaving without him."

"Ready, Mama," Daisy said, appearing in the pantry doorway. The little girl was dressed in long canvas pants, a shirt, and a little flannel coat. Over her back, she carried a little gunnysack with her own food supplies in it. She appeared completely ready, according to Jezzy's instructions. Then Jezzy realized the little twit only had one boot on.

"Where's the other boot?"

"Can't find it," Daisy whispered, cringing before Jezzy even responded.

"Well, you can't go with one boot. You only have one boot and I'm leaving your ass here." She wouldn't leave Daisy, of course. Daisy was the reason she did everything she did. She had killed for her Daisy and she'd do it again. But the child didn't know that, did she? Scare tactics always worked with little ones this age. "We're ridin' out in five, with or without you," Jezzy warned.

Daisy ran.

"Jezzy," Jehu said quietly. "I want you to do this for me. For us. For our family."

Jezzy spun around. She was as close to tears as she'd ever been. Haman was dead, Pots and Ahab dead. All she had left in this world was Jehu and Daisy . . . and that little part of Haman.

"All right," she conceded. "But if we're going to do it, we do it now, tonight. I want to put as much distance as possible between us and Nowhere from now till dawn."

"You won't be sorry," Jehu said.

Jezzy glanced at him over her shoulder. "No, you're wrong. I probably will be, but what the hell. Let's ride."

"They're comin'!" Pots cried, wiping at the big fat tears that ran down his cheeks. He was trying not to cry but he just couldn't help himself. Ahab was dead. His twin brother was dead. Ahab, the person he loved most in the world, was dead, and where were Jezzy and Jehu? Why didn't they come for him? Why didn't they explain that he never did any of the killing or robbing.

"They're not coming," Sheriff Dawson repeated without emotion.

"They are comin'." Pots sniffed and hung on to the jail cell bars. "They're comin' and they're going to get me out of here. I didn't do nothing wrong."

"They're not coming because they left you for dead, Pots," the sheriff said. "And robbing stagecoaches and killing people definitely rates in the 'something wrong' category."

"I didn't kill no one and it's not fair," Pots mumbled. "They left me and Ahab. They left us for dead. I wouldn't have left them. I wouldn't have done it."

"I'm telling you, Pots." The sheriff pulled up a stool. "You give us the whole story. The truth and the judge might be lenient with you. You said you didn't kill anyone, maybe—"

"I didn't kill no one. I swear I didn't. Everybody knows what a lousy shot I am." Again, against his will, the tears streamed down Pots's face. He'd been shot in the arm and the leg, and even though all the buckshot had been removed, his limbs still felt like they were on fire.

"Come on, Pots. Tell me what happened," the sheriff said all nice-like. "There's no sense in you protecting Jezzy and Jehu because they didn't try to protect you, did they?"

Pots fought a shuddering sob. "My arm hurts. It hurts like hell."

"You tell me a little about what's been going on at that ranch of yours and I might just be able to find a little whiskey to ease your pain."

Whiskey . . . Pots needed a drink. He needed it bad. And the sheriff was right, wasn't he? They had left him. They'd left Ahab dead on the road and they hadn't cared one lick, had they?

Pots wiped his eyes. "You'll get me whiskey? Now?"

"That could be arranged."

"All right." Pots gripped the iron bars. "They left me. What the hell do I care?" His gaze met Dawson's. "I'll tell, but I want the outrider. He's the one I want to talk to. He's the one I'll tell."

Twenty-two

"He wants *you?*" Mercy stood in the doorway of the front porch in the fading light, staring at Noah. Behind her she heard the faint sounds of men's voices as a dozen miners sat at the two tables in her dining room, enjoying one of her home-cooked meals.

Sheriff Dawson waited on the top porch step. He scuffed one boot and twitched his waxed mustache. "I can let you talk in private if you like," he told Noah.

Noah's hand rested on his gun holster. "Mercy, it's perfectly safe. Pots is behind bars."

Mercy fought the tears that burned the back of her eyelids. Edgar was dead because of the Atkins family. Dear Edgar, who had been so full of life this morning at breakfast, dead because of those bastards. She didn't want Noah near Pots. As far as she was concerned, Noah's duty was done; he had protected the banks' money. He'd saved lives. It was time for Sheriff Dawson to take over.

Mercy twisted a dishcloth in her hand and bit down on her lower lip. She didn't know how much the sheriff knew about her relationship with Noah, but obviously he knew something.

"Mercy, I need to go. I won't be long. You'll be fine here."

Mercy glanced at the sheriff. "Jack, will you give us a minute?"

"Sure," he said, glancing away bashfully. "Not a prob-

lem, like I said." He pointed in the direction of the jailhouse. "I need to get back anyway. I left my deputy with
the prisoner, but—"

"But you don't want any jailbreaks," Mercy said for
him.

Sheriff Dawson nodded, because of course that was on
his mind. It was on everyone's mind. Would Jezzy and
Jehu Atkins try to come back for their brother?

Mercy waited until the sheriff was out of earshot before
she spoke. "I don't want you to go," she said flatly. "Your
business with the Atkins boys— *Family,*" she corrected
herself, "is done. There's no need for you to go to the
jailhouse tonight. You belong here with us."

Noah swept off his hat and wiped his forehead with a
red handkerchief he pulled from his pocket. The sun had
set, but it was still hot. The air was still and hung heavy.
"Mercy, I haven't explained the whole situation to you.
There hasn't been time."

She stepped out onto the porch and let go of the
screen door. It slapped loudly behind her and blocked
out the miners' clinking plates and voices. Her nerves
were on edge. "*What* didn't you explain?"

He started to speak, exhaled, and then started again.
"What happened out there today—it wasn't a simple robbery."

Her throat constricted. It was bad enough that the At-
kinses were the ones responsible for the hold-ups and
deaths. Even though they weren't her blood kin, Mercy
felt a certain sense of guilt by association. She just wanted
this to be over now. Pots was in custody. The law would
catch up to Jezzy and Jehu, and justice would be served.

But Noah was saying there was more to it. He was saying
the situation was more complicated and she didn't want
to hear it. Still, she couldn't *not* hear it.

"What didn't you explain?" she repeated. "What do
you mean, it wasn't a robbery?" She snapped the dishrag

in the air. "They tried to rob the stagecoach. It over-turned. Edgar was killed. Ahab was killed, and Pots was captured. Jezzy and Jehu got away, but the sheriff will find them." She rattled off the events as if she'd read about them in the newspaper, as if they weren't people she knew, people who had sat at her own table. "They shot at you, but you're all right," she finished shakily. "Everything's going to be all right now."

He closed the gap between them and took her in his arms. "Everything *is* going to be all right," Noah said forcefully. "I'm fine. I wasn't hurt and I'm not going to be hurt. I just need to go down to the jailhouse and talk to Pots. For some reason, he won't talk to Dawson. He wants me."

Mercy clung to Noah's shoulders. He was hot and sweaty, but she didn't care. So was she. She held on tightly to him because she was afraid. She'd come so close to losing him today. "You didn't answer my question."

Noah smoothed her damp hair away from her face and looked into her eyes. "It wasn't a simple robbery, Mercy. It was just meant to look that way."

Her lower lip trembled. She didn't understand, but she didn't know that she wanted to.

"It was an ambush," he went on. "Jezzy meant to kill us all and take the money so that it looked like a robbery. The boys rode in later for some reason and joined in."

"Why?" Mercy whispered. She was afraid to say it, but she had to. "You? She wanted you?"

He lowered his head and pressed his cheek to hers. "The sheriff and I think so."

"But why?" she breathed, turning her head so that she could meet his gaze again. "Because of me? Because I said I wouldn't marry Jehu?"

"Jehu wanted you to marry him?" His dark eyes lit with anger. "You didn't tell me that."

She gave a little laugh that was born of nerves rather

than humor. "I didn't tell you because it wasn't worth the waste of my breath."

He spoke slowly, thinking. "It could have been about you, but that seems farfetched. It also could have been Jezzy, because a few weeks back, she made me an offer I didn't take her up on."

Mercy immediately knew what he meant. He didn't have to explain. Jezzy had made sexual advances toward Noah and he'd spurned her. Mercy knew she should have been shocked, but she wasn't. Touching Edgar's still face at the undertaker's had been enough shock for one day.

"That's so bizarre," she said. "Even for Jezzy."

"I think you're right, but we just don't know, Mercy." Noah kissed the tip of her nose. "That's why I need to talk to Pots. He knows why Jezzy did it and I'll bet he's willing to tell."

"So you have to go," she said softly.

"I need to go."

Mercy knew that Noah had to be thinking what she was thinking. Alice had asked him not to go. She had begged him to stay with her. Of course Mercy wasn't afraid for herself; she was afraid for Noah. This wasn't the same thing at all, but it had to feel similar to him.

"If I asked you to stay here tonight and not go, would you?" Mercy asked carefully.

He paused, his dark eyes searching hers. "I'll stay here with you tonight if you want. I'll send word to Dawson that Pots can wait until morning."

To Mercy's surprise she felt a smile turn up her mouth. "That's all I needed to hear. Go, and I'll fix you a late supper. It'll be ready when you get home."

"Do you ever think about anything but food?" he teased, breaking the tension.

She smiled, lifting her palms heavenward. "It's my job."

His gaze met hers again, his eyes twinkling. "You're

sure about this? I can stay if you want. I'll sit right on this porch with a rifle in my hands all night long if that's what you want, Mercy darlin'."

She laughed and stepped away, pushing him away. Her heart was still pounding but she knew she had to let him go. It was just a short walk to the jailhouse and back. Jezzy wouldn't try a jailbreak. Not tonight. Not even Jezzy had the guts to do that. "I wasn't worried about myself; I was worried about *you*," she explained. "But you're right, it's safe enough. Go on." She shooed him. "What do I need you hanging around here for anyway? I've got a table to clear." She waved him off again. "Go on, because the sooner you go, the sooner you'll be back." She gave him a sassy smile. "I love you, Noah."

"I love you," he answered.

She waved, and he was gone.

Inside, Mercy found Jacob sitting on a kitchen chair across from Tinny. They both just sat doing nothing, staring at nothing.

As Mercy passed her son, she brushed her hand over his shoulder. Jacob looked pale and drained and Mercy wished desperately that she could take his sadness away. It was what all mothers wished for their children, wasn't it? But she wouldn't trivialize his pain. She knew how much Edgar had meant to him, even if he had known him only a short time. "Did you eat something?" she asked.

He glanced up with sad eyes. "I ate a little, me and Pap."

For once, Mercy held her tongue and didn't correct her son's grammar. She walked to the sink to return to the pile of dirty dishes waiting for her. The men in the dining room were finishing up their meals. She could hear them talking about their day's work and the prospect of making a major silver strike.

"Do you feel like helping me out here, or would you

just like to turn in early?" Mercy asked Jacob. "I've got time to a read a little of *Robinson Crusoe*, if you like."

"If you need me, Mama," he said, his fatigue plain in his little voice, "I can help."

Her Jacob was trying to be strong, she knew. He was trying to be a man, or at least what he thought a man ought to be. Noah would be good for him. Noah was the first man she had ever known to cry.

Pap stretched and yawned. "I was thinking I might turn in early. Been a long, sad day."

Mercy glanced at her father. *Bless him,* she thought. Some people might say he was crazy and maybe he was, but he was also perceptive. He wasn't so crazy that he didn't know how to help his grandson when he needed him most.

"Pap's tired," Mercy said. "Would you mind helping him get into his nightshirt and lie down with him? I already laid out your red nightshirt. I could come in shortly and read to you." She leaned over Jacob's shoulder and whispered, "You know how he likes to be read to."

Jacob glanced up at his mother. "All right. I can do that."

She kissed the top of his head. "That's my boy. That's my Jake-for-my-sake." She walked back to the sink.

"Noah have to go back to the jail?" Jacob asked.

"I'm afraid so." She rinsed a dish and set it on the sideboard to dry.

"But he'll be home soon?"

"He'll be home soon," Mercy assured him. "And if you like, I can even send him in to tell you good night."

Jacob popped out of his chair. "As long as it's not too much bother."

"I'm sure it won't be."

Jacob took his grandfather's arm with one hand and the old man's hat with the other. "Come on, Pap, let's go."

Mercy watched from the corner of her eye as Jacob helped her father to his feet and slowly led him through the pantry and down the hall toward their room.

The miners finished up their meals, said their good nights, and excused themselves. Some went to their rooms in the hotel, while others left to go into town for a drink, or to head back to the mine.

After they were gone, Mercy cleared the table and went back to washing dishes. As she scrubbed, she kept thinking about Pots. She wondered what he had to say and why he needed to say it to Noah. She wondered if she should have gone to the jailhouse with him. After all, this could be about her, couldn't it? Jehu could have wanted Noah dead so that he could have Mercy.

She glanced at the door. Noah had been gone a good half an hour. Should she wait for him? It was what he wanted her to do, of course.

She glanced in the direction of the hall through the pantry. She could hear her father's gravelly voice and Jacob's higher pitched one as the two conversed, preparing for bed. They could certainly wait for their bedtime story long enough for her to run down to the jailhouse.

Of course Noah didn't need her. She was better to stay put.

Mercy's fingers found the ties of her apron and she whipped it off. "I'll be right back," she called down the hall.

"All right, Mama," came Jacob's voice.

Mercy didn't bother to grab her shoes or her bonnet. Before she knew it, she was at the jailhouse door and the sheriff was letting her in.

Noah glanced up at the sound of the door and his hand went instantly to his Colt.

"Just Mercy!" Jack Dawson hollered, probably guessing

rather than seeing Noah's reaction. They were both on edge, and probably would be all night.

Dawson had already put in a call for deputies and was in the middle of arranging a posse. He wanted some men to guard the jailhouse while others searched for Jezzy and Jehu. The sheriff wanted to get on the road before the trail got too cold. He'd already asked Noah if he'd be willing to lead the posse, as it was really his job as sheriff to stay with prisoners and protect the town.

Noah had said he would think about it.

Noah glanced through the hall into the main room to see Mercy coming through the door. She was red-cheeked and barefooted, her honey-blond hair spilling from the chignon that had been tight and neat this morning. He couldn't resist a smile. God, he loved her.

Noah glanced back at the prisoner and frowned.

Pots was busy cutting up a steak the size of a frying pan. He'd insisted on whiskey and a meal before he told what he had to tell.

Noah had tried to back out of having to stay. He just wanted to go home, climb into bed, and rest his weary muscles, with Mercy safe in his arms. But Pots Atkins would have no part of that plan. He said that if Jezzy and Jehu weren't coming for him, he wasn't taking the fall for them. He claimed he was innocent of any killing and mostly innocent of the robberies, and to Noah Ericson and no one else, would he tell his tale.

Noah wasn't sure what *mostly* innocent meant. He wondered, too, if Pots realized that the penalty for armed robbery, should he be found guilty, would likely be the same as the penalty for murder. Death by hanging. Nevada didn't take too kindly to stagecoach robberies, and hanging seemed to serve as a reasonable deterrent.

"What are you doing here?" Noah walked back into the main room of the jailhouse, his boot heels clicking on the rough plank floorboards.

Mercy was flustered, as if she'd run all the way there. "Well, I was going to use the excuse that I'd brought you and the sheriff supper." She opened her hands guiltily. "But I didn't think of that until I was halfway here, so I don't have any food."

Noah smiled. He was bone-tired, but right now a roll on Mercy Atkins's bed was an idea he couldn't shake. If he could get this confession out of Pots quickly, he might still have a chance of winding up there tonight.

"Jack, have you met my fiancé, the recently widowed Mercy Atkins?" Noah kissed her cheek as if they were still in the courting stage rather than the making love stage of their relationship.

Mercy's cheeks grew redder. She dipped a playful curtsy. "I believe the sheriff and I know each other well enough."

"Going to get married, eh?" The sheriff broke into a grin. "We figured as much. Just wondered when you'd make the announcement."

"We?" Mercy lifted a feather eyebrow.

"Sure. We—the whole town." Dawson smoothed the ends of his mustache. "We've been watching the whole romance from our front porches at night. We kept hoping someone like Ericson would come along. Everyone always thought you deserved better than Haman, so when Ericson did come along, we kept an eye on the two of you." He pretended to tip a hat he wasn't wearing. "We're mighty obliged to Tinny and Joe, playing checkers every night with the lamp lit. With our lamps out, we could always get a decent view."

Mercy squeezed her eyes shut, obviously embarrassed, but Noah just chuckled and put one arm around her waist. If they were caught they were caught, and what difference did it make? Noah intended to marry her and marry her soon.

"Don't worry." The sheriff reached for a tin cup of

coffee. "We never saw a thing indecent." He gave a wink. "Did get so we hated to miss a night, though."

"Hey, out there! You laughin' out there! Dawson!" Pots interrupted. "You find any biscuits? That there Mercy come to bring me biscuits?"

Mercy screwed up her mouth to make a retort, but her gaze met Noah's and she closed it. "Nothing I've got to say to him," she said quietly to Noah, "would be even close to being ladylike, so I'll not say anything at all."

"Smart woman." Noah squeezed her hand.

Dawson took a long drink of coffee before hitching up his gun belt and walking to the back. "No, we didn't get you any damned biscuits, Pots. You're lucky you're not eating hardtack with maggots. Now if you've completed your dining experience, we'd like to get on with the questioning. That is, unless you want dessert first."

"Dessert? You got apple pie out there?"

There was a loud bang from the jail cell as if the sheriff hit the bars with something.

"Je-sus!" Pots hollered. "You was the one who said it first."

"All right, Pots, are you ready to talk, because if you're not, Mr. Ericson is headed home for the night."

"No, no. I'm ready to talk, if you swear you're willin' to put in a good word for me with the judge."

"This shouldn't take long," Noah told Mercy. "You go home and wait now that there's been no jail break and you know I'm safe."

"I'd just as soon wait here if it's all right." She looked at him with her blue eyes so filled with tenderness and quiet strength that Noah couldn't say no.

"All right, but you shouldn't come inside. Sit here." He pulled the chair out behind Dawson's desk. "And you won't miss a thing."

Leaving Mercy in the main office, Noah walked back

to the jail cell where Pots was being held. It was the same cell the young thief had died in.

Noah hooked his thumbs in his jeans, wishing he didn't have to do this. He didn't want to hear about the Atkins family and whatever vendetta they had for Mercy or for him. He just wanted to go home. But if this would end it, Noah would sit through the confession, just to get it over with.

"All right," Noah said. "I got your steak and potatoes, I even got you the whiskey, now, let's hear it, Potipher."

"You swear you'll put in a good word for me?"

Pots pushed a forkful of potatoes into his mouth, and as grease dribbled down his chin, Noah lost his appetite. There would be no need for Mercy to fix him supper tonight.

"I'll do what I can," Noah grunted. "Now, start talking, because my patience is worn thin with you."

Pots grabbed the glass flask of whiskey and took a long pull. "You're sure they ain't coming for me?" His eyes became watery as if he were going to burst into tears.

"They're not coming for you."

Pots took another drink of the whiskey. "You want to know about the robberies, or about Jezzy, or you want to know about both, 'cause they's kind of connected a piece back. Kind of."

Noah swore under his breath. "Start from the beginning. Will that work?"

Pots screwed up his face. "The *way* beginning? Like three years back?"

Noah glanced at Sheriff Dawson. "The stagecoach robberies been going on that long?"

Dawson shook his head no.

Noah glared at Pots. "You're not making sense, but something tells me we're going to be piecing this story together anyway. So why don't you go ahead and get started, Pots, and we'll see if we can catch up."

The Atkins brother thrust a hunk of bloody steak into his mouth and talked between bites. "See, me and the boys, we'd ride around lookin' for a little fun. At first it was just shooting a cow or two, settin' fire to a barn or such. But Ahab, he always liked Injun women. Jehu, he liked 'em white." He took another bite of steak. "So sometimes we'd ride around, find us a 'vailable female, and . . . you know."

Noah's stomach did a flipflop. *You know?*

"You know." Pots avoided eye contact. "They'd have their way. Not me." He pointed to himself with the two-tined fork. " 'Cause I was always too chicken-shit. But the other two."

"You raped women?"

"Ahab and Jehu. Not a lot of women. I told you. And I told you, mostly Injuns. A few blackies. And just the one white woman. Then we'd take whatever they had that was good and ride off. We never hurt no one."

Something intangible crackled in the air and Noah felt the hair raise on the back of his neck. "Go back to the white woman," he said softly. He was getting an inexplicable feeling. A bad one.

"That's where Jezzy comes in." Pots motioned with the fork, potatoes hanging on the end. "See, she caught wind of what we was doin' and she followed us that day."

Noah stared through the bars at the big man straddling the stool, still eating steak and potatoes as he told of his crime spree. Noah's muscles tensed. He could feel his rage building with heat in his face.

Pots swallowed a big hunk of meat. "Well, Jezzy came up on us, seen what Jehu and Ahab done, and she went all crazy-like. She said they had to kill them because she could identify us. We usually wore bandannas, but Ahab forgot his."

"Them?" Dawson asked. "Go back. You said there was

one woman, but then you said your sister said you had to kill *them*. Who else did she say you had to kill?"

"There was just one woman and then the little girl. The boys didn't bother her none, but the girl saw us just the same."

"What happened then?" Noah said, feeling as if he were sleepwalking.

"Well, we wouldn't do it. See, us and Jezzy, we got different ideas. We don't like killin' much, but we never saw nothin' wrong with taking shit. Jezzy, she didn't think nothin' of pullin' a trigger." He licked his fork. "But you best not steal a pimple off a hog's ass and let Jezzy know about it."

Noah closed his eyes for a moment, trying to stay calm. If he lost his temper now, he would never hear the whole story. If he lost his temper, he'd kill the son of a bitch here and now and he'd never know what happened to Alice and Becky.

"Get on with the damned story," Dawson barked.

Pots nodded his head. "I'm gettin'. So we won't kill the woman and the little girl. But Jezzy does. She shot 'em in the head, takes the little baby, and tells us to burn the house down and make it look like maybe Injuns done it."

Noah suddenly felt as if the jailhouse walls were closing in around him. He couldn't breathe. He couldn't move. *"What baby?"*

"Well, the baby. The one in the cradle next to the fireplace."

An image of the house on the old homestead flashed through Noah's mind. He remembered the hooded cradle he'd built for Becky with his own hands. That cradle had remained at the hearth in anticipation of his and Alice's next child. "What happened next?" Noah clenched his fists.

"Nothin' happened. We burned down the house, went

home, and promised we wouldn't go to no more home-steads. Jezzy said the boys would have to stick to squaws and whores, or their own hands from then on."

"And the baby?"

Pots threw back the whiskey bottle and took another long pull. "Well, that's little Daisy, of course." He said it as if they were fools not to know it.

"And where was the homestead?" Noah knew the an-swer, but he had to hear it. He had to hear it out of Pots's own grease-coated lips.

Noah heard Mercy come to the doorway. He heard her hold her breath.

Pots screwed up his face. "Where?"

That was all Noah could take. He stepped forward, grabbed the iron bars and thrust his face as close to Pots's as possible. "Where?" he boomed. "Where was the home-stead you burned?"

Pots drew back, afraid. "Well, you know that. That's how we get to the stagecoach part with Jezzy."

"Humor me," Noah said thickly.

Pots scratched his head. "What?"

"Tell me!" Noah shouted through the bars.

Frightened, Pots came off the stool. "All right, all right. It was up off Washoe Lake. It was your old homestead."

Noah heard Mercy gasp. "Mine? My wife you raped and murdered? My daughter you murdered? My baby I never saw, you *kidnapped?*" He choked out the last word.

"Not me. I done told you that. Jezzy. She's really the bad seed of the bunch. Our pappy always said so."

Mercy appeared at Noah's side and firmly took his arm. "Daisy," she said, tears in her voice. "That's where Daisy came from."

"I'll be damned," Dawson swore. "So Jezzy found out who Ericson was and thought to kill him so he'd never find out about his daughter she took. But what about the stagecoach robberies?"

"That was us," Pots said excitedly. "We done that all on our own. Jezzy would never have let us take money from the stagecoaches."

Pots's words faded into background noise as what Pots had said settled over Noah. Images flashed in his head as he gripped the iron bars with one hand to steady himself.

He saw Jezzy's little daughter with her pigtails in the saloon. He saw Jezzy's daughter with her sad eyes. He saw Jezzy's daughter, afraid.

The truth fell over Noah like a shroud. These men had raped and murdered his family and taken his baby. They had his baby now.

The sudden shock of the reality hit Noah like a bullet in his gut. He flew at Pots, hitting the bars so hard that they rattled. "You son of a bitch," he shouted as he drew his pistol.

"Noah!" Mercy grabbed his arm.

"Now, Ericson," Dawson said. "You don't want to do anything crazy like that. If what he says is true—"

"It's true all right," Noah spat, so angry he was shaking.

"If it *is* true," Dawson repeated, "we need him for trial. Corpses don't testify, Ericson. They don't help you find kidnapped children."

The sheriff was right. Noah knew he was right. But it would have felt so good to put a bullet through Pots Atkins . . .

Noah slammed his gun into his holster and spun around.

"Where are you going?" Mercy hung on to his arm and ran to keep up with him.

"Now, Ericson, don't do anything crazy!" Dawson shouted after them.

"Where are you going?" Mercy repeated.

"Where do you think I'm going?" His gaze met and held hers. "I'm going to get my baby."

Twenty-three

She followed him out the door. "I'll go with you."

"No."

Noah stepped onto the sidewalk, his thoughts racing in a hundred directions at once. He knew there was little chance Jezzy was still at the ranch, but maybe he'd get lucky. She had to have gone back for the little girl, *his* little girl. Or maybe he'd get really lucky and Jezzy would have fled the state without her.

Either way, he had to get there fast.

But it would take too long to go to the livery stable for Sam. His gaze settled on the sheriff's horse. It was tied at the hitching post right in front of him. Dawson wouldn't mind if he borrowed his horse.

"I should go with you," Mercy insisted. She was concerned, but she wasn't dissolving into hysteria. Mercy was a strong woman. "Daisy . . . Your daughter knows me."

He began to untie Dawson's black gelding. "No, Mercy." Noah was firm because he knew he was right. "You have to stay here."

"But, Noah, I want to—"

"Mercy!" He let go of the bridle and grabbed both of her arms, forcing her to look him in the eyes.

Behind him, Noah heard Dawson coming through the jailhouse office, calling to him. "Don't you go off half cocked!" he shouted.

He ignored the sheriff. "Mercy," Noah said as gently

as he could under the circumstances, "I need you to stay here while I go for . . ." He couldn't bear to use the name. He would never have named a daughter Daisy. "My daughter," he finished. "I won't be able to ride safely if I'm worried about you. About *your* safety."

Mercy's eyes teared up. "I want to help you," she whispered.

"You can. I'm going to need a hell of a lot of help when I bring her home." Noah leaned over and kissed her hard on the mouth, trying to imprint the taste of her in his mind. "I love you," he said fiercely.

"I love you." Her voice quavered, but only a little. "I'll wait for you at the hotel. I'll wait for you both."

Noah let go of her, grabbed the reins, and vaulted onto the horse.

"Ericson!" Dawson shouted, running out of the jailhouse. "What the hell are you doing?"

Noah wheeled the horse around and headed out of town as if he'd never heard or seen Jack Dawson.

"You can't steal my horse!" Dawson shouted, waving his fist as he ran into the street. "For heaven's sake, Ericson! I'm the sheriff!"

It was only three, maybe four miles to the Atkins ranch from the little town of Nowhere, but it seemed to Noah that it was three hundred miles.

He knew there was little chance Jezzy was still there, or even that his daughter was still there, but he had to see for himself. And he had to see the place where she had been raised.

His daughter . . . Alice's child.

Noah recalled the last letter he had received from his wife. The one where she told him about Becky cutting her pigtails. Alice had said she had a surprise for him.

The surprise had been the baby, of course. She must have been conceived when Noah was home on leave.

It all made sense now. That was why there had been three crosses at the homestead. The neighbors had known there was a newborn. Everyone had assumed the child burned in the fire, and that there had been no remains. After Noah had returned and seen the grave, he'd been too grief-stricken to talk to the neighbors or get any details. Everyone must have just thought he knew about the baby.

Tears blurred Noah's eyes and he squeezed them shut for a moment. *His daughter.* He had to stay strong for his daughter. Alice and Becky were gone. There would be no second chance with them. But this daughter *was* a second chance, maybe his chance to truly be happy.

Noah rode into the barnyard of the Atkins ranch, scattering chickens as he galloped straight for the large, two-story frame ranch house.

There were no lights burning in the windows and the barnyard appeared empty. He rode right up to the front and dismounted onto the timber front steps. He threw the reins over the rail and raced across the open porch and in the front door, pistol drawn.

Inside the doorway, he halted, and waited for his eyes to adjust.

The house was silent. It felt empty.

He was in a large, high-ceilinged room where the walls were lined with great racks of antlers and the stuffed heads of various beasts: buffalo, elk, great-horned sheep.

"Hello!" He was almost certain no one was here, but he called out anyway, on the outside chance that there might be a little blond-haired girl hiding somewhere in the shadows. "Hello, is anyone here? I won't hurt you," he said in his best "daddy" voice.

Nothing.

Noah walked carefully through the great room, avoiding tripping over the shadowed forms of furniture. In the kitchen, he found embers still burning in a cast-iron stove. He lit an oil lamp he'd found on the fireplace mantel and continued his search through the house.

The little girl Jezzy Atkins called Daisy, his daughter, was only three. Noah expected to find toys throughout the house. His house, even as small as it had been, had always been scattered with Becky's corn husk dolls, leather balls, and bits of fabric that served as baby blankets and magic cloaks.

This house showed no signs of a child's presence. No toys. No small shawl at the back door next to the large coats. After searching several rooms, Noah began to wonder if he was in the wrong house. He wasn't, of course. The sign over the timber arch he had rode beneath had borne the Atkins family name and its brand mark.

But had his daughter really been raised in this house that was so grand and masculine and yet so devoid of warmth or any comforts for a child?

Noah opened the door to the downstairs sleeping room and went in. When he saw the trundle bed, hastily pushed only halfway under the larger poster bed, he was certain he'd made no mistake. This was where his daughter had slept. He knew it.

Noah picked up the corner of the log cabin pattern quilt and brought it to his nose. It smelled freshly washed, like sunshine and pigtails.

Again his eyes clouded with tears.

Then, as if a final confirmation, he spotted a tiny boot poking out from beneath the edge of the bed.

Noah picked up the boot with a hole in the center of the ball of the foot. He fought a sob.

One shoe.

It was the only real proof that his baby existed at all.

Slowly Noah walked back out into the room where he was surrounded by antlers and unseeing eyes. "I'll find you," he whispered, holding tightly to the boot. "Hang on sweetheart, Daddy's coming."

Mercy paced the kitchen floor, and when she thought she'd worn out the floorboards there, she paced the parlor floor. Where was Noah? She was going crazy with fear for him. What if Jehu and Jezzy had lain in wait and ambushed him again? What if he was lying dead or dying in the dark?

Mercy understood that Noah had to go after his daughter. She'd have done the same for Jacob in a heartbeat. God knew she'd have gone after *his* daughter if he'd let her. But Mercy couldn't bear the thought of losing Noah. Not now, not when it seemed that there was finally a chance for happiness for them both.

After Noah rode off on the sheriff's horse, Jack Dawson had cussed a blue streak and then sent word that he needed his deputies immediately. He wanted to send someone to give Noah a hand at the Atkins ranch. He couldn't leave his prisoner, with the possibility of a jailbreak, to go after Noah.

Mercy heard the sound of hoofbeats out front and she raced to the hall to peer out the front door. It was two men she didn't know, miners, no doubt.

She walked back to the kitchen. She had told Jacob she would read *Robinson Crusoe* to him tonight, but when she'd returned from the jailhouse, she'd been too agitated to read. She was afraid and upset and she didn't want Jacob to know it. The boy had enough to deal with today; he didn't need to be worried about his mama, too. When she'd listened at his door, all was quiet, so she'd known he was already asleep. She'd read an extra chapter tomorrow night.

So now she could do nothing but wait, and pray Noah and Daisy would come home safely.

Mercy went to the stove and put on hot water for tea. The kettle was just whistling when she heard Noah come up the front porch steps.

She ran to meet him and nearly collided with him in the front hall. "Was she there?"

Mercy knew the answer the moment she saw his taut face beneath the brim of his hat.

Noah shook his head.

"Oh, Noah. I'm sorry." She touched his sleeve. He looked vulnerable. Tired. Scared. "But we'll find her. We will."

"I know." He went into the kitchen. "I'll need food and the canteens. There was no one at the ranch. I found a couple of hands in the bunkhouse who said Jezzy and Jehu rode out with the little girl two to three hours ago. I'm riding after them. Tonight. I can't wait for dawn and Dawson's men."

She raced to the pantry and started grabbing whatever she could find that would give him nourishment on the trail. "But you're going to join the posse, right? You're not going to try anything foolish like a shoot-out with them on your own."

"The posse can catch up with me. I've got nothing against riding with them, I just won't wait for them." He tossed his hat onto the table. "Jake in bed?"

She nodded. She wished she could go with Noah. Of course she couldn't. She'd just hold him back. But she wished she could be with him, just the same. "He and Pap turned in hours ago."

"How's he doing?" Noah stood in the middle of the room, seeming to try to get his bearings. Talking about Jacob, about the family, seemed to calm him and give him direction. "How's he taking Edgar's death?"

Mercy stuffed biscuits into a little empty flour sack. "As well as can be expected. I'm still not sure he understands what death is yet. He didn't really know his father, so Haman's death never seemed real."

Noah nodded. "I'm going to kiss him good-bye, go up for some extra clothes, and then I've got to get Sam. Will you return the sheriff's horse for me?"

She dared a hint of a smile. "I can't believe you stole his horse."

She was relieved to see him smile back.

"I didn't steal it. Just borrowed it." He kissed her cheek as he passed her in the pantry. "I'll be right back."

Mercy threw the rest of the biscuits into the bag and tied it in a knot. She was just dropping it onto the table when she heard Noah call to her.

"Mercy?" His voice was sharp with tension. "Mercy, where's Jacob?"

She turned her head toward the pantry where the little hallway to the addition fed from. "In his bed. What do you mean, where is he?"

The moment the words came out of her mouth, an eerie feeling crept up her spine. "Jacob! Jacob!" she called.

Mercy raced through the pantry, down the hall, and shot through the bedroom doorway. "Jacob?"

Noah jerked the quilt out of the bed Tinny and Jacob shared. "He's not here."

She stood in the doorway, frozen in horror. Jacob was gone. Tinny was gone. There was no one in the room, only an empty bed and an open window.

"Oh, my God," Mercy whispered.

"Tinny!" Noah shouted. He rounded the bed and his gaze fell to the floor.

Mercy couldn't see what he was looking at, but she knew, she knew. "Pap!" she screamed as she grabbed the bedpost and swung around the foot of the bed.

Her father was lying on his back on the floor, his nightshirt tangled around his skinny thighs, his eyes closed. Blood trickled from a cut across his forehead.

Was he dead?

"He's all right," Noah said, surely knowing what she was thinking. "He's breathing."

Mercy and Noah kneeled at the same instant. Noah grabbed Tinny by the shoulders and lifted him to a seated position as gently as if he were an infant.

"Tinny, can you hear me?"

Tinny's eyelids fluttered.

"Pap?" Mercy took his bony hand and squeezed it. "Pap, honey, where's Jake? Where did Jacob go?"

Slowly Tinny opened his eyes.

"Pap?" Mercy's heart pounded in her chest and her mouth was so dry that the words would barely come out. "Pappy, you have to try and speak. Where's Jacob? Where's my son?"

Slowly Tinny's eyes focused. He looked at Noah and then at Mercy. "Gone," he said simply.

"Gone?" The word came like a croak from Mercy's throat.

"They took him."

"Who?" Mercy already knew who, but she had to hear it. She had to have proof.

"You know," Pap said, his voice fading in and out. "One of those fat Atkins boys. Hell, they all always looked the same to me. I don't know who."

"Jehu?" Mercy asked, attempting to sound calm so she wouldn't frighten her father any further. "Did Jehu take Jacob?"

Tinny nodded. "Him and the hussy woman, the sister."

"Jezzy?"

"That's her." He wiggled a finger. "Jezebel. Wrapped Jake up in a blanket and hauled him right out the window. The girl was the one that actually came in, 'cause the fat one couldn't fit through the window. I tried to stop 'em. Me and Joe both." His voice trembled. "That was when she hit me with the handle of her pistol. I don't remember nothin' after that."

Mercy's lower lip trembled as she turned her gaze on Noah. "Oh, my God, they took Jacob, too."

Noah reached out and grabbed her arm with his free hand. "Mercy, listen to me."

She stared, unseeing. "I was going to read *Robinson Crusoe,* but I didn't. I didn't come back to check on him."

"Mercy! You can't do this. You've got to keep yourself together so we can find them." He squeezed her arm. "We'll find them."

Mercy's mind spun, threatening to whirl out of control. Jacob gone? Her son? They took her son *and* Noah's daughter? How was it possible?

But Noah was right. She knew he was right. She couldn't waste precious energy or thought considering what she could have done or should have done. That served no purpose. She had to concentrate on getting the children back now. Both of them. If she wanted to, she could fall apart later, when they were both safely in her arms.

Mercy turned her gaze on her feeble father. "Pap, this is important." She already felt steadier as she worked up a plan in her mind. "Did you hear where they were going? Where did Jehu and Jezzy take Jacob?"

Tinny's forehead creased as he seemed to try to jog his memory. "West," he said. "To California. To California to find gold . . ."

Half an hour later, Mercy and Noah had tucked Tinny back into bed and gotten Mr. McGregor out of his bed to come sit with her father. Noah had retrieved his horse and saddled him. He returned to the kitchen to find Mercy dressed to ride, filling canteens of water.

Noah stood in the middle of her kitchen, hat in his hand.

She glanced at him. "I'm almost ready. Did you saddle the dapple for me?"

"I don't suppose I can convince you to stay here with Tinny and wait for me to bring the children home?"

She tossed him two canteens of water. "You suppose right." She grabbed the flour sacks of food and her homemade bedroll. She'd also packed pants and a shirt for Jacob. As far as she could figure, he was still in his red nightshirt, but his birthday boots were gone, so at least his feet were protected.

"Mercy—"

She threw up one hand. "You're wasting your breath, outrider," she said tersely. "As I see it, we've got two ways to do this. We can find our children together, or we can do it separately. I love you dearly, but I'll be damned if I'll sit here at my hearth and bake biscuits while a child of my womb is out there somewhere with those bastards." She pointed with one trembling finger.

"Mercy, Mercy." Noah grabbed her, food sacks and all, and pulled her into his arms. "It's all right. We'll go, you and me together." He kissed her forehead. "And no matter what happens, we'll have each other, all right?"

She searched his brown eyes for the strength she desperately needed. *"All right?"* he repeated firmly.

She closed her eyes for a moment. "All right," she breathed. "Together."

"Now let's go," he said. "Dawson said the posse won't leave until dawn at the earliest, so we'll go on our own. They'll be following our trail, but they'll be hours behind us."

She tossed one of the food sacks over her shoulder and reached for her bedroll, and Tinny's old rifle. "That's fine with me. No witnesses. That'll give me a chance to take the first shot at Jezzy Atkins."

Twenty-four

"Shut up, Daisy," Aunt Jezzy shouted, twisting in her saddle.

Jacob lowered his gaze so he wouldn't have to look at his hateful aunt.

"Shut up or I'll shut you up," Jezzy growled. "You hear me?" Then she turned back around.

Daisy, who rode in front of Jacob on the same horse whispered, "But I'm cold, Mama." This time she only said it loud enough for Jacob to hear.

"Shh," Jacob soothed. "It'll be all right. It's almost dawn, and then it will get warm again. I promise." He tightened his arms around her skinny waist and tried to pull her closer to his body for warmth. He didn't have to bother with the reins because Uncle Jehu had the horse on a lead line.

"It's going to be all right," Jacob said in a whisper. "Because my mama and Noah are going to come for us. You know Noah, the outrider?"

She shook her little head and her blond pigtails that stuck out from her head.

"You're going to like him. At first when you look at his face, you think he might be mean, but he's not," Jacob went on, hoping he could calm his cousin down by talking to her. He'd only ever seen Daisy a couple of times and never really talked to her because she was just a baby girl. But right now he knew it was his job to take care of her, to protect her until his mama got here and set Aunt Jezzy straight. "I love Noah and he's going to marry my mama, maybe, and be my papa since mine is dead."

"Don't have no papa," Daisy whispered. She had settled down in his arms and wasn't shivering so much.

"Well, maybe you could come live with us. Your mama don't act like she cares much for you anyway. You could live with us, and you could use my mama and Noah for your mama and papa. They're awful nice most of the time. Mama reads me big books and Noah plays checkers with me. Would you like that?"

"Do they let you have baby mice friends?" the little girl whispered.

Jacob thought for a minute. "Well, I don't know. I never had mice for friends, but I had a snake once. Mama hated him, but she let me keep him anyway. Just not in the house." Jacob held on to Daisy with one hand and began working on the hem of his nightshirt again. "So I guess you could have some baby mice. I can ask when we get home, if you want."

"I like baby mice friends," Daisy said.

Jacob tore another little piece of fabric off his nightshirt and dropped it. It fluttered out of his hand and into the darkness behind them. He had gotten the idea from a story his mother once read to him about someone leaving breadcrumbs to find their way. He didn't have breadcrumbs, so this was the best he could do. Hopefully Noah could track red pieces of nightshirt as well as someone could track breadcrumbs.

Jacob didn't know why his aunt and uncle had taken him out of his bed and brought him here, but he knew his mother and Noah would come for him. Jacob knew that his job right now was to be quiet and not make Aunt Jezzy and Uncle Jehu mad. Uncle Jehu was already in a bad mood because he was hurting bad and bleeding a lot, but Jacob was trying not to make him madder. Jacob just rode along, pretended he wasn't cold or embarrassed to be riding around in his nightshirt, and held on tightly to Daisy so she wouldn't fall off the horse.

Jacob didn't think he would like the little girl, but he did. She was tough like him. Tough enough so maybe he wouldn't mind her coming to live with them. He didn't want to tell Daisy and upset her or anything, but the way he figured it, Aunt Jezzy and Uncle Jehu were going to jail for taking him away.

Jacob kept his arm around Daisy as she leaned against him and drifted off to sleep. With his other hand, he worked on the torn tail of his nightshirt.

Little girls couldn't go to jail, so Daisy would be looking for a place to live. Jacob was sure his mama wouldn't mind having her. And he thought it might even be fun to have a little sister to play with, especially if she had pet baby mice.

"Is it another one?" Mercy lifted her reins and brought the dapple around, back to where Noah had stopped.

When they'd left town, the biggest question had been which way to go. Mercy thought they should head south for Carson City, but Noah believed Jezzy would want to stay away from any settlements. They had considered riding north, around the Washoe Lake, but ultimately, they had headed west. Noah said it was just a hunch, but he thought Tinny might be right. Mercy had thought they were both crazy. West to California, for gold? Jezzy was going to kidnap two children and then go gold-digging?

But Noah had insisted on riding west and it was at dawn's first light that they picked up the first piece of Jacob's red nightshirt and the Atkins's trail.

"Yeah. Looks like it." Noah dismounted and picked up another little piece of red fabric. "You've got one smart boy there, Mercy." Noah looked up at her from beneath the brim of his battered hat. He was grinning.

"He's bright all right. The question is, is he naked, too?"

Noah laughed and walked around a little, scuffing at the hard red earth. They had passed through the foothills and were now climbing into the mountains, following an old, dry riverbed. "We're catching up with them. This is the second place they've stopped since we picked up their trail." He ground his boot in the dirt. "And someone's bleeding."

Immediately Mercy's nerves became raw again. "Jehu, right? Jehu's got to be bleeding. You said he'd been hit."

Noah grabbed the horn of his saddle and swung up onto his horse. "It's Jehu's blood, all right."

"You're sure. You don't think one of the children—"

"Mercy, honey, just ride." He motioned with a gloved hand. "You can worry when your son and my daughter are safe. Right now, you just ride and you don't think and you don't feel."

Mercy urged her dapple into a trot, which was as fast as they could go now that they were in denser foliage and the trail was growing steeper. "That's what it takes to be an outrider?" she asked.

"That's what it takes. Let's go." He made a clicking sound between his teeth and urged Sam forward, past Mercy. The beating sun was almost dead overhead.

"Jesus H. Christ, Jehu, we can't keep stopping so you can get your frigging breath." Aunt Jezzy reined in her horse. "How much breath do you need, for shit's sake? You're riding a horse!"

The horse Jacob was riding stopped and started munching on some leaves on a tree. Sometime after dawn Aunt

Jezzy had taken his horse's lead line so now he rode behind her and not Jehu.

Uncle Jehu dismounted slowly with a groan, mumbling something.

"What?" Jezzy snapped.

He mumbled again.

"Again?" Jezzy flared. "Jesus H.! You're worse than a two-year-old. Daisy can hold her water, why can't you?"

" 'Cause I'm pissin' blood, all right, Jezzy?" Jehu whipped around and Jacob saw how white his face was except for where his cheeks were fiery red. Jehu was sick now. Sick and bleeding.

To Jacob's surprise, Aunt Jezzy didn't say anything else. Uncle Jehu walked slowly into the bushes.

"I gotta pee," Daisy said quietly.

Jezzy glanced over at them. "What?"

"Me, too," Jacob said, trying to be brave even though Aunt Jezzy's shouting scared him. "I got to pee, Auntie Jezzy. Daisy does, too. Awful bad."

"Fine." Aunt Jezzy threw her hands in the air. "Why don't we all take a break? Maybe I could fry up some bacon and make some biscuits and coffee. I suppose you'd like that, too."

Jacob was hungry, so hungry that his stomach was growling, but he wouldn't tell Aunt Jezzy so. He'd starve right to death or eat the saddle before he told her.

"Well, what are you waiting for?" Jezzy waved her hand. "Get off the horse and go take your piss!"

Jacob thought his aunt was going to help little Daisy down, but he guessed not.

Daisy looked at the ground that seemed a long way down, even to Jacob from up high on the big horse.

"I'll get down and help you," Jacob whispered in Daisy's ear.

The little girl nodded.

Jacob wiggled over in the saddle until he could position

himself right. This was going to be tricky with Daisy in his lap and the ground so far down.

He swung one leg over and flopped onto his belly, then slid down. He hit the ground with a plop and didn't even fall over. He quickly smoothed his red nightshirt, hoping his aunt didn't notice he'd torn a good bit off so that it hit above his knees now.

"Come on." Jacob waved his hand. "I won't let you fall," he told his cousin.

Daisy threw one leg over just as he had, and he caught her around the waist as she slid down. He meant to catch her in his arms, but she was slippery and heavier than he thought she would be.

Jacob hit the ground on his bottom and Daisy fell into his lap.

"Ouch," Jacob said, pushing her up and jumping up to rub his bottom.

"Ouch," Daisy echoed. She was wearing only one boot with just a sock on the other foot. Jacob wondered where the other one was, but he didn't ask.

"All right, hurry and go pee," Jacob whispered in her ear.

Daisy's eyes widened as she stared into the trees.

Jacob looked at his aunt who was drinking from her canteen and not paying a bit of attention to them. He looked back at Daisy.

"All right, I'll go with you and I'll just turn my back, all right."

"Just turn your back," Daisy said.

Jacob realized she was repeating everything he said. He guessed she'd been doing it for hours now. If she was going to do that all the time, he might have to reconsider letting her move into his house and letting her be his sister.

"Go on," he said.

Daisy walked into the trees, back in the direction they'd come. But then she didn't stop.

"I think that's far enough," Jacob said. He was really feeling dumb now, with it being broad daylight and him wearing nothing but his boots and his nightshirt.

Daisy kept walking, stocking foot and all.

"Where are you going?" he asked, running to catch up with her.

Daisy stuck out her lip. "Going to your house and get some baby mice."

Jacob glanced over his shoulder. He'd thought about trying to get away, but he hadn't wanted to leave Daisy behind and he didn't think she could run like he could.

"Daisy, I don't think your mama is going to like it if we just walk off."

She walked faster, swinging her little hands. She was wearing a hat now, one that looked just like Uncle Jehu's except that it was smaller. "Going to get baby mice," she repeated.

Jacob took one look over his shoulder in indecision and grabbed her hand. "All right," he whispered. "But let's run a ways. She'll know we're gone before long."

Hand in hand Jacob and Daisy started down the mountain they'd just rode up. Jacob didn't know what he'd do once he got down the mountain, but if Daisy was going, he was going.

Just as Jacob ducked a low-lying branch, he heard Jezzy calling Daisy's name. When she didn't answer, she called him.

Jacob tightened his grip on little Daisy's hand and ran faster. A minute later, he heard his aunt's voice louder, like she was closer and he heard hoofbeats. Now she was really mad.

* * *

"Did you hear that?" Mercy pulled up her horse and halted to listen.

"What?"

"Listen," she said softly. She rubbed the back of her sweaty neck with a handkerchief. "There." She fluttered the handkerchief. "Hear that?"

"Sounds like someone calling someone," Noah said, listening carefully.

Her gaze met his. They picked up another piece of Jacob's nightshirt not a hundred yards back. They were still on their trail and getting closer by the hour. "Sounds like a woman's voice to me."

"Jezzy," Noah said.

They both urged their mounts forward, up the mountain, watching, listening. The wind made a whispering sound in the trees, birds sang and squirrels and chipmunks scrambled through the underbrush, chattering.

Again, Mercy heard the voice. Loud. Angry. It had to be Jezzy.

"Let me go ahead," Noah said, lifting his rifle from where it hung on the saddle.

Mercy retrieved hers. It had been a while since she'd loaded and shot a rifle and she'd never shot this one, but if it came to Jacob's life, or the life of anyone she'd come to love, including Daisy's, she wouldn't hesitate to use it against Jezzy or Jehu. What would one more murder be on her conscience?

"Daisy Jezebel, you get your ass back here right now!" a voice shouted from up the mountain.

A second later, Mercy heard the sounds of something or someone running toward them, pushing through the weeds and low-lying branches on the path.

"Daisy! Jacob!" Jezzy shouted. She was still out of sight, but Mercy was certain she was coming right down the mountain at them. "I'll skin both of you alive, you little brats. Ask me if you can take a piss! You can hold it next time until we reach Baja!''

Mercy tightened her grip on her rifle, her blood pumping loudly in her ears. Her heart felt as if it were going to burst out of her chest.

Noah turned around and signaled for Mercy to be quiet.

She nodded.

Stay behind me, he signaled. *Stay back.*

She nodded again, but remained right behind him.

The sound of someone or something approaching became louder and closer. Was it Jacob? Had Jacob fled from Jezzy?

Mercy spotted a flash of red amidst the green pine needles and leafy foliage of the mountainside. Something red, running straight for her.

Twenty-five

"Noah!"

"Get back!" Noah shouted.

"No! It's Jacob!" Mercy kicked the dapple in the flanks and burst past Noah, startling him and his horse.

"Mercy!"

"Jacob! Jacob!" Mercy cried, riding straight up the mountain.

"Mercy, damn it, get back here!"

When the first shot sounded, Mercy had no idea what the noise was. It wasn't until the second explosion that it registered Jezzy was shooting at her or at Jacob, or at both of them. Her first instinct was to shoot back, to protect her child. But as the flash of red nightshirt became bigger and closer, Mercy knew she couldn't shoot back. What if she shot Jacob?

"Jacob!" Mercy screamed. "Get off the path! Run!"

The little boy appeared around a bend in the dry river bed just ahead. It *was* Jacob! And God love him, he was dragging a little blond pigtailed girl along behind him.

"Get off the path!"

"Mama!" Jacob hollered, obviously terrified. "Mama, help me!"

"Run!" Mercy screamed. "Run to Noah!"

"Mercy, turn around!" Noah called from right behind her.

"Pull up!" Mercy shouted at Jezzy as Jacob and Daisy

flew by her horse. "Pull up, Jezzy, or I'll shoot you off that goddamned horse!" Mercy threatened.

Jezzy appeared around the bend, headed straight down the mountain toward Mercy, rifle aimed.

"Jezzy!" Mercy screamed.

Jezzy pulled the trigger without warning.

Mercy acted on instinct, even before Jezzy fired. She reined hard to the left, straight into the dense under-brush. The dapple reared as it hit a pine branch. Mercy lost her balance and slid off the saddle, still clutching her rifle.

"Noah!" she screamed in warning as Jezzy fired an-other shot from her repeating rifle.

Mercy didn't know what happened next. She knew she was falling, and landed hard on an outcrop of rocks. An explosion of pain seared her thoughts as her head met the ground. And then there was nothing but blackness.

"Mercy!" Noah shouted. Everything was happening so fast, all at once, and yet in Noah's mind, he saw each event occur separately, in slow motion.

Jacob and Daisy ran by, unharmed.

Jezzy fired on Mercy before Noah could get in front of her.

When Mercy tried to ride off the path, her horse reared, and as another shot ricocheted through the air she fell before Noah could get to her.

Noah went crazy with fear and anger. Had Jezzy shot Mercy? Was she dead?

Still Jezzy rode straight for him, firing her rifle like a madwoman. He had no idea why she hadn't hit him yet.

Noah lowered his head, mad as a bull, and charged. He didn't even bother to return her fire. Death by gun-shot was too easy for Jezebel Atkins. He wanted to hurt her; he wanted to see her suffer. He wanted to see her suffer as he had suffered, as Mercy might be suffering now.

Noah's thoughts ran wild and unconnected as he barreled up the mountain. *Take his children? Kidnap the daughter he never knew he had? Take his Jacob who was not of his flesh but who he'd come to love? Jacob who loved him, when he hadn't believed he was worth loving?*

He'd skin the bitch. He'd scalp her. He'd boil her in oil. He'd rip out her fingernails one by one and make her eat them . . .

Jezzy screamed in surprise as Noah rode straight into her. She tried to shoot him, but by then it was too late. He was too close. Noah let his rifle fall and yanked her out of her saddle with both hands.

The two tumbled off their horses. Jezzy's rifle flew out of her hands as they hit the ground with a jolt.

Jezzy reached out with both hands and grabbed hanks of his hair, screaming as if she were possessed.

"Hanging isn't good enough for you," Noah raged as he rolled over on the rocky path to pin her down. "You killed my family! You took my baby." Tears filled his eyes as he pinned her down and grabbed his pistol from his holster. "You took the baby I never knew I had!"

"Go ahead!" Jezzy screamed. "Kill me. Kill me now! Haman's dead. Ahab's dead, Pots is dead, and Jehu'll be dead by nightfall." Tears streamed down her face and her red hair stuck out in fiendish spikes. "I got no reason to live, outrider!"

"Pots isn't dead!" he shouted. "How the hell you think I figured it all out, Jezzy? Your brother ratted on you."

"Liar! Son-of-a-bitch liar!"

Noah cocked the hammer of his Colt .45 and pressed it to her temple. He was still so angry that his vision was clouded by a haze of fury. He wanted to see Jezzy dead. He wanted to see the bullet wound in her brain and see her bleed out onto the ground.

"Go ahead!" Jezzy screamed. "Kill me!"

Noah hesitated. He heard someone behind him. "Is that what you really want?" he heard Mercy say softly.

Keeping Jezzy pinned beneath him, Noah glanced over his shoulder. Thank God Mercy was all right.

Her hand closed over his shoulder. Behind him, Jacob and his little girl cried softly.

"If you really want to kill her, I'll understand," Mercy continued quietly. "Kill her if you want, but let me take the children down the mountain first. They shouldn't see this."

The steady pressure on his shoulder and the tone of Mercy's voice made the tears well in his eyes again. He loved Mercy. He loved her so much.

And he hated Jezzy Atkins.

Noah focused his gaze on Jezzy again. He wanted to kill her.

Didn't he?

But slowly his anger ebbed. Mercy and the children were safe. He didn't need to kill Jezzy.

No. He didn't *want* to kill her. He didn't want revenge. He wanted to see her pay for her crimes, for the murder of Alice and Becky. He wanted to see her pay for the kidnapping of his infant daughter. But he wanted to leave her punishment up to the courts. She wasn't worth his trouble, or another blot on his conscience.

Noah eased back the hammer.

When Jezzy realized what he was doing, she began to buck wildly under him. "No. No!" she screamed, spit and hair flying. "Do it! You take my baby, I got nothing to live for. Kill me now or give me the gun and I'll do it myself!"

Noah kept her arms pinned down with his knees and returned his gun to its holster. He took a pair of the handcuffs Dawson had given him, rolled her over face-down, and handcuffed her wrists together behind her. "Get up," he said.

"Fu—"

Noah grabbed her by the arms and hauled her to her feet. "Keep your filthy mouth shut, you hear me?" He whispered through gritted teeth as he dragged her toward a tree. "I won't have foul language around my children."

He lashed her, handcuffed, to the tree. "Where's Jehu?"

"I don't know!" she spat, nose running.

He grabbed her shoulder and shook her. She crumbled to the ground, her spirit broken. "Up the mountain. Dead, by now," she sobbed.

Noah turned to see Mercy a hundred feet away, kneeled in the center of the path, a child in each arm.

"You all right?" he hollered. "I've got to find Jehu."

"We're all right!" She waved him away, tears wet on her face.

Noah didn't have to hike far up the path to find Jehu, seated on the ground, leaning against a rock, dead, eyes open wide.

Noah closed his eyelids, thinking what a pity it was for a man to die this way. Alone, a murderer, a thief. He'd have Dawson's deputies, who couldn't be far behind them, take Jehu's body back to Nowhere for burial.

Noah went back down the mountain to join his family. He found Mercy still kneeling on the path, embracing both children.

"You were so smart," she said to Jacob. "We followed you right up the mountain with all those pieces of your nightshirt."

She turned to Daisy. "And you ran so fast. I thought that was lightning that went by me!" She hugged the little girl. Noah's little girl.

Noah reached them and halted, suddenly feeling shy. What was he going to say to his daughter now that he had her? How could he possibly explain to a three-year-old how much he loved her, even though he hadn't known she existed a day ago?

"Noah, I have someone I want you to meet," Mercy said, God bless her. "This is Daisy."

Noah's gaze settled on Mercy's sweet face. Her cheeks were wet with tears and blood trickled from her temple down her jaw. She hadn't been hit by Jezzy's bullet. She'd just been struck with a rock on the way down.

"Pleased to meet you." Noah squatted between Jacob and Daisy and offered his hand.

The little girl stuck out her tiny hand hesitantly and Noah kissed it. He closed his eyes. It was warm and soft, and she smelled something like Becky had smelled.

Jacob pulled away from his mother and threw his arms around Noah, almost knocking him over. "I knew you'd come for me, Noah! I knew you would. I told Daisy you'd come for us."

"Of course I came for you." Noah put both arms around the boy and squeezed him tightly. His warm body felt so good in his arms. He felt like home.

"Oh," Jacob said, thrusting back his shoulders. "I've got something important to talk to you about."

"That right?" Noah stayed where he was between the two children. He didn't hug Daisy because he didn't want to frighten her. For now, just being close to her was enough. There would be time for hugs and kisses later when she knew him better, when she understood who he was.

"Can it wait, Jake?" Mercy asked, standing, looking a little shaky.

"Don't think so, Mama." Jacob took the little girl's hand. "See, me and Daisy—"

"Daisy and I," Mercy corrected.

Jacob grinned. "Daisy and *I*, we were wondering if maybe she could come live with us, seeing as how I figure you-know-who is going to jail." He cast a disapproving look in Jezzy Atkins' direction.

Mercy glanced up at Noah, smiling. "I think that could be arranged. What do you think, Noah?"

He walked up beside his Mercy and put his arm around her shoulders. He was so damned proud of her, proud of Jacob, proud of his daughter. "I think we could use another girl around the house."

Daisy cupped her hand around Jacob's ear and whispered. Jacob whispered back, then turned to his mother. "One thing, though, she needs to know what you think about baby mice. If you like 'em?"

Mercy burst into laughter. "Baby mice?"

Jacob wrinkled his nose. "I'll explain it to you later, Mama." He tugged on Daisy's hand. "Don't you worry, we'll find you some baby mice."

Little Daisy looked up at Jacob and for the first time, Noah saw a smile light up his daughter's elfin face. "Baby mice friends," she whispered.

"Good night," Mercy whispered.

"Good night," Noah echoed.

Mercy pushed Noah through the bedroom door and closed it behind her. "You can't stand there all night and look at her, she'll never go to sleep," she chastised gently, taking him by the hand.

"You certain Tinny doesn't mind? Two children in his bed?"

Mercy led him down the hall, through the pantry, and into the kitchen. "He doesn't mind. He said Joe could sleep on the floor." She laughed, feeling joy from her toes to the top of her head.

"It really is going to be all right, isn't it?" Noah said softly, taking her in his arms so that they could gaze into each other's eyes. "Jezzy and Pots are in jail. The other

Atkins boys are dead and buried. I have my daughter, and you have your son. Together I think we could make a pretty nice family." He brushed his lips against hers, his voice low and sensual. "If you're willing to have me as your husband, that is."

Dead and buried. Noah's words echoed in Mercy's head. She couldn't bear to look him in the eyes, so she stared at a spot on his clean denim shirt. "More like if you're willing to have me."

"Mercy, Mercy mine," he whispered. He caught her chin with his finger and lifted it so that she was forced to meet his gaze. "What is it?"

"I told you I had a secret," she breathed, fighting tears. All of a sudden she was afraid, afraid this newfound happiness was fleeting. "I thought maybe I could just not tell you. Not bring you into it, but . . ."

"But?" he urged gently.

His arms felt so good around her waist and his voice was so gentle and understanding that it gave her the courage to tell him her awful secret.

"But I have to tell you," she said bravely. "And after I tell you, if you don't want to marry me, I'll understand."

"Not want to marry you?" He kissed her again. "Mercy, nothing you could tell me could make me not want to marry you. Nothing could make me stop loving you."

Mercy trembled. She didn't want to lose Noah, but she couldn't not be truthful with him, either. "I have to show you something," she said.

"All right."

She took his hand and led him out onto the back porch, into the yard in the darkness. Noah walked beside her.

She halted at the edge of her garden. A full moon cast long beams of bright light at her feet, illuminating the pea patch. The plants were dead now, withered by the

Nevada heat. She'd just not had time to pull them up yet. "This," she said.

"This? You want to show me your garden?"

She let go of his hand. She wouldn't cry. She hadn't cried that night. She wouldn't cry now. "The peas."

"Mercy, love." His dark-brown eyes pleaded. "You're going to have to give me a little help here."

She bit down on her lower lip. "The pea patch," she whispered. "It's where he's buried."

He never even flinched. "Who?"

Noah's tone was so devoid of judgment that Mercy would be grateful to him for the rest of her life for it.

"Haman."

"You buried Haman here?"

She wrapped her arms around her waist, trembling. "Yes."

"When?"

" 'Sixty-four."

"How'd he get here, Mercy? I thought he was off fighting the war."

"He was supposed to be," she said in a tiny voice. "But he came home absent without leave. He came home in the middle of the night. He was awful drunk, Noah. He . . ." She took a deep, shuddering breath and went on. "He came home drunk and he hit me. When I resisted his advances, he . . . he tried to rape me. He pulled out his Army issue pistol and he said he was going to blow my brains all over the wall so Jacob could see them in the morning."

"I'm so sorry, Mercy," Noah breathed.

He reached out to take her arm, but she pulled away. She didn't want him to touch her, not yet, not before she got it all out.

He seemed to understand. "So that was when you shot him? Sweetheart, that's self-defense."

Mercy shook her head. "No. I . . . I didn't do it."

Noah waited in the moonlight, his handsome face drawn with the pain he felt for her. "Who did, then?"

She stared at the shriveled pea plants. "Pap," she said simply. "Pap heard the commotion and came to my defense. He shot and he killed Haman right in the hall."

"Oh, Mercy."

This time she let him wrap her tightly in his arms and kiss the top of her head. "Mercy, Mercy, sweetheart, why didn't you tell me a long time ago?"

Tears streamed down her face. She just couldn't stop them. It was almost as if she was crying now for what had happened that night. "Pap doesn't even remember it. I— I had to bury Haman. I had to hide it, else they would have put Pap in jail."

"Shh, shh," he soothed, smoothing her wind-blown hair. "It's all right. It's all right."

"I knew it was wrong," she sobbed. "But I couldn't see Papa go to jail. I couldn't tell Jacob what his father was, what he tried to do."

"Shh." Noah brushed her tears with his palm and kissed her trembling lips. "It's all right, Mercy."

Her gaze met his. "Do you think I should tell Sheriff Dawson?"

Noah thought a moment. "No."

"No?"

He took her hand and led her back across the yard. "No, I don't think you should tell because it would serve no purpose. The Army has declared him dead; you're a widow free and legal. Let Jacob believe his father was a war hero." Noah sat down on the porch step and pulled her down onto his lap. "The way I see it, you did Haman Atkins a favor, burying him out in the pea patch, hiding his shame."

Mercy laughed and brushed away her tears. "You don't think I'm a bad person?"

He pulled her tightly against him, back to his chest.

"No," he whispered in her ear. "I think you're a good mother, and a good daughter, and if you'll have me, I think you'll be an even better wife."

Mercy turned in his arms and lifted her chin to receive his kiss. "I love you, outrider," she whispered passionately.

"I love you, Mercy. And I'm glad you're mine." He grinned. "I've needed Mercy for a long, long time."

Epilogue

Three Years Later

With her hand, Mercy shaded her eyes from the bright noonday sun. "Alison, please tell your brother it's time to put down the fishing rod and come have something to eat."

"He won't listen." Six-year-old blond, pigtailed Alison shook her head in exasperation. There was no remnant of the shy, frightened Daisy Atkins she once had been. "He and Papa are having a contest to see who can catch the most fish. Pap's counting." She turned up her pretty nose. "You know how they are, Mama. *Men.*"

Mercy knelt to unload the picnic basket, chuckling. "Just go tell all of our *men* that the fried chicken is waiting."

"Yes, ma'am." Alison skipped away, swinging a stick and singing as she went.

A minute later, Noah appeared. "Supper ready? I'm starved." He plopped himself down on the blue quilt she'd laid beneath the willow tree. It was the same willow tree beneath which they'd celebrated Jacob's seventh birthday.

"Did you forget something?" Mercy lifted an eyebrow.

He stretched out and grabbed a chicken leg from the plate Mercy had unwrapped. "What's that?"

"The children? My father?"

"Eh, they'll be along. Jake challenged Alison to a fishing duel and I guess she's taken him up on it. Tinny and Joe are overseeing the fairness of the contest." He waved the fried chicken. "You know you won't get her off that bank until she wins now."

As he waved the chicken past her again, Mercy took a bite.

"Hey!" he protested. "That's my chicken."

Mercy pressed her hands to his chest and gave him a push. "Yours? And who fried it up?"

"You," he conceded. He finished the chicken and tossed the bone, licking his fingers. "And fine chicken it is. Best fried chicken in Nevada."

She handed him a glass jar of fresh lemonade.

He lifted the jar in salute. "Best lemonade, too."

She laughed and leaned over to kiss him. He tasted of sour lemons, sweet sugar, and the sunshine of the May day. "Actually, it's nice to be alone for a few minutes," she said, lowering her tone sensually. "It seems as if we never have enough time alone these days."

Noah stretched out on his back and pulled her over him. *"Feels* nice to be alone." He lifted his hips to meet hers.

"You are shameless!" Mercy protested.

They both laughed and she pressed her mouth to his again. "But I love it just the same."

"What's this?" Noah lifted the necklace of fresh flowers she wore around her neck.

Mercy brushed her hand over the loose-link chain of daisies. "Alison made it for me. Isn't it pretty?"

He smiled and brushed back her honey-blond hair, looking up into Mercy's eyes. "She's so happy, Mercy," he said softly. "You wouldn't have thought it could have happened, but it's almost as if she's become someone else. I don't think she remembers Jezzy or any of them."

"Shh," Mercy whispered, pressing her finger to his lips.

"No need to speak of the dead. But you're right; that part of her life is gone. I think changing her name was a good idea. It helped her leave that old life behind."

He kissed her finger that still rested on his lips. "I think having a loving mother like you did it."

"And a loving father."

Noah grinned. "We make a good team."

She grinned back. "You've got that right, outrider."

Their lips met and Mercy felt the same thrill she had felt the very first time Noah kissed her. In fact, the pleasure was stronger, more intense, because of the family ties that now bound them.

The year after Daisy-turned-Alison joined them and Mercy and Noah were married had been a difficult one, but it had only made their love for each other stronger. Pots and Jezzy both stood trial. Pots was sentenced to a prison term because he had played minor parts in the robberies and committed no murders. He later committed suicide. Jezzy was sentenced to hanging for the murders she'd committed. In many ways the sentence had been difficult for Mercy. On one hand, she was glad to be rid of the woman and her evil ways, but in another it was hard to see anyone die.

The Atkins ranch was given to Jacob as the only living relative of the family, and Noah and her son now spent a great deal of time there, running it. Mercy's hotel continued to profit, and even though the money was no longer necessary with their income from the ranch, she refused to give it up.

She moaned softly as Noah lifted his hand to caress her breast. He always knew just how to touch her. He knew how to touch her body and her heart.

But just as their kiss deepened, the baby wailed from his basket beneath the willow tree.

"So much for being alone," Noah said, pulling back and rolling his eyes.

Mercy laughed as their three-month-old son wailed louder. "He's possessive of his property."

Noah buried his face in the cleft between her two voluptuous breasts. "His property? I don't think so. These are just loaned out and he'd better keep that in mind."

Laughing, Mercy rolled off him and started to rise to retrieve the hungry baby.

"No, let me get him," Noah said. "You sit and rest."

Mercy sat at the tree's trunk and began to unbutton her dress. "Rest? Do I look so haggard that I need rest?"

"No," Noah said, scooping up his crying son and jiggling him gently. "I just want you to get a little rest for tonight."

"Tonight?" She reached out for the baby.

"Tonight." He winked. "When I can have you all to myself." As the baby nuzzled her breast, Noah leaned over and kissed her on the mouth.

She glanced up. "That a promise, outrider?"

He grinned beneath the brim of his battered hat, his dark eyes twinkling with the undying love she knew he felt for her. "You bet."

ABOUT THE AUTHOR

Colleen Faulkner lives with her family in southern Delaware and is the daughter of bestselling historical romance author Judith French. Colleen is the author of twenty Zebra historical romances and is currently working on her twenty-first, which will be published in February, 2000. She loves to hear from readers and you may write to her c/o Zebra Books. Please include a self-addressed stamped envelope if you wish a response.

BOOK YOUR PLACE ON OUR WEBSITE AND MAKE THE READING CONNECTION!

We've created a customized website just for our very special readers, where you can get the inside scoop on everything that's going on with Zebra, Pinnacle and Kensington books.

When you come online, you'll have the exciting opportunity to:

• View covers of upcoming books

• Read sample chapters

• Learn about our future publishing schedule (listed by publication month *and author*)

• Find out when your favorite authors will be visiting a city near you

• Search for and order backlist books from our online catalog

• Check out author bios and background information

• Send e-mail to your favorite authors

• Meet the Kensington staff online

• Join us in weekly chats with authors, readers and other guests

• Get writing guidelines

• AND MUCH MORE!

**Visit our website at
http://www.zebrabooks.com**

ROMANCE FROM JANELLE TAYLOR

ANYTHING FOR LOVE   (0-8217-4992-7, $5.99)

DESTINY MINE   (0-8217-5185-9, $5.99)

CHASE THE WIND   (0-8217-4740-1, $5.99)

MIDNIGHT SECRETS   (0-8217-5280-4, $5.99)

MOONBEAMS AND MAGIC   (0-8217-0184-4, $5.99)

SWEET SAVAGE HEART   (0-8217-5276-6, $5.99)

Available wherever paperbacks are sold, or order direct from the Publisher. Send cover price plus 50¢ per copy for mailing and handling to Kensington Publishing Corp., Consumer Orders, or call (toll free) 888-345-BOOK, to place your order using Mastercard or Visa. Residents of New York and Tennessee must include sales tax. DO NOT SEND CASH.

ROMANCE FROM FERN MICHAELS

DEAR EMILY   (0-8217-4952-8, $5.99)

WISH LIST   (0-8217-5228-6, $6.99)

AND IN HARDCOVER:

VEGAS RICH   (1-57566-057-1, $25.00)

Available wherever paperbacks are sold, or order direct from the Publisher. Send cover price plus 50¢ per copy for mailing and handling to Kensington Publishing Corp., Consumer Orders, or call (toll free) 888-345-BOOK, to place your order using Mastercard or Visa. Residents of New York and Tennessee must include sales tax. DO NOT SEND CASH.